STEEL'S FATE

T.L. HEINRICH

Published by Beautiful Fire
Edited by Maria D'Marco & Dan Heinrich

For Aunt Sooz,
Who loved books.

ALSO BY T.L. HEINRICH

The Vigilantes Universe

The Rise of Heroes

Serpent's Return

Shadow's Torment

Steel's Fate

The Heroes of High Tide

Fahrenheit's Ghost

Fire & Ice

WINTER-1962

CHAPTER ONE

The cafe was crowded in the middle of the day. Men and women chatted at their tables in a flurry of French that Lionel had a hard time following. Bright winter sunshine streamed in through windows that looked out onto the cobblestone streets. The occasional car or Vespa zoomed past, muting the pulsing rhythm of American rock music that spun through the air.

Lionel sat at a table by the window with a good view across the street, not at all worried about being caught by the woman he spied on. His blond hair was dyed a dark brown, black rimmed glasses perched on his nose. His usual style had been replaced by that of the young artists and poets he saw wandering in and out of shops and cafes. He looked, for all the world, like just another young Parisian enjoying a coffee while reading a book of obnoxiously deep poetry.

He glanced at the upscale restaurant across the street, with its large windows and air of snobbery. Though he lounged in his chair, the perfect picture of *joi de vivre*, every muscle in Lionel's body was tense as he watched Victoria Veran.

She sat erect like a dancer, ankles delicately crossed and swept to the side, a hint of a smile gracing her lips, and any trace of jet lag deftly covered with a dusting of powder on her porcelain skin.

The man across from her, his bald head shining with sweat, seemed oblivious to Victoria's one-eyed, broad-shouldered body guard sitting at the table behind him.

Baritone sticks out like a sore thumb, and it's not like she needs him with that strength serum coursing through her veins. Maybe she just likes the intimidation factor.

Lionel stirred some sugar into his coffee and took a sip, not really appreciating the rich flavor as he studied the mundane scene across the street.

There has to be a reason she's meeting him. Either that or I'm wasting a perfectly good afternoon in Paris.

With the grace of a viper, Victoria pulled a slip of paper out of her purse and handed it to the man across from her. As he read it, the man's face paled and he shook his head.

The more Victoria talked, the more the man looked like he was about to vomit until he finally nodded, his eyes wide in defeat and fear.

After a few more sips of her drink, Victoria got up and gave the man a broad smile before departing the restaurant. Baritone trailed behind her.

Lionel didn't bother following the dark car that Victoria climbed into. He already knew her hotel and room number thanks to a very chatty, very amorous maid.

I should send her flowers, though she did say it was fun like she hadn't expected anything after. Still…I'm not a complete cad.

The man Victoria had terrified sat there for a minute longer and paid the bill. When he finally stumbled out the door, Lionel threw some cash on the table and followed him. He had to know what Victoria had asked of him and why.

Maybe he can help me if I help him.

For two years now, Lionel had lived with the effects of poison that gave him uncontrollable fits of rage. He'd left Jet City with Marco hoping to find a cure. They traveled to Metro City with a scrap of hope to cling to and a few thin leads. For a little while, being with Marco and having the search for the cure to focus on had helped. Then, one night, Lionel's control had snapped, and he nearly killed his best friend.

He couldn't stand the guilt and fear that he might do something like that again, so he fled. Eventually, Lionel found himself in Switzerland trying to be a devoted son to his invalid mother. But the decision had haunted him, and every day Lionel wished he could return to his old life. The fact that it was impossible felt like an open wound that he didn't know how to heal.

Then one day, completely by accident, a British woman had barged into his sullen life with bullets, secrets and an undeniably strong will.

He smiled at the memory and fidgeted with the ring she'd given him.

Maria had helped him believe in himself again, to see that he had something to offer in this fight. If not for her, he'd still be hiding in Switzerland.

Lionel snapped out of his memories when he realized how far ahead the man was. If he didn't focus, the man would slip away.

Putting on a little more speed, Lionel closed the distance quickly. The man pulled a handkerchief out of his coat pocket and mopped his brow even in the cold winter air.

Victoria must've done a number on him. That could be useful.

He came to an intersection where he and the man waited at the corner to cross. The man was mumbled to himself in French as Lionel passed, wanting to take advantage of the man's distracted frame of mind. There was a small alley up ahead and Lionel ducked into it. He waited

3

as others passed, and when he saw the man, Lionel reached out and pulled him into the alley. The man tried to yell, but Lionel covered his mouth.

"I'm here to help," Lionel said in French.

The man stared at him, his corpulent body shaking.

"If I let you go, will you be quiet?"

The man nodded and Lionel took his hand off the man's mouth.

"I swear, I told her nothing!" he said. "I'm loyal to Apollo Industries, I swear it!"

At the mention of his stepfather's business, Lionel felt the bitter taste of hate on his tongue even as his mind reeled.

What the hell does that bastard have to do with all of this?

But he kept his expression hard, showing nothing.

"I'm not with Apollo," Lionel replied. "I'm...well, with other parties."

The man swallowed.

"I don't know the other Coalition members, except for Victoria. I will not betray Apollo."

Coalition? Now that's...interesting.

Lionel filed that away, pretending he knew what the man was blubbering about.

"What if I wanted you to betray Victoria Veran?"

The man let out a little sob.

"She-she is too powerful. You have no idea. I only wanted to focus on my work, my experiments! No one would fund them until Apollo came along. I don't care about the Coalitions goals or any of that. I just want to do my work!"

Lay down with dogs, you get fleas, little man.

"Look," Lionel said. "I'm not connected to the Coalition, but I want to help you."

"Why?"

"Let's just say that you might have something that will help me."

The man thought about it for a moment and shook his head.

"You don't know how powerful…if Apollo knew I was talking to another party, not just Veran…"

"You let me worry about that, okay?"

"You swear you will protect me from Veran? At least until I can get word to Apollo?"

Lionel didn't want to help anything his stepfather was involved in. But if it meant finding out what the hell the Coalition was and getting his cure, he'd pretend all damn day.

"Yeah, I promise."

"I am Monsieur Fritz."

"You can call me Steel."

An hour later, Lionel was back at the one room apartment Logan had rented for him. His mind reeled in disbelief as he sipped a drink and went over everything Fritz had spilled.

The fact that his stepfather Jason James and Victoria Veran were somehow in a secret group doing God only knew what made the hair on Lionel's neck stand up. His stepfather was formidable, no one got in his way when it came to business. Not if they were smart.

"But what the hell are they doing? Jason doesn't exactly respect intelligent women, or any women. So why partner with one like Victoria? They'd try to eat each other for breakfast at every chance."

Lionel cocked his eyebrow.

"Now that would be entertaining to see."

In spite of the humor in that thought, Lionel felt genuine

fear at what those two could accomplish together. He'd seen just how far Victoria was willing to go to get her way.

The memories of the Park Side Massacre shot through his mind and Lionel flinched.

Hundreds had died that day. Women, children, criminals and cops.

Victoria had justified it as necessary to convince the city to let her protect everyone from-

"People like me."

He flexed a hand, seeing the blood of those he'd killed on it, the blood of those he'd lost control around.

And Alice's blood.

The day of the Park Side Massacre he'd pulled her out of the dumpster where she'd landed after falling from the fire escape. Holding her in his arms, seeing the odd angle of her arm and leg, barely feeling her breath, her face covered in blood, Lionel had thought he'd killed her. If not for the rage he'd been lost in, she would've let him pursue Phantasm onto that fire escape, it would've been him who had fallen. With his strength, near invincibility and accelerated healing, Lionel would've gotten hurt but not nearly as bad as Alice.

Even if he found a cure for the rage, Lionel could never shake the fear that one day he'd mess up and Alice would die.

Or be a cripple, like Mom.

He downed the glass of bourbon and poured another.

Sixteen and too sure of himself, Lionel had lost his temper around Jason and lashed out. But it wasn't his cruel stepfather that had been hurt, it was his mother, standing just off to the side where Lionel couldn't see her.

That was the day Lionel realized that the power he possessed was dangerous to those he loved, that he had to keep a distance if they were going to be safe.

"But soon, at least one of these problems will be a thing of the past."

A grin lit up his face and, for the first time in a long while, Lionel had hope.

Fritz had recognized the poison and said that he could likely engineer a cure within a few weeks. The catch was that Lionel had to keep the man safe until he'd finished one last project for Jason.

"I wish I could find out what he's working on...but first things first. Get the cure, find Alice and Marco, help them finish Victoria once and for all. And then..."

It was a sentence he'd tried to finish many times.

Would Alice give him another chance? Would Marco?

The dream of going back to how things were before Park Side was a child's game, one that Lionel had stopped playing the night he'd lashed out at Marco in Metro City. But after helping Maria in Switzerland, Lionel thought that there might be a way to forge a new future. Whether that meant the three of them together or him alone, he didn't know. All he knew was that he wanted the chance to find out.

The ring on his pinkie caught the light and he ran a finger over the strange design.

Maria had given to him as a way to find her in the future.

"You're a good man, Lionel."

"I hope you're right Maria. I really do."

CHAPTER TWO

The candle's wax dribbled in small beads onto the crystal holders. Their dancing light caused the red table cloth to shimmer under the gleaming silverware and white plates. Glasses clinked, accenting the soft music that filtered through the small restaurant.

"I've always wanted to come here," Alice said to the man seated across from her.

He smiled. "I'm glad I chose correctly. It's one of my favorite restaurants. How is your duck?"

"Perfect."

He raised his glass of wine and sipped, never taking his brown eyes from her face. Alice schooled her features into an amused, but submissive, smile and dutifully took a bite of the greasy duck.

"I will admit," he continued. "I was shocked that you agreed to come to dinner with me."

"Why is that?"

"Well, I thought you were firmly engaged elsewhere."

Alice laughed, a false, silvery sound. "With whom?"

"Dennis Drummond."

Now the laugh was more on the genuine side. Dennis

Drummond was the son of the former Mayor and had less personality than a lump of overcooked oatmeal.

Still, I had to make it look good. If I were just another debutante, he would've been a good catch.

"Unfortunately, Mr. Drummond just wasn't what I was looking for."

She let her gaze linger on his, her lips parting ever so slightly. The effect was nearly perfect. His pale skin flushed and he took a longer drink of his wine.

"You," Alice continued, "Mr. Parker, are not just fascinating, but intelligent, generous, and have something... well, I can't quite put my finger on it, but I know that I like it, very much."

His smile turned more predatory. "I am very glad to hear it."

Their dinner continued, with the conversation descending into a slow-witted, predictable discourse that was insulting to Alice's intelligence. But, when she felt it impossible to swallow one more moment of condescension, she remembered what Mrs. Frost had told her at the start of all this.

"Men like these do not favor women who are too intelligent. Err on the side of stupidity, if you have to."

And so, she did for the rest of the four-course dinner, of which only the dessert was hers to choose.

At the end, Mr. Parker helped Alice from the chair, pretending that the cane he handed to her didn't make him want to wince in discomfort. Like the gentleman he was, Mr. Parker also helped her into her white Chimera fur coat. He did a decent job of wearing a relaxed smile as he walked beside her limping gait out to the valet station at the front of the small expensive restaurant. The winter air was dry and cold, cutting through the warmth of her coat and the thin material of her light pink dress and sending a chill through Alice.

"I had a wonderful time, Mr. Parker," Alice said.

"Please, call me Jared. And know that I did as well. Perhaps we could have lunch next time, or if you like, we could go to the symphony. I have orchestra seats."

Alice smiled. She did enjoy the symphony, but the thought of going with him was not appealing in the least.

"I would be delighted," she said instead, following Mrs. Frost's other advice on dating society men.

"It will be vital to keep them interested, to make them believe they have a chance. A rejection after a date will discourage them and you will quickly have a bad label. At the very least, give a halfway answer, they will not know the difference."

Her cream-colored Cadillac pulled up, it's blood red seats nearly glowing in the light of the street lamps. Jared helped her into the car, smiling all the while. But, as she pulled away, Alice was sure he was just as relieved as she for the evening's end.

"They will tolerate your limp and your low birth, to add my fortune to theirs. It is the only kind of marriage they truly care about."

"Was it a good evening, Miss?" asked her driver, Patrick Seville.

"As pleasant as could be expected."

"That's a shame."

Alice chuckled. "Yes, I suppose it is."

Patrick handed her a thick, green Filofax and a small packet of mail.

"Miss Jones said to tell you to review the report from Dr. Allen first."

"Thank you, Patrick."

Alice opened the sealed envelope that had her name written on it in Gerald's blocky handwriting and began reading.

"Evidence suggests that a group of four orphans, calling themselves the Prides, are powered, though in what way I do not

know. Their aberrant behavior has drawn the attention of one of their neighbors, who has contacted child services. If we do not act soon, they will be split up and put into a system that is not prepared to deal with them."

Alice felt her heartbeat quicken.

"I have also discovered the existence of two more powered children within the Children's Home. I don't know how they've so well hidden for this long, but if not for the keen observation of Mrs. Shannon, I'd have never known.

The Pride children are particularly resistant to my attempts to convince them come to the Children's Home. They insist that they want to meet you, to make sure that it's really safe. My suggestion would be for both of us to visit the Pride children at the Spiral Falls apartment building in Park Side. If we wait and petition through regular channels, we risk losing them to the system, or worse."

Her thoughts began to whirl with implications of this news.

"The eldest brother, Simon, is the one you must convince. He's held them all together, though I don't know how."

She and Gerald had suspected there would be more powered children making appearances in the coming years and she had asked Gerald to keep his eyes open for them. A few had surfaced here and there, mostly from school reports of strange violence or emotional distress. Alice had gotten quite good at talking to families about their children and encouraging them to help the child feel safe. A few parents had asked if Alice would be willing to train them, but she had firmly declined that responsibility. Not only could it weaken the in-roads she'd made with Victoria, but it might reveal too much about who Alice really was.

What can I do for the orphans? They have no parents, no support…I can't adopt them.

She winced at the thought of being anyone's caretaker.

There were too many times she felt she was just barely taking care of herself.

Gerald and I will figure something out. In the meantime...

She opened her Filofax and scanned through notations for the next few days, looking for what she could reschedule in order to help the Pride children.

After the massacre, there had been so many children left behind. At first it was overwhelming and Alice had wondered how they would ever find homes for all of them. But, in the end, the numbers reported had been surprisingly small, and the children taken to the Diana Miller Children's Home were much less than expected.

Not for the first time, that fact brought an itch to the back of her mind. As if something was not right about that, something she should know.

Maybe Uncle Logan could look into it? Now that he's Editor in Chief of the Chronicle, and Jet City's pride and joy Pulitzer winner, I bet he'd be able to get some answers.

The next envelope in the pile was a report from Frost Consolidated. Once it became clear that Mrs. Frost would be in no condition to run a multi-national company, she had signed everything over to Alice. There had been a frantic scramble by the board to keep Alice from taking over, but to no avail. With her usual forethought and take-no-crap attitude, Mrs. Frost had made it impossible for the board to do anything but capitulate. And ever since, Alice had been working overtime to prove herself.

The newest contract between Frost Consolidated and the Department of Defense was a compromise on her part, a way to appease the board so she could make other decisions without much interference. Still, Alice wasn't sure how she felt about making money off a bomber that could kill hundreds with a flick of a switch. She put the report back into the envelope before opening the last one.

It was a letter from Victoria, detailing how wonderful Paris had been.

A sour taste coated Alice's tongue as she read it and her jaw tightened. This had been the hardest part of the last year and half.

Getting her body strong again, after the near fatal injuries from the Park Side Massacre. Forcing herself to let go of the hollow pain left by Marco and Lionel's abandonment. Telling herself every day she didn't need them, until she believed it. Training every spare minute. Learning to speak French and Japanese. Being taught the ins and outs of Frost Consolidated's business involvements. Meeting the pompous members of the board. Hiding her intelligence from them and others. And navigating the mind-numbing world of dating in upper class circles.

All of it had been necessary to gain the trust of Phantasm's alter ego, Victoria. As the real mastermind behind the Park Side Massacre, Phantasm was also responsible for the murder of thousands driven insane by her fear gas.

But of all the things Alice had been doing the past few years, cultivating the right relationship with Victora was the most important. Victoria needed to believe Alice was beaten and that she was her friend and confidant, so that when the time came to defeat her, Alice would hold powerful cards.

She re-read the letter, examining the words for any hint of what Victoria was really doing in Europe.

There's no way she's vacationing. Not when the Science Foundation is so close to opening...perhaps this visit to a 'friend of her fathers' could be a German scientist now living in Paris. Maybe Uncle Logan might have an idea. He still has friends in Paris from the war.

"Miss?" Patrick said.

Alice jumped and looked up. They were parked at the

front of the mansion, the fancy outside lights casting the white mansion in a warm glow.

Patrick came around, opened her car door, and gave her a helping hand in getting out.

"At the risk of being impertinent, you work too hard, Miss."

Alice smiled. "You're probably right, Patrick, but I don't have much choice. I'll need the car tomorrow after lunch."

Patrick nodded. "Good night."

"Good night."

Alice climbed the steps to the front door with a wince. The wrap around her right knee had become too tight, making her limp more pronounced.

Inside, the foyer light was low, and Alice's uneven gait echoed strangely as she hung up her coat and went to the library.

A cheerful fire blazed in the huge fireplace, reflecting off the blue and green striped couches and chairs. Dark wood book cases stretched floor to ceiling along three of the four walls, a small side board with simple decanters sat to one side, and round tables of the same dark wood were scattered around.

It was to one of the large chairs that Alice limped, sitting down with a sigh. She unwrapped her right knee and flexed it several times.

"How was your evening?" said a quiet voice behind her that could only be Miss Jones.

Miss Jones had been brought in to take over Alice's rigorous training schedule when Mrs. Frost was no longer able to handle it. Initially, Alice hadn't been comfortable with the tall, reserved woman, but soon came to admire her keen mind and strict discipline. No one could ever replace Mrs. Frost, but Alice was thankful for Miss Jones' experienced presence at her side.

"As terrible as expected," Alice said.

"Well done."

Alice snorted, rubbing her knee.

"How was *your* evening?" Alice asked, taking in the remnants of Miss Jones' disguise as an aged janitor.

When Alice had gleaned all she could from her pretense of being Victoria's friend, Miss Jones had offered to go undercover at the Science Foundation. Alice had assumed it would be as a secretary or something like that, but Miss Jones had shown up in baggy coveralls, her cropped red hair covered by a bald cap, and deep wrinkles covering her normally smooth skinned face. She was tall and rail thin, but as the Janitor, her shoulders slumped forward, producing the appearance of a bowed back. In her disguise, Miss Jones looked exactly like an aging night janitor, who talked to himself.

Miss Jones began peeling off the segments of synthetic wrinkles and placing the pieces into a paper bag.

Alice turned away and kept stretching her knee.

I can never get used to that.

"It was fruitless, but not," Miss Jones answered.

"How so?"

"The files I was planning on pinching had been moved, a whole filing cabinet of them. It was a recent thing, too, because I just saw them two days ago."

Alice frowned. "Why would Victoria move them in the middle of her vacation? If she was worried, why not move them before she left?"

"Excellent question. My guess is that something happened on her trip and she's feeling the need to be more cautious." Miss Jones peeled off a huge strip of wrinkled skin from her forehead.

"Where were they moved to?"

"The lab in the basement, the one I haven't been able to get into…"

"Damn. Do you think you could, if need be?"

"There are cameras down there, it's how I was discovered the first time. And the locks are key pads."

"We should talk to Rose, maybe she could come up with something. Though I don't want to give her any extra work, since she just started managing Atlas Books."

"If that's all," Miss Jones said, walking to the desk in the room and pulling out a large personal calendar, "I think I will go over your schedule for the week and then turn in. I assume we will be doing our usual run tomorrow?"

Alice nodded, and walked to the door, her cane silenced on the thick carpet.

"Yes, thank you Miss Jones. I think I'll check on Mrs. Frost before I turn in," Alice said.

"Good night, Miss Seymour."

———

Alice stepped into the spacious bedroom now doubling as a hospital room. The heavy, dark green drapes were pulled back a little, letting faint moonlight into the room. A low fire crackled in the hearth, while two tall lamps barely illuminated the space around Mrs. Frost, who lay in the hospital bed that had replaced the palatial four poster bed she'd once slept in. The best equipment money could buy surrounded her. Two different IVs fed sustenance and pain relief into her body. Heart monitor chords snaked their way from her chest to the machine, which gave a soft, intermittent beep.

Comfortable, dark green arm chairs sat on either side of the hospital bed, along with a cherry wood table, where a radio and a few books sat, untouched.

Gerald was sleeping in one of the chairs, his feet up on a matching ottoman, and his head crooked awkwardly to one side.

She touched him on the shoulder and he jumped.

"It's just me..." she whispered. "I just...I can sit with her for a while. Why don't you go to bed?"

Gerald rubbed his bloodshot eyes. "She was asking for you an hour ago."

"I'm sorry I wasn't here."

"She wasn't awake for very long, but if she wakes up again, she'll be glad to see you."

Alice wanted to ask how she was doing, but knew that was a stupid question. The cancer in Mrs. Frost's stomach had sapped her strength and made her unable to eat anything, leaving her a weak shadow of her former self.

For a few minutes, they both just stared at the emaciated figure on the bed, grief stinging their eyes.

Mrs. Frost had never been a large woman, but the force of her personality often made people forget that. She'd resisted the hospital bed that Gerald had ordered for her, insisting that she was more comfortable in her own. But Alice and Gerald knew the real reason: Mrs. Frost had known that once she lay in the hospital bed, and the burning oblivion of morphine coursed through her veins, it would be the beginning of the end.

"There's one more fight I have to win," she had said. "Then...I can rest."

Alice had worried that Mrs. Frost was talking about defeating Phantasm, which would take far longer than the old vigilante had left in her. And, in a way, she was.

It took months of campaigning, threatening and other-wise just being herself, but Mrs. Frost successfully blocked Victoria's attempt to create a special, enhanced police force.

The day after the news broke, Mrs. Frost finally began accepting the occasional morphine shot from Gerald. It wasn't long after that first shot that Mrs. Frost had succumbed to the hospital bed and its comforts.

"I am still in charge," she had said, pointing a bony finger at Gerald and Alice. "Do not forget it."

Alice guessed that Gerald had used his healing powers to prolong Mrs. Frost's life, and a grateful guilt lanced through Alice every time she thought about it. But, in the last few months, something had begun to change.

Mrs. Frost slept more and more, until she was barely awake anymore. And when she was, she often talked about people who weren't alive, as if they were. Alice hated when Mrs. Frost realized her mistake. Seeing her fear and embarrassment was almost too much to bear.

"She's...she wants to go, doesn't she?" Alice whispered.

Gerald's smile was horribly sad. "Yes, but I think she's waiting for you to tell her that you're ready."

Alice let the tears slide down her cheeks.

One more good-bye...how many more to come?

"I'll be in my room, if you need anything," Gerald said, standing slowly.

As gently as possible, Alice took Mrs. Frost's bruised, frail hand in hers and held it.

"I'm sorry I wasn't here earlier. I was out with Jared Parker, he of the dull conversation and railroad money."

She forced a smile on her tear stained face.

"Miss Jones says I'm making good progress with Japanese. My staff work could be better when we train, though I did disarm her with the Si yesterday, so that's something."

Alice wiped her tears away, not wanting Mrs. Frost to see them if she should wake up.

"Victoria moved some files to the basement lab this week. I think if we get Rose to help us beat the security system, we might be able to get Miss Jones down there, but I'm not sure if this is the right move."

Alice laid Mrs. Frost's hand back on the coverlet and began to pace in front of the bed, twirling the cane in her hand as she walked. The muscles around her knee were starting to warm up and loosen.

"If she fails, it could tip our hand, not that I think Miss Jones would talk, I just...we've been lucky up to now. Everything Miss Jones has stolen she was able to return before anyone knew it was gone, at least as far as we know."

She looked at Mrs. Frost, hoping for something, but she laid as still as before. Turning away, Alice began pacing again.

"It was my idea to spy on the Foundation in the first place," Alice continued, feeling some small comfort in her one-sided conversation with Mrs. Frost. "But you confirmed that it was a good idea, and told me to let Miss Jones do it. You can look at things in business, and with Victoria, and see the shape of them in a moment; while I need more time. I'm afraid that in that extra time, it will be too late – like it was with Park Side. If I just could've seen earlier what she was going to do – even a day – I could've stopped it."

"Nonsense," said a raspy voice.

Alice jumped. "You're awake!"

"It would seem so..."

Alice went to the small freezer they'd installed in the room and came back with a cup of ice chips. She spooned a few into Mrs. Frost's mouth and sat the cup on the table.

"Where...were you earlier?"

"Out with Jared Parker."

Mrs. Frost made a face. "You can do better."

"That goes without saying."

Mrs. Frost's chuckle was weak, but it sparked a gleam in her eyes.

"I wanted...to talk to you. You must...beware of Victoria...she's not what she seems."

Alice felt her heart squeeze. "I know."

"No! You do not!" Mrs. Frost's face was fierce, and then a confused frown softened her features.

"I wanted…No, that's not what I wanted…to say. What was it?"

"You can tell me later."

Mrs. Frost pressed her fingers around Alice's hand. "You and I both know…later might not come. Oh now, do not…cry. No tears. I have lived…such a life! And when I die…I leave you here…my pride…the best of me."

Alice remembered Gerald's words and forced herself to really look at Mrs. Frost. She could see the suffering Mrs. Frost had endured all this time, just because Alice couldn't let her go.

I've needed her, I couldn't have done all this, become who I am without her.

But Alice knew that wasn't entirely true. Shame sliced at her heart as a tide of grief rose up within her. It was time to say good-bye.

"I had it easier than you," Mrs. Frost looked down at the cane that dangled from Alice's wrist. "All I had to do was punch serial killers…and be as…eccentric as I pleased. But you…you have a more difficult path. This false injury…the mask you must wear…I am sorry you must bear it."

"It was the only way to finish this."

"Was it? You could've…done things differently. An easier way…but that is not you, is it? No, do not…misunderstand me. I admire it…this stubborn fire…you remind me of…someone I loved once…she was…so full of life…"

Mrs. Frost's eyes glistened with tears, her gaze becoming far away before snapping back to Alice's face.

"But here…listen. I know…you are afraid…you feel guilt. Do not deny it…I can see. You are careful…distant… at first that was good. But…the time for that is passing. Careful is now…a weakness! You must trust your true strength…"

Mrs. Frost managed to raise a gnarled hand and poke Alice in the chest with one bony finger.

"In there I had…what I thought was strength…alone, always. I thought…it was necessary and I…didn't mind, not really. After Emily…alone was fine. But now, having you…"

Mrs. Frost smiled, a wheezing breath coming from between her parched lips.

"Diana…she knew I think…but you…you are stronger than…either of us."

She coughed and Alice offered another spoonful of ice chips, which Mrs. Frost hungrily accepted. Alice wasn't sure exactly what to make of her words. Over the months their conversations had become fairly one sided, with Alice doing most of the talking and Mrs. Frost mostly asleep or barely listening. This was the most Mrs. Frost had spoken to her in weeks.

"I don't feel strong most of the time," Alice admitted.

"Doesn't matter. Actions…perfection…I pursued them…never satisfied. You…don't have to be that way."

Alice felt confusion and frustration at those words. She'd pushed herself every day for years because that's what she thought was needed. And now, Mrs. Frost is telling her…what?

"I am not trying to be-" Alice began.

"Do not lie…to a dying woman. Driven is good…but alone…alone is empty. I am so glad…I have you…and Gerald."

Mrs. Frost opened one of her hands lying on the covers and Alice took it. She could feel every bone through the thin skin and tears came to her eyes.

"Thank you…Alice," Mrs. Frost whispered. "Thank you…"

"You've given me so much more than I've given you."

Mrs. Frost opened her mouth to speak and instead shook her head.

"Someday…you'll see."

"Alright," Alice said, wiping her tears away. "In the meantime, do you want me to read to you or anything?"

"Has it…snowed?"

"Not yet."

Mrs. Frost looked toward her window. "I wanted to see it…one more time."

"Do you want me to open your curtains a little more?"

Mrs. Frost nodded.

Alice tied back the heavy drapes with cream colored ties and looked up into the clear night sky. She wasn't a fan of snow, but wished that it would for Mrs. Frosts sake all the same.

"There," Alice said, forcing a smile. "If it snows you can…"

She turned and saw that Mrs. Frost's eyes were closed and her thin chest rose and fell at odd intervals. Coming back to the bed, Alice took Mrs. Frost's hand in hers again and tried to speak. There was something she needed to say, but the more she tried, the more elusive the words became. In the end, she settled for a light kiss on the old vigilante's wrinkled forehead.

"I'll stay for a while. In case…in case you want to say anything else or if you…I don't want you to be alone."

Alice settled into one of the chairs and covered up with one of the many blankets laying around. She stared at Mrs. Frost for a very long time, expecting the beeping of the heart monitor to cease. But Mrs. Frost just slept.

And after a while, Alice slept, too.

CHAPTER THREE

"Only a mile left," Miss Jones said ahead of Alice.

"Okay," Alice breathed.

The winter air was wet this morning, coating the low shrubs and ground in a hard, white frost. It crunched under Alice's feet as she ran through the wooded area behind the Frost Mansion.

She heard the change in Miss Jones' steps seconds before she saw the punch coming. Grabbing Miss Jones' wrist and pulling her forward, Alice tried to pull her off balance, but Miss Jones wasn't fooled and landed a solid punch to Alice's side. Recovering quickly, Alice elbowed Miss Jones, trying to bring her down.

"Good," Miss Jones said, stopping to rub her midsection. "Next time, do not use brute force to bring down your opponent. Your short stature is a powerful weapon because your adversaries—"

"Won't think of it. Yeah, I know."

Miss Jones gave a short nod, turned, and they continued running.

Alice followed, her pride bruised more than her side.

After they had run a few more yards, Miss Jones whipped around to throw a wooden practice knife at Alice.

Where the hell does she hide those things?

Alice effectively dodged the first two, then felt the third graze her thigh. She rolled into a somersault and punched Miss Jones in the solar plexus, then leapt up and landed an upper cut. Miss Jones stumbled back, but did not fall. Instead, she drew a fourth practice knife and pressed it to Alice's stomach before putting it back in its sheath.

"Better," Miss Jones said, then turned and sprinted away.

Alice smirked and followed her.

They were about to finish their run when they came within sight of the house, and Alice attempted to attack Miss Jones. Within moments, Alice found herself on her back, staring up at thick gray clouds.

"You would've had me, but I heard your initial step," Miss Jones said, helping Alice up.

"Good to know."

"You are improving. Endurance, forethought, discipline, all are vastly improved from when we first began. You should increase your meditation time another fifteen minutes, it will help your healing and mental acuity."

Alice cringed. She managed about half an hour of meditation before her body began to feel as if it were going jump out of its skin.

I can't deny its effectiveness though, especially since she won't let Gerald heal me half the time.

They went through a back door beside the vast kitchen, where a squat, kind-faced woman was stirring something on the stove. Alice smiled at her and followed Miss Jones down a set of stairs to the gym. They passed a huge dark room on the way and Alice stopped to stare at it.

When she was recovering, Alice had suggested that they create a room where she could practice fighting while affected by the Fantasy fear gas, just in case her mask failed. Gerald and Rose had managed to come up with a close imitation of the gas and Alice had gotten pretty good at working within its effects. But, the last time she'd practiced, something very different had happened.

She shivered, remembering the paralyzing fear that had taken hold of her, the way her muscles had contracted and her whole body felt like one big cramp.

"Miss Seymour?"

"I wonder if I should try again," Alice said, nodding at the room.

"Why?"

"In case…"

"You loathe defeat."

Alice looked up at her. It was said so simply, without condemnation or the intention to teach.

"I can relate to that," Miss Jones continued. "It is not defeat to treat things with intelligence, however. Knowing when and how to do that is not easy. You will learn. Shall we start with the punching bag?"

After a hot bath that managed to soothe many of the sore muscles that were now a normal sensation in her body, Alice settled with a sigh onto a soft chair in the small dining room and took that first, glorious sip of coffee. Her long dark hair felt like it was coming out of its pins since she'd rushed through her morning beauty regimen, what there was of it anyway. Alice played with a few of the bobby pins that held her half up-half down. Once satisfied that they were secure she helped herself to a generous helping of scrambled eggs, bacon and homemade biscuits that were laid out on the sideboard.

Weak morning sunlight streamed in through the gauzy

white curtains, falling on the light wood floors, table, and chairs. A small fire a year ago had necessitated a complete redecoration of the small dining room, and Alice had been the one to make the final decisions about it.

As a result, it was perhaps the lightest room in the entire mansion. Where every other room had rich, deep colors, this one was in light shades of pink and green.

Alice loved how much it reminded her of the dinning room in her aunt and uncles home and intended to redecorate most of the rooms on the main floor of the house in the same style as soon as she had the time.

Perhaps I should ask Miss Jones to schedule time with a few decorators. It would be nice to have it nearly finished by next year.

The thought took her a bit by surprise. Planning such a thing had nothing to do with Victoria or training for whatever was coming. And, usually, that's what she thought about. The fact that planning for something as simple as redecorating was jarring, it made Alice feel uneasy.

I'm not that out of touch with life...am I? Is that what Mrs. Frost was getting at last night?

"Good morning," Uncle Logan said, kissing her cheek and snapping her out of such thoughts.

He put a newspaper on the table and proceeded to help himself to some breakfast.

Though he had a room in the mansion with an attached study, Uncle Logan didn't stay there often. Preferring instead to remain in the large, two-story rambler that he and Aunt Diana had bought when they were first married. Alice understood completely, and would've been heartbroken if he ever decided to sell it. Still, there were times she missed seeing him every day. His duties as Editor in Chief of the Jet City Chronicle kept him busier than when he was a reporter.

"I didn't expect to see you this morning," Alice said.

"I thought I'd come by. I can be late a few times, now that I'm in charge."

He sat down with a full plate next to her and began to eat.

"Good morning, Mr. Miller," Miss Jones said as she walked to an empty place at the table.

Uncle Logan nodded at Miss Jones and opened the newspaper.

"Don't you already know what's going on?" Alice said.

"I like to read it like a normal Joe," Uncle Logan said, wrinkles appearing at the corners of his brown eyes as he smiled. "And besides, how else am I supposed to know who you're dating?"

Alice choked on her coffee. "You have someone writing about me?"

"Not *you* specifically. It's the society page, and you just happen to be big news for that page right now."

Alice grabbed the page Uncle Logan was holding up and groaned at the picture of her and Jared Parker taken a few days ago at the library fundraiser.

"You could do better," he said.

She scowled at him. "It's all part of the job."

"Thank God."

"Besides," she said, a wicked grin lighting up her eyes, "It's not as if I'm dating someone half my age and employed by me."

Now it was Uncle Logan's turn to choke. "Oona is not half my age!"

"Ten years," Miss Jones said, not looking up from the crossword puzzle she was working on.

"And," Uncle Logan continued, "she's not my employee."

"Not anymore," Alice said. "Isn't that a bit unfair? She loses her job just for dating you?"

"She—I didn't do that! She was going to resign to start

that women's magazine, before I started dating her, you know that!"

Alice held up her hands in surrender. "Don't get so upset, I'm not judging or anything."

Uncle Logan eyed her a moment more before returning to his breakfast and newspaper. "She's not half my age."

Alice couldn't stifle a giggle.

"Would you like to go over your schedule for the day?" Miss Jones asked, opening Alice's Filofax.

Though she phrased it like a question, Alice knew it was anything but.

As Uncle Logan and Alice ate, Miss Jones discussed a meeting with an investor from Japan, who was in town for two days, as well as what Alice might want to do about the government contracts for the bomber. Alice used to like numbers and balance sheets. The simplicity of it had always been comforting. But that was before she saw the reports for Frost Consolidated, which were complicated, as one would expect with a multi-national corporation. It had taken her the better part of a year, but Alice was finally able to decipher the complex graphs and reports from various departments and agencies.

"You changed your afternoon appointments?" Miss Jones asked.

"I need to go into Park Side. Gerald has found a group of powered children and needs me to talk to them."

"You don't usually do that, any reason in particular?" Uncle Logan asked.

"They just need some reassurance."

"I think that's great. You're taking an interest in…well, things like that."

Alice knew what he wasn't saying: That she was looking past Victoria to other people that needed her help. It grated on her more than a little, but then she remembered how she felt before he came into the dining room and wondered, just for a moment, if he might be right.

No time to examine that. Maybe later.

Alice forced a smile to hide her discomfort and said, "That reminds me. Could you look into the number of orphans reported from the Park Side Massacre versus the number that have been found?"

"I suppose. Why?"

"Something doesn't feel right. With all the casualties from that day, there should be more of them."

Uncle Logan sighed. "Alice, do you think that maybe there aren't, because they died that day, too?"

"I've thought of that. But...no, something isn't right, I can feel it."

"Alright, I'll see what I can find." He stood and kissed Alice on the forehead. "I better go. Shouldn't be too late. Good-bye, Miss Jones."

"Mr. Miller," she said, nodding her head.

Once Uncle Logan was out of the room, Miss Jones asked, "Have you given any thought to what we discussed last night?"

"The files? Yes – and I think you should try. I'll talk to Rose after the meeting with the Japanese investors and see what she can come up with. If it's important enough for Victoria to hide, then we need to know about it. Might be the key to figuring out what she's going to do with the Foundation."

Miss Jones nodded. "You will need a rather public alibi, just in case anything goes wrong. We don't want Victoria to suspect you."

Alice cringed. "Jared Parker wants me to go to the symphony with him this weekend."

"That would be quite perfect. Why don't you ask your uncle and Miss Ruiz to go with you?"

"Why?"

Miss Jones shrugged. "It might ensure more press that way. And, I do believe you should get used to the idea of Miss Ruiz being around."

Alice knew Miss Jones was probably right, and although she felt far too old to be jealous of someone taking Aunt Diana's place in Uncle Logan's life, she had to admit she was feeling just that.

She's nice and smart. Hasn't tried to force her way into my life. Why is it so hard to just let him have this? Maybe if I spent more time with her...

"Alright," Alice said, standing up, "I'll call Uncle Logan today."

"And Mr. Parker."

"Yes..."

"Remember to wear blue and green to the meeting."

Alice nodded, barely noticing the way her body ached as she walked out of the dining room.

———

The meeting with the Japanese investors went better than Alice had hoped. They complimented her language skills and the tea she had flown in special for them. For perhaps the first time, Alice felt that she was ready to take over, that she could not only maintain what Mrs. Frost had built, but could help it grow.

Patrick opened the door of the car for Alice and she stepped out in front of Atlas Book Company. She took a moment and gazed at the familiar store front. Her eyes took in every brick, her ears every door squeak when a customer opened it – no matter how much WD-40 they used. She admired the display of new books in the window and made a mental note to pick up a few of them. Then, her gaze traveled, against her will, up to the loft above. Huge windows looked out onto the street and Alice closed her eyes and saw the place where she'd lived for a brief time.

The shining floors, tall book shelves…Elvis singing from the stereo in the corner…marinara simmering on the stove…

"Miss?" Patrick said.

Her eyes snapped open to see Patrick holding out the bags of sandwiches they had stopped off for on the way to the store. Alice took a deep breath and smiled.

"Thank you, if you want to come in…?"

"If it's all the same, I think I'd like to visit an old friend down the street."

"Of course. Be back in an hour?"

He nodded and walked down the street.

The door squeaked and the bell above rang as she stepped inside. The smell of lemon furniture polish and paper embraced Alice, bringing a wave memories with it: her aunt behind the counter, Uncle Logan picking Alice up when she fell asleep on the rug in the children's section, Lionel and Marco surprising her after so many years.

This is why I don't come here anymore…

Pain gripped her chest and she pushed it away. There was business to be done. Memories could be cried over later.

Only later never comes…

Gritting her teeth, she walked to the counter at the back, her uneven gait making hollow sounds on the old, dark wood floor.

A tall, lanky black man was behind the counter, a pair of square, dark rimmed glasses on his nose. A stack of books sat on a stool beside him and Alice could see half-a-dozen boxes to the left of the counter. His dark eyes were intent on an open ledger, and he was murmuring something as Alice approached.

"Problem with the books?" she asked.

His eyes jumped up to hers, startled out of his thoughts. Then he grinned, showing slightly uneven, white teeth.

"Just double checking the figures, Miss Seymour."

"I've told you before, Derrick, call me Alice."

"That feels, if you don't mind me saying, a little strange. You're my boss."

"And I'm not that much older than you. It feels even more strange to hear you call me 'Miss Seymour'. Alice, okay?"

Derrick nodded. "Sure, I'll try."

Alice handed him a thick sandwich wrapped in wax paper.

"Is this what I think it is?" he asked.

"Francisco's, of course! Do you think I'd bring any other sandwiches here?"

Derrick was about to unwrap it, but stopped.

"Go on, I'll watch the counter for a little while," Alice said.

"Thanks."

Derrick walked into the tiny back room, which was really more of an entry way for the upstairs loft.

She looked around the shop that had been like a second home. The shelves and thread-bare rugs were the same, but what was on the shelves had changed a bit since she was running things. Now there were books on civil and women's rights, some eastern philosophy and two shelves packed with texts on Islam. There was also a prominent display of poetry by Negro authors, and a small section of jazz records.

Alice picked up a book from the Islam section, a thick, bright blue one with the word *Quran* on it. She'd heard about Islam on the news relating to a civil rights leader. Not one for religion of any kind, Alice had simply filed it away in her mind for another day. But Rose had been talking about it more, and so had the men and women who'd begun to frequent Atlas Books, so Alice's curiosity had been piqued.

"Getting religion?" said a voice to her right.

Alice smiled and turned to look at her old friend.

"Not exactly."

Rose's dark hair was perfectly bobbed, its curls straightened and shining. She wore a simple pair of dark blue pants with a white and blue sweater, which hugged her curves and made her look like a college undergrad.

"Where's Derrick?" Rose asked, leading Alice back to the counter.

"In the back, eating," Alice said, and handed Rose a sandwich.

"Francisco's, yum!"

"I need a favor."

"Color me surprised."

There was a sharpness under the playful tone in Rose's voice and Alice hesitated.

"If you're busy—"

"No, it's alright," Rose said and nodded to Derrick, who'd just walked in from the back. "I need to talk to Alice for a little bit. You alright to watch things again?"

Derrick gave Rose a wide smile. "Sure."

Rose smirked and turned away.

"He's cute," Alice whispered, as they climbed the stairs to the loft.

"Derrick? He's alright."

Alice laughed. "Don't even try to play coy with me. I saw how he looked at you."

Rose opened the door to the loft and stepped inside. "Yes, but my other career could make having a relationship hard at the moment. And…I don't know if I want one anyway. I've got enough going on."

Alice walked in and stopped, taking it all in. Rose had kept most everything the same, even the punching bag in one corner. The drapes were a darker shade though, and Alice could tell that she actually used the stove and kitchen utensils. The tiny bedroom was decorated in dark blues and reds, with a shade drawn over the small window. And there was a large blanket thrown over the leather couch, as if to cover it up.

I can still smell cinnamon...

"Alice?"

The sound of her name jolted her out of her memories.

"If you want to go to the mansion—"

"No." Alice shook her head. "I'm fine, really. I'm glad you've made it your own."

Rose studied Alice for a moment, and took in a breath as if she were about to say something. Alice could guess that she was about to make sure the apartment didn't bother Alice, or something else meant to simply check in. Rose had been doing a lot of that lately, and Alice didn't want to hear it

So, she waved toward the punching bag and said, "I didn't think you sparred anymore."

Rose's face became tight and she shrugged. "I just... there's a lot, that I want to do. Best be prepared is how I look at it. You want to eat while we talk?"

"Sure," Alice said, ignoring the small pinch of worry in her mind. "Plates still where they were?"

Rose nodded. "What's the situation?"

Alice laid out the dilemma of the security system that Miss Jones needed to beat and why. They sat at the familiar, dark brown kitchen table and ate the gourmet sandwiches as Rose jotted things down in a small notebook.

"Where is this exactly?" Rose asked. "The room..."

"Do you still have copies here of the Foundation blueprints?"

"Yeah," Rose set her sandwich down.

"Wait. Let's eat first. I feel like I haven't just talked to you in a very long time. How is it running the store?"

"The store is pretty easy, except for some of the other owners around here. They haven't been too happy with all of the Negro customers. Thank god they just give me dirty looks and don't take it any further though."

"I'm sorry that's happening. I'd ask if I could have a word with them, but I think that would just make it worse."

"It would yeah. It's annoying but nothing has happened and they don't try to keep the customers way from our shop. Just their shops."

"Bigoted idiots."

Rose nodded.

They sat in silence for a few minutes, eating their sandwiches. A tension that Alice couldn't name settled around them, and for the first time in her life, she felt disconnected from Rose and couldn't figure out why.

"How's your civil rights work going?" she asked, desperate to break the silence in the room.

"It's...you know, why don't I get those blueprints now? I'm going to need to get back down to the store soon. There's a delivery coming."

"Did I say something wrong?"

"No, you didn't say anything," Rose said. "I'm gonna get those blueprints."

Alice nodded and set her sandwich down. There'd been tension between them for months now. Every time Alice came to Rose for help, whatever it was grew. Today was the worst it had been and Alice didn't think she could ignore it any more. She also knew that she just didn't want to talk about it right then.

Rose came out of her room, where a small safe had been installed. She carried copies of the blueprints, as well as three files full of suppliers, contractors and scientists working with Victoria on the Foundation.

"Thought maybe one of these might tell us a little more about the security system, if they'd had any part in installing or creating it."

"Good thinking."

They pored over the papers, which Alice had practically memorized from studying her own copies. After an hour, they had a pretty good idea of what the security system was and who had taken part in the installation.

"I might be able to get more information from this company," Rose said, tapping her pencil on a name, "tell them we need something special for the shop...I don't know..."

"I could have Miss Jones call and say it's for the mansion. Everyone knows how eccentric Mrs. Frost can be."

"How is she? I know I haven't been over... It's just really hard to see her that way."

Alice took a deep breath. "She's...I don't think it will be much longer. She sleeps a lot and even when she is awake she's not always coherent."

"I'm sorry," Rose squeezed Alice's hand. "I know what she's meant to you."

"And you, too. I'm not the only one whose life was changed by her."

"No, you're not," Rose said. "I miss her. The strength in her very presence...the way she'd tell me to do better. She pushed me until I could push myself."

Alice nodded. "I know what you mean."

"At least now she can move on knowing we will be alright."

Will I?

The question struck Alice's mind with the force of a bullet and, for a moment, she could only stare at the table.

"Alice?"

"Yes...yes, she can be at peace, that's true. We've both

found our place in the world. I think that's what she wanted."

Rose bit her bottom lip, her long, calloused fingers drawing shapes in the water on the counter top.

"Do you ever feel," she started, her voice low and halting, "like you're starting to outgrow your life? As if someone is pushing the walls and ceiling in on you, little by little, and you didn't even notice until it was too late? And now you're just stuck in a box?"

Alice opened her mouth, then closed it. She'd felt like that once, just before Mrs. Frost had offered her the chance to become Serpent. And since then, she had felt the world open to her, unfolding opportunities in a myriad of colors and shapes. Not all of it had been good, or something she'd want in her life constantly. Some of it had hurt worse than anything, and other things had driven her to the point of terror. In the midst of everything, though, Alice had always felt grateful that her life was so big.

Rose walked to the floor-to-ceiling windows that looked out onto the city, her arms crossed in front of her. She looked older and more serious than when they'd first set their feet on this path.

Before Mrs. Frost, Rose had almost no opportunity to use her gifts. And then, Mrs. Frost had given her a lab and unlimited resources to invent and experiment, as long as she aided Alice in her endeavors. That had been almost three years ago, and Rose had become not only a genius inventor, but a self-educated scientist in several fields. Alice had seen her scrutinize every book she could get her hands on, teaching herself to read Russian and French, just so she could learn about the latest breakthroughs.

Giving the management of Atlas Books to Rose had made Alice feel like she'd given away one of her most precious possessions, but she'd wanted Rose to have something more than a dark lab and a secret intelligence.

Maybe she didn't want it though. What if I did the wrong thing?

"I thought," Alice said, choosing her words carefully, "that your life was...maybe not perfect, but good. That you had a lot of what you wanted."

"People change, Alice. At the beginning, what Mrs. Frost gave me was the chance of a lifetime. But now...I see a world out there, of people like me – or maybe not just like me, but they think like me. I write letters to other scientists under a false name, to protect you, and a few have wanted to meet me and I have to say 'no', because—"

"It might endanger all of us."

Rose nodded. "I couldn't go to college, because my father seems to think that someone there is going to want to kill me. I can't talk to my few friends about what I'm most passionate about, because they can't know what I really do! I go to protests about equality and rights, and then all I hear from the black men I meet is how it's my duty to bear and raise up the next generation of educated and strong black children. As if I should have no other aspiration!"

"I know what that's like."

Rose sighed, her face becoming tense. "Alice...I love you like a sister, but there are times I get so frustrated with you."

Alice stared at her. "What did I say?"

"You don't know how it is for me!" Rose's voice burst out of her like pressure from a under a lid. "Because until today you've never bothered asking. And to be honest, I don't know how things are really going for you either. I see you, running around to this business meeting and that, I hear about your training and you ask me for this or that but whenever I ask about *you*, there's a wall up."

Alice stared at Rose for a moment, and then felt herself stiffen. She'd gotten sick of everyone fawning over her the first few months after the Park Side Massacre, practically every conversation had been about how she felt and if she was really sure about her plan.

After a while, Alice simply changed the conversation and people stopped asking. It had been a relief to not feel like every emotion or word was being constantly scrutinized for meaning. But now, Alice wondered if Rose had ever stopped.

"So that's what you've been angry about these past few months," Alice asked, her voice hard. "Me not talking about my feelings?"

"In a way. I mean, when was the last time you and I just sat and talked about…nothing?"

"I don't know, but we've changed, haven't we? Are we the same girls who used to giggle about boys or listen to music and dissect every lyric?"

"No but-"

"Then don't expect us to act the same! We've grown up and our relationship has to grow up, too."

"So part of growing up is you treating me like your employee instead of your friend?"

Alice's mouth hung open. "What does that mean?"

"Have you been listening? I just told you!"

"I thought you liked this work! I thought you wanted to help me bring Victoria down!"

"I do, but-!"

A knock echoed in the loft and both women jumped at the sound.

Rose ran a hand over her hair and went to answer the door.

"Sorry to interrupt," Derrick said from the door way. "But, the delivery is here and they need your signature for it."

"I'll be right down," Rose said.

Derrick glanced at Alice, and then back at Rose. "You okay?"

Rose's smile was stiff. "Of course, thanks, Derrick."

He nodded and walked down the stairs back to the store.

Rose stood at the open door, leaning against it as if she needed its support. Alice took several deep breaths and straightened her blouse. Anger at Rose's accusations ran hot through her body. And, underneath it, a horrible sense of guilt. If Rose was right, even a little, then she'd been neglecting one of her best friends and treating her like...

A servant.

Alice cringed at the thought.

"I'll have something for the security system in a few days," Rose said.

Alice wanted to say something to make this right, to return them to what they'd been even a few months ago. But one look at Rose's hard expression and Alice knew that only a very hard, very uncomfortable conversation could begin to solve this.

So, she just nodded.

"Thank you, I appreciate that," Alice said, walking past Rose and down the stairs.

As Alice walked through the shop and got into her waiting car, her heart felt like a lead ball in her chest. When Marco and Lionel went away it had been like losing a part of herself, but having Rose had always been a comfort. What if she didn't even have her anymore?

Perhaps she's right. Maybe I have been neglecting her. Though, it's not as if I've had a lot of time the last two years.

Alice sighed. Rose had always seemed to understand what Alice was going through and what she needed, so Alice never thought she had to worry about her feeling left out or wronged. Then again, their friendship had never been through something like this.

She looked out the window, at the new signs in some of the shop windows.

"*No Negroes*" wasn't something Alice had grown up seeing, though the implication was clear in many shops north of Park Side. Now, with the increased demonstrations and riots, many shops were starting to make plain the kind of people who were and weren't accepted. Even ones that didn't have a problem a few years back were starting to refuse service to anyone who was black.

It's not just me focusing on Victoria that has Rose on edge, it's everything. She's got to be feeling the tension all around. And…I haven't been there for her.

Patrick turned the car down the street that ran along the waterfront. The Science Foundation came into Alice's view and her jaw tightened.

I'm so close to finishing this, to making Jet City safe from Victoria. When that's done, I'll make sure to spend more time with Rose. She's…I can't lose her too. I'll make this right, I just have to finish what I started first.

Alice closed her eyes and tried to use those thoughts to bury the seeds of doubt and guilt that had started to plague her. To her frustration, it didn't work.

CHAPTER FOUR

The last thing Alice wanted to do after the fight with Rose and the memories that assaulted her mind at Atlas books, was to go to Park Side. But she'd made a promise and time was a factor.

As they drove into the southern most part of Jet City to the neighborhood where she'd grown up in and met her best friends Lionel and Marco, Alice felt her heart constrict at the way it had changed.

Historically, it was considered the run down part of Jet City, the place where the undesirables were pushed. Alice had known, as had all the children she'd grown up with, that they were in the poor part of town. But it hadn't bothered her. She'd had the store that sold penny candy, the grocer that sometimes gave her an orange or apple, and a dozen other places where she'd felt safe and happy.

She had ignored the fact that a lot of the people living in Park Side turned to crime to survive. And Alice had no idea that the businesses that survived often had to pay protection money. Park Side was just the place where she had lived, laughed, and played with her friends. Though there were plenty of bad memories attached to this place, there was enough good for Alice to feel a pang at what was now happening to it.

After the Park Side Massacre had devastated an entire block and killed hundreds, those that could, had fled to other cities or towns. Those that couldn't were evicted from their run down apartments, as the rich of Jet City bought up the buildings in an attempt to "clean up" Park Side. Businesses that had existed for generations were closed because the owners couldn't afford the increased rent. Families were pushed out of their homes with meager compensation for the lives that they were being forced to abandon.

We pushed them into this part of the city, told them to make do and they did. But now that this land could be profitable, we strip it from them and force them out once again.

She felt sick with it, the hypocrisy and greed that she was inextricably a part of as the heir to Frost Consolidated. Mrs. Frost had bought up a couple of blocks worth of apartment buildings in the hopes that others would see that profits could be made by simply improving Park Side for the people that already lived there, but no one cared. Alice knew that the renovation of those buildings was costing Frost Consolidated more than they were likely to see in profits for a good long while, but she also knew that it was worth it if they could help some of those families keep their homes.

"I just wish we could've done more," she said aloud, as she saw the bulldozed remains of three different buildings.

She recognized one of them as the old candy store that she, Lionel, and Marco had visited. Another place was where their childhood nemesis, the Dorn brothers, had lived. The only evidence of their existence now was the crumbled remains of a few brick walls and a handful of wooden beams. A sign exclaimed that new apartments were being built.

"The Future of Beautiful City Living is Here! Reserve YOUR Apartment Now!"

Alice scoffed in disgust and looked away.

But soon, as they neared the middle of Park Side, where once a warehouse had stood, Alice's eyes clouded with tears.

It was in that spot that she had last fought side-by-side with Marco and Lionel. Where they had failed to stop Phantasm from killing so many innocent people. Where Alice had almost died after falling three stories into a trash bin.

"Could you pull over Patrick, just for a minute?"

"Of course, Miss," he answered, his voice low.

She got out and limped to the entrance to a small memorial park, where a plaque read *"In Memory of Those Who Died, We Will Never Forget-July, 1960".*

The ghosts of that day trailed behind Alice as she walked through the ivy-covered gate and into a simple garden. She could see the booths that had been crowded into the space, the cement slab in the center. Now, there were just bushes along a narrow path. The smell of caramel corn drifted on the air for a moment, and then faded to the cold emptiness of winter. Alice could almost hear screams echoing around her, but it was just a distortion of the fountain splashing in the center of the garden. Her heartbeat began to speed up and she had to stop, leaning heavily on her cane. Closing her eyes didn't help, as it only brought the images of that day into sharper focus.

Pale clouds of fear gas...shapes...people...blood... pain...smoke!

A hand grabbed her arm and she yelped. Without thought, she grabbed the hand and threw a punch where she knew a stomach would be. Someone grunted, and blocked her next attack.

"Alice!" Gerald said, hands on her shoulders.

She halted with her arm cocked back for another punch,

eyes wide as she stared at Gerald. Then all the strength went out of her and she sagged against him.

He held her tight, and Alice could feel the cool sensation that went with Gerald's healing powers.

"I'm alright," she whispered.

It's nothing you can heal.

"Why did you come here?" he asked.

"I've driven past it so many times...I don't know. It seems to be a day for memories."

"These might not be the best ones to drudge up."

Alice stepped out of his embrace and smiled. "I know. I just...I never went to the dedication and I just wanted to see it. Just once."

"It's prettier in the spring. Now it's a little..."

"Dead?"

Gerald gave her a wry grin. "C'mon, the Pride kids are expecting us."

They stepped out of the garden and Alice was about to get into her car, when someone called out to her from across the street.

"Hello, Mr. Marsden," she said, smiling on the outside while wanting to give the man a very unladylike gesture.

Mr. Marsden was tall and fit, with graying blond hair and gave off an air of European aristocracy, despite the fact that his family was new money. He walked casually across the street to Alice, taking his time, as if he owned it.

Which in a way, I suppose he does...

"How good to see you," he said, squeezing her hand in both of his. "What brings you to Park Side? I was under the impression that you disliked this neighborhood since the massacre."

Alice extricated her from his and resisted the urge to wipe it on her skirt.

"I do not come here often, that's true, but I have business in the area."

"Ah, finally going to sell those rat traps Mrs. Frost bought?"

It took a great deal of self-control for Alice to bite back the response that leapt to her tongue. She shook her head, getting control of her temper.

"No, I am inspecting some of the renovations actually. I want to make sure the contractors aren't cheating us."

"I would've thought that...well, perhaps it is none of my business, but I had thought that you, being young and forward thinking, would've wanted to sell those buildings, now that you have control of the company. You know, the future is in middle class families, when it comes to real estate, not...well, these people."

Alice's smile felt stiff on her face but she held it nonetheless. "You know, Mr. Marsden, I hadn't thought of it like that. You seem to have a very keen business mind when it comes to real estate."

If he'd been an actual peacock, Alice knew she'd have seen his tail plumage ruffle and his chest puff out.

"I don't like to brag but, I was one of the first to invest in Park Side."

"Really?"

"Oh, yes. I could see that there was a gold mine here after that awful attack. People were leaving as fast as they could, and so I thought, why not buy the terrible buildings and turn them into apartments for decent, upright citizens? I love Jet City, you understand, and would never want anything like that unfortunate incident to occur ever again. Ensuring that good people are here is the best way to do that."

Alice nodded, only half listening.

"Well," he continued, "your properties are prime real estate, if you don't mind my saying. Close to a school and a park, within walking distance of a very nice neighborhood.

You could have the apartments rented before you even finished building them!"

"You think so, really?"

"Oh, yes! I'd be happy to help, if you should like. A young woman like you should be thinking of other things, wedding dresses, babies, that sort of thing."

Alice laughed. "Well, I will keep that in mind. Thank you for your advice."

"Oh, I remember why I came over to talk with you. My nephew is coming back from Sweden in a few days, and I was wondering if you would like to meet him."

Well he's not subtle, is he?

"Your nephew?"

"Yes, he hasn't been here in quite some time and I thought that someone close to his age to befriend might make him feel a bit more at home."

"I would be delighted. Please call and have my assistant set up a lunch. Now, I'm sorry to end this, but I really must be going."

"Oh yes! Of course, I am sorry to keep you. And remember what I said, about real estate."

"Don't you worry, I will."

The apartment building where the children had been trying to eke out an existence was one that Alice and Mrs. Frost had purchased right away. It was in good condition compared to others in Park Side, and the renovations were nearly complete. The only thing Alice had asked of the residents was to take care of one another.

She hadn't meant for them to spy on each other and call Social Services when one apartment played too much loud music, but what was the use of complaining about that now?

The newly-repaired stairs shone with a dark stain finish as Alice climbed to the second floor. The apartment doors were new, and the smell of fresh paint and plaster lingered in the air under the various cooking smells.

When she knocked on apartment 206, a short, stocky teenage boy answered the door, his bright green eyes narrowing.

"You the social worker?"

Alice smiled. "No, I'm Alice Seymour and this," she gestured behind her, "is Dr. Allen from the Park Side Clinic."

"Hello, Simon," Gerald said. "Can we come in?"

Simon shrugged and opened the door wider, his square face set in a tight frown.

Alice heard what sounded like a cartoon playing from the living room nearby, and the smell of toast burning made her nose itch. She glanced into the small galley kitchen, where a new stove gleamed and the new fridge already had a small hand print of something that might've been jelly.

"This the woman from the home?" Simon asked Gerald.

He nodded. "She wanted to talk to you and the others about coming to her Children's Home instead of going into the system."

Simon sighed, a sound far too heavy and adult for someone that looked barely sixteen.

"What did he tell you?" Simon asked, his voice low.

"That you and a few of your siblings needed special help."

The boy's green eyes snapped up to hers, a glint of distrust shining in them. She held the gaze with a gentle smile on her lips and, eventually, he softened.

"We're not related, not technically. But special help... that would be nice. The littlest one, Judy, she's pretty scared. It started for her right after her mother died a month ago, but she hid it until…well, until someone tried to grab her last week."

"And is she the only one?" Alice asked.

Simon snapped his fingers and white sparks appeared. At first Alice thought it was fire, but then she saw the hair stand up on his arm and the lights began to flicker.

"I've had to learn the hard way to control it," Simon moved his fingers and a white ball of electricity began forming in his hand. "And I can be discreet when I need to." He released the ball gently and the lights returned to normal. "But the others? They're just learning."

"Can I meet them?" Alice asked, schooling her voice and features into a peaceful neutrality.

Simon looked at Gerald, who nodded, and the two headed for the living room. Alice followed them and soon saw three children sitting around a fuzzy television watching a cartoon cat and mouse singing.

The youngest, Judy, had dark skin and hair that was braided in two pig tails and looked like she was eight, or nine at most. She ducked behind a thread bare throw pillow on the couch the moment she saw Alice. The other two, twin boys with large brown eyes and light brown skin, were probably ten or eleven and stared up at her with naked curiosity.

The TV turned off with a pop that could only be from the loss of its electrical connection, and Alice shivered at the raised hair on her body as Simon drew the power into himself.

"Hey!" said one of the twins.

"This nice lady has something to say, and we're gonna listen," Simon said, his hand closing over the ball of electricity.

Alice smiled as four pairs of eyes settled on her. She sat down on a chair with so little stuffing the springs were digging into her bottom, hands resting on the head of her plain black cane. Outside, she looked calm and peaceful, inside her stomach roiled with nerves.

"I'm Alice, and I promise I don't want to hurt you. I want to give you a safe place to be who you are. Maybe even to find a family—"

"We have a family," one of the twin's said. "We don't need—"

"Mateo, zip it!" Simon said. "She's on the level, might even be one of us for all we know, so we're gonna listen."

"What's your power?" asked the other twin.

"Sam, quiet!"

"I'm not one of you," Alice said, "but, I have known people like you."

"Did you know the Vigilantes?" Sam asked, his dark eyes shining.

A familiar pain squeezed Alice's chest and she ignored it. "In a way, yes, I did."

"Are they...are they monsters?" Judy asked from behind her pillow.

"No, they're not. They're heroes."

"Like we could be," Mateo said, puffing out his chest.

Alice couldn't help a smile. "Someday, if you work very hard and are very brave and good, yes, you could be a hero, too."

"The Social Services will be here tomorrow," Gerald said. "They won't care if you want to stay together. Since you're not blood-related, they will split you up and send you to different places."

"But we're like family," Judy said, her large brown eyes peeking out. "We took a vote, and now we're all Prides."

"Yes, but that's not what they look at," Alice said. "But if you come with me, I promise that you will be together. Not in the same room, we have boys' rooms and girls' rooms, but you will see each other every day. And you won't have to be afraid of being who you are."

"Is everyone there like us?" Simon asked.

"No, so you won't be able to use your powers just whenever. But no one will ever do anything bad to you because of your powers."

"So, the others kids know?" Mateo asked.

Alice sighed. "In a way. Some of them have seen kids like you. Some of them are like you."

Simon looked at the three other kids. "This is probably the best thing we've got coming. I can't look out for you if we get split up. I won't make you do anything you don't want, but…I think this is what we should do."

His simple speech seemed to do the trick, because the twins stood up in one fluid motion and smiled at Alice.

"Judy?" Simon asked, holding out his hand. "I think you can trust them."

Very slowly, the little girl lowered the couch cushion and Alice had to clench her jaw to keep from gasping.

The child was slight, a faded blue dress hanging on her frame. But that wasn't what made Alice want to run to the child and hug her tight. It was the bright pink hash marks that covered her little mouth.

Alice looked at Simon. "What happened?"

Judy looked down at the new carpet and nodded, as if giving Simon permission.

"The kids in her building found out about her and one day they cornered her and sewed her lips shut."

"Judy," Gerald said, kneeling down in front of the little girl, "has a very special voice. She can make vibrations that will hurt bad people, or destroy things."

"Like buildings," Simon said, "which…you heard about the apartment that collapsed a month back?"

"Yes…"

Gerald took a deep breath. "They blamed it on structural problems, but that wasn't it, not really. The same kids cornered Judy again and she got scared."

Fat, bright tears fell from Judy's pointed chin. "And Mama...I didn't mean to..."

Gerald held Judy's little hand, wiping her tears away. "We know sweetheart, we know."

"I don't want to hurt anybody else," she whispered. "If you can help me, I want to come live with you."

Alice felt her chest once again tighten, and, maybe for the first time in her life, she wished that she could take the little girl into her own home.

Maybe...No, am I crazy! She'd be safer at the Children's Home.

"I believe," Alice said, "that we can help you. All of you. We will find a way, I promise."

"But you don't know what *our* powers are," Mateo said.

Alice smiled at the boys' sudden enthusiasm. "Well, what are they?"

The twins grinned at each other. Mateo disappeared completely, the only evidence he was still there was an ecstatic giggle. Sam put his hands out and something that looked like a huge soap bubble surrounded him.

"Simon?" Sam said, bouncing on the balls of his feet.

Simon rolled his eyes and threw a small ball of electricity at the bubble. It evaporated in a puff of sparks.

"Judy, wanna give it a try?"

The hint of a smile played at the corners of the girls scarred lips, but she shook her head.

"Alright, now you," Sam said, nodding at Alice.

"What about me?" she asked.

A disembodied voice behind Alice made her jump. "Hit the bubble, silly."

Alice took a swing at it with her cane and it bounced off.

"That's pretty impressive," she said.

"'Pretty impressive'?" Mateo said, reappearing next to her.

"Yeah," Sam said, the bubble disappearing. "I think that

deserves at least a 'Wow! You guys will one day be the best heroes in all of Jet City!'"

"Or something equally cool."

Alice laughed. "I will admit that you will be very good heroes, someday."

Mateo shrugged. "That'll have to do."

"I will send a car for you tonight," Alice said. "You can take whatever you want with you, just be ready at five. You'll have dinner at the home, I think it's fried chicken tonight."

"Will you be there?" Judy asked.

Alice bent down and brushed a dark curl from Judy's face. "I will come see you tomorrow, find out how you're settling in. How does that sound?"

Judy nodded.

Simon walked Alice and Gerald to the door. When he looked up at them, his green eyes were bright with tears.

"Thank you," his voice was rough. "I don't...I'm not good at whatever this is."

"I think you've done a very good job," Alice said. "They've been lucky to have you. But, you don't have to do it anymore. You can be their friend, not their father."

Simon nodded. "We'll be ready tonight."

———

Alice and Gerald walked down the stairs and out to the waiting car. For a while, they were both silent as the construction of Park Side faded into the bright store fronts and packed traffic of downtown Jet City.

"Any idea why we are suddenly finding so many of them? And so young?" Alice asked.

Gerald shook his head, blowing out smoke from a newly-lit cigarette. "I've been trying to figure that out, but I don't know. Could be trauma of some kind brings it on, or genetics."

"I wish there was a way to find out."

"To what end?"

Alice stopped and thought about that. Finally, she shrugged. "I don't know I'm just...I feel very out of my depth with this."

Gerald patted her hand. "You're doing fine, really."

"But I'm starting to see that it might not be enough," Alice said. "These kids...they need something more than what we've done so far. They need protection, they need to know how to control their powers. No one should be afraid of themselves or walking out their front door, just because they're different."

"What do you want to do?" Gerald asked.

"I don't know. I still think a private school would have a target on it, but I don't know what else to try."

"Let me think about it. We've got a little time."

Tell that to Judy...

Alice's jaw tightened at the memory of the little girl's scarred lips, the way she was afraid to speak.

Just as they were pulling into the Frost Mansion's circular drive, tiny white flakes began floating to the ground. Alice smiled, a few flakes melting against her round cheeks when she stepped out of the car. She looked over at Gerald, and he smiled at her.

I hope Mrs. Frost wakes up and sees this.

CHAPTER FIVE

"You sent flowers," the busty red headed maid said as she nibbled Lionel's ear.

"It seemed the thing to do," he grinned, thoroughly enjoying her rather skilled attentions.

"Hmmmm....I loved them."

"I'm glad."

He kissed her long and deep before pulling away as if he were about to leave.

Lionel had felt genuinely guilty about using this woman after their first hurried encounter in a supply closet. But she didn't seem to mind the casual nature of the dalliance, had seemed to prefer it actually.

"Where are you off to?" she asked. "More spying on the rich blond woman?"

Lionel shrugged.

"Ah, you have more questions."

"Only if you," he kissed her neck, "have more information."

"I do. But you have to give me assurances that it will be worth my while."

Lionel picked her up and set her on his lap. After a few

minutes of carefully teasing ministrations, the maid was a panting, groaning puddle.

"You can have more," he said, "if you tell me what you know."

"Oh *mon chere*, you are a tease."

Lionel kissed her. "Only for you."

She chuckled, a deep, seductive sound.

"Alright then. She's got a reservation for Le Jardin Dore at eight o'clock. She's bringing," the maid planted a kiss on Lionel's lips, "a short Russian man."

"Do you know his name?"

"No. He didn't seem the friendly type. I don't even know how he got into the country."

She planted biting kisses along his neck, her breath hot on his ear as she asked, "Why are you so interested in this woman? What is she to you?"

"It's business, that's all."

"Oh, well then. I suppose I'm not really jealous."

"That's good, you shouldn't be," Lionel said, nibbling her breasts. "Now, for your reward, my dear."

She buried her hands in his hair and gasped.

Le Jardin Dore was a new night club that catered to some of the richest tourists in the world. The clothes of a Parisian artist wouldn't get Lionel past the front door.

With great care, he unzipped a large garment bag and stared at his dark blue suit. Memories flooded his mind. Memories of Alice and her smile, her voice.

That blue dress I bought her...the way she'd looked at me, kissed me...

It was a lifetime ago, yet Lionel could swear he still felt her lips on his.

He would always love her, always want her. Some

people just became a part of you after a while, and Alice had been lodged in his heart since the moment he'd first seen her smile. Though Lionel knew that after Park Side things could never go back to the way they were, he sometimes still yearned for the future that would never be.

Tears clouded his vision and Lionel shook his head to dislodge the thoughts of grief and loss. He had to focus and find out what he could. Crying could come later.

He took a deep breath, rallying whatever strength had kept him going all this time, and got dressed. When he was done, the image of a starving artist had been replaced by a handsome socialite with dark hair and glasses. Lionel hoped Victoria was distracted enough not to look too closely at him tonight. The suit made him appear much like he had in Jet City.

"Though people see what they want, as Maria said."

The winter air was dry and brutally cold when he stepped outside and climbed into a cab.

Le Jardin Dore was across town from where his tiny apartment sat, so by the time Lionel arrived, he was a mere ten minutes ahead of when Victoria would be there.

The outside of the nightclub was bedecked in gold flowers winding up two green columns, gold and blue doors that were opened by opulently dressed men who didn't even meet his eye. His shoes sunk into the thick carpet in the foyer as he checked his coat and then walked to the maitre'd with a swagger that had half the men and women watching him with hungry gazes

"Reservation?" asked the maitre'd.

"No," Lionel said, his voice bored as he pulled a cigarette out of a case and lit it.

The maitre'd looked him over and Lionel simply stared right back.

"Ah well, you see we are very busy-"

"Here, this might help."

He slipped the man a business card with his real name and the logo of Apollo Industries brazenly printed on its white surface.

The man frowned and then, as if a literal light bulb had gone off in his brain, his face brightened.

"Oh, but of course, yes! I am so sorry! We have a table waiting for you."

Lionel's face betrayed none of the worry his mind was reeling with. If his father came in, if anyone from Apollo was here meeting Victoria, this would get messy fast.

"How is that possible when I-"

"Oh, I'm sorry, I meant, we always have a table for Jason James' son."

"I see."

The maitre'd hesitated, a sychophantic smile on his face.

"Well? Am I going to stand here all night?" Lionel asked, inwardly cringing at the harsh tone he laid on.

"No! No, pardon, I am so sorry. This way."

The man skittered ahead of Lionel and ushered him into the gorgeous garden themed dining room. A table awaited him near the center of the room and just a few feet from the stage where a floor show would take place very soon. He would be in the direct eye line of anyone and everyone.

Victoria will spot me as soon as she walks in.

"No," he said, letting nerves coat his tone with frustration.

"I-I'm sorry, sir? This is the best table-"

"I'm sure it is but you see, I don't want to be the center of attention tonight. Put me somewhere that prying eyes won't notice if I go home with a woman who isn't my girlfriend."

The maitre'd's smile changed into something wolfish and he nodded.

"But of course, yes. Like father like son, eh?'

Lionel clenched his jaw and nodded.

Sure pal, if I was a sadistic asshole with a God complex.

The next table was off to the side in what would be the shadows of the room once the floor show got under way. It also had the advantage of being out of the general vicinity of most of the rich and annoying that frequented the night club.

"This," the maitre'd said, gesturing to a non descript door to the left, "is a private exit where you can leave whenever you wish, with whomever you wish and no one will be the wiser."

"Thanks," Lionel said, sitting down and not giving the man a second look.

A waiter scurried over and Lionel ordered a whiskey sour, something he hadn't indulged in too much in the last few months. He'd nurse the drink instead of guzzling half a dozen through the course of the night like he wanted to do.

At precisely eight o'clock, Victoria walked into the room, golden hair piled high on her head. Her cool blue eyes scanned the room in a lazy arc that was meant to show indifference, but Lionel knew better. She was looking for someone or something.

Trailing behind her was Baritone, leaving confused and repulsed people in his wake. Lionel didn't see anyone who fit the maid's description of a short Russian and wondered if she might've gotten it wrong.

Victoria sat down at a table a mere five feet from the one the maitre'd had tried to place Lionel in and whispered something to her body guard.

Baritone nodded and left the room. Though a moment later, Lionel spied him standing in the very back, glaring at everyone with his one good eye. Victoria smiled and chatted with a few other society matrons, their bodies squeezed into couture dresses that would cost the yearly food budget of an average family.

The minutes stretched to an hour, and the short Russian

didn't show up. Lionel ordered food and ate with bored distraction as he watched Victoria, who didn't seem at all bothered by being stood up. Though outwardly, he looked as if he were having a decent time, inside Lionel's body hummed with tension. He fidgeted with the ring on his pinkie and tried to not order a fourth drink to calm his nerves.

When the lights for the floor show finally dimmed, Lionel lit another cigarette and sat back to see what the psychotic villain would do.

Before the first verse of the first song had finished, a short, very muscular man with a neatly trimmed beard walked up to Victoria. She kissed his cheek and he kissed hers with a familiarity that had Lionel wondering what they were to one another.

As the man sat, a glass of dark, amber liquid appeared at his left hand, which had a briefcase cuffed to it. After the Russian had taken a slow drink from the glass, he unlocked the hand cuff and handed the briefcase to Victoria. Her smile broadened to show her white, perfect teeth and she handed the case to Baritone, who cuffed it to his own wrist and skulked back to his spot at the rear of the club.

Short Russian I presume. I wonder what's in the case. And if the US government might be interested in why a woman like Victoria was meeting with a Russian.

Victoria and her visitor settled in for an intimate discussion as the singer and dancers performed a few feet away from them.

After ten minutes, Lionel realized that Victoria had chosen her table well. From his vantage point it was hard to see them through the feathers and glittering costumes of the performers. Though he couldn't read lips, Lionel could tell by their body language that the discussion was important.

At one point, the smile Victoria had worn all night was

completely gone, her brows knit together and her eyes shot cold daggers at the Russian. She said something, jabbing her finger into the table to make her point. Her companion shook his head and looked away. Under his beard, Lionel could just barely make out the tense set of his lips before dancers blocked his view of the man.

Just as Lionel once again caught a glimpse of them, the entertainers had begun their finale and Lionel couldn't see the table at all. He leaned to the right, trying to see around the dancers, not at all subtle if someone had been looking his direction.

When the chaos of the song had ended, Lionel's stomach dropped.

The table was empty and Baritone was gone as well.

Damn it! I need to know where that man is going.

He threw some money on the table and left through the private entrance the maitre'd had mentioned. It led out to a narrow hallway that Lionel sprinted down. There was a door at the end of the hall that let out into the cleanest alley Lionel had ever seen in his life.

He looked to his left in the direction of the street and ran toward the cars. If he could get to the end of the alley and catch a glimpse of Victoria leaving-

A fist crashed into Lionel's face, the impact lifting him an inch off his feet right before he fell onto his back.

Stars careened through his vision, and Lionel shook his head to dislodged the shock.

Was that Victoria?

Her strength serum had left quite a few bruises on his body when they'd fought, but she'd never lifted him off the ground before.

"You're probably wondering, 'how did he do that?'" said a voice in heavily accented English.

Lionel's head swam from the blow, something that had honestly never happened to him. Once his vision had focused, he could see the Russian standing over him, a malicious grin peeking out from under his beard.

"Strength serum?" Lionel asked, getting off the ground.

The man shrugged. "If you want to call it that. You see, I was once strength champion. Amateur, of course. So, what I have, the 'serum' as you call it, made more, better."

Lionel backed a little away from the man, who as at least six inches shorter than him but evidently just as strong.

Or stronger. That's new.

"It's good finally meet you Mr. Lawson. Or is it Steel? I can never keep up with you hero types and your multiple names."

"Call me what you like."

"How generous."

"And you are?"

The Russian laughed.

"You expect me to spill it like that? Well, since you are so fond of code names, you can call me Mishka."

And with a barreling rush, Mishka knocked the wind out of Lionel and pinned him against one wall of the alley. Lionel gasped in shock as pain lit up his right shoulder.

Pushing passed it, he brought his fists down on Mishka's back to get the villain off of him. With no small measure of satisfaction, Lionel heard the man grunt in pain just before he landed a blow to Lionel's gut.

"Victoria said you were formidable," Mishka said, backing up as if getting ready for another run.

"That's nice of her," Lionel said, gasping for breath.

Lionel feinted to the left and then delivered a right hook to Mishka's face, not bothering to hold back the full strength he possessed.

If there was ever a time I could use a good surge of anger...

Mishka stumbled back and spat blood onto the ground. Without waiting to see if the man was alright, Lionel pressed his attack, coming at him with a rapid sequence of jabs to the face and body. He managed to back Mishka against the opposite wall of the alley and was taken off guard when the man rallied to deliver a blow to Lionel's midsection and then his side.

Lionel felt the breath leave his lungs in a violent rush, and the pain of his lower back muscles seizing. His body doubled over, and Mishka took the opportunity to give Lionel a brutal upper cut that had his teeth clattering together and his jaw screaming in pain.

"You're playing the hero in a game you don't even understand," the Russian wiped blood from his mouth as he stood over Lionel, who found himself once again on the ground. "You think it's just about your city, yes? But you are so blind, much like Victoria. The world is waiting. You could be so much more. A gGd with people bowing at your feet. And yet you throw it all away."

"You're talking about the Consortium then?"

Mishka paused, eyes narrowing.

"And how would you...? Ah, yes, I see. Victoria...you were too sure of yourself, my dear. Pity."

Lionel was surprised at the tender tone in Mishka's voice and also that he seemed unaware of what Victoria was doing.

He didn't have time to unpack all of it, before Mishka seized Lionel's hair with one hand and punched in him twice with the other.

Pain exploded across Lionel's face, his vision going fuzzy as his mind struggled to clear.

He'd been in so many fights, he'd been injured in more than a few. But never, in all the years he'd had his powers, had anyone been able to get the upper hand like this man suddenly had.

And for the first time, Lionel was afraid.

"It's a shame," Mishka said, "you would've made a

wonderful addition to our arsenal. I'm surprised the other American never found a way to use you, he's so fond of weapons."

Mishka pulled back for another series of blows when a horribly familiar voice cut through the pain filled fog of Lionel's mind.

"She doesn't want him dead," said Baritone, standing a few feet away. "He's going to help her get what she wants."

"I know what Victoria wants, and she has become short sighted because of it."

"There are rules to this sort of thing."

The Russian swore and let go of Lionel's hair.

"If he survives whatever she has in store for him, then he's mine."

"Sure. C'mon, she's waiting for you."

Mishka gave Lionel one last kick to his midsection before walking away.

The moment the former vigilante tried to stand, his legs folded under him. He'd come very close to dying tonight and it would take longer than usual for his body to heal.

He was grateful for the tidiness of the alley as he crawled to the nearest wall and leaned his aching head against it. Every muscle screamed at him, and his lungs felt on fire as he tried to get air flowing through them again.

Why does Victoria care if I'm alive or not? And what the hell was Mishka talking about? There's something more behind his words. I can feel it.

A loud groan escaped his lips as Lionel felt a bone snap back into place. He could feel the bruises and internal injuries beginning to knit, the sensation felt like hundreds of hot bees crawling under his skin. Lionel breathed through the worst of it as his body stabilized itself.

Once his mind cleared enough that Lionel could think of something other than agony, he decided to run over everything that was said, trying to distract himself from the healing still taking place.

Victoria doesn't want us dead, she's going to use us and Mishka seemed disappointed in her...she'd over stepped...but how? What if...what if the Consortium doesn't want us gone but just controlled...He called me a good addition to—.

"Arsenal," Lionel's eyes became wide as he jerked upright. The sharp agony in his back told him that was a bad idea and he fell back against the wall. "What if the others aren't wanting us eliminated just controlled?"

A sick feeling settled in Lionel's gut that had nothing to do with his muscles shifting as they healed.

"Apollo is known for it's weapons...and Jason is a greedy, conniving man...but how would they do it?"

Lionel shook his head. It was absurd, not to mention terrifying. He knew there was likely something to it, but the variables wouldn't come together and form a picture the way they did for Alice.

At the thought of her, something else fell into place and Lionel felt sick.

"The only reason I'd help Victoria is if she had Alice and Marco. She's planning something for us. I have to call Marco...warn him..."

But then Lionel realized that maybe Victoria wanted him to do that because she wanted to find Marco.

"Damned if I do and damned if I don't."

Now anger began to worm it's way through his veins, but it was weaker than usual, and did nothing to help him heal faster. Lionel could only sit there in the cold and fume about what to do.

By the time he was able to get off the ground without feeling like he was going to vomit, the night was far gone and Lionel was starting to worry that Victoria might know that he'd contacted Fritz.

I've got to check on him...make sure...

He got to the end of the alley before having to admit that he was still in no condition to take defend anyone. Ignoring the horrified looks of passersby, Lionel hailed a cab and went back to his dingy apartment.

I could call Fritz...but the man spooks too easily. He'll bolt. No, I'll visit him tomorrow, and every day if I have to so I can keep him safe.

The creaking, old bed that was several inches too short for his frame had never felt so good as it did tonight when he fell into it, fully clothed.

CHAPTER SIX

The rest of the week passed in a steady stream of business meetings and visits to the Children's Home to make sure the Pride children were settling in. Alice realized during her third visit that it was the most she'd spent at the Children's Home in months.

Today she'd been in time for Thursday afternoon milk and cookies in the common room. Sam was nursing an upset stomach in his room and Simon was sitting with Judy and another girl by the bookshelf, reading to them. Mateo, as per usual on these visits, was staying with Alice and asking questions about the Vigilantes and what it was like to live in a mansion.

"Hey, you gonna finish that?" Mateo asked, pointing at her half eaten cookie.

She smiled. "Nope, all yours."

He shoved it into his chocolate smeared mouth and Alice laughed.

She realized with a start that it was the truest laugh she'd had in a very long time.

"Ok, watch this now," Mateo said, disappearing.

Alice felt the ghost of a touch on her coat pocket and grinned.

Reaching out with reflexes that had been honed over the last two years, her fingers closed over a small, invisible hand.

"Hey!" Mateo said, reappearing. "How did you do that? Are you sure you don't have powers."

Alice crossed her heart. "I swear."

"Then how?"

"I'm just very observant."

Mateo crossed his thin arms and studied her. "I'll just have to practice then."

"Heroes generally don't steal."

"Except from the bad guys."

Alice started to say that even that was a bad idea and then she thought about what she'd been doing to Victoria over the last few years. And then, to her further surprise, she realized how little she'd thought about her mission while she'd been with the children.

When I'm here, with them, I don't think about Victoria or what comes next. I'm just...happy.

"Miss Seymour?" Mateo asked.

"Yes?"

"You ok?"

"Yes, why?"

"You just...got this look on your face...kinda sad."

Alice smiled. "No, I'm not sad. But, I do have to go."

"Ok, but come back on Sunday. There's supposed to be cake and if you don't eat yours I'll get two pieces."

"I bet you could get two pieces even if I'm not here."

Mateo looked down, his smile fading. "Yeah but...I like it when you're here."

Alice hesitated, then reached out and took the slight boy in her arms. "I like it too."

"Then come back, ok?"

"Ok. Cake on Sunday."

Mateo smiled a broad, toothy grin at her and skipped out of her arms.

She watched him run to Simon, who waved good-bye to her.

Several of the other children said their good-byes as she made her way to the door, a few even daring to hug her since they'd seen Mateo do it.

When she got downstairs and to the main entry way, Gerald was just coming inside.

"How are they?" he asked.

"Adjusting well I think."

Gerald put a hand on her upper arm and held her gaze. "How are you?"

A jolt of irritation lanced through her, though the smile she gave him wasn't as stiff as usual, and it felt a little more honest than in the past when she said, "Fine, just fine."

Gerald smiled back. "Good. I will be back at the mansion in an hour, I just needed to check on a few of the children."

"I will see you there."

"Miss Seymour," Miss Jones said as Alice stepped into the Frost Mansion. "I was instructed to tell you that Mr. Parker will arrive promptly at seven to pick you up for the symphony tonight."

"But it doesn't start until eight," Alice said, shrugging out of her coat.

"I believe he wants to have cocktails prior."

Alice sighed. "He would. Alright, could you call Uncle Logan and have him meet us wherever Jared is taking us for cocktails?"

Miss Jones nodded. "Francis will arrive in an hour to set

your hair, and Jacques will not be far behind. I drew a bath for you upstairs."

"Thank you. Do you need anything for tonight?"

"No, I believe that what Miss Allen has procured will do nicely."

Alice pretended to brush lint off her black skirt. "How was Rose when you saw her?"

Miss Jones didn't say anything until Alice looked up. "She seemed a little out of sorts and very anxious to attend her civil rights meeting, for which she was late."

"Oh, well…thank you, Miss Jones."

"It is interesting," Miss Jones said as Alice began climbing the staircase. "She asked about you, as well."

Alice smiled. "Did she?"

"I have many jobs for which Mrs. Frost hired me. A go-between for two friends who are fighting is not one of them, but all the same, let me just say that in circumstances like this, it is best to speak directly to the person who is angry."

Alice felt her face begin to flush and turned away. "Yes, you are right of course."

As she climbed the rest of the stairs to her bedroom, Alice felt a sudden fatigue settle onto her like a weight. She sank onto the huge bed with its soft blue and white duvet and mounds of pillows. She longed to just lay down and let herself drift off into a deep nothingness. But sleep was elusive on the best of nights, with Alice often finding herself roaming the house, like some ghost looking for something.

Or someone.

She cringed.

Lately, her thoughts turned more and more to Marco and Lionel. Though they were always there, lurking in the back of her mind, Alice was usually very good at keeping them at a distance. Until recently, that is. Perhaps it was the realization that the end was fast approaching. Or maybe it was seeing the closeness of the Pride children. Whatever the reason, the memories were harder to push away these days.

The small clock down the hall chimed the quarter hour and Alice sighed. If she wanted a bath she'd better do it now.

And then to be painted and fussed with like some prize dog that everyone wants to own, while Miss Jones gets to have all the fun. If only my date was remotely interesting.

As she shed her black skirt and sweater, Alice's gaze fell on a small book with a bright green cover and gold lettering that lay on her desk. She walked over and ran her fingers over the cover.

"Why's a raven like a writing desk?" she said, a bitter-sweet pain in her chest. "I guess we'll never know, will we?"

"Vous avez l'air parfait!" Jacques said, clapping his hands.

"Merci, beaucoup," Alice replied, grateful that she now understood more than just a few phrases from the Frenchman.

Mrs. Frost had been the one to give Jacques seed money for his first boutique, and as a thank you, he had agreed to design clothes for Alice and remain in Jet City for a little while. That had been almost a year ago, and he seemed in no hurry to leave.

Alice hadn't been enthusiastic at the thought of having someone design thousands of dollars' worth of clothes for her, but when she saw what Jacques could do with a simple bolt of green fabric and her curves, she had relented.

For tonight, Jacques had created a gorgeous dark blue silk dress that draped over Alice's body, giving it the illusion of height. As she stared at the lofty, intricate pile of hair atop her head, and the way the dress fell over her body and down to her feet, Alice felt like a Grecian Goddess.

"You need a few more pins," Francis said, hands on her round hips. "Perhaps…"

She reached up and placed three more diamond-studded pins in Alice's hair.

"There! Now she's perfect."

Tiny dots of light twinkled in Alice's dark hair. She had worried that diamond studded hair pins would be too much, what with the large, teardrop, sapphire earrings and matching bracelet she also wore. But in the end, she had to agree with Francis, it was perfect.

"S'il ne propose pas ce soir, il est aveugle!" Jacques said.

Alice laughed outwardly, but inside, she cringed.

I hope Jared doesn't propose, it would be awkward to have to turn down another society catch.

After Jacques and Francis fussed over her for another few minutes, Alice grabbed her cane and went into Mrs. Frost's room to say good bye.

Hot air hit Alice the moment she opened the door and the smell of something…

Douglas smelled like that just before…

She looked at Gerald, who was taking Mrs. Frost's pulse. When he looked up and met her eyes, Alice's stomach dropped.

"Soon…" Gerald said as Alice silently stepped closer to the bed.

Mrs. Frost's breathing was erratic, with a strange rattling sound to it. Her face was slack, skin sagging against bones which had become terribly prominent the last month.

"Maybe I shouldn't—"

"You know what she'd say."

"Yes, but…I don't want…"

"But you need to."

Alice looked up at Gerald, whose gaze was devoid of judgment.

"Alice..." His voice was soft, full of understanding. "She always understood you better than you thought. If you're here, she may try to hold on for your sake, so you don't have to see her die."

Tears burned in her eyes and she held them back. He was right, and a part of Alice wanted to stay for that very reason. But instead, she bent down, pressing a light kiss on Mrs. Frost's forehead. A hint of red lipstick made a garish patch of color on the pale skin and Alice gently wiped it off with a tissue.

"I'll come see you when I get home," Alice whispered. "Tell you about how awful the date was."

Alice could swear she heard a soft, grunting laugh beneath the labored breathing, and smiled.

The bored socialites of Jet City exited the theater in a glittery mass and made their way to the waiting bartenders for a little intermission refreshment. Alice limped slowly with her cane, Jared Parker's hand lightly cupping her elbow.

"Can I get you a club soda?" he asked.

Looking up between her artificially long lashes, Alice smiled. "If you wouldn't mind. I am afraid I'd be trampled with this cane."

"Of course. Miss Ruiz..." Jared said, turning to Uncle Logan's date and barely concealing his disgust, "...can I get you anything?"

"Champagne, please?"

Jared nodded, his smile tight.

Oona's large brown eyes caught Alice's, flashing a smile as she lit the cigarette at the end of a crimson holder that matched the clingy dress she wore. Alice had to admit, her

Uncle had a type. Statuesque and athletic, Oona Ruiz was a few inches taller than Uncle Logan, and as tall as most of the other men in the room. Her red-brown hair was pulled back into a simple knot, with strategically-placed strands left loose to accent her long neck and heart-shaped face. The crimson dress made her light brown skin appear richer somehow, and Alice found herself wondering how Oona seemed to ignore all the leering and judgmental looks she attracted.

"I was relieved when your Uncle told me you weren't serious about Mr. Parker," Oona said, her voice low and sensual.

"He's an interesting distraction."

"I've dated a few of those in the past." Her brown eyes shone when they found Uncle Logan talking to Jared as they waited at the bar. "But these days, it's quite different."

Alice fought the urge to roll her eyes.

"I am very glad you invited me tonight," Oona continued. "I have wanted to get to know you better. Perhaps next week, we could have lunch? Your uncle told me that you like the International Quarter, there's a wonderful Chinese restaurant there."

"That would be nice. Miss Jones can set something up."

Oona blew a stream of smoke from between her crimson lips and turned to Alice.

"You know that I have no intention of replacing your aunt, don't you?"

Alice had to admire her directness.

"You couldn't if you tried." Alice had meant to sound playful, but came out hard.

She expected Oona to be angry or turn away. Instead, the tall woman smiled.

"Finally, honesty."

Alice's face burned, but with anger or embarrassment, she couldn't tell.

"I want him to be happy, but this is very hard to watch, you have to understand that. In the end, it doesn't matter if I like you or approve. If you make him happy, and don't hurt him, that's all that matters."

"If your uncle didn't see you as a daughter, then you might be right. But he loves you. And if you won't accept me, it will be very hard on him. You see that, don't you?"

"Unfortunately."

"I'm not asking to be your best friend, or even another aunt. I would settle for just being on friendly terms for now, with the hope of becoming real friends later."

"Do you…?"

"Love him?"

Alice nodded.

"I could, with time I could be very much in love with him," Oona's eyes twinkled. "Age difference and all."

Alice chuckled. "He really doesn't like talking about that."

"No, he doesn't. But it's quite fun to see him squirm when I bring it up. Ask him sometime what grade I was in when he was at college."

Jared and Uncle Logan were making their way back toward them, tight smiles on both their faces.

"I will," Alice said, as a little of the dislike she'd felt for Oona faded.

"Sorry that took so long," Uncle Logan said, handing Oona a slim champagne flute. "Did you two have a nice talk?"

Subtle, real subtle.

"Yes," Alice said, taking a sip of her club soda. "We decided to have lunch next week."

Uncle Logan visibly relaxed, his gaze sending a silent 'thank you' to Alice.

The rest of the short intermission passed with Jared doing his best to ignore Oona, without seeming outright rude, and Oona seeming not to care or notice. By the time they were making their way back into the theater, Alice had a bit more respect for her.

They had just settled into the richly upholstered seats when an usher jogged down the aisle toward them. Alice's heart jumped into her throat before she'd read the note he held out to her.

"Thank you," she whispered.

Uncle Logan's rough hand grabbed hers and squeezed. "Is it...?"

Alice nodded as she read the simple message.

"I suppose that's not unexpected," Jared said.

"No," she said, standing. "I have to go."

"But, there's nothing you can do. Might as well enjoy the rest of the—"

"I wish to go," Alice said, a hard glint in her blue eyes.

Jared stared at her as if she'd transformed into something unrecognizable, and Alice realized that the mask she'd worn so effectively all this time had slipped.

"Please," she said, forcing her face into a more passive expression. "I am sorry, but...please."

"You can ride with us," Oona said.

Uncle Logan gave Jared a hard stare and ushered Alice out into the aisle. As the three of them made their way up the aisle, Jared stood with a deep frown on his face and watched them.

"I think that's the last time you'll have to see him," Oona said once, they were all in the car.

Alice couldn't think of anything to say.

———

The car had barely stopped before Alice bolted from it. She silently cursed the wrap around her knee, as it restricted her movements. Everything felt too slow. Opening the door, running up the stairs.

When she was finally in front of Mrs. Frost's bedroom door, Alice stopped, her heart hammering, tears falling. She couldn't seem to make her feet move, her body frozen at the entrance to the room.

A heavy hand fell on her shoulder.

"I can go first if you want," Uncle Logan said.

She shook her head and finally opened the door.

Despite everything Alice had been through with Gerald, she'd rarely, if ever, seen him cry. But the first thing she saw was Gerald sitting by the hospital bed, face buried in his hands. His sobs were low and ragged. It cut Alice to the quick to see him like that, and any strength she had left evaporated. She stumbled to the bed, sight blurred with tears. After a moment of blind groping, she found Mrs. Frost's hand. It still held the smallest hint of warmth and she pressed her lips to it, tears wetting the wrinkled flesh.

Beyond the sounds of crying, Alice noticed an odd silence in the room and realized what was missing: beeping machines and the rattle of Mrs. Frost's breathing.

And with that reality, she broke down. Heaving sobs shook her body and she clutched the edge of the hospital bed, her cries joining with Gerald's in the room that now felt so terribly empty.

At some point, Uncle Logan brought a chair to her and Alice sat down. Eventually, her tears stopped and she simply stared at the green and violet carpet, wrung out and raw.

"Alice?" Uncle Logan said, kneeling in front of her.

His eyes were red, and Alice was surprised at how upset he was. He and Mrs. Frost were never friends, but maybe he'd grown to respect her.

How could anyone not? Especially after knowing everything she did…who she was…

Alice pressed a small hand to her chest. It felt as if someone had drilled a hole there, and now a tiny hollow feeling was taking root.

"Alice…" Uncle Logan said again.

She looked at him.

"The funeral home is here to take her away. I don't think you should stay for that. Why don't you come downstairs, have a little breakfast?"

"Breakfast?" she said, her voice hoarse.

That's when she noticed the pale light of a winter sunrise coming through the window, illuminating the patches of snow on the bushes and lawn.

"I don't…I can't leave her," Alice said, looking at Mrs. Frost.

But someone had covered the body with a sheet and Alice felt a strange revulsion fill her.

That's not her anymore. She's gone.

Fresh tears filled her eyes and she began to cry again, but quiet this time. When Uncle Logan helped her from the chair and walked her out of the room, Alice didn't look back.

CHAPTER SEVEN

Alice woke with a start, feeling as if something wasn't right. What had happened the night before? Was it a fight? Was she…?

"No, it was…"

And that's when her head began to throb and her eyes felt as if someone had rubbed sand into them. She took a moment, sitting on her bed, trying to process what she'd lost. Mrs. Frost had been dying for some time, but the longer she held on the more Alice felt as if this day would never come.

"But it has."

Alice pressed the heels of her hands to her eyes to stop the tears that began to build. She'd cried enough last night, and there would be plenty of time for more tears later. Now, there were things to do.

Not funeral arrangements though. Mrs. Frost had taken care of all that a year ago. There were just a few papers to sign that finalized Alice taking over Frost Consolidated, and then Alice had to speak at the memorial, but that was nothing too difficult.

Miss Jones, the mission last night. I wonder if she got the papers and what they have in them? We'll have to get Rose to analyze them...Mrs. Frost is gone.

All of this swirled around in Alice's mind, simple but overwhelming.

I need to clear my head.

She flung the covers aside and stood up, only to fall back onto the bed. The pain in her head was now beating out a harsh rhythm, and she felt a terrible nausea sweep through her. She barely made it to the bathroom before vomiting. Sitting on the cool linoleum afterward, she leaned against the huge claw-foot tub. The pain was finally starting to ease and she could move without feeling like her head was going to explode.

She closed her eyes and concentrated on her breathing, as Miss Jones had taught her, to stop the incessant spinning of her mind. She'd started to let go, finding a pinprick of calm, when a memory burst in her brain.

Marco was holding her, the warmth and strength of his arms soothing her grief.

The effort of pushing away the memory was hard on the best of days, but on a day like this, it was impossible. The pain of his absence blossomed out from her chest and into her arms and legs. It was pointless to try and stop the tears. Her throat tightened and soon she was drowning in the pain of losing Marco, Lionel, and now, Mrs. Frost. Her sobs echoed in the large bathroom, startling her at first. How long had it been since she'd allowed herself to cry? Really, truly cry?

"I wish you were here," she sobbed. "Why aren't you here?"

When Alice opened her eyes, she could see the phone on her bedside table and a terrible longing took hold of her. She needed to hear Marco's voice.

Rising clumsily to her feet she went to the phone and picked it up before reason could once again take over. She knew Gerald called him every once in a while, she'd found the number on the phone bill and had memorized it.

She dialed the number with quick strokes, her hand shaking as it held the receiver to her ear.

I'll hear his voice and hang up...I just need to hear his voice, that's all.

It rang and rang, but no one picked up.

Alice dropped the receiver back into its place and buried her face in her hands.

It was well past lunch by the time Alice got dressed and came downstairs, and though she hadn't eaten since the night before, she had no appetite.

Voices came from the library and Alice was about to make her way there when a familiar figure walked out of the small study that Miss Jones used as an office.

Rose wiped her eyes with a hankie and leaned against the door frame, her shoulders sagging.

Alice walked up to her, a little unsure since the last time they spoke was the fight. But when Rose opened her red rimmed eyes, her face crumpled in a sob and Alice threw her arms around her.

They held each other and cried, heaving, snotty sobs into each other's sweaters. And Alice realized that this is what she needed. Not an empty phone call to Marco, but Rose, who was here now, who had stayed and been there for her all this time.

"I'm sorry I wasn't here," Rose said, her face buried in Alice's shoulder.

"Don't be," Alice said, her arms tightening around Rose. "You're here now."

Rose nodded.

They held each other for a little while longer and then

stepped back. When they took in the wet stains on each others shoulders, they both started to laugh through tears that were still falling.

"I'm sorry," Rose said, wiping Alice's shoulder with her hankie.

"Me too," Alice said, doing the same.

She paused and looked at Rose. There was so much they needed to talk about, but one thing Alice knew she had to say before anything else.

"Rose, I'm-."

"You're awake," Uncle Logan said, walking toward them. "I was starting to worry."

He hugged her tight, the familiar smell of peppermint and cigars on his clothes. She hugged him back, the feeling of allowing herself to be comforted an odd thing after all this time of being so strong, so sure.

I still am though...I just need this, just for a moment.

She stepped back and gave Uncle Logan a lopsided grin, wiping a few tears away.

"You hungry?" he asked.

"No," she nodded toward the library. "Is that where everyone is?"

"Yes," Rose said, "I just need to get some files in Miss Jones' office and I'll be right in."

Alice wiped her eyes and nose then followed Uncle Logan to the library.

"You don't have to hide how you're feeling," he said just before they went inside.

"What?"

He nodded toward the hankie clutched in her hand.

"You've never had to," he said, "we all know the pain you've been in and we don't care."

"I-I just want to work. I don't want to-"

"Be weak?"

Her jaw clenched.

"I know," Uncle Logan went on, his unshaven face tender. "You are the furthest thing from weak, Alice. Crying or not."

"It doesn't feel that way," her voice was a harsh whisper as she tried to keep a reign on the tears that started to fall once again. "I can't think when I'm like this, it s just...I can't."

She wiped her eyes once more and swept past him into the library. A cheerful fire was crackling away, and a shining coffee pot sat on a side table with cookies and small tea cakes. Miss Jones and Gerald stood around, papers spread out on the coffee table.

Gerald's smile was sad and he gave her arm a small squeeze.

"Do you want something to eat?" he asked.

"No, just coffee for now."

She felt Uncle Logan's worried gaze on her as he came back into the room. Alice tried to ignore it, poured herself some coffee and took a few sips. The hot liquid coursed through her, giving her a much-needed jolt of caffeine.

I have to focus now, there's still a job to be done.

"How did it go last night?" Alice asked, turning to face Miss Jones.

"You don't have to worry about this right now," Uncle Logan said. "Take a few days off and—"

"I can't," Alice said, feeling her body tense at the thought. "Miss Jones, what did you find?"

"Rose was just trying to decipher that," Miss Jones said, nodding toward the door way.

"It's not good," she said, walking through the doorway.

"I asked Miss Allen to come take a look at the papers when I realized they were beyond my scope of expertise."

For the first time, Alice noticed the fresh bruise on Miss Jones' cheek and the cut on her upper lip.

"Was there trouble?" Alice asked.

"More than usual. The electronic barriers weren't the only thing in my way. There were enhanced guards."

Alice frowned. "We haven't seen enhanced since Park Side. I assumed she'd given it up."

"These weren't like the ones in the past."

"How so?"

"They appeared to be…empty, somehow. As if their free will, their ability to think on their own was removed and replaced with a single-minded purpose: Guard the room."

Alice took a large swallow of coffee. "I saw some like that at Park Side actually, but I thought they were an anomaly."

"If they were, they aren't anymore."

"It took me a few hours," Rose said, pouring herself a cup of coffee, "but I think I know what they're doing."

"Besides the enhanced?" Alice asked.

"Those papers aren't about enhancement, but rather stripping powers away."

Alice felt her stomach drop to her toes. "What?"

"They have been experimenting with how to block or eliminate the genetic ability that some people have to develop powers. From what I can tell, they're reverse engineering something that a German and American scientist had developed just prior to the war."

Gerald set his coffee cup on the saucer with a loud clink, and walked to a nearby window. Alice frowned, wondering what could've upset him, then kicked herself. They just lost Mrs. Frost, of course he's raw.

Putting her attention back on what Rose has been saying, Alice asked, "You mean like the strength serum Victoria created?"

"No, this is different. These scientists actually found a gene they believed could be manipulated and changed to allow people to develop powers. Victoria and her team are attempting to isolate that gene and destroy it or hinder its development, so that people no longer develop powers."

"Would it take powers away from those who have them?"

Rose nodded. "But, from what I can tell from the data, the longer a person has had powers, the riskier the procedure. In theory, if they could stop it before it starts or soon after, the person would experience very few side effects."

"What about the opposite?" Uncle Logan asked. "Would she be able to activate powers with this?"

"According to the data that's what this was originally used for," Rose said. "So, if she could stabilize the serum, then yes. But Victoria doesn't seem interested in that."

"How would this affect anyone without the gene?" Alice asked.

Rose shrugged. "Likely, it wouldn't do anything at all beyond maybe a little nausea."

"Does it say in what form she's making the serum? Injections or—"

"Gas?" Rose asked.

Alice nodded.

"You don't think…" Uncle Logan started.

"Why not? She's done it before. And if it only affects those with the gene, then it poses no risk to everyone Victoria says she's trying to protect."

Rose began flipping through the papers on the coffee table. After a few minutes, she stood up.

"There's one reference to gas, a recent one. In the test, the gas dissipated too quickly, but there's a reference to other tests." Rose looked up at Miss Jones. "Was this everything?"

"Yes, although the file drawer looked as if it had been tampered with and, in addition to the enhanced men, there was a particular person that seemed to be in charge. He may have taken some of the files before I got there."

"The one in charge, do you recognize him?" Alice asked.

"Yes, he's there a lot at night. I thought he was head of security, and he might be, but what he'd be doing with files is a mystery."

"Maybe he was moving them again," Uncle Logan said.

"But he'd have a key for that," Alice said, rubbing her forehead, which had started to throb again. "Unless he wasn't the one who tampered with the lock. In any case, he's not important. What's important is what Victoria is planning on doing with this gas or serum."

"She hasn't had a successful test yet," Rose said. "Or at least not one where the test subject has survived."

Alice stared at her. "Are you saying she's tested this on powered people and killed them?"

"I don't know if it's her, but there are references to tests as recently as three months ago."

A sick angry heat began to spread through Alice as she imagined innocent people being tortured and killed just for being different.

Victoria can't see that she's become what she most despised.

"Do you really think concern for their survival would stop Victoria?" Uncle Logan asked.

"Before Park Side I would've said yes, but now? I doubt it," Alice said.

"What we should ask," Miss Jones said, "is how this fits in with the Science Foundation. Is she using it as merely a cover or is there a wider plan at work?"

Alice looked around the room and realized that Gerald had been silent through the entire conversation. He stood at the large window, staring out at the snow-covered gardens smoking a cigarette, his face tense and thoughtful.

"Gerald? Do you have thoughts?" Alice asked softly.

He blew smoke out and closed his eyes.

"Gerald?" Uncle Logan said, walking toward him. "What's wrong?"

Gerald shook his head. "I don't want Rose anywhere near this."

The statement took all of them by surprise, but none more than Rose.

"What? Why?" Rose asked.

He took another drag. "You have other things you could be doing. Didn't we have a talk about that on the way over here?"

"Yes, but Mrs. Frost would've—"

"Wanted you to be safe!" Gerald's voice echoed in the room, and everyone fell silent. Alice couldn't remember ever hearing him yell, and had seen him truly angry only a handful of times. But now his face wore a fierce glare that made Alice take an instinctive step back.

"I want to finish this," Rose said, unfazed by her father's outburst, "and I'm sick of you laying down the law without an explanation. I'm not a child anymore and I don't have to do what you tell me."

"I made a promise to your mother to keep you safe, and I intend to keep it."

"Then tell me why!"

Gerald's jaw clenched and unclenched, the cigarette pinched tight in his fingers.

"It's complicated," he finally said, his voice rough.

"Not good enough," Rose said, crossing her arms.

Gerald took one last drag and stubbed the embers out in the ash tray next to him.

"It's going to have to be."

Rose's brown eyes blazed. "You've kept this secret my whole life, telling me that every restriction was for my protection, but you never told me from what! Well, no more! This is my life and I'll live it how I want!"

Rose grabbed her gray pea coat off a nearby chair and walked out of the room. Seconds later, Alice heard the front door slam.

"Do you want me to make sure she gets back to the book store alright?" Uncle Logan asked.

Gerald nodded, eyes on the floor.

Uncle Logan patted Alice's arm as he left, and kissed her on the cheek. "I'll come back in a few hours to check on you."

Alice nodded.

"I will ask the cook to bring you a sandwich," Miss Jones said to Alice. "You can't be missing meals."

Eating was the furthest thing from Alice's mind, but she didn't fight Miss Jones about it. She put the files down and finished her coffee, feeling awkward alone with Gerald.

He lit another cigarette and stared out the window again. Alice poured another cup of coffee, her mind automatically picking at the thread that somehow could connect Gerald to what they were just talking about.

"Have you figured it out yet?" Gerald asked, his voice rough.

"Almost."

He nodded. "I figured you'd be the one to do it. If you hadn't been so distracted with Victoria all this time you probably would have by now."

Then something clicked into place for Alice and she almost choked on her coffee.

"It has to do with that research, and where it came from."

Gerald didn't speak.

"The experiments before the war," she continued, "they were trying to bring out the potential powers and you were one of the test subjects, weren't you?"

"Yes," he whispered.

His voice was so full of pain that Alice flinched.

"Did they force it on you?"

He shook his head. "I volunteered, but I wasn't told everything."

Alice waited as he finished his cigarette, and at last, he stubbed it out and turned to her.

"Those men, if they're still out there, are a different breed, Alice. I escaped, but I've never forgotten what they were like, what they could do."

Alice's eyes bulged as realization hit her. "Rose's intellect, it's a power, isn't it?"

"It might be. I don't know. It was always a risk if I ever had a child. All I know is that if they found her…"

"She deserves to know, to understand why you've been like this."

Gerald nodded. "I know, but this is different. You're just going to have to trust me. Please, don't tell her."

"I won't, but you have to promise me that when we've beaten Victoria, you will talk to her."

He paused, running a hand over his graying hair before he said, "Alright."

CHAPTER EIGHT

The cold cut through Lionel's heavy jacket in bursts of air and snow as he made his way to Fritz's apartment

It had been more than a week since Fritz had agreed to help Lionel, and almost as many days since his confrontation with Mishka. In that time, Lionel had spent most days either in Fritz's apartment or outside of it making sure that no one was trying to harm the scientist.

While Fritz had become annoyed and rude with Lionel's constant hanging around, Fritz's eighteen year old daughter had taken a liking to Lionel. The last few days he'd been there, she had played her cello for him and talked about the conservatory in Switzerland she was going to attend. Lionel could tell the young woman was smitten, but he kept a respectful distance.

Though now that I think about it, I'm not sure Fritz is happy with me talking to his daughter even if I do show respect.

Her music had been a welcome distraction for Lionel, who had nothing to do while guarding Fritz and his daughter except to try to unravel the questions keeping him up at night.

How would the Consortium use powered people as weapons?

Why would Victoria would be a part of a group like that in first place? And, maybe most important, how can I protect Alice and Marco from whatever Victoria has planned?

He asked himself these things for the hundredth time as we made his way to the apartment building. It did nothing except increase the tension in his body, which made him frustrated and more inclined to give in to his anger at the wrong times.

Lionel took a deep breath of cold air to try and calm himself. It hurt his lungs but also snapped him out of his ruminations. It did no good to dwell all this, he knew that. The fact that he was trying to be logical and unwind these mysteries but couldn't was only making him more disheartened.

"If only I could call them," he said to himself, knowing that would be foolish.

There were just too many variables that Lionel couldn't see through, and he didn't want to put them in any more danger than they were already in.

He stopped at the gilded doors of the apartment building and stomped some of the slush off his boots. It had been built post war in the new modern style that was taking all the elegance out of Paris, in Lionel's opinion anyway. The structure stuck out in sharp contrast to the classic designs and grace around it.

Before entering the building, Lionel took a few deep breaths to steady his mind. It was no use worrying about any of this when he couldn't do anything about it. Not without the cure anyway.

First things first.

Lionel stepped inside the lobby, his shoes echoing on the polished wood floor. The furniture looked like something out of a modern housewife's dream, with its orange and red womb chairs and Langley couch. Lush potted plants lurked in the corners, and modern lamps stood at attention every-where to illuminate the large space.

Lionel looked up at the concierge, ready to hear the latest joke the man seemed to revel in torturing him with. A smile froze on Lionel's face.

This man, giving him a stare that bordered on hostile, was not the usual concierge. In fact, no one in the unusually empty lobby, was who they they should be.

"Name, sir?" asked the concierge.

Lionel forced his smile to remain as relaxed as possible.

"Mr. Steel to see Monsieur Fritz."

The man hesitated, just a half second, before using the lobby phone to call up. Lionel sighed in apparent impa-tience and looked around the room slowly. There were only two other men in the lobby besides the fake concierge, but that didn't mean there couldn't be others in the building somewhere.

Something has happened. Either Jason found out I'm here, or Victoria knows Fritz isn't cooperating. Either way, I have to get up there.

"Monsieur Fritz is busy," the concierge said as he replaced the lobby phone.

"Oh that's alright, I'll wait," Lionel said, smiling.

"I'm afraid that's not-"

Lionel punched the man in the nose just as the other two moved toward him. One of them threw a knife at Lionel. It hit his back with a good amount of force, the tip of the blade lodging into his flesh just enough to stick and then fall with a clatter to the ground.

The now familiar burn of anger started to warm Lionel's veins and he let out just enough to make his focus sharper. Before it could run amok, however, he clamped down on it and hoped he could keep it at bay long enough to save Fritz without raging out.

Lionel let out a feral grin and motioned for the assailant

to come at him. The man hesitated as if caught off guard by what he'd just seen. Lionel used the opportunity to kick a nearby end table at the man. It hit him in the gut hard enough to knock him to the floor.

The last man rushed Lionel when his back was turned. Just before he was able to get close enough for a hit, Lionel pivoted, caught the man's hand and twisted, feeling the bones of his wrist break. The man yelled in pain but didn't stop. He drew a knife with his other hand and stabbed up toward Lionel's diaphragm.

Lionel felt the tip of the blade just barely pierce his tough skin. In response, the former vigilante delivered a brutal punch to the man's jaw and and he fell to floor.

Anger, hot and bright began to build like water behind a damn. The pressure was becoming hard to withstand and Lionel took in large gulps of air to try and steady himself. He wanted the edge the rage gave him, but not at the expense of control.

The doorman, who had recovered from the blow by now, rushed toward him with a wicked looking club spiked with nails.

Where the hell did he keep that?

The doorman swung wildly at Lionel's head as the vigilante took several steps back to avoid the impact. He was so focused on not getting hit by the club, that he didn't notice the rug scrunched up on the floor. The heel of Lionel's shoe caught on it, and he couldn't move fast enough to avoid the nails, which raked down the left side of Lionel's face. He gasped, vision going red as fury started to take over.

No!...No, I will not...give in!

He looked up in time to see the club coming at him again. With a snarl, he dodged to the side to avoid another blow. Out of the corner of his eye, Lionel saw the first assailant trying to get up from the floor.

Afternoon light glinted off the nails sticking out from

the doorman's club, which was sweeping in an arc straight for him. Taking a chance that his powers would protect him enough, Lionel grit his teeth against the anticipation of pain and raised his forearm to block the club. The nails pierced his skin and the pain set loose some of the anger Lionel had kept at bay. He wanted to kill this man, to rip his arms off and listen to the screams as he bled out.

No I don't...Keep it together!

The doorman stared up at him in shock as Lionel simply ripped the club from his flesh. It was the perfect opening for Lionel to hit him with the blunt end of the club. The man dropped like a stone to the floor and Lionel didn't even bother worrying about if he'd killed him or not.

The last assailant ran up and hit Lionel across the back with a pipe. The impact reverberated up Lionel's spine, and though the pain was minimal, it still managed to anger him more.

The former vigilante turned as if nothing had happened at all and delivered three brutal punches to his face. He was about to go in for a fourth when he saw the red on his knuckles, the way the man hung there, limp and unconscious.

It was so tempting to just keep hitting him until his face was a bloody pulp.

With a shout, Lionel threw the man down. He gulped air, sweat pouring off him as he tried to calm down. He couldn't go up to Fritz's like this.

But what if...I can't wait, he could be dead already.

The line between self control and blind rage was thin, but it was still there. Lionel took a deep breath and ran to the stairs. If there were others that had been alerted, he didn't want to get caught fighting in a tiny space like an elevator. Lionel could feel the wounds on his body knitting back together, skin and muscles stretching until they met and healed.

Once he reached the sixth floor, Lionel cracked open the door from the stairwell and peeked out into the hallway. There were no signs of guards or anything out of the ordinary, yet Lionel's senses were on high alert after the fight.

That can't be all. Neither Victoria nor Jason are that stupid.

The quiet was shattered with a shriek of terror that sent Lionel bolting down the hall to Fritz's apartment.

"Please! Not my daughter!" screamed Fritz from somewhere inside.

With one kick, the door was forced open, hanging off its hinges.

Lionel ran inside the entryway and into the spacious modern living room in time to see a man punch Fritz's daughter.

The thin line holding back his rage snapped.

With a growl, Lionel stalked across the room, picked up a nearby vase and smashed it into the man's face. He screamed, blood and glass shards all over his visage. But that wasn't good enough.

Lionel punched him, full force. The man's head snapped to the side, and in a distant place in his mind, Lionel knew he was dead even as he kept hitting him.

Someone screamed nearby, a terrified, ear splitting sound. Lionel knew it was the girl, that she was screaming because of what he'd just turned into. And he didn't care.

A hard object slammed into Lionel's back and he dropped the now unrecognizable man he'd been pummeling.

Another assailant had been hiding in the apartment and thought to get the jump on Lionel. But the moment Lionel turned around, the man's eyes became huge and he stumbled back. Lionel advanced on him, bloodied fists clenched and ready.

The assailant started picking up things and throwing them at Lionel, who barely felt the impact. When Lionel got close, he simply reached out, picked the man up by his collar and threw him across the room like a rag doll. He crashed against a nearby wall and slid down, dazed. Lionel picked him up and slammed him into the wall again, leaving a dent in the heavy plaster.

Inside, Lionel was shouting at himself to stop, but his pleas were like a whisper in a wind storm, lost and without significance.

He pulled back his fist and punched as someone outside himself shouted for him to stop.

That's not Alice…who…?

The more he punched the man, the louder the shouts.

If it wasn't for the piercing sound of a gun shot, Lionel might've stood there beating the man until all that was left was shattered bone and bloodied muscle.

The sensation of suddenly being back in control of his body was always disorienting, followed closely by revulsion. The first thing he saw, was the bloodied face of the dead man before him. He let go of the man's throat and stumbled back. Blood seeped between his fingers, sticky and warm.

As the fog in his mind cleared, Lionel heard someone sobbing behind him.

H spun around and saw Fritz holding his daughter in his arms, the back of her head bloody.

"No," Lionel whispered.

"You were warned," said a man out in the hall.

Lionel turned and started to go after him when he realized that more men could be coming for Fritz.

"We have to go," he said, making his way to the scientist.

"No, no!" Fritz cried, shaking off Lionel's hands. "You are death! Look! Look around you!"

Lionel didn't have to. He knew exactly what he'd done.

"I won't hurt you, I'm calm now-"

"This poison, it was made to make men like you killing machines for Apollo! You will die as the monster they've made you!"

A sick feeling spread in Lionel's gut as Fritz screamed the very thing that he'd feared for so long now.

"No, with your help-"

"I will not help you! They were only here to intimidate me. You stomping in, killing them...it made them kill her... my baby."

Lionel's throat became tight. He wanted to reach inside himself and pull out the part of him that had done this, to tear himself to pieces.

I killed her...I killed that girl as sure as if I'd pulled the damn trigger. And I can never make it right but I can try to save her father.

"Fritz, I'm so sorry," he said. "Please let me protect you."

"You don't care about me. You only care for your cure."

It brought Lionel up short and he closed his mouth. Was that the only reason he felt compelled to save Fritz, so he could live without this deadly rage controlling him?

Fritz walked around his daughter's body to an ornate desk across the room. Unlocking the second drawer he pulled a piece of paper from a folder and marched back to Lionel.

"Your cure is in America," he said, shoving the paper into Lionel's chest. "I hope you choke on it."

Lionel clutched the paper and stared at the man. He wanted to run out the door with the information and leave Fritz with his anger and grief, never looking back.

I should but there's something I have to know.

"What's Apollo want with powered people?" he asked.

"You don't know anything," Fritz spat. "You are a brute! You ask these questions to me when my daughter is...you go to hell!"

Lionel took a deep breath and decided to use the only weapon available to him. He would truly feel like a monster after this, but he had to know if Apollo had intentions to go after Marco.

He took two steps toward Fritz until he towered over the man and made his face as hard as he could.

"Answer me," Lionel said, his voice low and hard.

To his credit, Fritz held Lionel's gaze, though his lip trembled and fear rolled off him in waves.

"I don't have any contact with the test subjects," Fritz finally answered.

The phrase brought images of labs and cages to Lionel's mind and he shoved it away.

"But you know something, don't you? What does Apollo have you working on?"

Fritz looked down at his dead daughter and shook his head as if to say *"What does it matter now?"*

"Equations for formulas, chemistry."

"For what?"

"To aid people like you in becoming more of a monster, and then surviving the process."

Lionel was taken aback and stared at him.

"You're telling me Victoria-"

Fritz laughed.

"No, she is the only sane one I think. She wanted me to give them equations that would do the opposite, that would strip powers. Then I was supposed to report the results to her so she could replicate it."

So she's at odds with her other partners, sabotaging their efforts. If she's alone in this, that could make her desperate and desperate people do terrible things.

"Now," Fritz said, "you have what you wanted, leave! Leave!"

With heavy steps, Lionel walked out of the apartment.

Fritz started sobbing again, and Lionel's heart squeezed

at the sound. If he'd stayed away from Fritz then maybe Apollo wouldn't have found out that their scientist was compromised.

I can't dwell on that now. I've got to save those I can…if I can. She could do something that would make Park Side look like Christmas if she's not stopped.

Lionel clenched his fists and heard the crinkle of paper.

His cure! He'd gotten so distracted that he'd almost forgotten he held the one thing he'd wanted for the last two years. Lionel looked down at the paper Fritz had given him.

There was an address. Specifically, Marco's address.

"He found it," Lionel's stomach dropped. "And if Victoria knows Marco has this,…I have to find him before she does. And maybe together we can stop her once and for all."

CHAPTER NINE

Alice looked out at the crowd of black-clad businessmen and their wives, society dames and their husbands. The tinkling of glasses and a low hum from the ballroom's heating system was the only sound as she looked down at the speech she'd written the day before.

Though she knew that public displays of mourning were frowned upon by the assembly before her, Alice couldn't push away the tears that made her large eyes gleam. The prim and proper of Jet City would just have to deal with a little real emotion. She took a deep, shaking breath and put on a smile.

"Ladies and gentlemen, thank you for coming here tonight to celebrate the life of one of the pillars of Jet City. Rebecca Frost was...well, how to describe such a person? She was one of the first women to successfully hold together a business empire that, to this day, stretches across the world and has influenced the lives of thousands. Committed to making Jet City better, she founded the Philanthropic Society, a group that continues to strive for the betterment of Jet City's unfortunate and needy."

Alice licked her lips, a ball of grief sitting in her stomach like a lead balloon.

"I was fortunate to be the recipient of her knowledge and guidance. I can't say she was a friend, because she was more like a mentor — or a drill sergeant."

Empty laughter floated on the air.

"But all the same...I will miss her." Alice's voice broke. "Terribly."

The room became thick with discomfort.

Wiping a stray tear away, Alice forced a thin smile back on her face.

"She made me swear that there would be no sappy speeches, yet here I am, breaking her rules one last time. So, let us raise our glasses and toast the life of a woman whose like we will never see again."

Alice turned to the portrait behind her, hiding the way her face crumpled and her stomach clenched. No one noticed that she stayed up there longer than necessary, because once the toast was done, they all went back to speculating as to why one of the richest women in the country would leave her holdings to a nobody young woman.

At least that's what the women were talking about. The men were wondering how they could get their sons and nephews to catch the new heiress's eye.

"Miss Seymour?" said a soft voice to her left.

Alice glanced up at Miss Jones. "Make sure everyone has enough to eat and drink, and then call my car. I won't be staying."

Miss Jones nodded, handing Alice her cane.

"Of course. Do you want me to cancel your appointments tomorrow?"

"No," Alice said, hobbling down the stairs.

Miss Jones nodded and went to do her job.

Alice smiled at the hollow platitudes lobbed at her from

various people. She could see the questions and avarice shining in their eyes.

I'd trade every cent Mrs. Frost left me if I could have that old woman by my side again.

"Miss Seymour?" said Mr. Marsden. "My darling girl, I am so sorry."

She gave the odious man a sad smile and leaned on the cane.

"Mrs. Frost was an amazing woman," he continued.

"Yes, quite. And, by the way, thank you, Mr. Marsden, for the more than generous donation you made this week to the Children's Home."

He waved away her thanks and motioned behind him, to where a young man stood. He was tall and thin, with wide gray eyes and blond hair. Though most of the young men in the room could barely hide their distaste of Alice and her cane, this man showed a curiosity that took Alice by surprise.

Mr. Marsden smiled. "May I introduce my nephew, Matthew Marsden."

Alice nodded, measuring her tone to make sure it was appealingly meek. "My pleasure. I am sorry to meet you under such sad circumstances."

Matthew nodded. "Yes, Mrs. Frost was an extraordinary woman."

"She was," Alice said, appreciating the sincerity in Matthew's voice.

"Matthew was just telling me how excited he was to see the newly-finished water front. Perhaps you could show him around?" Mr. Marsden said.

"Uncle, I'm sure Miss Seymour has other things on her mind just now."

"True. But a stroll on the boardwalk might be a nice distraction during such a sad time."

Alice wanted nothing more than to tell Mr. Marsden

what a complete ass he was, but instead she kept her mask of demure civility firmly in place. She was about to excuse herself when Matthew spoke up.

"Miss Seymour, I apologize for my uncle's insensitive behavior. I would, of course, be delighted to get to know you better outside of such sad circumstances. But I would never presume to barge in on your grief."

Alice stared at him. She didn't know what to say to such sincerity.

"Thank you," she finally said. "I am deeply touched by your concern."

Matthew nodded and guided his red-faced uncle away from her. And for the first time since she started dating boring, egotistical men whom she hated, Alice was intrigued by someone.

But not now. It's…not now.

She turned, and almost collided with a hugely corpulent man who smelled of sweat and bourbon.

"Miss Seymour?" he said, his voice wheezing.

She gave him a soft smile.

"Hello, Mr. Burton, how wonderful that you delayed your European trip for the memorial. It would've meant so much to Mrs. Frost."

Burton's chest puffed out even more, straining his already bursting buttons.

"Of course, of course. May I introduce my son, Samuel?"

Alice's face felt stiff with the brilliant smile she wore as she listened with apparent rapture to the equally corpulent Samuel expound on foreign trade and what she should do.

"You make some very interesting points. I confess, I had not thought of that before," she said, once Samuel had taken a breath.

"I would be happy to speak with you more extensively, perhaps, over dinner?"

"Oh, what a lovely thought. But I make it a rule to never talk business after three o'clock, I get tired so early."

"Well, then, lunch?"

"Yes, please call my office and my assistant will set something up."

Alice made slow progress toward the door as two more young men were pushed forward to meet her. One was barely able to keep his eyes off her cane while his father droned on about Mrs. Frost's brilliant business acumen and how it took years to learn.

"I would be happy to act as mentor, should you need further guidance," he said.

Alice nodded and smiled, the perfect picture of a meek young woman, in too deep to really know what to do with the millions she'd just inherited.

The second rich young man shoved forward by his ambitious father wasn't much better.

"I really do think that, in cases such as yours, that women should have the help of a veteran of business affairs, don't you? I mean, a business empire such as Mrs. Frost left, needs careful management, and women such as yourself are far too inexperienced in such matters to do a proper job. Not to mention that I'm sure your mind will be preoccupied with finding a husband and raising a family."

Alice grit her teeth as she smiled benignly at him and nodded.

"I confess, I do feel a little out of my depth."

"I would be happy to assist you."

"That is so kind. Everyone has been so willing to help me with this new position I find myself in. It's so generous!"

The young man's smile slipped. "I see, well, I don't wish to be one of many."

"Oh." She infused her smile with a little seduction. "I don't think anyone would ever say that about you."

He smiled back at her. "That's good to hear. Dinner, perhaps?"

She giggled. "Why not? Next week? Call my assistant, she will set something up."

It took over an hour to finally make it into the car. When Miss Jones settled into the front seat, Patrick pulled away from the front of the hotel. Alice could feel the eyes of everyone on her as she sat with the upright posture and sad smile everyone expected.

"You will be getting a lot of requests for lunches and dinners for me," she said to Miss Jones.

"What shall I say?"

"Schedule them, but nowhere romantic. Make it clear that it is business and that I have other appointments after or an early flight. Something like that."

Miss Jones nodded. "You did well this evening."

"Thank you," Alice said, leaning back against the red leather.

Images of the funeral played behind Alice's eyelids. She looked out her window, desperate for a distraction, when she caught sight of a tall, blond man with his arm around a tiny red head. Alice sat upright, her heart pounding in her ears.

"Miss Seymour?" Miss Jones asked.

Alice was about to call for Patrick to pull over when the man turned around and she could see his face.

She slumped, like a deflated balloon, and felt tears spill down her cheeks.

"I thought…" she shook her head. "Nevermind."

"Do you need anything?" Miss Jones asked, her voice bordering on tender.

Home…I want to go home. But my home left and he's not coming back.

She opened her mouth to tell Patrick to keep driving

when sirens pierced the night. Two police cars flew past them, with two more following a second later.

A dark foreboding settled in Alice's stomach.

"Follow them," she ordered Patrick.

"Miss—" Patrick began, looking back in confusion.

"Just do it!"

They were soon forced to an abrupt stop by a blockade of the street around the Children's Home. Dense smoke hung around the cream-colored structure, which reflected the garish blues and reds from the lights of the police cars. When Alice jumped out of the car, a horribly familiar, sickly sweet smell met her nose.

"No," she said, not bothering to grab her cane as she hobbled toward the blockade. "No!"

"Ma'am I'm sorry but—" a young officer said, stepping in front of her.

"That's my Children's Home! Let me through!"

"We have a situation. If you could just—"

"Let me through!"

"What the hell is going on here?" said a boxy-looking man in a long coat.

"Sir, this woman says—"

"I'm Alice Seymour! This is my Children's Home. I demand you let me through!"

"You do, huh?"

"At least let me talk to whoever is in charge. I have a right to know—"

"Lady, we're not even sure what's going on. You wait here."

"But! Wait!"

The man walked away and the young officer gave her one last look before following him. Alice let out a grunt of frustration and began pacing along the barricade, trying to see anyone who might tell her anything.

After a few minutes Miss Jones arrived with a short man with a military style hair cut walking next to her.

"You Alice Seymour?" he asked, his voice full of irritation.

"Yes."

"I'm Sergeant Don McComber, you can call me Mack. Come with me."

Alice thanked Miss Jones with a look and took her cane as she tried to keep up with Mack.

"What's the situation?" she asked.

"We're not completely sure," he admitted. "We got a call saying that there was a Fantasy gas attack. Honest, we thought it was a hoax, hasn't been one of those since…well, you know when. But, the first officers on the scene confirmed it. Kids were going crazy, and there was a sign of a bad fight. The lady that runs this place, she was affected pretty bad."

"Mrs. Shannon? Where is she?"

"On her way to the hospital, along with the man that we think is the gardener, you got one of those?"

Alice frowned. "Yes, but he doesn't live here."

Mack scratched his head. "Huh, well, he was dressed like a gardener or janitor. Anyway, the gas was contained at first to just one wing of the place before spreading."

Alice's hand tightened on the head of her cane, already knowing the answer before she asked.

"Which one?"

"The one to the right," he said, pointing.

Alice met Miss Jones' eyes.

"Get a hold of Gerald. Tell him what happened and to get here as soon as he can."

Miss Jones nodded and ran off.

Alice studied the wing of the Home where the powered children lived, her stomach in knots.

The windows on the first two floors were broken,

curtains fluttered like ghosts in two of them. She could see scorch marks on the outside of one, as if it had been blown out by fire.

Or electricity.

The sickly sweet smell of the gas was already fading, and now Alice could smell ozone and smoke.

"How many of the children were affected?" she asked.

"Mostly the ones in that part of the house," he said. "But when it spread a few others that had gotten up became affected, too."

Alice nodded. "Take me inside."

"Miss, I'm not sure—"

"I survived the Park Side Massacre, and I run this Children's Home. Take me in there."

Mack swallowed, a new respect in his green eyes. "Alright."

Even with Mrs. Frosts death, Alice had made good on her promise to come to the Children's Home on Sunday for cake with the children. They'd been happy, playing with the other children without fear. Alice could tell that for the first time in a while, they felt safe.

And then someone came in and did this.

She tried not to think about what might've happened to them in the midst of Fantasy gas, the things that they saw or did. She had only been exposed to the full strength gas once, but the memories of what she saw and felt still haunted her. That, combined with what she'd seen the people at the Park Side Massacre do, meant that Alice got very little sleep most nights.

They'll be alright, they have to be…they have to be.

Alice took several deep breaths to calm her racing heart and climbed the stone steps leading up to the beautiful, stained glass double doors. One was hanging askew and glass from the other crunched under Alice's feet. They walked through the entryway and into the main hall, and saw that the large staircase in the center of the room was littered with clothes, bits of wood and toys.

"The unaffected children were kept in their wing of the house," Mack said. "I have a couple of my men staying with them. I think they might've scrounged up some cookies from the kitchen once it was cleared."

Alice nodded. "Have you taken any of the children to the hospital?"

Mack looked down at the floor. "Well, now that's a complicated question."

Alice's stomach sank. "Why?"

"Well…were you aware, Miss Seymour, that you were housing some…let's see how do I put this?"

"Powered children?"

Mack nodded. "I got nothin' against powered people, if they keep to themselves and don't hurt anyone. And if they're kids, well…seems obvious I don't have a problem. But…well, if you don't mind me saying so, seems kind of dangerous keeping them all in one place."

"Thank you for your opinion, but please answer my question. Have you taken any of them to the hospital?"

"No. We…damn, I hate saying this, but we had to lock some of them in rooms until the effects of the gas wore off. Paramedics have cleared most of them with minor bruises and cuts."

Alice frowned. "It's worn off already?"

He nodded. "My memory was that it lasted a bit longer than this, but maybe because they're powered—"

"That shouldn't matter," Alice said, forgetting that she shouldn't know much more about the gas than the general public.

Mack frowned at her, but didn't say anything.

"Are they calm now?" Alice asked.

"Most of them, but there were two that haven't calmed

down. They keep screaming for the vigilantes to come and help them."

Alice took in a ragged breath and she began climbing the stairs as fast her legs could take her.

"Wait!" Mack said, grabbing her arm with his meaty hand. "You can't just walk in there."

Alice looked down at his hand and when he let her go, she simply turned and continued walking up the stairs.

"Damn it," Mack whispered a few moments before following her.

The horrifically sweet smell of the gas was stronger once Alice turned a corner and started walking down the main hall of the east wing. Her entire body tensed and sweat began to trickle down her spine and under her arms.

It's alright. It's dormant, you'll be fine.

But her heart wouldn't slow down and she had to pause once to catch her breath.

Think of the children. They need you now, more than ever. You promised to keep them safe. Just calm down!

As her mind cleared, Alice could take in her surroundings, which didn't exactly help to keep her calm.

The cream and blue striped wall paper had been shredded horizontally on one side, and a nearby door had a hole in it as if someone had simply punched their way through.

The dark blue carpet was dotted with toys, clothes and other items Alice couldn't identify in the dim light. She looked up and noticed that most of the hall lights had been shattered. In her mind, Alice went through the list of powered children they were housing, trying to figure out who might have done what while under the effects of the fear gas.

It didn't help.

"Miss?" Mack said behind her.

"Where…where are the children?"

"I don't—"

"Just tell me. I can handle myself."

"We put the ones that had calmed down in the library at the end of the hall. And the two that were still screaming… well, they're in the last two rooms there."

Alice took some deep breaths and walked to the library. She could hear low whispers and some crying before she opened the door. Books were stacked in neat piles on the hard wood floor, two of the larger book cases were toppled over and glass sparkled on the floor by the window. Most of the lights had survived whatever happened, illuminating half a dozen frightened faces.

"Miss Seymour?" one of the boys said.

"Yes, I'm here. We're going to get you back to your rooms as soon as possible. We just needed to keep you safe."

"Until they come to take us away, right?" he said.

"Marcus, isn't it?"

He nodded.

"No, Marcus, no one is going to take you away."

"But…" A teen girl raised teary brown eyes to Alice. "What we did…everyone knows and…"

The kids turned away from her, a few continued to cry.

She walked further into the room and sat by a Hispanic teen named Gloria and another girl, Mary, whose red hair hid the small gills on her neck.

"Whatever happened," Alice said, looking at each of them. "It wasn't your fault. The Fantasy gas…it makes you lose control, see things that aren't there. I won't let anyone blame you for this."

"How will you stop them?" Marcus asked.

"You let me worry about that."

"Why?"

"Because I made you all a promise, and I keep my promises."

"No way," he said. "I'm not sticking around waiting for someone to cart me off to some lab."

Alice frowned. "What do you mean?"

The kids wouldn't meet her eyes.

"I can't help you if you won't talk to me. What lab?"

"It was a rumor," said Mary, her voice a little hoarse. "We had heard in Park Side that if anyone knew you were different, that a van would come and take you away."

"One of the boys who disappeared," continued Gloria, her hair starting to change color. "He escaped and came back to the place we were staying. He said they...did stuff to him. And when they were finished he couldn't do anything anymore."

"Where is he?" Alice asked.

Gloria shrugged as her hair became white. "He got sick and...we never saw him again."

"Did he say where the lab was? Was there water nearby? Anything at all will help us find out what's going on."

"You think the guys from the van did this?" asked Paul, a young Negro boy. His lips never moved, and Alice was startled to realize that he'd spoken telepathically.

"I don't know," Alice said, carefully schooling her features to not be affected by the powers going off around her. "But regardless, I want to stop anyone who hurts you."

"In the gas," whispered Gloria, the air around her shimmering as she made a circle motion with her hand. "I saw this."

Alice couldn't help but gasp as images appeared in the circle the girl had made with her hands.

Good God that kind of power...!

Three men, one that looked like their gardener and the other two dressed completely in black. All three had gas masks, and were walking through a chaos of children screaming. Sparks exploded in the picture, and then Alice saw Simon Pride, electricity flying from his fingertips. His head jerked back and he fell to the ground in a heap. Then Judy ran up to him, her brown eyes filled with terror. She began to open her mouth, and also fell to the ground. Alice saw a tranquilizer gun in the hand of one of the men in black. The other picked both children up as if they weighed nothing. They walked with terrible confidence through the chaos around them – and that's where the images stopped.

Simon and Judy! No, no, no! But where is Sam and Mateo?

Gloria crumpled to the floor, gasping for breath.

"Did you...see?" she asked.

Alice brushed Gloria's now brown hair away from her face. "Yes, I did. Thank you for trusting me like that."

She raised her head, brown eyes sparkling. "It felt good...to do something with it for once."

"Excuse me?" Mack said, stepping into the room. "But, uh, I think the other two are ready to come out, but I'm..."

"Afraid?" Marcus said.

Alice shot him a warning look before smiling at Mack. "Thank you, Sergeant, I'll be right there."

Marcus snorted as Mack left the room.

"You will never win them over if you continue to act this way," Alice said to him.

"How am I acting, huh? He's terrified of us. The only difference is now everyone will be free to act that way to our faces instead of behind our backs."

Alice sighed. "There are more people willing to give you the benefit of the doubt than you think. But whether they do that, is partly up to you."

Marcus looked away from her, his face flushing.

"Now," she looked around at the rest of the children. "You can go back to your rooms. I'll have cleaning crews come in tomorrow to help put this place back together. In the meantime, collect any of your belongings and try to get some sleep. We will sort this out, I promise."

After a few hugs, Alice limped into the hallway and followed Mack down the hall to one of the bathrooms.

She knocked on the door. "Hello? It's Alice Seymour, you're safe—"

"Miss Seymour?"

Alice covered her mouth to stifle a sob of relief when she heard Mateo's voice.

"Yes, it's me," she said, opening the door.

Mateo threw his long arms around her waist and hugged her tight. A moment later Sam came barreling around the corner, hugging both of them.

"They took Judy and Simon!" he said through tears. "You have to call the vigilantes and get them back! You have to!"

"You promised to keep us safe!" Mateo sobbed. "You have to get the vigilantes to save them!"

Alice hugged them and a hot, piercing anger began to rise from deep inside.

Just you wait kid, Victoria won't know what hit her.

CHAPTER TEN

The basement gym in the Frost Mansion was cool, but Alice's body dripped with sweat. She grunted and yelled with each punch and kick to the bag. All she could think about were the cries of the children, their fear and the experiments that Victoria was doing.

On children. Does she have no conscience left?

She yelled again as she delivered a furious series of punches to the bag.

"Time," Miss Jones said. "And, your uncle is here."

Alice wiped her face with a towel. "Gerald told him."

"It would seem so."

Miss Jones looked down.

"Say it," Alice said.

"I don't need to. You know the risks. I will not treat you like a child."

Alice was taken aback, a sudden anxiety filling her gut.

Was she making the right decision by deciding to train in the fear gas room again? She shook her head. There wasn't room for doubt now.

"Did you find anything?" Alice asked. "Was the gardener conscious yet?"

"The gardener was found dead in his hospital room this morning," Miss Jones said. "Apparently, one of the nurses accidentally gave him the wrong drug."

"Victoria's quick with the loose ends, I'll give her that."

Miss Jones nodded. "There are two possible locations where children could be held for experimentation. But getting inside without tipping our hand may be difficult."

"I'm not too concerned about that. Just find me a way in. We've got to start somewhere before...just get me inside."

"Miss Seymour, you have been perfectly willing to allow me into the field up to now. I believe that-"

"No."

"If I may," Miss Jones said, "this is bordering on reck-lessness. If you are discovered, all you've done these past two years will be thrown away. You have to keep the main objective in mind."

"I am, it's all I seem to be able to think about. But she can't get away with this, I can't let her."

Miss Jones sighed, a small sound filled with disapproval.

"Very well then. I will help Dr. Allen prepare the room."

Miss Jones opened the door and Uncle Logan swept past her.

"Alice, this isn't safe," he said.

"The gas is back in play," Alice took a drink from a canteen. "It made sense to scrap the fear gas room when Victoria hadn't used it in over a year, but now she has — and on children."

"I know you're upset, but—"

"No, I'm not. I'm furious and I'm focused."

"Yes, but exposing yourself to more fear gas, after what happened last time, how does that do anything except put you in danger?"

"I have to be ready."

"Have you thought that she might be trying to draw you out with that attack last night? Or distract you while she does something somewhere else?"

"And while I sit around trying to figure all that out, she could be plotting the next Park Side!"

Uncle Logan put his hands on her shoulders, and squeezed. "Alice, that wasn't your fault."

"Two years ago, I waited too long, wanting to figure it all out. I can't do that again; don't you see that? She's going after children that I promised to protect."

"I know, I just wish...I wish you weren't going there alone."

Alice felt her eyes itch with sudden tears. Of all the things he could've said, this was the most unexpected. Uncle Logan had been furious when he found out that Marco and Lionel had gone, knowing that she wouldn't stop just because they'd abandoned her. She had always thought that he had taken the, "good riddance" stance. But his words painted a different picture, and brought up the one thing she'd been trying not to think about since last night.

Mateo and Sam's insistence that she "call the vigilantes" had stuck in her mind. By the time she'd gotten home very early the next morning, all Alice wanted to do was find Marco and Lionel, wrap her arms around them and then plan how to take Victoria down, just like old times.

She had indulged such thoughts for about five minutes before taking a sedative and falling into a fitful sleep.

They left everything unfinished. I won't mourn their absence when I need my energy elsewhere.

"Yeah...well," she said finally, turning away. "It's just me, that's all there is. I'm enough, I'm going to have to be."

Uncle Logan let out a long sigh. "You're not alone, you

know that right? You have me and Gerald, Rose, Miss Jones. And we're here for you, in it with you, whatever you need."

"Thank you," she whispered. "I know you've never liked me doing this—"

"Stop right there," Uncle Logan said, holding his hand up. "It doesn't matter what I wanted. There are many times I just wish you'd stop and listen, especially lately. But no matter what happens, no matter your mistakes or how stubborn you are, I'm proud of you, Alice. No matter what happens, I'll always be proud of you."

"I try to listen you know," she said, letting him hug her.

"I know," he said into her sweaty hair. "You're just too much like...well Mrs. Frost and your aunt. It's one hell of a combination."

She chuckled in spite of the maelstrom of feelings inside of her. For a moment, she wished she could be a little girl again, when a kiss and a chocolate milkshake could make everything all better.

But this helps too.

The fear gas room had a two-way mirror on one wall, with a control panel behind it where Gerald monitored the amount of gas released. Miss Jones controlled the secret doors set into the wall that would open at random intervals, revealing an innocent or an adversary. And, sometimes, Miss Jones would suit up and attack, but she never told Alice when this would happen.

Alice stepped into the room and waited. The lights dimmed so that she could barely see what was in front of her, and the familiar hissing of gas made her pulse quicken.

The first few times she'd tried this, inhaling the gas on purpose had been the hardest part. She hadn't even lasted long enough for the secret doors to open. But eventually Alice was able to extend her time until she could withstand twenty minutes of exposure.

Of course, that had been before the last time, when something had changed.

Focusing her breath and her mind, Alice shoved aside any fear and took in the gas.

She allowed all her senses freedom, not just her eyes. A shuffling sound to her left made her duck down just as a whoosh of air shot past her. Not knowing if that was her mind reacting to the gas, or Miss Jones, Alice kept low to the ground. A familiar stickiness seeped through her skin, and she didn't have to look down to know it was blood.

Swallowing the bile in her throat, she focused on the shadowy figure in front of her. A cry died in her throat as she saw more clearly who it was.

"Marco?" she whispered.

A maniacal laugh echoed around her, getting louder with each repetition until she had to cover her ears with her hands to drown it out.

A kick to her face sent Alice flat on her back. She rolled to the right just as a fist crashed down beside her. Looking up, she saw a hulking figure looming over her, a primal scream ripped from its lips.

She didn't know if it was a pure illusion, or something her mind was layering over Miss Jones, but she knew that laying there to find out wasn't smart.

Flipping back and onto the balls of her feet, Alice fired lightning fast punches at its abdomen before the massive figure disappeared like smoke.

A cry for help came out of the fog, followed by something landing on her back. She grabbed it and realized that it was an innocent. Easing the dummy to the ground, she turned back around and was punched square in the face.

The careful control over her emotions disappeared and

she felt rage such as she'd never experienced before. It took over her whole being, her body shook with it, and the rational part of herself was held prisoner by its power. She lunged at the assailant, tackling them to the ground, her fist flying without thought to accuracy or mercy. Spittle flew from her lips as the delicious freedom of pure, unhinged rage flowed through her body.

In the back of her mind, Alice saw who she was punching. Felt the crunch and pop of Miss Jones' broken nose and how hard Miss Jones was fighting to get the Vigilante off her. But that didn't stop the fire coursing through her, and the dark freedom of holding nothing back.

Another figure crashed into Alice, and they tumbled onto the mat.

"Stop!" Uncle Logan's voice echoed in her mind.

"No!" she growled, kicking her uncle in the face.

She could see him trying to defend himself against the onslaught of her punches and kicks, but he couldn't. Blood appeared just above one of his eyes and Alice yelled in fury.

That's when something sharp bit into her neck from behind. She let out a bellow of anger at the person who dared do that to her. And then crashed to the mat. No matter how much she fought it, sleep dragged the monster she'd become away.

Alice tried to open her eyes and moaned in pain.

"What...happened?"

"You went rabid," Gerald said, a tinge of anger in his voice.

Confusion masked her memories at first, but then flashes came back to her in startling clarity.

"Uncle Logan! Miss Jones are they—"

"Easy," Gerald said, his hand on her arm, "or I'll have to give you another sedative."

"But…I…did I—"

"They'll be alright," he said. "I healed most of the bruises."

"Oh god," she whispered, covering her face with shaking hands, "I could've killed them. I…I wanted to…I wanted to kill someone…"

Gerald sighed and took her pulse.

She glanced down at herself and saw that she was in her bed, her shorts and t-shirt soaked in sweat.

"How long?"

"About two hours."

She moaned. "I need to get up, to apologize."

Gerald was surprisingly strong. His calloused hands flew to her shoulders, holding her in place.

"You need rest."

Alice closed her eyes, but flashes of what had happened in the room played behind her eyelids.

"Why did I react this way? Last time it wasn't anger, it was terror."

Gerald frowned. "I don't know. Maybe you've had too much exposure, maybe something triggered it. Like the Children's Home."

"Maybe," she sighed, pushing memories of the room away.

She brushed long strands of hair from her face and winced in disgust at the clothes clinging to her sweat covered body.

"I need a bath."

Gerald gave her a long, hard look.

"If you're in there longer than an hour, I'm sending Miss Jones to check on you."

She saluted as he helped her sit up.

A bath, then she'd find out what Miss Jones had discovered about the two locations. With any luck, she'd have a way inside one of them soon.

CHAPTER ELEVEN

The next afternoon, an unwelcome surprise arrived with the mail. Alice stared at the thick, cream colored invitation, with blue letters curling elegantly.

Victoria Veran would like to cordially invite you to a special reception for The Science Research and Exploration Foundation.

A special presentation will be followed by a private tour of the Foundation by Victoria Veran herself.

We hope you will be able to join us.

"What is she playing at?" Alice said, jumping up from her chair in the library. "Why steal children, release fear gas and now do this? How does it all connect?"

"Calm down," Uncle Logan said. "You're too worked up."

"You're damn right I am!"

Uncle Logan poured her a cup of tea from the green and

purple pot sitting on a nearby table. She waved it away as she paced, chewing on her lip.

Her mind whirred in and out of possibilities, always coming back to the look on Simon and Judy's faces in that apartment where she'd promised to protect them.

I'm failing again.

She shook her head, trying to dislodge those thoughts.

"Maybe it would help to find out who else is invited to this thing," Uncle Logan said.

Alice stopped pacing and felt a small jolt of relief go through her.

"That's not a bad idea. Could you get me that guest list?"

"Shouldn't be hard, especially since I'm on it."

"You? But…oh…Editor in Chief of the paper."

Uncle Logan nodded. "How much do you want to bet that the guest list is filled with influential people from Jet City?"

"I'm not influential."

"I think Victoria has been putting on as good a face as you. Be careful Alice, something about this doesn't smell right."

She patted his shoulder. "As careful as I can be."

Miss Jones stepped into the room, a file folder in her hand.

"What have you found out?" Alice asked.

"A request was made for a delivery truck to arrive at the Foundation late tomorrow night, and then take something to a small air field south of Jet City."

"You think that the children are at the Foundation?"

"For the moment, it's the only location I am certain of as a possibility."

Alice nodded. "Alright."

"I can stake out the delivery—" Miss Jones began.

"No," Alice said. "I'm going to do it."

Miss Jones and Uncle Logan stared at her.

"It's time," she continued. "I'm tired of letting everyone else do all the work. Victoria hasn't come back to the city, so even if I'm spotted, there's no guarantee anyone will know it was me."

"But, what if something goes wrong?" Uncle Logan asked.

"Then I will deal with it."

He shook his head. "Alice—"

"I'm in the best shape of my life. And if I'm masked, not as Serpent, but like Miss Jones usually is, then chances are they will just assume it was her again."

"It is a risk," Miss Jones said. "If they unmask you—"

"They won't."

"Take Miss Jones with you, at least," Uncle Logan said.

"She doesn't need me," Miss Jones said.

Uncle Logan held her gaze, a scowl deepening the lines on his scraggly face. "You better be right."

Alice took his hand. "I know you're scared for me, but I'm ready. I promise."

He sighed. "It's hard...All I can think of is you in that hospital bed."

"I don't want to be injured like that again either, so I'll be careful."

Uncle Logan smiled, but it looked forced. "Anything I can do?"

"Get me that guest list?"

"Of course. See you for breakfast tomorrow?"

Alice nodded.

When they heard his car drive away from the front of the house, Miss Jones turned to Alice.

"I meant what I said, you are ready. But I would be remiss if I didn't point out that this could be exactly what Victoria wants. To draw you out and know for certain that you are still Serpent. She won't trust you if she has doubts around that."

"I know, but I have to try."

Miss Jones gave a short nod. "Your Mandarin lesson is in an hour."

The waterfront renovations had sped up in the last year. Instead of moldy, crumbling stores, there was now a thriving tourist business. Curio shops, cheap restaurants that sold greasy fish and fries, and souvenir shops sat alongside elegant restaurants like The Elliot and small hotels with rooms so expensive, only a select few could afford a night there. The Science Foundation was built between where the waterfront met the downtown streets of Jet City, a statement of sorts for anyone visiting: we are the future.

Alice sat on the roof of a small apartment building across from the Science Foundation, trying her best to ignore the cold seeping through the black shirt, pants, reinforced gloves and balaclava she wore.

She had to admit it was an impressive place. Two tall buildings stretched up to the sky, with a smaller one between. The odd, but beautiful, circular shape signifying the different schools of scientific thought. It was encased above and on three sides by glass that looked frosted from the outside, but from the inside gave a clear view of the streets and sky. It was the center building that would be open to the public, with ever-changing exhibits and lectures.

Alice studied the smaller building, wondering if that would be where the special tour would take place and what kinds of things Victoria could do in a space that size.

She waited for over an hour, seeing nothing but a few

pedestrians at this late hour. Finally, a mid-sized delivery van pulled up, with no markings on the sides. It backed up into the narrow side alley that Alice assumed doubled as a loading dock. The van blocked her view of the side door, but she could guess that it was more than a simple delivery entrance.

Delivery entrances don't have high tech locks with combinations that change every week.

It was time.

Alice climbed down the fire escape and ran across the street. Keeping to the shadows, she crouched down between two trash bins by a small shop next to the Foundation. The side door opened, spilling pale light out onto the loading dock. Four men carried a long gray tube into the van. It had a similar shape to a coffin, but was metallic, with buttons and dials on the side.

"Be careful you don't jostle it too much," said a man that was supervising. "Last time the cargo arrived with a concussion."

"Yeah, yeah. We do our best."

Alice clenched her hands into fists.

Cargo? How could they think of a child as cargo?

She kept still until the door closed and the van began to pull away. Then, she jogged behind it and hopped onto the back bumper, holding onto a bar that ran horizontally above the van doors. The van picked up speed for a few blocks, and then stopped at a light.

Alice was just beginning to believe that no one knew she was there, when someone pulled on her shirt from behind and threw her to the frozen street.

The shock made her slow to respond to the meaty fist careening toward her face. She dodged to the side, but it still managed to glance off her cheek.

Alice rolled and came up on the balls of her feet. Dodging another blow, she kicked the man's stomach, then delivered a quick jab to his face. His nose snapped, but he didn't stop. She heard a snarl from the back of his throat as his hands reached for her. She ducked under his clumsy grab and punched him in the stomach.

The van began to move again and Alice tried to take a step toward it but the man seized one of her arms, and pulled her back. She pivoted and kicked him in the groin with one fluid motion. He fell to the cold street, clutching himself and whimpering.

With a squeal of tires, the van careened around the corner and was now out of sight.

But it can't go far on these one-way streets.

She took off at a dead run down a side alley that intersected with the next street. The asphalt was slick underfoot and she barely avoided slipping.

When she reached the end of the alley, the sound of an engine drew close. Alice crouched low and when the van slowed for the corner, she jumped, grabbing the side mirror on the passenger side. The man sitting there stared at her, shocked. Alice punched through the window, barely feeling it with her reinforced gloves. The man flinched and reached for the gun in his belt holster and fired at her. She jerked to the side, and barely missed the bullet.

With a quick motion, Alice captured the hand with the gun and twisted it, feeling the familiar pop of displaced bones. The man screamed and the weapon fell from his hand.

The driver of the van jerked the steering wheel, causing the van to swerve wildly. Alice was unprepared as the passenger door swung open and she found herself dangling from the large side mirror with her feet almost touching the front wheel. The passenger leaned out of the open door, trying to shake Alice loose.

She pressed her feet to the side of the van as she held onto the open door and pushed off. The momentum slammed the door against the man's body. He gave a cry of shock and pain and then fell to the street when the van swerved again, opening the door.

Alice swung her body around the open door and into the passenger side of the van. The driver fired his gun, grazing Alice's arm. She punched him across the face as the van careened through an intersection and swerved onto the sidewalk. It crashed into a large city garbage can, before the driver corrected it back onto the street.

Alice delivered a jab to the drivers face once more. He couldn't fight her and drive at the same time, and she was going to use that to her advantage.

The van swerved again, grazing a parked car.

He tried to punch her, but it was sloppy and she dodged it easily.

With swift movements, Alice reached into the small pouch at her waist and pulled out a garrote that she quickly looped around the man's neck. Pulling tight, back and up, she hoped she remembered the right amount of pressure to knock him out, not kill him.

The driver flailed, kicking the gear shift. The van groaned and began slowing. Then the driver kicked the gas and sent the van lurching forward.

Alice pulled harder and in a few, very long, moments, he stilled. She checked his pulse, relieved that he still had one.

The van was creeping down the street now. Alice opened the driver's door, shoved the unconscious man out, and then climbed into the driver's seat, wanting to get as far from the men as possible.

She was a little short for the way the seat was positioned, but made do, easing the gear shift back where it needed to be. Knowing that the tube in the back was probably too heavy to carry, and not entirely sure who was in it,

Alice decided to drive the van through the back of Mrs. Frost's property.

My property now...

The thought brought her up short and she shook her head.

There wasn't time for wherever those thoughts would take her.

Alice took a roundabout route, in case anyone had followed her. The dirt road through the wooded part of her property was bumpy and full of holes, making the drive take much longer than Alice liked.

When she reached the edge of the wooded area, Alice turned the ignition off, knowing that someone would've seen the headlights and be coming out to see what was going on very soon.

She went around back and opened the doors. The metal tube was there, small lights flashing on its side. A loud, muffled sound was coming from it, as if someone was awake and terrified.

Alice jumped into the van and looked on the sides of the tube to see if there was a release of some kind. She found a dial next to the latch of the lid. Hoping she wasn't doing something dangerous to whoever was inside, Alice turned the dial and heard a pop from the latch.

Lifting the lid, she saw Simon's panicked face. His arms, legs and torso were strapped down, and his clothes had been replaced by a loose gray shirt and pants. Wires ran under the neck of the shirt and Alice assumed they were attached to his chest to monitor his vital signs.

"Who are you?" Simon demanded. "Why...why am I here? What did you do with Judy?"

Alice debated for all of two seconds whether to reveal herself to him.

"I don't know what happened to her," she said, taking the mask off, "but you're safe now."

Simon stared at her as the sound of footsteps reached Alice's ears.

"M-Miss Seymour?"

"Yes, and I know you've got a lot of questions, but right now, I think we need to figure out how to get you out of there."

"I can't use my powers," he said, fear lighting up his green eyes. "What...what did they do?"

"I don't know. But we'll figure it out, I promise."

***

Simon sat on the edge of a large comfortable bed as Gerald took his pulse. The room was one of many guest rooms in the mansion that Alice had yet to explore. She'd been surprised when Gerald had led Simon to it, especially considering it was spotless and smelled faintly of laundry detergent and lemons.

Alice paced on the thick dark brown carpet, waiting for Gerald to finish his exam.

Simon jumped and Alice knew that Gerald must have used his healing powers on the young man.

"He's clean of neurotoxins," Gerald said, when he'd finished. "But there is a residual of something that I don't recognize. His body appears to be burning it off. My guess is that the IV they had in him was pumping a drug into his system to dampen his powers."

Simon rubbed the inside of his arm where the needle had been.

"Anything else?" Alice asked.

"He also had a sedative in him, but not through the IV." Gerald turned to Simon. "Your body must've burned that off sooner than they'd expected. Something to do with your powers, probably."

"How long have you...?" Simon asked Gerald.

He gave a little smile. "A while."

Simon's tired, frightened eyes swung toward Alice. "And you? How long have you been a powered person?"

"I'm not," she said. "I just…well, it's complicated."

He shook his head. "This is all so crazy."

"You need rest," Gerald said, pulling the cream and brown comforter down so Simon could get underneath. "Tomorrow we'll work out anything you remember and see if we can find Judy."

"I heard her," he said, making no move to get under the covers. "She was crying. I think…I think they must've dampened her too or something because I know she would've screamed."

"Simon," Alice said, sitting down next to him, "you need to rest."

"No, I promised I'd protect her. You promised! We have to find her."

"We will. But not tonight."

Simon sighed, and slowly crawled under the covers.

Alice felt her gut twist as she made her way downstairs to the library. She'd hoped to recover both kids tonight. And even though she was happy to have found Simon, the fact that Judy was still at the mercy of Victoria gnawed at her.

"Your turn," Gerald said, once they'd reached the library.

"It's not bad," she said, looking at where the bullet had grazed her.

Gerald arched his eyebrows.

"Fine," she said with a sigh.

The familiar sensation of ice and fire coursed through her veins as Gerald healed the bruises on her body and knit the skin back together on her arm. Once he was done, Alice felt more relaxed than she thought possible with everything going on.

"You need rest, too," Gerald said, going to make himself a drink.

"In a little while. What do you think they were going to do with him?" she asked.

"I'm not sure. The address we found in the van was for a small airstrip just south of Jet City. They were obviously sending him somewhere."

"Metro City," Miss Jones said, coming into the library.

"How do you find these things out so quickly?" Alice asked.

"It's my job," Miss Jones replied. "The flight plan was filed for a final destination in another small airstrip on the outskirts of Metro City."

"Does Victoria have any labs or property there?"

Miss Jones shook her head. "She could be working with someone. There are several new labs within the city limits and a few more just outside. One on the outskirts recently burned down and there was some mystery surrounding the circumstances, as well as the man who ran the lab. But none of it is connected to Victoria."

"That we know of," Gerald said.

Miss Jones nodded in agreement. "We do have someone in Metro City that might be able to shed light on what happened there, if need be."

Alice felt her stomach drop. She knew that Miss Jones meant Marco. She remembered calling him barely two weeks ago, and how the ache of being so close to hearing his voice had left her raw for days. Alice still caught herself longing to be held by him one minute and imagining yelling at him in pained fury the next.

If he wanted to be here, he would. Still, if it could help us find Judy....

"Fine," she said, "ask him for any information he might have but make it clear we are not asking him to come back."

"Of course," Miss Jones said. "Purely informational. In the meantime, we will look into any other possible locations for Judy. I will inform you when I have something."

Alice nodded, trying her best to push thoughts of Judy, scared and alone, out of her mind. But when she did, Marco was there. She'd never had a real reason to try and contact him before this.

I want to be the one but...no. I can't.

"Do you want me to say anything to Marco for you?" Gerald asked.

"No," she said, walking out the door.

CHAPTER TWELVE

Towers of steel and glass surrounded Lionel, the incessant honking of horns a symphony that echoed off the buildings as snow fell in trembling flakes onto his coat. Slush, gray and sad, was piled up on his right, while the warm air from a deli and dry cleaners brushed against him on the left. The smell of bodies and wet exhaust stung his nostrils.

Compared to Paris's elegant avenues, Metro City was a lumbering Neanderthal.

And Lionel couldn't be happier to be in the midst of it.

I'm almost home. I just have to get a cab, talk to Marco and then…Jet City and Alice.

He had tried to hail several, but all had passed him by. Finally, he managed to get a dirty yellow beast to stop for him and gave the cabbie the address to Marco's boxing gym.

The cabbie glanced at Lionel in the rear view mirror and shook his head.

"You got the build of a boxer kid, but with that face, you should be out on the other coast making movies."

Lionel gave him a crooked grin.

"Thanks. Could you step on it."

The cabbie shrugged and pulled into traffic, eliciting several honked horns and one very rude gesture from nearby motorists.

At first they crawled an inch at a time and Lionel wondered if the cab driver was intentionally taking the slow route to get more money from him. But then the driver cut off two motorists and began a wild criss-cross of the downtown streets in an attempt to get Lionel to Little Italy. If he hadn't been nearly indestructible, Lionel would've feared for his life.

Once they reached the business district of the city, traffic once again stood still and Lionel found himself gazing up at the black and silver high rise that was his stepfather's place of business.

"Impressive, huh?" the cab driver asked, pointing at the building.

"Yeah."

"I'll have us outta here in a jiff, don't worry. C'mon! You drive like my dead grandmother!"

Lionel tried to ignore the building, but his gaze was pulled back to it as they sat there. The name Apollo was emblazoned in harsh block letters above the silver and glass doors. A pretentious fountain of the god fighting a python and looking fierce dominated the small courtyard that preceded the building. It all was set up to intimidate and impress.

What the hell do you have to do with all of this?

It was a question that had haunted him since he knew Jason James was involved with the mysterious Consortium. Though he wouldn't put it past his stepfather to use powered people as weapons, he also knew that the risk involved was huge. There would have to be some guarantee that Jason wouldn't be implicated if it all went to hell.

Is that why Victoria is part of this Consortium? A scape goat?

Or are you really arrogant enough to believe that you won't get caught?

The thoughts whirled in his mind, like the snowflakes that had started falling heavy and wet around the cab as they finally got out of traffic. By the time they pulled up to the boxing gym, Lionel had shoved the unknowns about his stepfather to the back of his mind. There were more important things to deal with at the moment. Jason would have to wait.

He gave the cabbie a generous tip and stepped out. Men and women walked down the well-shoveled sidewalks with paper bags of groceries or sundries. Children ran past, hats askew on their heads and mittens trailing behind them, dangling from strings inside their coat sleeves.

Snow had frosted the overhangs of the shops, like a life-sized gingerbread village. Here, the smell of baked bread and coffee lingered in the cold air, like a siren beckoning him to come inside and get warm.

Instead, he crossed the street and pulled on the handle of the boxing gym. It refused to open.

"The gym is closed," someone behind him said.

He whirled around to see a tall Negro woman, her hair covered in a bright red hat that matched her coat and boots.

"I'm looking for Marco Mayer," Lionel said. "I'm...an old friend."

The woman's frown deepened, her lips pressing together.

"He's out at on a case. If you want to come inside, I can take a message."

"Sure, thanks."

The woman unlocked the front door and they stepped inside. The smell of paint and other chemicals involved in construction hit Lionel's nostrils. The floors gleamed in the low light between mats full of equipment, some old, some new. A boxing ring sat in the middle of the enormous space, its ropes missing.

"C'mon," said the woman, waving a hand for him to follow her.

They walked through the main gym, past the locker rooms with their smell of old sweat and laundered towels, and through a storage area to a small office.

"Mr. Mayer is very busy these days," the woman said, tossing her coat down onto the old office chair, "but if you give me your name, I can let him know you stopped by."

"It's a delicate situation. Is there anyway you could call wherever he's at or tell me? I'm happy to-"

"Sorry," she gave him a tight smile. "I'm afraid not. Name?"

Lionel felt a surge of frustration and anger. Who the hell was this woman and why was she keeping him from Marco?

Maybe she's working with Victoria...maybe he's not out on any case at all.

"Is there a problem?" she asked.

"Yes, actually," Lionel said, crossing his arms so that his muscles bulged extra large. "I need to talk to him. It's urgent and I have a feeling you know exactly where he is and won't tell me."

"You're right. I do. And I'm not going to tell you, so you can-"

The blow to the head was a shock in and of itself. The fact that it came from behind him and he didn't hear it was even worse.

He pitched forward from the impact, and a surge of heat flew over his head.

The smell of something burning stung his nostrils and Lionel frowned in confusion.

Bar-b-cue?

He turned and looked behind him and saw a man

batting flames from his face and torso in a panic. As Lionel watched, the flames gathered into a ball and shot back toward the woman behind the desk. The man fell to the floor with a heavy, wet sound that made bile rise to the back of Lionel's throat.

"He with you?" the woman asked.

"Not that I know of," Lionel replied, staring at her. "You…You can-"

"Yeah, and now you need to leave."

"I need to find Marco. It's life or death."

"I'm sure it is."

Lionel grit his teeth and caught the woman by the arm, digging his fingers into her skin. Her eyes widened and a split second before heat rushed through his hand, Lionel realized his mistake.

He yelped and let her go, seeing the sign of first degree burns on his finger tips.

"I don't know who the hell you think you are-" she began.

"Lionel Lawson. I'm an old friend of Marco's from Jet City! And if I don't find him, men like that," he gestured to the burned heap in the doorway, "are going to find him."

"Wait," she said, "Lionel…but…"

"But what?"

"He went to Jet City to find you. He has a lead on your cure."

Lionel breathed out a sigh of relief.

"He's safe then."

"I guess. He called this morning to tell me he landed and he was going to lay low for a few days. I assumed he told you."

"No, he didn't know where I was."

The woman nodded.

"Sorry for the…well, the singeing."

"I shouldn't have grabbed you," Lionel glanced at the burned corpse and swallowed. "What should we...?"

The woman sighed.

"I'll take care of it."

Lionel had no interest in finding out how the woman would 'take care of it.'

"I'm Colleen," she said. "And before I call my clean up guy, I need to know if I'm going to have to fight off anymore of these goons. We just had this place redone."

"I don't know actually," he said. "But if he was here for me then I should leave."

"We have a back entrance."

Colleen motioned for him to follow her and stepped over the dead man as if it were a perfectly normal occurrence. Lionel did his best not to look at the corpse, but the smell was lodged in his nostrils and he knew he wouldn't forget it anytime soon.

They walked into the storage area, which was much larger than Lionel had thought. Boxes were stacked at least as tall as he was, and some old boxing equipment sat in a corner, along with remnants of an old sign and furniture. He wondered what kind of life Marco had built for himself here, and who Colleen was to him. Was she a girlfriend or just a friend? He always knew that Marco loved Alice, and for some reason he had never made any move to tell her. Maybe he'd found comfort with someone else, or at least found a friend to lean on.

Colleen unlocked a heavy looking metal door and peeked out, the smell of wet garbage wafting into the storage room.

"Okay," she said, "it looks clear."

He stepped around her and into the cold afternoon.

"If you go left at the end up that way you'll hit the next street and you can catch a cab."

"Thanks and if you talk to Marco, tell him I'm coming home."

She gave him a genuine smile.

"He'll be excited to see you."

I hope so.

Lionel turned left down the alley and peeked around the corner. He saw people walking down the sidewalks, smiling at each other or just hurrying on their way. No one appeared out of place or waiting, but then what did he expect? Someone with a sign that said "We're coming for you?"

With a whispered prayer to no one in particular, Lionel stepped out and began a brisk walk down the street to the stop light. He knew Colleen had said he should get a cab, but he didn't want to leave any of these men on her doorstep. So he walked another block, hoping that if they had been waiting, they would follow him and not stick around.

He wondered who sent this man. Was it Victoria or Jason? And why? Were they looking for him or for Marco? There were too many questions, and too many powerful enemies.

Maybe I should try calling Alice. If Marco is there and he's with Alice, I can at least warn them about what's happening.

Spying a phone booth up ahead, Lionel sprinted down the sidewalk. He barely fit inside and didn't bother closing the doors. Alice's phone rang and rang without any answer. With his heart beating out a panicked rhythm in his chest, Lionel tried Logan's and no one was there either.

"Damn it! Someone pick up the phone!"

Next he tried Mrs. Frost's house.

"Hello, Frost Mansion," said a woman's voice.

"Hello is-"

Something pierced Lionel's skin at the back of his neck, hot and sharp.

"Hello?" the woman asked.

"I..."

The strength in his hands vanished as he felt the world spin around him. Lionel could feel his legs turn to jelly seconds before he collapsed onto the filthy floor of the phone booth. He looked up as someone replaced the receiver and saw Baritone staring down at him.

"Bastard," Lionel managed before succumbing to darkness.

There was a scent of flowers and the sound of Chopin to greet Lionel as he regained consciousness. It confused him because, though he'd drifted off plenty of times during a symphony, he knew that he wasn't sitting in a theater.

Theaters generally don't tie their patrons to the chair.

His vision was distorted when he opened his eyes, which sent a wave of nausea through him. He groaned and tried to blink away the problem.

Soon, his eyes adjusted and he could see the grossly palatial surroundings.

A huge four poster bed with a green and gold duvet and a mountain pillows sat a few feet from him, taking up a large part of the space. A gold gilt mirror hung above an enormous fireplace, reflecting the large windows behind him, which were shrouded in gauzy curtains. A dressing table, chairs and side tables all made out of delicately carved rose wood were to his right. Under his feet was thick, dark green carpeting, that smelled like it had been freshly shampooed.

The ropes around his feet and hands were thick, but Lionel knew that they couldn't hold him.

With a grin, he jerked his arms up, expecting the

stinging snap of the bindings. Instead, he just got rope burn.

A deep frown cut across his face and he strained against the ropes once again, his face going red with the effort.

They didn't so much as budge.

He concentrated, trying to figure out what was going on. With a jolt of fear, Lionel realized that somehow his strength was just out of reach, as if someone had put up a wall between himself and his powers.

"What the hell...?" he mumbled.

A woman's angry voice from an adjoining room barged into his confusion.

"I killed traitors, intruders who have been using *my* Foundation, *my* private sanctum as a—a warehouse for children test subjects!...Of course I didn't! Children are too dangerous to use for something like that, even orphans with no family to complain about their disappearance...No, I don't know who it is. Those men died without saying a word. But when I do find out—...Don't you threaten *me*, I've done nothing wrong....Fritz was looking for a way out, everyone knew that..." the voice paused for a long time, a heavy sigh punctuating the silence.

Lionel's mind was quite clear now, and he was trying to absorb every word he could as his mind reeled with the information.

Someone is taking kids for test subjects and pinning it on Victoria? What kind of rotten bastard...? Wait... Fritz was working on something for Apollo, an enhancer for powered people, and the poison...he said Apollo had made it to turn people like me into weapons. What if...Oh my God.

A sick feeling spread throughout Lionel.

The person Victoria was talking to was clearly one of her partners in whatever nefarious plans the Consortium had up their sleeve. And if Jason, as a member of that group, was indeed turning powered people into weapons, what better way to do it, than to get the person while they were young, malleable and won't be missed.

And then pin it on someone else. Especially if he despises her.

"Very well," the woman finally said, her voice taut with anger, "I will await your advice. But if I find anyone else from his organization, I will deal with them as I see fit....Yes, I'm planning on going ahead with the special tour...Well then, you'll just have to make sure it doesn't get into the press then! Unless of course you want me to let Mishka know what you were really doing in Russia last year...No, I didn't think so."

There was a loud clang as the receiver was slammed back into its cradle, then muffled words.

He struggled against his bonds, desperately trying to break free before his captors could come into the room.

"Awake already!" said a horribly familiar voice. "And dear, do stop struggling before you hurt yourself."

Lionel looked toward the doorway and saw a beautifully cold woman smiling at him.

"Victoria," he said.

"It's good to see you, too."

"What have you done to me?"

"A lovely little serum has cut you off from your powers temporarily so that we could have a little chat."

"Why would I want to spend any time in the same room with you?"

Victoria laughed.

"So rude! I would've thought the boarding schools your stepfather had sent you to would've taught you better manners."

"Speaking of the dear old son of a bitch, how is he these days?"

"How should I know?"

Lionel grinned.

"Come now, don't play coy. You two were at the

museum benefit three nights ago, thick as thieves. Or so the papers say."

"We both love art."

Lionel considered pushing it, but didn't want to lay his entire hand out for her to see at the very beginning. So, instead, he just shrugged.

"Fine, keep your secrets. Just know that Jason doesn't really like women. At least not ones he can't use and throw away."

"Thank you for the advice. Now," she walked over to a well appointed side bar, poured herself an already mixed martini and took a sip, "I want to discuss an arrangement with you."

And here's why she didn't want me dead. But I can't be too eager to know it.

"Unless it's you giving me the cure to what you infected me with two years ago, you can jump out that window."

"Again, so rude. You know I can't do that. Besides, isn't it freeing to be yourself, no restraints, no rules? Just you in all your monstrous glory."

"And here I thought you hated all us 'monsters'. You sound rather fond of us."

"Hated you? My dear man, I just want what I'm sure you and Marco and everyone else with these powers wants."

"Our extinction?"

"For you to be as you once were, as you were supposed to be before," her lips twisted into a sour expression, "some men overstepped the laws of nature."

"Isn't that what you do all the time? Your strength serum? The fear gas? You over step the laws of nature all the damn time. Not to mention the laws of basic compassion and decency. Park Side showed that."

Her glare pinned him to the chair and she set her glass down.

"Park Side was a terrible necessity. Do you have any idea how much better off that place is now?"

Lionel snorted.

"You can wrap it up in as many altruistic things as you want. You're no better than the men you derided a moment ago."

Victoria's face hardened into something cruel and cold. It made Lionel pull back even as he forced himself to look her in the eye.

"I'm better because I'm willing to be called a monster to make the world a better place," she said, her voice a harsh whisper. "I'm willing to make the hard choices to prevent the kind of world that led to the last great war. What are you willing to do? To sacrifice? Anything?"

"Yes. I already have."

"Poor baby, you had to live in palatial exile in Europe. Self imposed, I might add."

"Because of what you made me!"

The anger began to rise in his veins and for the first time in a year, Lionel welcomed it. He wanted to let the monster inside of him loose, let it pound Victoria Veran into a red paste of flesh and bones. But evidently with his powers locked away, that surge of anger was useless.

A cruel smile spread on her lovely face and she stepped toward him.

"You want to kill me, don't you? And yet, you say you're not a monster."

Heat rocketed through his body and sweat dotted his forehead. His body trembled with the raw power just beneath his skin, held in check by whatever she'd given him. It was beyond frustrating, and yet he was also grateful for it.

"I won't give you the satisfaction," he said. "I control me, and my fate. Not this poison, not you."

"Oh Lionel," she said, raking her fingers through his hair.

He flinched back from her touch, but she grabbed a handful to keep him looking up at her.

"You're right," she said, "you do have a choice. You can stay with me and do what I say and Alice won't have her life stripped from her. Or, you can fight me and I can ruin her precious little secret identity."

His mouth went dry as his heart sped up.

"What are you talking about?"

"One word from me and everyone will know that Alice and Marco are two of the Vigilantes responsible for the Park Side Massacre. They'll be arrested and whether or not the courts convict them, the public will crucify them."

"If you really could you would've done it already."

"No," she let go of his hair and stepped away, "it feels a little too...well, impersonal. When I defeat Alice, and I will, I want to look her in the eye and be the last thing she ever sees."

"You stay away from her!" he screamed.

"Poor man. Go on, get all your frustration out."

Though he may not have been able to rage, that didn't stop Lionel from seeing red at Victoria's words. Fury beat against the barrier of the serum inside of him, demanding release that he physically couldn't give.

Lionel grunted and then roared at her, jerking his arms up against the ropes. He could feel the fire of rope burns, the warmth of blood as his usually tough skin was torn open.

After a few minutes he slumped against the bonds, the fury leeched from him just enough for his mind to once again be able to think.

"What do you want?" he asked, his voice low.

"I thought you'd never ask, "she sat on the bed grinning

at him. "You will do what I say until the Science Foundation special tour that I'm hosting."

"Why?"

"Because I can't have you running around the city, causing trouble. I also want no questions. No snooping. No running to your little friends and telling them anything. Not that you'll be in a position to know much."

"You want me to willingly stay in a cage until whenever this party is?"

Victoria laughed.

"No, of course not! I want you to be my new lover. Or at least appear to be. That way, no one will question why you are seen with me at the theater, dinner and so on."

Lionel stared at her, sure that the woman had cracked at last.

"I know," she continued, "it seems strange. But humor me in this and I swear to never reveal who you or your two cohorts really are."

If he appeared with her in public, it would get back to Alice. Society news that strange and out of the blue would travel at lightning speed.

There's no way Alice would believe that I'm...would she? It would be a way for Victoria to twist the knife, to get at Alice and throw her off before whatever this event is. And if I'm with her, I might hear or see something. Especially if I make her think I'm defeated enough to not be a threat. This could be a way to learn more about what's really going on.

"Well?" Victoria asked. "I can see the wheels working in your little mind."

"Fine," he said, voice hard, "I will be your little toy."

She smiled.

"Very good. Now, we have some things to take care of while we're here and then it's back to Jet City. Be a good boy and go to your adjoining room where someone is waiting to take your measurements for some new clothes.

And then you have an appointment so we can do something about your hair. Really, what were you thinking dying it such a dull color?"

With one knock on the door, Baritone strode in with another guard, who cut Lionel loose from the ropes. When Lionel looked into his eyes, a chill ran down his spine. The man stared with a vacant yet feral expression, as if he were no longer human.

Lionel turned away from that haunting gaze and saw that Baritone had the same briefcase Mishka had given to Victoria. He whispered something in Victoria's ear, giving Lionel a glare full of hate.

"No," she said, "we'll store it at my office. The new safe should be secure."

Then her cold gaze swung to Lionel as he stood to his feet.

"And oh yes, I almost forgot."

With a nod of her head, the guard took a huge syringe off the dressing table and, before Lionel could think to stop him, plunged it into Lionel's neck.

"I can't let you have access to all that strength and anger, not when I know how much you hate me."

It was like cold fire raced through is veins. He gasped and doubled over in shock and pain. A few seconds and it was over, leaving Lionel with a terrible sense of loss. His powers were locked away even further now.

"You'll be getting one of those every six hours. Enjoy the reprieve from your rage, dear boy."

And with that, Baritone escorted Lionel to his new prison.

CHAPTER THIRTEEN

Alice paced the soft carpet in the library, narrowly avoiding being tangled in the phone cord as she did. A fire crackled in the fireplace and a pot of tea sat untouched on the coffee table. She could smell roast from the kitchen and wished that she were able to sit down and enjoy the cozy comfort around her.

Instead, she paced a little faster and sighed.

"No, I haven't found anything out yet," Alice said into the receiver.

"We need to find her," Simon said on the other end of the phone, his voice sharp and hard. "You don't know what it was like. I could handle it, but Judy? Miss Seymour, she won't survive it, she'll...I don't know."

Alice thought about the stakeouts she'd been on for the last two nights, and felt a fresh wave of frustration lance through her.

The only thing I can do is sit and stare at the Science Foundation like a damn gargoyle, waiting for something to happen! We have no more clues, no direction, nothing!

Taking a deep breath, Alice tried to bury those thoughts.

She couldn't let Simon know just how desperate the situation was, but she did have to give him some measure of honesty. He deserved that much.

"I want to find her as bad as you do," she said. "Just trust me that we're doing everything we can, it's just…the trail has gone cold at the moment."

Simon sigh was broken, as if he were holding back a sob. She wanted to run out into the night and do something, anything. But, as Miss Jones had told her half a dozen times, there was nothing to do but wait and see if something came up. The Foundation security had been increased the last few days, and Miss Jones couldn't get into the places she could before, so there was nothing more direct that they could do.

And the phone call to Marco had apparently been useless. Or at least that's what Gerald's sparse explanation had told her.

Something else is going on there. Something he doesn't want to tell me. And I'm not sure I want to know.

"Have you settled back into the Children's Home?" Alice asked, anxious to divert her attention far away from Marco.

"Yes. Mateo and Sam aren't leaving my side. It's a little annoying."

"But understandable. Are they not making other friends?"

"To be honest, none of us are. After the gas attack, the not powered kids are kinda staying away."

It was hard to hear the bitter edge in Simon's voice and Alice cringed.

"I'm sorry," she said to him, "just try to stick with the other powered children until I can figure something out. And be careful. I've added some security there but who knows if it will be enough."

The library door opened and Uncle Logan stepped in, a manila file folder in his hands.

"I have to go," she said, "but please, call at any time, I mean that."

"I will, thank you again, Miss Seymour. And," his voice dropped to a rough whisper, "I haven't told anyone about you and I won't. You can trust me. But, when you go after whoever took Judy, I want to come, too."

"I thank you for keeping my secret, but there's no way—"

"She's like my sister. I won't sit back and let you do all the work. I want to help."

"Keeping yourself and Mateo and Sam safe is helping."

Simon sighed again. "Fine. But I want you to train me."

Alice's eyes widened. "Y-You want what?"

"You to train me. I want to do what you do."

"I don't...I mean, I'm not—"

"You think about it."

The receiver clicked as Simon hung up, and Alice stared at it with her mouth open in shock.

"He's going to be a problem, I can feel it."

"Is everything alright?" Uncle Logan asked.

"Uh...No...Yes...I-I think so. It's nothing that needs thinking about right now. What do you have for me?"

Uncle Logan planted a brief kiss on her cheek. "Well, hello to you, too."

"Sorry, I know I've been all business, it's just..."

"I understand. I was the same when I was chasing a story."

He handed her the file folder and went to pour himself a whiskey. Alice began reading the names listed on a piece of paper, and her heart dropped to her toes.

"The mayor, police chief and commissioner, district attorney, the City Council, the top businessmen in the city and…editor in chief of the Chronicle…They're all invited to the special tour," Alice's mouth became dry. "She's clearing the decks."

"Looks that way," Uncle Logan said, downing his whiskey in one swallow. "And as prestigious as this Foundation is becoming, no one will want to miss that special tour. My question is: what does this really get her? Besides killing everyone that stopped her special police force."

Alice tried to calm her mind so she could think logically and tie all the pieces together. But for the life of her, she didn't see how the serum or gas that Victoria was creating to strip people of powers could be tied to the special tour.

She paced around the library, the soft sound of her footsteps and the crackling of the fire the only sounds in the room. Her mind went through every piece of information she knew about Victoria and what she wanted. But no matter how Alice bent and twisted it all together, none of it made any sense.

"I just don't see how it's connected!" she burst out. "What does the serum have to do with this? How does any of it line up?"

"Stop for a minute, get some distance and maybe you'll see it."

"I can't stop."

"Why not?"

"You know why not."

Uncle Logan sighed.

"How long are you going to blame yourself for Park Side?"

"You act like I shouldn't."

"Exactly."

"I should've seen it then," Alice said, stepping away from him to look out the window, "and now, here we are. I swore it would be different this time. How long have I been waiting, pretending to be her friend in the hopes of seeing what she'll do next? What has it gotten me? Nothing but confusing pieces of a puzzle that I can't see, just like last time."

Uncle Logan came to stand next to her, his warm presence comforting.

"Not everything bad that happens is your fault," he said, his voice low and kind. "Just because you're a hero doesn't mean you'll always have the answers. You've got to accept that, sometimes, even when you do your best, give everything you've got, that it just won't be enough."

Alice closed her eyes, the weight of it all pressing down on her. A part of her knew he was right. But another part, a much louder, stronger part couldn't accept it.

They stood in silence and stared out at the back garden. It was drenched in twilight, the half-melted snow practically glowing. A small fountain stood silent from the freezing temperatures, and all the plants looked fragile and sad in their winter slumber. Alice usually loved the twilight, the depth and beauty of the light as it colored the world cobalt before descending into darkness. But she could take no pleasure in it now. All she could think about was the lives that had been ruined in Park Side, because she wasn't the hero she needed to be.

And now? How many will die this time?

She looked down at the list still clutched in her hand, as memories of the meetings with the mayor and police commissioner played in her mind.

They'd sworn that as long as they were in power, Victoria would never get what she wanted. She was so furious. She even let slip that she'd —

"Oh my god!" Alice said, jumping with the sudden realization.

"What?'

Alice walked away from the window, pacing once

again, but this time in an effort to keep up with the furious speed of her mind.

"What if..." she said, her voice shaky with energy. "What if...you said it yourself, she's clearing the decks...right?"

Uncle Logan nodded.

"Half this list opposed her when she wanted the special police force. Now she's developing a gas or serum that will strip people of their powers. But how many people will line up for a 'cure' that might leave them dead or injured?"

"You think she's getting rid of anyone who might oppose using it without the public's knowledge or consent?"

"I think that's one reason, maybe the main one."

"If that's the case, she must be closer than we thought to perfecting it."

Alice nodded as she kept pacing. "Special elections would be needed to replace the politicians, and with the rest of the wealthy families in turmoil from losing their patriarchs—"

"Those that seek election would likely turn to Victoria to help them," Uncle Logan said.

"She could even promote herself as a leader. City Council or something."

"The city would need leadership, someone to come in and bring order to the chaos this would create."

Alice nodded. "And we both know, Victoria believes she's the best person for such a job."

"Alright," Uncle Logan rubbed a hand over his haggard face. "How will she do it? She has to stay unsullied."

"I don't know," Alice admitted, "but this, at least, is a start."

She felt her shoulders relax, and knots she hadn't known were there suddenly began loosen. She felt like she could breathe again.

"Excuse me," Miss Jones said, stepping into the room, "but you have a phone call." The subtle tension around her thin lips made Alice's peace evaporate.

"Who is it?" Alice asked.

"Mrs. Veran is calling for you from Metro City."

Alice took a deep breath, concentrating on keeping her voice soft, relaxed.

"Hello, Victoria," she said. "Is everything alright? I thought you'd be in Europe a little longer."

"I wanted to return early, especially when I heard about the trouble at the Children's Home," her voice was oozing sympathy, like honey from a full comb. "Is everything under control?"

"Oh, yes, that was horrible. The children were terrified. But besides some cosmetic damage to the inside of the home, everything is fine."

"It must've been so very hard to hear about that dreadful gas after what you went through in Park Side. Are you sure you're alright?"

Alice tried not to grit her teeth. "Well...it was so... memories of before...I feel sick just thinking about it."

"My dear girl! You shouldn't have had to be reminded of all that."

The words felt like ash in her mouth, but Alice pressed on.

"Thank you. I'm glad my uncle was here to help."

"And I'll be home soon to help as well. In fact, I contacted the rest of the board of the Children's Home, since I am the second highest officer next to you, and let them know that if at any time you seem too affected by what's happened, they should let me know. I would be happy to take over for you, if you need me to."

Cold fury blazed through Alice's bones, her knuckles turning white as she gripped the receiver.

"Alice?" Victoria asked. "Are you still there? Have I lost you?"

"No," Alice said, her voice raspy until she cleared her throat, "no, I'm here. I'm just very surprised you spoke with the board behind my back."

"Now, dear heart, it wasn't like that. But we both know you aren't good at asking for help. And I just didn't want your aunt's legacy to suffer, because you were trying to be brave and soldier on. You don't have to do that, I'm here for you."

"Thank you, that's very kind."

"Of course, my dear."

"Well, if that's all—"

"Oh, one more thing. I would very much like to have dinner with you when I return. I have someone I'm just dying for you to see."

Fear joined the anger coursing through Alice, making her gut churn.

"Really? Who might that be?"

"Uh-uh, I want it to be a surprise. I fly in tomorrow, so how about the day after? The Elliot, eight o'clock."

"I would be delighted."

"Wonderful. I will see you then."

Alice slammed the receiver back on the cradle and let out a loud, throaty groan.

"What did she want?" Uncle Logan asked.

Alice told them the gist of Victoria's call, her voice harsh with emotion.

"Any idea who this might be?" Alice asked, when she was done relaying the conversation. "No reports or rumors about her with someone in Europe?"

Uncle Logan shook his head. "I asked some of my reporters over there to keep an eye out for her, but she saw no one more than a handful of times. And it was always business related or old friends from the war."

Alice looked at Miss Jones, asking the same thing.

"No, I'm sorry," Miss Jones said.

"I don't want to be blindsided by her, so, if we could find out who this person is, that would be helpful."

Both Miss Jones and Uncle Logan nodded.

"I'll see what I can find out," he said.

"As will I."

"We also need to try and figure out how to stop this tour," Alice said.

"That could be tricky," Uncle Logan said.

"Agreed," Miss Jones said.

"Well, we have...how many days?"

"Nine," Miss Jones replied. "I could try to find something out tomorrow night at the Foundation."

Alice nodded. "See if you can discover the lead scientists on the gas. Maybe we could...I don't know, put them someplace so Victoria doesn't have access to them, throw her timing off. And I'll look over the blueprints we have. Maybe Rose could come up with some way to damage the structure, make it unsafe for anyone to visit."

Uncle Logan stared at her. "You're talking about kidnapping and destroying a building?"

"Not destroying, damaging," Alice said. "I wouldn't do anything when there were people in there. And as far as the scientists go, I won't harm them, just...give them an enforced vacation."

"Alice, this is...it's not like you. Are you sure you want to consider this? Something could go very wrong, and then what?"

Alice paused, chewing on her bottom lip. Doubt whispered in her mind, at odds with the guilt that seemed to permeate everything these days.

"If I could've stopped Park Side by crossing the line just a little...," Alice said, shaking her head.

"Then you wouldn't have been a hero," Uncle Logan

said. "You have to find a way to let this fear go. It's clouding your judgment."

Alice nodded, trying to believe that she wouldn't need to cross a line to beat Victoria this time. But doubt had its icy claws too deep in her mind and she wondered what it would cost her to see all this finally done.

CHAPTER FOURTEEN

Alice patted her half-up, half-down beehive before stepping out of the car in front of the Elliot. It was the only outward sign of how her nerves were bouncing around like maniacal bees. She'd changed dresses five times before settling on the first one Jacques had chosen for her-an emerald green satin number with a square neckline just low enough to show some cleavage, that clung to her curvy hips and waist. It created a look that would be alluring to any man, even with the cane and the wrap around her knee. If she had to endure hours of dinner conversation with Victoria, at least she'd look and feel good doing it.

With a slow movement, Alice stepped out of the car and drew her knee length, white fur coat around her as a burst of cold wind whipped through the covered entryway. Once inside, she couldn't wait to hand it to the coat check attendant, as the temperature was wildly different.

"Oh, Miss Seymour, how delightful to see you," the impeccably slender maître d'hôtel said, his smile tight.

Alice returned his smile and followed her sleek guide until he stopped at a table beautifully laid with shining silver and crystal. As she took the proffered seat, she saw golden dots of light cast on the dark water from the newly-constructed seaside shops, and the small islands in the distance.

She ordered a club soda and scanned the dining room, habit dictating that she get a lay of the land before Victoria showed up. Once that was done, Alice tried not to think about the fact that Miss Jones hadn't found anything last night to help them stall the special tour.

Her thoughts were interrupted by a familiar voice and her jaw clenched briefly.

"Darling!" Victoria called out, walking toward the table, her blue satin dress swishing with each step. Her usually pale skin was tinged with color, and her hair looked like spun gold in its perfect bouffant.

Mr. Graves, or Baritone, as Alice still thought of him, walked with a perpetual scowl behind her, one eye scanning the restaurant. Alice had almost gotten used the man's presence everywhere Victoria went.

His eye landed on Alice and his lips spread in a sneer. She smiled at him, and nodded, as she usually did, and then tried to pretend he wasn't standing off to the side, glaring.

Victoria bent down and gave Alice a quick kiss on the cheek.

"I'm so sorry I'm late. Have you been waiting long?"

"No, I've enjoyed the view," Alice said, barely able to keep her voice even and soft.

Victoria's face became sad, though her eyes still shone.

"I am so sorry I wasn't here for the memorial, it must've been so difficult for you."

It was easier with you not there.

"I understand," Alice said. "But I am more curious about this person you wanted me to meet."

At that, Victoria's grin reappeared. "Not just any person."

Alice looked to where Victoria nodded and felt her whole body go numb and hot and painful, all at once.

Walking toward her, with all the lethal confidence of a god, his tall, broad body clad in a double-breasted dark blue suit, square face tanned, a fierce light in his navy eyes...

"There you are, what took you so long?"

Lionel's full lips twisted in a cold smile.

"I thought you wanted me to make an entrance."

Victoria hit his chest and leaned toward him. He kissed her, and Alice felt her heart constrict.

Memories of the crooked smile he used to give her over a plate of Marco's pasta, how he'd held her the night they'd kissed, the way his blue eyes would hold hers with such fire. All of it crashed through her mind. The boy he used to be, the man he'd been, both so kind and everything Alice thought she'd ever wanted.

Alice found herself staring at him, unable to move.

Say something! Do something!

"H-Hello, Lionel," she said, inwardly cringing at the shock and pain in her voice.

He nodded, his eyes barely grazing her.

When he sat down, Lionel looked at her again before ordering a whiskey sour for himself and a glass of champagne for Victoria.

Alice could feel Victoria's eyes on her, picking up every nuance. She knew that she should hide her feelings under the well-worn mask she'd constructed, but it was too much of a shock. Her face flushed and her hands began to tremble before hiding them in her lap.

"I gather from your reaction that this is a pleasant surprise?" Victoria asked, her smile friendly on the surface. Underneath, however, Alice could see the pleasure Victoria was experiencing at her "surprise".

She held Victoria's gaze, shock turning to anger. It took

every ounce of discipline Alice had to make her mouth relax and produce a natural smile. Unclenching her hands and taking a deep breath, she laughed.

"It's an amazing surprise! How long has it been Lionel? Two years?"

He took a long pull from his drink and shrugged massive shoulders.

A part of Alice didn't believe he was really so cavalier about seeing her, but the fact he didn't bother giving her an actual answer still managed to sting.

"Well, I suppose it doesn't matter," she said. "Where did you two meet?"

"That's a rather funny story, isn't it darling?"

Lionel's lips ticked up into a tense smile and he nodded.

"Do you want to tell it or shall I?" Victoria asked.

"You're the better storyteller, you always have been," he said, a sharp clip to his words.

For a split second Alice swore she saw Victoria's gaze turn icy and then it was back to the gushing, love struck woman she'd been when she first walked in the door.

"I do so love it! Well, you see, Lionel..."

Alice may have looked like she was engrossed in the tale, but her mind tuned it out. Why was he with her? What was the angle? Did he know what he was doing? Was he plotting to kill Victoria, and if so why hadn't he done it yet? Did he really want to be with her? Had he changed that much since Park Side? What had he been doing all this time that could've changed him so completely?

Lionel shifted in his seat through Victoria's tale, fidgeting with a ring on his pinkie finger and looking about as comfortable as a man wearing a hair shirt.

I know exactly how he feels. But if he's this uncomfortable, why is he with her? Good god I wish I drank!

"That is quite a story," Alice said once it was done, her face starting to hurt from holding the smile.

"After Tony, I never thought I'd find another man I'd want. But, I suppose I'm quite lucky."

Alice glanced at Lionel, who was accepting his second whiskey sour from the waiter. She wondered if Lionel felt lucky.

"Well," he said, "should we order?"

Alice would've given anything to not sit across from them for another two hours, pretending not to be full of hurt and fury. But there was no way to leave without giving away how she felt. And tactically, it was smart to stay and see if Victoria or Lionel would give anything away.

The small talk while waiting for the food was excruciating. Alice was grateful that she had the memorial to talk about, and even joked with Victoria about the rich young men that suddenly decided to take notice of her. During the stories, the first course was laid in front of them. Alice picked at her food while Lionel ate with his usual gusto.

"Which will you choose?" Victoria asked as the waiter cleared their plates.

Alice laughed. "I really can't say. Right now, I just want to focus on getting to know the company better."

"Yes, establish yourself first, let the board know that you mean to lead straight away."

"I am not very interested in marriage, anyway. I may never marry."

"Oh, come now! Not every man will try to rule you. The trick might be to get one that you can command. What do you think, darling?" Victoria asked, her long hand resting on Lionel's forearm.

He shrugged. "If she doesn't want to marry, why should she?"

Alice swallowed, wishing the dinner would be over so she could go punch something.

"Quite right! Here's to independence!"

Victoria raised her champagne flute and they toasted.

Alice caught Lionel's eye above the glasses, and for a brief moment, she could see pain and longing. She was reminded of another night, so long ago, when the two of them sat across from each other in this restaurant. So many possibilities in front of them, so many hopes.

Tears itched her eyes, and Alice looked down at her food, hoping Victoria and Lionel didn't notice.

Get a hold of yourself! This isn't the time for memory lane.

The next course was soon served and their conversation turned to Victoria's European trip. Alice was a little relieved that all it required of her was to look like she was listening.

As the evening wore on, and Lionel's cold demeanor didn't change, Alice's hurt began to transform into anger.

He'd run away when she was lying in a hospital room, broken and scared. And for what? To find his cure? Or just to run, because he couldn't handle it all anymore?

Alice managed to just barely avoid dessert, mentioning an early meeting with an investor. If Victoria suspected that it was a lie, she didn't act like it.

As they were getting their coats, Victoria pulled her in for an embrace.

"It was so good to see you tonight," she said.

"Yes, I'm glad you're back."

"And I hope I will see you at the upcoming tour of my Foundation."

Alice silently kicked herself. She'd been so preoccupied with trying to hide her feelings about Lionel that she hadn't even tried to steer the conversation toward that.

She forced a wide smile on her lips.

"I wouldn't miss it. Lionel, it was lovely to see you again."

"Yes, I suppose it was."

Alice's hand tightened on her cane while she tried to keep her face relaxed. She could feel Lionel's gaze on her as she walked out to the car, her gait more halting than usual.

Once in the car, her emotions sprang from the box she'd trapped them in, crashing through her. She waited until they were a safe distance from the restaurant before letting her tears flow freely.

Alice gave up all pretense of walking with the cane the moment the front door of the mansion closed. Her anger and shock had blossomed into something so intense she was shaking with it. All she could think of was Lionel's cold smile, the gentle kiss he planted on Victoria's lips, the flush of happiness on her face.

"Alice, there's—," Uncle Logan said, coming out of the library.

"I'm sorry Uncle, but not now," Alice said, stalking past him.

One foot was planted on the bottom step of the staircase when a soft voice sounded in the foyer with all the power of a bullet piercing her heart.

"Alice…"

In her darkest times of loneliness and fear she used to conjure up that voice, used to imagine what he'd say to her to keep her going, and then regret the exercise. It was always too painful, so she'd stopped.

And now, there it was, that voice. Not imagined, but very real.

Turning around, Alice's lips parted in complete shock.

Marco looked the same, but very different. He was dressed in a brown trench coat and plain blue suit, hands shoved in the pockets of his pants. His dark hair was a little too long on top, large chunks falling across his forehead and into his brown eyes, one of which looked bruised, as did his cheek. There was a hardness to the angular planes of his face that hadn't been there before, as if he wore a perpetual scowl. The most striking difference, however, was the thick, well-trimmed beard, which gave his long, thin face an appearance of fullness.

Alice couldn't help it. She laughed. A high, furious sound that echoed harshly in the foyer.

"I gather you've seen him," Marco said.

"Yes, I have. And now, having you here makes my night complete."

"Can we talk?"

She threw her hands up in the air. "Why not?"

Uncle Logan reached out for her arm as she passed him. "Listen to him, please? He might be able to help."

Alice took her arm from his grasp and stared at him. "Y-You knew he was coming, didn't you? That's what Gerald did when he called. He didn't ask for information. He asked him to come back."

Uncle Logan sighed. "He didn't, no. But I did."

She couldn't have been more shocked if her uncle had slapped her across the face.

Alice looked away to where Marco waited in the library and shook her head.

"I don't know what to say to you," she said.

"I know. It's OK."

Uncle Logan placed a quick kiss on the top her head and walked up the stairs to his private suite of rooms.

Tears once again threatened to spill down her cheeks and Alice forced them back. She wanted her anger, not her grief, to carry her through whatever Marco was going to say. As much as her instinct was to trust him, she couldn't bring herself to be vulnerable with him.

Once the library door was closed, Alice began to pace, swinging the cane at her side. When she finally stopped, Marco's eyes were hooded in a deep frown.

"You going to explain what I saw tonight?" Alice asked, her voice sharp. "Did you set this up or—?"

"No. My partner in Metro City told me that he came by, and the visit ended because someone came in and attacked him. I have no idea what he's doing. His only thought the last time I saw him was to find a cure. Maybe he's getting close to her to find one."

"You lost touch with him?" Alice felt her body begin to shake. "You left to help him, to make sure he didn't do anything stupid, and you lost track of him?"

Marco's lips thinned "It's not that simple. He left for Europe and told me not to follow."

"And what did you do after that? Did you try to find him or did you just throw in the towel, like you did here?"

"I asked your uncle to have his European contacts keep an eye out—"

"Oh, you made a phone call! Bravo!"

"That's not fair," his voice was low.

"No, it's not. Nothing about tonight is fair! Seeing him like that after all this time and now seeing you!"

Marco opened his mouth to speak, but Alice cut him off.

"You left me to clean up this mess! And one phone call from my uncle and you're back?"

"I didn't—"

"I went through hell getting my body strong again after Park Side! I swallowed every ounce of hatred to get close to Victoria, made her trust me, so that I could find the right time to stop her." Alice began to walk toward him, her grip on her cane tightening with every step. "I have waited and watched for the perfect moment to finish this, and now that it's almost here, you two show up like you're going to save me or help me? Did you really think I needed your help? Because I don't!"

She stopped mere inches from Marco, face flushed, eyes glittering with fire. Marco stared at her, and Alice couldn't tell if he was angry, or sad or both. And there was a part of her that didn't care.

He opened his mouth to speak, and shut it again. Alice wanted him to try and apologize. Wanted to hear his excuses so she could hurl at him all the pent up pain and anger she'd been living with. But he just shook his head and turned away.

"You can stay here tonight," Alice spun around on her heel. "But tomorrow, you're gone."

CHAPTER FIFTEEN

Lionel paced the large 'room' he'd been given in the base-ment of the Science Foundation, a drink in his hand.

When he was first escorted here, he wondered if Victoria had outfitted this for him special or if it had been for her own use before he'd arrived. Whatever the reason, every-thing about the room was comfortable and expensive, from the large bed with it's headboard of carved mahogany, to the thousand dollar crystal glasses and assortment of liquor. The adjoining bathroom was at least half the size of the room with a two headed shower and soaking tub that Lionel could more than fit inside.

The three security locks were an interesting addition, as were the vents that pumped knock out gas into the room when they cut his next injection too close.

It had been hours since the dinner at the Elliot. Since seeing Alice again for the first time in almost two years. But instead of begging her forgiveness for leaving her in the hospital, instead of wrapping his arms around her and holding her like he'd thought of a thousand times, he'd helped Victoria to plunge a knife into Alice's heart.

The scenes replayed in his mind, over and over in a loop he couldn't stop.

The rules had been clearly laid out by Victoria before they'd left for the dinner. He was to adore her in both words and deeds, he was to be as cold to Alice as possible and give absolutely nothing away.

A sour taste coated his tongue at the memory of how Victoria's body had pressed against him, the feel of her lips on his. He'd wanted to vomit right there at the table and had chosen instead to drink the guilt and bile away.

Alice had tried so damn hard to hide her pain and anger throughout the dinner, but Lionel could see it. And if he could see it, he knew Victoria could too.

Relishing her pain the whole damn time like some sadistic ghoul.

There had been so many times he'd been tempted to throw the lie aside and tell Alice the truth. But the moment he would wet his lips to speak, Lionel thought of what would happen to Alice if Victoria made good on her threat.

But was it better to hurt her like that tonight and save her all that? Was it really? Or am I just too much of a damn coward to do what was right?

Victoria had been delighted when they'd left the restaurant, patting his hand and telling him how good he'd done, as if he were her dog.

"Maybe I am…"

The thought brought a snarl of anger from his lips and he threw his glass of scotch against the wall.

A guard peeked into the room and glared at him, one of the few who weren't blank eyed enhanced zombies.

"What," Lionel said, "it's not like she doesn't have eleven more!"

The guard said nothing and left Lionel alone once again.

He wanted to smash every piece of furniture in the place, to destroy this gilded cage and Victoria with it. His steps were fast and his breath came out in huffs as he paced the room. Finally he stopped and took a few deep breaths. This was what Victoria wanted, to have him so twisted up inside that he wouldn't be able to think.

"I was never much good at thinking though," he whispered to himself, "that was always Marco and Alice's department. But if I'm going to make Victoria pay for this, if I'm going to make all this worth it…I have to try."

He took a few more deep breaths and sat on the bed, head in his hands.

The first thing that ran through his mind was Alice, standing there staring at him, a cane clenched in her hand.

No one had mentioned that Alice used a cane, and he'd had a damnably hard time not staring at it.

Is it real or artifice? After what happened to her…Dear God, the way she looked at me!

In all the years they'd known each other, Alice had never looked at him with such fury or hurt.

Lionel shook his head, trying to dislodge the memory. If he kept thinking about Alice and what happened tonight, he'd be right back where he started.

It was difficult to work past it all, and Lionel kept finding himself thinking about when he, Marco and Alice were together as friends and vigilantes. The memories were so bitter sweet that they brought tears to his eyes.

"We were really good together."

The statement jolted something inside of Lionel and he sat up.

We almost beat Victoria, when we were together. This…what she's doing with me. She's trying to keep us from becoming a team again, she's driving wedges between us. And I think it's because together we could beat her, and she knows it.

The locks on the door clicked and Victoria stood in the door way.

Lionel's hands clenched into fists and he didn't bother to hide the murderous gleam in his eyes.

"The guard tells me you threw a glass?"

"I was bored."

"It sounds like you have some excess energy to burn. And, since I don't want you breaking anything else in this room, you may have a little time in our training room. No weights, not ropes. Just the running track and the punching bag."

"Why would you let me do that?" he asked, eyes narrowing.

Victoria shrugged. "Maybe I like to watch you sweat."

Yeah, I'm sure you do.

Thirty minutes later, two guards escorted Lionel to a half mile track stashed in the underground maze that was Victoria's secret facility under the Science Foundation. The anticipation of letting off some steam had already helped his head begin to clear. He knew that Victoria wasn't being generous with this little work out session, there was a reason for it.

Does she want me away from my room for some reason?... Maybe I'll just happen to hurt myself and need to go back early so I can see what she's trying to hide...

He wasn't in any hurry to return to his palatial cell, but if it meant throwing Victoria off her stride, even for a moment, then he was willing to sacrifice some free time.

And maybe I'll discover something useful.

Just before Lionel walked through the door to the indoor track, he saw an old janitor, bent over and slowly mopping the floors. There was something about him, something decidedly out of place.

"Hey you," said one of the guards, "what are you doing down here?"

"I wuz jus' moppin'," said the janitor, his voice slurred. "Jus'...moppin'."

The guard turned to look at his partner, who shrugged.

"Don't look at me, I don't keep track of the janitor schedules."

The first guard sighed.

"Fine, old man, just finish this hall and go back up stairs."

"Yep," the janitor said.

Lionel's instincts itched in the back of his mind. Something was off about this man but what? He lingered, and met the eyes of the old janitor. They were sharp and calculating, as if the man were sizing Lionel up.

He turned away, quickly trying to unravel this new, strange piece of information.

That's not a janitor. Who...? Alice? No...that's not her but... could she have a spy here?

He glanced back, but the guards were closing the door behind them, cutting off the old man and his sloshing mop and bucket.

"Better get to it," the first guard said. "We haven't got all night."

Lionel flashed the guard a one finger salute as he took off down the track.

As he ran, Lionel felt his mind ease into the rhythm of his body and begin to soothe his emotions. He could think a little better now, even if his powers and his anger were locked inside of him like a snarling animal in a cage.

The janitor had to be a spy of some kind but was he from Alice or Jason? If the man worked for Alice, Lionel might be able to get a message to her. If he worked for Jason...well, that was a risk Lionel might just have to take.

The more he thought about how Victoria was using him,

the things she'd said, he knew that whatever her plan was it hinged on keeping the three of them apart, and somehow also having them at the Science Foundation tour.

Why? What is she going to do there?

A distant sound, the bass clang of something heavy either being set down or dropped, reached Lionel.

That could be what she didn't want me around for.

His stride faltered, and with his next step, he stumbled. With what he hoped was perfect deception, Lionel began to favor his right ankle.

"Hey, what's wrong?" asked one of the guards.

"Oh...my ankle. I think I stepped wrong," Lionel said, limping over to a nearby bench.

He made a show of examining it while his mind feverishly worked to figure out how to get a message to Alice. If he found out something tonight, he couldn't just sit on it.

"Are you gonna run some more or what?" the guard asked after a few minutes.

"I think I need to go back to my room," Lionel said, wincing as he tried to stand.

The two guards said something to one another that Lionel couldn't hear. They looked worried and finally one of them shrugged.

"Fine," the first guard said, "we'll take you back."

They didn't offer any help, and that was fine with Lionel. He went as slow as possible, stopping to rest a couple of times. It looked like he was in pain, but really he was listening and looking. The janitor was nowhere to be found, unfortunately, but as of yet, Lionel didn't have anything to report.

He started to wonder if maybe he'd gotten it wrong and Victoria was telling the truth, when he heard the sound of crates being moved in a nearby room. As he stopped next to the door where the sounds were coming from, Lionel was able to peek inside and see that half a dozen of the enhanced guards were moving crates. The crates warned that the contents were under pressure, a picture of a gas canister next to the warning.

Fear gas? Again? Will she use it at this tour?

"Get moving," the guard said, shoving Lionel.

He stumbled past, picking up the pace in the hopes that he could see a little more of what was going on elsewhere. When they walked past Victoria's office, she was on the phone and Baritone was shoving papers from a briefcase into a large wall safe behind Victoria's desk.

That's the briefcase that's been cuffed on his wrist a couple of times…what would she need safeguarded that much?

"I don't care what it takes, kill that story," she said, "and find out why those buildings haven't been finished, they're now months behind."

She looked up and saw Lionel stumbling past. Her eyes widened as anger tinged her fair cheeks with red. She snapped her fingers at Baritone and waved at the door. The large man slammed it in Lionel's face and the guards prodded him forward.

I wonder if what she's complaining about here has anything to do with what she was mad about in Metro City?

Whether or not it was connected, Lionel took no small amount of pleasure at the thought that someone had thrown a wrench in Victoria's perfectly controlled world.

Now if I could just figure out a way to use this to somehow help Alice…

Once the door to his room snapped close, Lionel began a series of leg strengthening exercises. Working his muscles usually helped his mind to focus, and he'd need all the focus he could get if he was going to fight Victoria.

This special tour is the key and whoever is causing trouble in her organization is making her scared that it won't go off the way she wants. That means if I can figure out what the real purpose of it is, I can throw a wrench in it from here.

He ran through the possibilities as he switched to military style push ups, sweat dripping off the end of his nose.

If I'm going to find out anything, I need to get Victoria to not see me as a threat and ease up security.

As he finished his last set of push ups and moved to sit ups he still had no clue how to accomplish this.

It wasn't like Victoria would just give him what he wanted, and even if he had months, there was no way Victoria would ever really trust him.

After almost an hour of exercise, Lionel had nothing except more questions and frustration. Taking a warm shower in the large bathroom helped to loosen his tight muscles and the headache that started to take root behind his eyes, but that was all.

There has to be a way...but what?

He was so lost in thought that he hadn't heard the bedroom door open and was startled to see Victoria perched on the edge of his bed, a glass of bourbon in her hand.

With a quick motion, Lionel tied the towel he was drying his hair with around his waist and swallowed. Victoria turned to look at him over her shoulder and revealed the tiniest hint of a smile at his discomfort.

"My, my. I can certainly see why Alice has been captivated all these years."

He clenched his jaw against what he wanted to say to her and went to retrieve his pajamas from the wardrobe.

"How is your ankle?" she asked.

Lionel silently cursed himself. He'd been so shocked to see her sitting on his bed that he'd completely forgotten about his fake injury.

"Better thanks."

"Good to hear. I have a few public appearances coming up over the next week. I'd hate for you to be unable to attend."

"Tonight wasn't enough?"

Victoria's answer was a feral smile.

"I'd like to get out of this wet towel. Do you mind?" he asked, holding up his pajamas.

"Not at all," she answered, turning around.

"Is that all you wanted to know, how my ankle was?"

"How did you like dinner? Was it nice to see Alice again?"

Alice was gorgeous. But you I wanted to stab with my steak knife and watch you bleed out all over the table.

"It was a fine steak," he said instead.

Victoria laughed as he walked to the bar and poured himself a drink.

"What do you think our Alice will do now that she knows you're mine."

"You really think she believes this little farce?"

"You better hope she does," Victoria said, her eyes gleaming as cold as ice, "because if she causes too much trouble, I will be forced to take certain actions."

Lionel held her gaze with a flinty one of his own. To her credit, Victoria didn't seem to mind.

"I can't keep her in check from here," he said.

"You think I'll just open the door and let you go?"

"No. But, you must have a very low opinion of Alice if you think this little charade will make her stop coming for you."

"I never said it would. But it will make her suffer, and that's a good start."

And throw her off her game. Obviously, Alice wasn't rattled enough tonight. Or Victoria needs to make sure Alice just continues to be…I might be able to use this.

"Fine," he said, taking a sip of bourbon. "I'll be your kept man. But I want something else out of this."

Victoria snorted. "My dear, you are not my type."

"Well thank god for small favors. No, at the end of this

Science Foundation event I want my freedom and my cure. Then I want you to leave us alone."

Victoria's lips spread in a slow grin that made Lionel feel like the mouse that had just walked into the cat's trap.

"What makes you think I have—"

"Cut the crap, Victoria. We both know you've killed just about everyone who could possibly create the damn thing. The only reason you'd do that is so you could keep control of me."

She took a long pull from her glass and nodded.

"Very good, Lionel. Apparently your stepfather is wrong. You're not just a pretty face."

"So you do know him?"

"We've had a few business dealings with one another over the years."

"That must've been charming."

"He's a competitive ass to be quite frank."

"And not above eliminating the competition at all costs. You're lucky he hasn't come after you."

If he hadn't been looking for it, Lionel would've completely missed the way her gaze shifted and her lips tensed.

Something just fell into place for her. I wonder if she hadn't known it was Jason before now.

"Yes, well," she said, her smile tight, "I've never given him reason to, as you say, eliminate me."

Lionel took a sip to hide his smile.

Her words may have said one thing, but her tone said quite another.

"In any case," he said, "do we have a deal?"

"What...? Oh, your cure and freedom. Fine, yes," she said. "Except for one thing. I will leave you and Alice alone if you leave the city and never come back. Jet City is mine."

"Getting Alice out of here—"

"I'm sure you'll think of something."

"Fine."

She smiled at him and patted his cheek like a mother would a child before walking out of the room. He felt his blood boil, but the fury was just outside of his reach, like his powers.

Of course Lionel knew that Victoria could be lying to him about having the cure just to keep him in line. Most likely, whatever she had planned included his and the rest of the vigilantes' deaths. But if there was one thing that Lionel still believed in, after all this time, it was Alice.

She'll figure out how to put all this together and beat Victoria. I've just got to wait this out, find out what I can and hope that damn janitor is on her side.

Even her mild sedatives didn't do much except give Alice a few hours of restless slumber. When she awakened for the fourth time and saw that it was close to her usual wake time, Alice decided it would be pointless to stay in bed while her mind and body hummed with so many thoughts and feelings.

Unlocking the gym, she stretched a little before attacking the punching bag with quick, hard strikes.

She had expected her mind to clear in a few minutes like it usually did. But after a half hour, Alice still couldn't see her way through the torrent of emotions that Lionel and Marco's return had caused. On one hand, she yearned to have them sitting on either side of her, like they had so often in the loft, listening to music and eating Marco's food.

But she was also burning with anger at their return. After all the time she'd spent trying to get used their absence, accepting that it was up to her to finish Victoria, they both show up and upend her life once again. That thought made her even angrier and she punched the bag harder. She couldn't afford for anything to become messy and unpredictable now. She was too close the end of this. And even if they all survived and triumphed, they'd never be what they were. Those days were gone.

So, what was the point in having them here?

Tears began to blind her vision and she yelled in frustration, landing blow after blow onto the bag. What good was it to mourn any of that again? Yet here she was, wasting her energy, doing just that.

The door clicked and she looked up to see Marco walking toward her. He was in loose sparring gear, but Alice could see that he'd put on more lean muscle, and he moved with a quiet determination he hadn't possessed when he left Jet City. It made her body burn with a sudden desire for him, which she shoved down with vehemence.

Without a word, Marco stood on one side of the sparring mat and got into a ready stance.

Alice hesitated, afraid of the emotions burning in her.

Marco met her gaze, eyebrows drawn low over his brown eyes. With a small motion of his hands, he beckoned her onto the mat.

Before she could stop it, her body propelled itself toward him. She came in with several fast punches. He blocked most of them and caught her wrist. She spun out of his reach and kicked him in the back. He pitched forward and rolled, coming up on his feet and kicking her in the chest as she barreled toward him.

Landing flat on her butt, the air knocked out of her, Alice was grudgingly impressed, but no less angry.

Squaring off again, Alice feinted a punch, but spun with an elbow to Marco's stomach. He grabbed hold of her arm and flipped her over his hip. He was about to come down for a pin, but she rolled and kicked him first in the face, then the stomach, as she grabbed his arm and pulled him down to the mat.

Jumping on his back for a pin, Marco surprised her by rolling over so quickly that Alice didn't have time to adjust. He tried to pin her down, but she wasn't going to give in to him that easily. They grappled on the mat, each looking for the opportunity. Alice saw it first, and elbowed him in the solar plexus, shoving him to the ground and pouncing onto his chest.

Her fist was cocked back, ready to punch him. Alice stared into those achingly familiar brown eyes that held hers with such understanding and admiration. Slowly, her arm lowered and she just sat there, the fury draining out of her second by second. Her posture slumped, eyes closing, as a painful longing began to take hold of her.

This is what I get for letting my guard down.

Marco's fingertips grazed her ear as he tucked a strand of hair back. The touch sent a fire through her body, and she tilted her head, just a little toward his hand. She wanted to bury her face in chest and feel his arms around her as she cried out all the fear, anger and grief of the past two years.

All the months of healing my broken heart, becoming strong without him, and in one night, I'm falling apart.

Gritting her teeth, Alice sprang off him and walked to the small refrigerator that held a few canteens of water. She kept her back to him as she took several, long drinks.

"What happened to your face?" she asked, wanting to talk about anything except how she felt.

"Someone didn't like the outcome of my last case. Private investigator occupational hazard, I guess."

"You became a PI?"

"Yeah."

A thick silence fell between them, full of everything they weren't saying. It weighed on Alice and she was tempted, once more, to pour everything out. She took another drink from the canteen and slammed it down on the table next to the fridge.

"Let's get something straight," she said, her voice harsh as she sought to cage her feelings. "I've done all the work here, not you. You follow me and my lead or you can go back to Metro City, which I'm sure you're going to do anyway, when it's all over. But you'll be back there quicker if you fight me."

"Is that all?"

Her body tensed as she felt him walk up behind her. Instinct wanted to turn and embrace him. But the rest of her wouldn't dare.

"Why did you come back?" she finally asked, not sure if she was asking for information or something else. "Was it… was it just because Uncle Logan asked?"

Marco sighed, the sound laced with fatigue.

"Alice I wanted to call you a hundred times but…I don't know why I didn't. Then when your uncle called and told me that you might be able to use my help I…I just thought it might be time to come back and finish this."

She wasn't sure what to say. The fact that he'd missed her, that he'd wanted to talk to her made Alice feel relieved and angry all at once. She wanted to trust him as she once had. But if she did and he left again, then what?

"What information did you find?" she asked instead, her voice unsteady.

"It was about Lionel's cure."

Alice spun around. "You know where the cure is?"

"Victoria has it. But the cure isn't so…it will strip him of his powers, similar to the gas or serum that Gerald was calling me about."

Her gut twisted. "Is it permanent? Does he know the cure exists?"

"I don't know the answer to either. The information I have indicates that it most likely would be permanent. And, I'd bet Lionel is getting close to Victoria to get it."

"That might be why he's with her, but why is Victoria with him? She doesn't do anything without a reason."

"So Lionel is part of her plan."

"It would seem so, I just don't know how yet. And neither does he. Idiot!"

She started pacing along the edge of the mat as she turned all the pieces over, trying to see if she missed anything.

"He'll probably be at this tour she's giving of the Science Foundation," Alice said. "So, that's two out of three of us that she's guaranteed to be there. That's no coincidence...she's settling it all."

"If she attacked Lionel at the boxing gym, then it's a good bet she was looking for me. She knows I'm here," Marco said. "When is the tour?"

"Seven days."

Marco rubbed his long fingers across his forehead.

"That doesn't give us much time."

"No, it doesn't." She smoothed her hair back and stepped to one end of the mat. "I guess we should keep working then."

"Do you want to fill me in on what's been going on?" Marco asked, dodging her punch.

"Sure." She rolled under his kick and landed a punch to his back.

As they sparred, she told him more about Victoria's cure, the special tour, and the kidnappings. The fact that it started, just a little, to feel like old times simultaneously grated on Alice's nerves and made her wistful. When the time came, would she be able to remember that they could never go back to the way things were, and let him go?

CHAPTER SIXTEEN

"I understand we have a new house guest," Miss Jones said at breakfast that morning.

Alice felt her toast turn to ash in her mouth and forced it down with a generous gulp of coffee.

"Until after the Science Foundation tour. Then," she felt her eyes itch with tears as the next words left her mouth, "he'll be on his way back to Metro City."

Miss Jones paused.

"I see," she said. "Well, it will be good. You could use an ally in this fight."

"Because I can't do it on my own?"

"Because a smart warrior uses all the resources at their disposal and does not throw away a fellow fighter."

Alice took a long pull from her mug and tried to reign in her annoyance at the fact that Miss Jones was likely correct.

"Shall we go over your schedule?" Miss Jones asked.

"Yes," Alice said, feeling relief at an excuse to talk about anything but Marco.

It didn't take long to go over the few appointments Alice had for the day and they were just finishing when Uncle Logan came into the dining room. Alice took a long drink of coffee and avoided her Uncle's gaze by focusing on the cold toast on her plate.

"Can I have a few minutes alone with Alice?" he asked.

Miss Jones nodded and walked out, a hint of curiosity in her gaze.

Uncle Logan sat down next to Alice, who still wouldn't look him in the eye.

"Why would you tell him to come? After all this time?" she asked, her voice rough.

"Because you need him."

Alice's gaze shot up at him, her face flushing.

"I do not!"

"I'm not saying that when the chips are down you can't handle yourself."

"Then what the hell are you saying?"

Uncle Logan sighed. When he began to speak again, his voice was firm but not angry. Like when she was a little girl and he had something important to say but he knew she wouldn't want to hear it.

"When you first started this, I told Mrs. Frost that I didn't want you to end up like her."

"What, successful and independent?"

"Alone."

What Mrs. Frost had told Alice during their last conversation rose up in her mind, stark and clear. She tried to push it away, but it stayed fast.

"She told me," Uncle Logan went on, "that you wouldn't be like her, that you were smarter, stronger because of what was in there."

He pointed at her heart, just like Mrs. Frost had.

"And you think Marco is, what, my heart?" she said, the words sticking in her throat.

"I think that if anyone was going to get through to you it would be him. You have a special connection and when no one else could reach you, he always could."

"So I can cry and wail about what I've lost?"

Uncle Logan stood to his feet with a sigh of exasperation.

"Sometimes you really are the most stubborn woman. Would it be so bad to cry a little? To get mad about it all? To just talk to me, to Rose?"

"What good would any of that do? It doesn't give me back anything I've lost. And while I'm doing all that, Victoria is out there with her plans, always one step ahead!"

"Well at the very least you would stop walking around like the only thing that matters is getting revenge on that damn woman!"

"It is all that matters!"

Alice stared at her uncle, who stared right back, their eyes wide in shock.

"Oh my god," she whispered, putting a shaking hand over her mouth.

"Alice-" Uncle Logan said, reaching out for her.

She sprang up from table, knocking her chair over and sprinted to the door.

Alice felt the walls of the mansion closing in on her. She hadn't meant to say that to her uncle, she didn't even want to believe that she really felt that way.

"I don't," she whispered, brushing tears off her cheeks. "I...can't..."

But the nagging feeling that she did indeed believe it was taking root in her mind and there was no way to out run it with her usual exercise regimen. No, Alice knew she needed a mental distraction, and quarterly reports fit the bill perfectly.

She asked Patrick to get the car and threw her coat on over the red and black blouse and slacks she wore. In a few minutes she was nestled in her Cadillac, trying to focus on the papers she'd brought with her.

They were halfway to her office in downtown Jet City when the sounds of shouting and police sirens invaded the car.

"What's wrong, Patrick?" she asked.

"Not sure, Miss."

A man ran in front of them as they were turning by City Hall. Patrick almost didn't stop in time, and the man's hand hit the hood of the car as he ran past, leaving a red mark that could only be blood. A policeman tore after him, night-stick drawn.

More shouts and screams met Alice's ears and she looked out her window with dread churning in her gut.

Police surrounded a large group of people in front of city hall. Some still held signs, while others were fighting one another or the officers.

A bottle shattered against the window Alice was looking out and she jumped back.

"Miss Seymour," Patrick said, his voice tense. "I can't turn the car around, traffic is blocking us in and I don't think it's safe on foot."

"You're likely right, Patrick."

Another man ran toward them, but he didn't get far. A policeman hit him over the head and he went down. But the officer didn't stop hitting him, even though Alice could see blood flowing from the protester's head.

Alice grit her teeth and felt her heart race at the sight of the brutality.

Before Patrick could stop her, she bolted from the car, barely remembering to use her cane.

"Stop!" she shouted at the policeman. "You'll kill him!"

The officer jumped up, bloodied night stick at the ready when he saw her cane and expensive coat.

"What the hell is a woman like you doing here?"

"Watching you kill a defenseless man."

The policeman snorted. "Go back to your mansion, lady, let us handle these thugs."

She knelt down and winced at the swollen eye and broken nose of the unconscious man on the ground.

"He's defenseless," she said.

The policeman pulled him up under the arms and dragged him to a nearby car. Alice watched him toss the man in the back seat and walk away.

A bottle sailed past her head, and another crashed to the ground nearby. She heard a woman scream and looked toward the group of protesters. The police had stopped merely surrounding them and were now actively assaulting the men and women.

"Miss!" Patrick said, running up behind her. "You shouldn't be out here!"

"These people didn't do anything!"

"You don't know that."

Alice looked back at the protesters and gasped when she saw a familiar face in the crowd.

"Rose!" she said.

The sudden, real possibility that she could lose Rose to this chaos made her gut plummet to her toes.

Ignoring Patrick's further protests, Alice limped as quickly as possible toward the group.

A policeman shoved her away when she got close.

"This ain't no tea party!" he said.

"No kidding!" she said, side-stepping his next move and rushing toward Rose, who was about to get clubbed.

Alice swung her cane up and blocked the officer's night-stick. She forced his arm down, then jabbed him in the stomach with the end. The officer doubled over and Alice pulled Rose through the throng of people.

"Alice, what are you—"

Rose shoved Alice out of the way and caught the wrist

of another officer, who was about to hit Alice over the head. The officer got a hand free and backhanded Rose.

Alice swung her cane at the officer's knee caps and the man went down.

"We have to get out of here," Alice said, pulling Rose back toward the car.

"I can't, Derrick and—"

Someone screamed.

Alice could see a gray cloud far to the left of the protesters, who were being pushed further away from where she and Rose were standing.

A sharp, brutal memory slammed into her mind. Gray gas, screaming people doing horrible things to one another...

"Gas...it's...no...no..." Alice's throat began to close.

"It's not fantasy," Rose said, clasping Alice's face between her hands. "It's okay, look at me, Alice. Look at me!"

Alice whimpered. She heard Rose but still felt herself getting lost in the nightmares of Park Side.

A sharp slap landed across Alice's face, followed by another.

The pain got through the terrifying fog that had taken over Alice's mind and it began to lift.

"Alright," she said, her voice rough. "I'm...alright."

Alice's body shook, and she was, for the first time, glad for the support her cane offered.

"Good, because I've got to get Derrick."

Rose moved like she was going to run toward the gas and Alice clamped down on her arm.

"Are you crazy?"

"I have friends in there!" Rose wrenched her arm free and took off.

Alice hesitated, terror threatening to take over once again. But she couldn't let Rose go into all that alone, she wouldn't. Taking a deep, shaky breath, Alice hobbled after her, dodging the panicked protesters and the police.

Her eyes began to tear and she coughed as she reached the outskirts of the gas.

"Rose!" she yelled, barely able to see her friend in the chaos.

Someone crashed into Alice and she fell hard onto the pavement. Footsteps ran past her, then someone stepped on her hand as she tried to get up. She looked up and got hit across the face by someone's foot as they ran wildly past.

Each time she tried to get up, someone knocked into her, sending Alice back down to the ground. She could feel the hot stickiness of blood on her face from a cut above her eyebrow and her back was starting to feel like someone had taken a tire iron to it.

I survived Park Side and dozens of fights only to be trampled to death. That's just—

Hands reached under her arms and Alice found herself being half-carried, half-dragged through the chaotic crowd.

"I got you, Miss Seymour."

Alice smiled with relief as she recognized Derrick's voice.

"It's Alice," she said. "And you can put me down now."

"You're too slow," Rose said. "No offense."

"This way," Derrick said.

Derrick shifted Alice until he was carrying her a little more securely. She felt like a jostled bag of meal as Derrick ran after Rose.

There was an opening ahead, where the police didn't seem to be paying much attention and it would get them around the corner from what was now a riot.

They had almost made it, when two men stepped out to try and block them. One had a baseball bat and the other a tire iron.

"Where do you think you're going with her?" one of them said, pointing the tire iron at Alice.

"They're getting me to safety," Alice said, using the tone she often did with the board of Frost Consolidated. "So, if you would be so kind as to move, I would very much appreciate it."

They laughed.

"I'm sorry, Your Majesty, but these have to be taught a little lesson, and if you're on their side...well..."

"Rose," Alice said, tossing her the cane she still miraculously had.

Rose didn't hesitate.

Catching the cane, she pivoted and smacked the man with the bat across the face with it, leaving a bright red slash of blood.

"Put me down, Derrick," Alice insisted.

"Go!" Rose said, delivering a side kick to the man with the tire iron as he tried to rush her.

"But—" Derrick said.

"For God's sake!" Alice said, pushing off of Derrick's chest as she wiggled out of his grasp.

She half fell onto the ground and looked up in time to see the man with the bat punch Rose across the face.

Behind her, Derrick snarled and kicked the man who'd hit Rose.

The one with the tire iron saw Alice and lifted it up like he was going to beat. She couldn't get to her feet quickly with the wrap around her knee, so she hit the only place she could reach: his groin.

Two punches and he fell with a shrieking cry, clutching himself.

Alice looked up to see the man with the bat unconscious on the ground, Rose standing over him with the cane in her hand.

"We better get out of here," Alice said, stumbling to her feet. "Before anyone notices what we just did."

Rose nodded and handed her the cane.

"Do you want me to—" Derrick began.

"Thank you, but I can manage," Alice said.

Derrick's eyes slid to the man she'd punched in the groin.

"Yeah, guess so."

They ran around the corner and down one block from City Hall, none of them speaking.

"Is that your car?" Rose asked, nodding to the next corner.

Alice grinned when she saw Patrick waving frantically.

"Yes."

They ran to the Cadillac and dove in, just as two police cars barreled past them.

Patrick turned around, his usually neutral face a mask of anger and panic.

"I know I risk dismissal, but what, in God's name were you thinking, Miss?" he said.

Alice smiled. "I wasn't, which was fool hardy, I know. But I couldn't stand idly by, you should know that about me by now."

Patrick shook his head. "Reckless...where to, the hospital?"

Alice looked at Derrick and Rose and they shook their heads.

"Atlas Books," Rose said.

Patrick nodded once and started the engine.

"What started all that?" Alice asked. "I've never known you to riot before."

"We didn't," Derrick said, his voice hard. "Someone threw a bottle at us—"

"Three," Rose said, her voice quiet as she stared out the

window. "They threw three. Joseph, Mark and Celeste all got hit. I don't even know if they're alright."

"The police were already there," Derrick said. "As if they knew something was going to happen."

Alice sighed. "I'm sorry. You sure you don't want to go to the hospital, see if your friends are there?"

"They wouldn't be there," Derrick said.

"The police don't take us to the hospital," Rose said. "They take us to jail and if we survive, then fine and if not...well, one less to make trouble."

"That's..." Alice was at a complete loss for words.

She knew it was bad between the activists and many of the people in power, but somehow, she never thought the result was murder.

"I can call the station," Alice said. "See if I can find out if your friends are there and get them proper medical attention."

Derrick frowned. "Why would you get involved in this?"

"Because it's the right thing to do."

"Thanks," Rose said, "but I doubt you'll be able to do much. Records seem to disappear if someone asks too many questions. Just ask your uncle. He's been covering a lot of this."

Alice stared at Rose, a sudden guilt coursing through her.

I've only looked at a newspaper to see how it helped my own interests. I haven't bothered to see what was going on outside of my own world for...how long?

"Maybe," Alice said, ignoring her emotions so she could think logically, "if I call one or two of my lawyers, send them down to the station. And then Uncle Logan coordinates with the local television news to have cameras and reporters on hand to see the conversation between the lawyers and the police…They won't be able to hide, at least not as much as before."

Derrick and Rose stared at her.

"You'd do that?" Rose asked.

"As soon as we get to the loft, I'll make a few phone calls. One lawyer in particular would be especially good in this situation."

"Thank you," Rose said, her voice rough with emotion. "I just… thank you."

Alice smiled at her old friend, who gripped her hand and squeezed.

"Hey," Derrick said, leaning to look more closely out the window. "Could you stop the car?"

Patrick pulled over. "What's wrong?"

"I see a couple people from the protest."

Rose leaned across Alice and looked out the window. "That's Jen and Albert."

"I should find out if they're alright," Derrick said.

"Go, I'll catch up with you later at the bookstore."

"Okay, I'll be over tonight."

Rose nodded and Derrick darted out of the car.

"Are you two…?" Alice started to ask.

"No. He might want to, but…no."

Patrick drove away from the curb and a tense silence descended on the two old friends. Alice wished that she knew what to say to make up for all the months of ignoring what Rose was going through.

Finally, Rose spoke, her voice soft.

"Thanks for running into all that for me," she said. "It was reckless, but…it means a lot that you'd do it."

"Of course, you're…Rose, you're one of my best friends. I don't know what I'd do without you."

"Me, or what I give you?"

Alice looked down, her throat tight. "I deserve that. I

haven't been a good friend, or any friend to you for a while now."

Rose didn't say anything. When Alice dared look up, Rose was frowning at her with tears in her eyes.

"What?" Alice asked.

"It's just...I've been really worried about you and really hurt for months. And I had this great speech all planned and now-"

"I've ruined it haven't I?"

"Yeah."

They threw their arms around each other and began laughing through their tears.

"I'm so sorry," Alice said. "You're more important than all the gadgets and things in the world!"

"I know," Rose said. "And don't think I don't love hearing this but, what brought this on? Last time we talked you didn't seem to hear anything I said."

Alice sighed as they separated. "It's complicated."

"Well," Rose said, as they pulled up to Atlas Books. "We could talk over a cup of coffee."

"You sure? You've just been through something terrible back there."

"I have, but between the two of us, one of us always seems to be getting over something terrible these days."

Alice laughed, wiping her eyes. "I guess that's true. Alright then, yes, I'd love some coffee."

They went straight to the back door and up the staircase to the loft. Alice didn't really want to be there, especially with Lionel and Marco back in town, the memories were more potent than ever, but she went in anyway.

Wasting no time, she called one of her many lawyers while Rose cleaned the blood and sweat from her face. It took a few minutes to convince him that this was worth his time, but she eventually did. The call to her Uncle was tense, and she could tell that he wanted to know what had happened but he didn't ask.

When she hung up the phone, Rose had come out of the bathroom, her face washed and a fresh set of clothes on.

"Well?" Rose asked.

"The lawyer and Uncle Logan are on their way, along with a couple of photographers. The television news is already there but Uncle Logan is going to try and make sure they're admitted with the lawyer. Which, honestly shouldn't be a problem, the man loves the media attention."

"Let me call dad real quick to let him know I'm alive, and then I'll get the coffee going," Rose said.

"I'm going to clean up a little in the bathroom."

She could hear how stiff Rose's voice was as she talked with Gerald and wondered if the man was ever going to come clean to his daughter.

The cut above her eye was minor, though it had bled plenty. Alice managed to clean off the dirt and blood from her face and hands, though her coat and slacks were ruined.

"All for a good cause," she said to herself as she walked out of the bathroom.

The rich smell of coffee began filling the apartment and Alice pulled mugs out of the cupboard. Rose dug around in the pantry and found a box of cookies and they sat around the table, more relaxed with one another than they'd been in a very long time.

"So," Rose said, "what's going on?"

Alice took a deep breath and began to tell her about seeing Lionel with Victoria, and then coming home to find Marco in her library. As well as discovering that Uncle Logan had told him to come and why. The words were difficult for Alice to find at first, and she realized just how long it had been since she'd really told anyone anything that had to do with how she felt. Once she got going, however, Alice found the words tumbling out, along with more tears than she felt comfortable with.

Rose just listened, giving Alice a spare hankie when she needed it.

When she was done, Alice felt lighter, as if someone had taken a weight off her that she didn't realize she'd been carrying.

"What are you going to do about Marco?" Rose asked.

"What do you mean?"

"Well," Rose poured them both more coffee, "he's here to help you fight Victoria, but there's this...well, how you feel about him to consider."

Alice shrugged. "He's here to help and then he'll leave. There's not much point in worrying about any of that."

"But it's still there, you can't just bury it."

"Why not? I've been doing a pretty good job of that so far. Why not a little longer?"

"And then what?"

Alice sighed.

"I don't know. But I can't get caught up in all that right now. No matter what anyone tells me, I know that will only be a distraction."

"Then, you have one choice I guess."

"And that is?"

"You have to let him in enough to fight beside you, but not so much that it hurts when he leaves."

"Exactly," Alice nodded with far more confidence than she felt. "That's exactly what I'll do."

Rose held her gaze before taking a sip of coffee, a smile playing at the corners of her lips that Alice chose to ignore.

"That's enough about me," Alice said, "tell me about Derrick."

"Nothing to tell. He wants more and I don't."

Now it was Alice's turn to examine her friend with a look.

"Why is that?" she asked.

Rose sighed. "Because my life is too complicated right now."

"Are you sure that's all?"

"No."

"Well then?"

"Okay," Rose leaned forward, "I'll make you a deal. When you tell Marco how you feel, I'll give Derrick a chance."

"What?"

"You heard me. We both have complicated lives and if you're encouraging me to give Derrick a chance then you need to give Marco one too."

"He doesn't want a chance," Alice said, a sudden burst of fear and anger rising up. "I think his leaving made that pretty clear."

Rose chewed her bottom lip.

"I used to think that your anger at them would fade with time. That you'd see why they left and you'd forgive them. Instead, you've clung to it. Now that Marco is back, you'll have no one to blame but yourself if you let this keep you from being honest with him."

Alice stood up and took her mug to the sink. After a moment Rose came up behind her, and she felt Rose's strong hand on her shoulder.

Tears filled Alice's eyes, falling warm down her cheeks as she let the truth rise up at last.

"Anger," she whispered, "is easier than being afraid they'll hurt me again."

Rose turned her around and embraced her. Alice's tears made wet stains on Rose's sweater but she didn't seem to care.

"It'll cost you more in the end to stay angry," Rose said.

Alice nodded against Rose's shoulder. "I know, I just… it's hard to let go and trust."

"But if you don't risk it, you will always wonder, always carry this hurt around. That's no way to live."

"I know."

The phone rang, and Rose ran to answer it as Alice wiped her face with a nearby kitchen towel.

"It's for you," Rose said.

Alice frowned and put the receiver to her ear.

"Miss Seymour?" Miss Jones said.

"How did you know I was here?"

"Patrick just checked in from Atlas Books, and it's a good thing he did."

"Why, what's wrong?" Alice asked.

"I have new information concerning the possible whereabouts of a certain person you've been looking for."

Alice's mouth went dry and her stomach twisted.

"Alright, I will be back in an hour."

"There is no rush. Nothing can be done until tonight."

"Understood. Thank you."

Alice replaced the receiver, and pressed her palms to her eyes.

We've found Judy…Oh God, we've found her!

"Everything alright?" Rose asked.

"No, but maybe soon it will be."

CHAPTER SEVENTEEN

Once Alice returned to the mansion, she drilled Miss Jones on the two locations. Both were abandoned warehouses in the southernmost part of the Warehouse district, but only one had the structural integrity and proper wiring to have heat and lights.

"That's the one then," Alice said.

"Will you be taking Mr. Mayer with you?" Miss Jones asked.

Alice paused. Though it would be the logical and safe thing to do, the thought of spending hours on a rooftop with Marco didn't appeal to her.

"Yes, she will," Marco said, walking into the room.

"I can handle a little surveillance."

"And if something happens? If the little girl really is there?" Marco asked. "You just going to charge in by yourself?"

Alice felt heat rise to her face.

"If Victoria sees you or hears about Shadow returning-"

"What if he dresses down?" Miss Jones said. "He can wear the same black attire you do when you've gone out."

Alice sighed.

"Alright, Marco, you can go to the other location, that way we cover both," Alice said.

Marco hesitated before nodding.

"And I will go to the Foundation tonight, see if I can find out anything else there," Miss Jones said.

Four hours later, Alice shivered in her thick black clothes and balaclava as she crouched on the roof of an abandoned warehouse. Tiny flakes of snow had started to fall an hour ago, and the sidewalks and rooftop was beginning to turn pale.

She forced her mind to focus on the dilapidated brick warehouse across from her instead of the chill seeping into her bones. Lights had appeared, faint and low in the windows, and a car was parked out back. She'd seen two men go inside a while ago, carrying bags of food, but that had been the only movement all night.

Boredom and frustration were an impatient combination inside of Alice. She swung her arms around and tried to stretch out her stiff legs. Heat began to work its way back into her limbs, but her body was even more restless than before.

Maybe if I go down and look in the window. I've got to do something before I freeze to death.

She jogged to the side of the building, saw the fire escape she'd climbed and stopped. There was a half second when she couldn't make her body move. She closed her eyes and took some deep breaths. Then, with a hitch of fear, she climbed onto the creaking fire escape. Each step she took made the rusted metal stairs shake, and Alice remembered another fire escape – at Park Side. The one that came off the side of a building and broke her body.

The rusty stairs under feet trembled and Alice fell to her knees, heart hammering, sweat beginning to course down her back in spite of the cold.

"It's not…I'm not there…this is…different…I'm not… I'm not falling…"

A whimper sounded in the back of her throat as she crawled to the next set of stairs. She stayed hunched and shaking on the step, unable to make her body move.

"Focus…your breath…" she whispered to herself.

Every instinct screamed for her to stay there and cry. Instead, she stumbled through the fog of terror and concentrated on her chest as it moved in and out, in and out. At first, it was too fast, and she knew it, but she kept focusing until her breathing calmed. Her muscles followed, unwinding until she felt like she could move. Though sweat still coursed down her trembling body, she knew she could make it down.

Unconcerned about how loud she might be, she ran down the rickety steps, and jumped off the fire escape before finishing the last set of steps.

She sprinted away from the towering reminder of one of the worst days of her life and bent over, feeling like she might vomit.

"No…don't you dare," she said to herself, taking in gulping breaths.

A fist careened toward her.

Alice didn't have time to dodge, so the full force of the punch landed square on her face, sending her stumbling back into the shadows by the warehouse. She could feel her nose break, a bright explosion of pain across her eyes.

A tall, thin man came at her again, this time with a kick to her stomach, which knocked the wind out of her.

"You must be the little menace I've heard about," he said, swinging his fist down at her again.

Alice darted to the side and rolled on the filthy, frozen ground.

She sprang up behind him on her knees and punched the man in the kidneys. His cry of pain echoed in the dark and Alice had a moment of panic. She couldn't have him alerting anyone else.

Sweeping his legs out from under him she straddled him quickly, high on his chest and pressed down with her forearm onto his wind pipe. His eyes bulged and he tried to swat her away, but no matter how many slaps to the face Alice took, she didn't let up until he was unconscious.

She spat blood onto the frozen, cracked sidewalk and sprinted across the street, doing her best to ignore the throbbing pain from her broken nose.

The windows of Victoria's warehouse were filthy, and Alice couldn't see anything beyond a few blurry figures.

I've got to know if she's there.

Alice tried the side door. It was unlocked and well oiled, much to Alice's shock. She crept into a small room filled with dust-covered boxes and moth-eaten cloths. A sign in cheerful letters said: "Super Strength! Come see the world's strongest man! And his invincible partner!" The boxes had old shipping labels from Metro City on them and inside were pieces of machinery and moldy award ribbons.

She heard talking in the next room and crept to the doorway. The main floor of the warehouse stretched out before her, filled with rusted machinery covered in ragged tarps. The center of the room had been cleared to make room for two tables. To the side of these tables, sitting on strange looking metal stands were three—

Metal tubes! One of them must be Judy!

Alice counted four men and found herself wishing she'd asked Marco to come along after all. Instinct told her to wait and go get help, but she was afraid the tubes would be gone by the time she got back.

With silent steps, she stole into the main room.

Picking up a small metal pipe, she threw it at the man closest to her, hitting him square in the back of the head. That alerted the other three sitting around the table, drinking beer and playing cards. They sprang up, one of them drawing a large handgun from his shoulder holster. Alice dove to the right as bullets pinged over her head. The tightly-packed machines provided the perfect cover for her short frame and she slithered between and under them as the men searched for her. She ended up behind the man with the gun, and with no weapon of her own. Rushing him was risky, but she had to get the gun out of play.

Alice climbed silently onto the nearest piece of equipment, then tapped the metal. The man snapped his head around, toward the sound just as Alice leapt from her perch. The man realized what was happening and tried to turn back, but he was too late. Alice wrapped her arm around his neck and her legs around his back. Within seconds, she had him on the ground.

His face slammed into the concrete floor and the gun fell from his hand, discharging.

Two down.

The third man dove for Alice as she got to her feet. She sidestepped, drove her elbow into the man's stomach, then pivoted to face him. Two brutal kicks to the stomach and one to the face and the man collapsed to the floor.

A bullet pinged on the table next to her, and Alice dropped into a crouch.

"Come out, you little vermin," he said.

Alice could hear his shoes on the dirty floor as he walked slowly around the table.

When he was at the right spot, Alice shoved it into him and knocked the wind out of the man. Jumping up onto the table, she ran at him, as the man raised the gun and fired. She screamed as hot pain lanced through her shoulder.

He pointed the gun at her again. This time, he had a clear shot of her head.

Alice froze, knowing how this would end – but the shot never came.

Instead, the man began crying and backed away from her. Dark tendrils wound around him. In a few seconds, he was a blubbering mess on the floor and Marco stepped out into the dim light. His shadows had found a dark, terrible memory inside the man's mind.

Eventually, the man's cries died down and he looked like he'd simply fallen asleep. The shadows unwound from his body, flowing back to Marco like children to their father.

Alice climbed down from the table, barely containing a hiss of pain. She could feel Marco's angry eyes on her, but all that mattered was the children in those tubes.

Unlatching the first one, Alice threw up the lid and stared.

"I-I don't…"

It was empty.

She ran to the next and opened it. Then the next.

All were empty.

"No…what would be the purpose—?" she began.

Then the reason hit her.

Alice kicked the nearest tube off its stand and screamed in anger.

"The tubes at the other location were also empty," Marco said. "When I saw that I knew that this was—"

"A trap."

"Or a distraction away from wherever they were hiding Judy. Either way, you were going to need help."

Blood began to drip down her arm from the wound on her shoulder and the throbbing in her face was fast becoming worse, but to Alice it was all distant.

"I'll never be able to find her now," she said, the sense of failure beginning to carve a hole in her gut. "They know

I'm onto them and they'll make sure she's in a place I won't be able to find."

"You don't know that," Marco said.

She waved his reassurances away.

"What is certain," he continued, "is that we need to get out of here, regroup and figure out our next move."

For the first time since he arrived at the warehouse, Alice looked at his face. The angular planes were hard, his lips set in a tense line. She knew that for all his calm demeanor, Marco was burning inside.

She followed him out the warehouse door to a small black car parked in an alley a block away.

"I'll get blood on it," she said.

"It's your car," he said.

Alice blinked and realized he was right, it was one of the eight she had in the garage.

"I...yeah, I'll have it cleaned, I suppose," she said, sliding into the passenger seat.

Marco raised an eyebrow as he settled behind the wheel. "You honestly didn't remember?"

"More important things on my mind, in case you hadn't noticed."

He pulled out from the alley a little fast, the tires squealing on the snowy pavement. The car fishtailed and a sudden dizziness threatened to make her sick.

"Slow down," she said, afraid Marco's driving would make her vomit.

"I don't want you to lose too much blood."

She closed her eyes, but the feeling got worse.

"Here."

Marco passed her a small box that Alice recognized as a first aid kit. She dug out a handful of gauze and pressed it to her shoulder, wincing.

They drove in silence through the dingy parts of the Warehouse district and into Park Side. Alice stared at the abandoned and half-torn-down buildings as snow began to fall faster. The tension in the car had become thick. Marco's profile in the dim light of the street lamps was hard and angry.

"You can say it you know," she said, wanting something to focus on besides her bleeding shoulder. "I won't break."

"Later."

"Are you sure? How do I know you won't run rather than say it in person?"

Marco actually flinched at her words, and Alice felt guilt behind her rage.

"You really want to hear it now?" he asked, his voice low.

"Yes, I really do."

"You were reckless. Not only could you have exposed everything you've been trying to hide all this time, but you could've gotten killed. You would have if I hadn't come when I did!"

"I had to take that chance!"

"You could've had me with you."

"Now we come to it," she said. "You're not angry I went out; you're angry I went without you."

"Your damn right I am!" he turned too fast and the car fishtailed again.

"Try not to wreck the car," she said, the nausea returning.

"You're the one who wanted to talk now."

Alice sighed. As much as she hated to admit it to herself, Marco was right.

"I'm sorry," she whispered. "I should've...I shouldn't have gone out alone."

Marco kept his eyes on the increasingly hard to see road, but Alice could detect a small softening of his face around the eyes and mouth.

"Thanks," he finally said. "I'm here to help, not get in the way."

"I'm glad you said that."

"Why?"

"Because there's something I need your help with. And I don't think you're going to like it."

CHAPTER EIGHTEEN

"You've lost your mind!" Marco looked at Gerald. "Both of you! Why would you expose yourself to Fantasy gas?"

"It's a weaker gas than Victoria's," Alice said, stretching the shoulder that Gerald had healed the night before. "And I have to be able to fight, no matter what state my mind is in."

Marco shook his head and retreated to the furthest corner of the gas room.

"If you really want to help me," Alice said, crossing her arms, "then this is what I need."

"What, torture?" Marco asked, his eyes hard.

Alice knew that Marco had never been completely comfortable with his powers, and because of that, this would be a very hard sell.

"You are safer than the gas," Gerald said. "I know how you feel about your gifts, but this isn't like attacking someone, not really. It's training."

"Wait and see what she thinks after five seconds of me toying with her mind!"

"I can take it," Alice said.

Marco glared at her. "You have no idea what you're asking of me."

She stepped up to him, her body a battlefield of compassion despite herself.

"Then, tell me."

His face hardened, thin lips disappearing under his beard as he pressed them together.

"I will be able to see you, every fear you've ever had. You won't be able to hide it from me. And that might mean other things, too. Desires, happy memories. I might see them all before I'm done. But," he closed the distance between them, his body like a taut string ready to snap, "the only thing you'll know is mind-numbing fear and panic. Is that what you really want me to do to you, Alice?"

She swallowed. The thought of him seeing all the desires she'd buried, the longing and desperation that haunted her on sleepless nights, it almost made her go back to the gas. But after last time, she wasn't sure it was safe anymore. What if she went rabid again, but this time it was harder to take her out of it? What if she eventually became lost in it?

"Is there a way I can shut you out of the places I don't want you to go?"

"Yes, but it could take years to—"

"Just tell me how."

"Alright, if you're sure."

She nodded.

He closed his eyes, resignation weighing on him.

"Imagine your mind like a house with many rooms. The things you don't want me to see are in the rooms with the locked doors. It sounds simple, but it takes practice. Before we begin, do this, lock the doors, and we'll see if it works."

Alice sat on the floor, hands resting on her knees in a meditative posture. After several minutes of concentrated breathing she did as Marco told her, locking up as many things as she could think of.

"Are you ready?" Marco asked, voice thick with hesitation.

She nodded, rising to stand on the balls of her feet.

The room darkened and a cold sensation crept along her skin. She could see the familiar dark tendrils wind themselves around her legs and arms. Instinct told her to panic, and she glanced around for Marco, but couldn't see him. Reminding herself that she wanted this, Alice pushed away the desire to run. Her mind began to itch, it felt like feathers brushing against her brain. A prickle went up her spine as she saw a murky figure move toward her.

She gasped and fell back, scrambling away.

Phantasm towered above her, impossibly huge. She laughed, no mask this time, but Victoria's own face. Next to her came Lionel, sneering down at her.

"Little snake, so silly to fight someone bigger than you," Lionel chided.

"Let's squish her, shall we?"

They laughed, a sound that grated against her soul like nails dragged across glass. She tried to calm her heartbeat, but it was out of control. Crawling away from them, she stumbled into a pile of something cold and hard. It stank; and at first, she was confused. But then, she saw hands, feet, arms, faces.

Screams tore from her throat as they began reaching for her, crying out to be saved.

She could hear Uncle Logan among them, and Gerald and Rose.

"All gone, all gone," Victoria said behind her. "Too little too late, weren't you?"

It's not real! Get hold of yourself!

Alice grit her teeth, her body shaking like a naked child in a snowstorm.

"No, I'm not!"

She swung at Victoria, the image dissolving and reappearing a few feet away. That's when something solid hit her in the face, sending her to her knees.

A foot connected with her stomach, knocking the wind from her. The dark figure stood behind her, arm hooking around her throat. Alice brought her elbow up into the person's stomach and heard a muffled groan. The tension on her neck eased, and as she reached back to hook the assailants leg, she heard Victoria's laugh. Then a high pitched screech of pain and a pleading cry for death.

She hesitated.

No, it's not real...he's fine...he's ok.

Victoria's laugh became louder, until it was all around her. The assailant hit Alice in the back, sending her sprawling to the ground.

The screams of pain intensified and Alice felt tears streaming from her face.

It's...not real! The house...the rooms...

Alice retreated from the assailant, using every bit of focus she could spare to see her mind as Marco had told her. Her adversary landed a solid kick to her stomach and slapped her across the face. Alice blocked two more kicks before landing her own. The split focus was costing her though, and her next blow was easily dodged, opening her up to being tossed to the ground. The screams continued to echo around her, Uncle Logan's cries of agony adding to the crescendo.

Find the room in your mind...!

Rolling up onto her feet, Alice retreated, her mind finally opening the door to her "house". A shadowy figure materialized in front of her, eyes black. Though his body was very much like Marco, dark tendrils wound in and around him, as if seeking shelter.

He turned to look at her. *"Alice?"*

A quick pain coursed through her mind, like a rubber band snapping against sensitive skin.

The agonizing noises around her disappeared, a thick silence taking its place.

The real Marco fell to his knees a few feet from her, eyes wide as he took gulping breaths. Miss Jones stopped her advance when she realized the exercise had somehow been stopped.

Alice felt her stomach heave and ran out of the room, vomiting just outside the door.

She was trembling as if cold, though her body was damp with sweat. It had been far more real than the gas ever was, not to mention more specific. Marco had dredged up nightmares she'd had right after Park Side, as well as fears she had thought long past.

His screams, more than anything else, echoed through her whole body and she felt her stomach curdle at the memory of it. Barely managing to keep from throwing up again, Alice sat against the wall.

Gerald ran around the corner, kneeling next to her.

"Alice—"

The door to the fear gas room flew open.

"Are you alright?" Marco asked, his voice rough.

She nodded, but couldn't bring herself to look at him.

"I...I tried to warn you," he said.

Alice flinched at the pain in his voice. When he hurried away from her, she wanted to call out for him, tell him it was alright, but the words couldn't get past her tight throat.

"Miss Jones," Gerald said, "help me get her to her room."

CHAPTER NINETEEN

"What is it now?" Victoria demanded, throwing her fur coat on the couch in her office. "What couldn't wait until after DeBussey? We had box seats!"

"Sorry," a ram rod straight man by the name of Dobbs said, handing her a piece of paper, "but there's been another theft. And this one's big."

Victoria flushed as she read it while Lionel waited for her to send him to his room. Instead she flew to her wall safe and began rummaging inside.

Did she forget I was here?

Lionel stood as still as possible in the door way, hoping Victoria continued to ignore him.

After he'd planted the idea that Jason was the one behind all the break-ins and thefts, Victoria had been increasingly tense and snappish. Last night Lionel had heard her rage for over an hour about an incident at her lab, and someone outbidding her on construction contracts that were supposed to be air tight.

And now this.

First time in my life I'm grateful for that bastards giant ego. If he can keep Victoria off balance, then we might have a chance at beating her for good this time.

After a minute, Victoria gave a sigh of relief and slammed the safe shut.

"We need to find those supplies," she said, picking up her phone and furiously dialing. "Get me the foreman, now!"

Two of her blank eyed guards scurried out to do her bidding, shoving past Lionel.

"It's happened again...I don't need to, it's Jason!...You know he's always hated me and now...Of course I've considered it..."

Lionel couldn't help but smirk at the sound of pure frustration in Victoria's voice. A movement to his right pulled his focus away from the spectacle. That same Janitor was slowly sloshing away at the floor.

Checking all around, Lionel saw that the hallway outside Victoria's office was devoid of its usual group of enhanced guards. Everyone in her office was furiously calling people on the multiple phones she had.

This was his chance, maybe his only chance.

Lionel walked as silently as he could in his expensive dress shoes and squatted down in front of the janitor.

"I need to get a message to Alice," he said.

"Jus' moppin'," the janitor said.

"Please? You have to tell her that something is going to happen at the Science Foundation event. Tell her nothing is as it seems even...."

The mop paused and the janitor looked up. Again, the gaze was too direct, too meaningful to belong to a simple minded old man. His eyes accused Lionel of being a traitor and he felt it like a stab to the chest.

"I'm not with her," he whispered, tears itching his eyes. "I...I did it to protect Alice, and try to fight from the inside. Please, please tell her?"

The man's eyes narrowed and he grunted.

A crash erupted from the office and Lionel looked over to see Victoria throwing her phone off her desk.

Good God...she's coming apart at the seams. This is either going to work brilliantly for us, or make her too erratic to predict.

He turned back to the janitor and grabbed a hold of the mop to get the man's attention.

"Tell her I'll be at the Children's Home fundraiser. Tell her to find me behind the banquet hall kitchens. Half past eight. Please?"

The janitor just stared at him before plunging his mop back into the bucket.

"I need to mop there," he said.

Lionel sighed. "Sure, sorry."

He moved to the side and was about to consider the whole conversation pointless when Lionel noticed how focused the janitor had become outside of Victoria's office.

He's listening.

Though, in all honesty, it wasn't hard to hear the woman as she screeched into another phone.

"You better find out who authorized that transfer of funds because it wasn't me!...Yes and the supplies. That high rise is supposed to be finished by now and I find out that the reason it's not is because someone has been authorizing...What?...Give me that name..."

The janitor looked back at Lionel and motioned with his head toward Victoria's door.

He wants the name.

Lionel nodded and moved with slow steps back toward the door.

Victoria tore a piece of paper from a pad and handed it to Baritone.

"Find him and get him here. We need to have a little chat," she said.

The bodyguard nodded and stalked through the door.

Lionel pretended to slip and crashed into Baritone, who dropped the note on the floor.

"Sorry, wet floor," Lionel said.

Baritone shoved Lionel off him and glared. The vigilante grinned, knowing Victoria had given the man strict instructions to keep his hands off Lionel.

However, that directive must've only applied to his face, because Baritone delivered a punch to Lionel's solar plexus before retrieving the slip of paper and walking out.

Lionel doubled over and fell to one knee, coughing. The noise alerted Victoria's men that he was outside the door and listening to everything. Rough hands picked him up and dragged him down the hall to his room.

Just before they rounded the corner, however, Lionel looked back and saw the last traces of a mop bucket being wheeled in the opposite direction.

I hope to God that man gets Alice the message.

"Wait," Victoria said from the hallway outside her office. "I need him ready to go in half an hour. We need to visit this place and I don't want him staying behind."

Lionel looked up and met her hard, suspicious gaze.

He could see the wheels working behind her eyes, and wondered if she'd simply kill him if things got too complicated.

Finally she turned on her heel and slammed her office door.

Distracting herself had become an art form for Alice, and her favorite way was to study all the information she'd collected about Victoria. It usually worked, but tonight, Alice caught her mind drifting between memories of Judy's scared little face, the images she saw in the gas room and the two men who'd crashed back into her life.

"I have to find Judy," she said, pacing her room. "I have to stop the special tour. And I must not go crazy in the process. Easy, right?"

She picked up a photo that Miss Jones had snapped on one of her many reconnaissance missions at the Foundation. It was of Lionel and Victoria getting into a black car, his stony, beautiful face glaring down at the villainous woman.

"Why are you with her?"

The question pierced her heart. Even if she no longer felt romantic feelings for him, Lionel was still someone she loved, and the thought that he would betray her was a brutal blow.

"You couldn't though," she said, tracing his face with her index finger. "I know you…or at least, I did."

She threw the photo on her bed with the rest of the useless pictures and gave a grunt of frustration. Her body hummed with energy and emotion, but it was too dark outside for a run.

"And Gerald would skin me if he found out I disobeyed his orders to rest."

She paced a little more, feeling like a caged animal with every step.

"I need to get out of here, get some distance from all of it."

A chuckle escaped her lips at the thought that she'd ever really let herself escape this mission. It had lived inside of her for too long, and she'd never be rid of it until Victoria was behind bars.

"Or I'm dead."

She stopped at her bedroom door, realizing that she'd never said out loud what she'd always known. It was the truth, cold and stark. If it came to it, Alice knew that she'd lay down her life without a second's hesitation.

Shaking her head to dislodge such gloomy thoughts,

Alice padded downstairs to the library, hoping for the peace of a good book in front of the fire and a cup of tea.

Accustomed to being the only one, besides Miss Jones, up this late, Alice was surprised to see Marco sitting in front of the fireplace in the library. He didn't see her at first, and Alice allowed herself the indulgence of simply staring at him.

His shirt was a little tight and she could see the outline of lean muscles in his back and arms. The firelight brought out dark red strands in his neat beard, which he absently ran his fingers down. The wrinkles above his nose were deep, brows drawn low over his eyes as he frowned, and a glass of something dangled from his long fingers. She could see his mind working behind the pain in his eyes, and felt her stomach tighten with guilt.

Forcing him to use his powers was something Alice never thought she'd do.

I hurt him today. How could I do that?

A picture came to her mind, of Marco staring up from below the tree she'd loved to sit in as a girl. His goofy grin beneath a too-large nose, wiry arms waving up at her.

Staring at him now, Alice felt much further away from him than the height of a tree. She ached to leap across the chasm, hold him and tell him how she'd missed him and wanted him. But they weren't children anymore, and not everything could be fixed with chocolate chip cookies and a hug.

The best I can hope for is just to get us all through this alive. I guess I'd be happy with that.

Marco started when she walked through the door, downing his drink and getting up.

"No, please stay," she said, picking a book from one of the shelves.

"I'm not in a very good mood, if you can't tell."

"I can." She plopped down in the chair opposite him, relishing the warmth of the fire.

They sat in silence for a while and Alice wondered if she should bring up what happened and apologize. But Marco's brooding silence was impenetrable, so she tried to read. When he finally spoke, she jumped in surprise.

"I tried to warn you," he said, his voice strained. "Tried to tell you how awful it would be. Why didn't you listen? Do you have any idea what it is like to do that to you?"

"I'm sorry, I never meant to—"

"It's taken me a long time to accept that my powers don't mean I'm a monster. But in there, today…?"

"I never meant to make you feel that way. I just needed your help."

"I thought you didn't, you made that pretty clear the night I arrived."

"Don't be petty, you know that's not what I meant."

"I knew that you would be angry with me, but treating me like this?"

She leaned forward, heat flushing her pale skin.

"Are you hurt by the lack of welcome? What did you expect, an enthusiastic embrace? We go in the kitchen and talk like old times?"

"No, but I didn't think you'd be so cold, so closed off. Not to mention reckless. Going out alone last night, using Fantasy gas, then using me? Are you wanting—"

She jumped up, sudden fury burning in her veins. "To finish it! You know, that thing you never bothered to do before you left?"

"You keep bringing that up, but you also keep telling me how you didn't need me to stay, so which is it?"

If he'd been close enough, she'd have hit him.

"You can leave any time, Marco. I'm not keeping you here."

"Damn it, Alice!" He covered the distance between them in two steps. "Stop pushing me away! I came back—"

"To help Lionel, I know!"

"And for you!"

The tenderness she saw underneath his anger made her speechless.

"I...needed to see you," he whispered slowly, as if it hurt him to admit it, "to know you were alright."

She frowned, shaking her head.

"Now, you care how I am?"

"You think I left because I didn't care? That's not it. I knew that the only way you and Lionel would ever be happy was if I helped him, and kept him safe until he was cured. I asked Gerald and Logan to do the same for you. I promised them I'd send Lionel back when he'd been cured. I love you...both, of you. I just wanted you to be happy."

"How could you think I'd ever be happy without you?"

The words were out before she could stop them, and the look on Marco's face was full of disbelief. She cursed herself for letting even that much of her true feelings out. It wouldn't do any good to tell him. He believed she loved Lionel. Even if he didn't, Marco had never given her a reason to think he'd felt about her in any way other than friendship.

Had he?

"Either of you," she added, and then her mouth ran away with her again. "We're a family. I'm not angry because I couldn't live without you. I'm angry that you didn't give me a choice in the matter. You just decided what was best for me."

Marco looked away.

"And then, you show up when everything is about to be finished, when I need to be focused, no distractions. It would've been bad enough with Lionel's surprise visit, but you, too..."

"Do you want me to leave?"

"No!" Her hand shot out and clutched the sleeve of his shirt.

His gaze held hers and Alice found herself inching closer to him.

"I don't want you to go," she whispered.

"Are you sure?"

She nodded.

Marco's eyes drifted down to her lips and Alice's heart hammered in her chest. She could feel his breath on her face and tilted her head up a fraction of an inch.

His jaw tightened and he took a step back, shattering the tension of desire between them.

"I'm sorry I left you the way I did," he said. "I shouldn't have said good-bye in a note, it was cowardly."

"And I'm sorry I made you use your powers."

Marco nodded, picking up his glass.

"I...how did you do that, by the way?" he asked.

"Do what?"

"Find me like that. No one has ever done that."

She sat down in the one of the chairs.

"Miss Jones has been teaching me meditation as a way to strengthen my mind. I just used some of those techniques and there you were."

"Did you...I mean, was there...what did you see?"

"I imagined my mind like a house, then I saw a door-way, and then you in the house. You were...you looked more frightening and powerful than I'd ever seen you."

Marco looked away.

"You really do have so much power, don't you?"

"Yes," he whispered.

"And you hold it in check so often. You don't release half of it, do you?"

He shook his head. "The last time I did..."

"Park Side?"

He nodded. "I could've stopped those people, every person there. That's how much power I have. But I would've crippled every person there, too. I—"

"You couldn't do that."

"No."

Alice heard what he didn't say, she could see it written in his eyes. If he had crossed that line, she never would've gotten hurt, Park Side would have been saved, and all those people wouldn't have died.

"It's not your fault," she said.

He sighed, a smirk on his lips.

"I don't believe that, but thank you. Park Side made me realize that I must learn to use my power in a better way, so I don't lose control. But even so, Alice, don't ask me to use my powers on you again, please? If there's even the smallest chance that I could really hurt you—"

"I won't ask you, don't worry. But even if I did, I know you wouldn't hurt me."

"How do you know that?"

She smiled. "I just do."

"So, what happened in that room was a walk in the park?"

She opened her mouth to answer, but the door to the library opened, and in stepped Miss Jones in her elderly janitor disguise.

"Who are you?" Marco asked.

Alice frowned, and then realized that Marco had never seen Miss Jones this way.

"It's Miss Jones," Alice said.

Marco's frowned deepened into confusion, and then shock when he saw Miss Jones peel off her fake nose.

"Did you find something?" Alice asked, ignoring Marco's gasp.

"Mrs. Veran was there tonight, railing at someone about money and supplies that had been diverted. It had to do specifically with her nearly complete high-rise apartment. If I had to guess—"

"Judy could be there," Alice said, before frowning. "She was angry about it? As if she didn't know?"

Miss Jones nodded and peeled off more of her disguise.

"That doesn't make any sense," Marco said. "Why wouldn't she know about something like this?"

"Mrs. Veran accused someone by the name of Jason when she was on the phone," Miss Jones said. "We have been assuming that Mrs. Veran is behind the disappearing children. But what if someone is merely using her organization as a cover?"

Marco rubbed his fingertips across his lips and sighed.

"What are you thinking?" Alice asked.

His eyes darted up to her, surprise shining in them.

She grinned. "It hasn't been so long that I don't recognize when you're turning something over in that head of yours."

"It's just a little spooky, that's all," he said. "My last case had to do with something similar to this."

"How similar?" Alice asked.

"A little too similar."

"And what was the outcome?" Miss Jones asked.

"It was a shadowy organization that took children with powers and amplified those powers. But they took kids that were orphans and…they had help covering up the disappearances. This sounds sloppy by comparison."

Miss Jones nodded. "That's because it was. If someone didn't want anyone knowing about the abductions, they wouldn't have made it so public."

"The use of Fantasy gas makes it…well, strange, don't you think?" Marco said. "Especially since Victoria wasn't even here. What did she have to gain by it?"

Alice felt her stomach clench and a terrible, awful thought take form.

"Did you dismantle this organization?" she asked.

"No, unfortunately not."

"What if I've been wrong?" she said, her voice choked. "What if I was so ready to blame Victoria that I dismissed the things that didn't add up?"

"What do you mean?" Marco asked.

"Miss Jones, you're sure Victoria seemed surprised by the missing supplies and money?"

"Absolutely."

"She has no reason to put on a show for your benefit, correct?"

Miss Jones' shoulders squared. "I have not been found out by her, if that's what you're implying."

Alice couldn't help a little grin. "I didn't mean to offend, but I had to be sure. Wait…you said 'by her'. Is there someone you have been found out by?"

Miss Jones hesitated, her eyes darting to the side.

"Mr. Lawson was there. He knows that I'm working for you."

Alice felt her mouth go dry. Words escaped her. All she could do was stare at Miss Jones, searching for what the woman wasn't saying.

"How do you know that?" Marco asked.

"He asked me to give you a message."

"What is it?"

"He says that the Science Foundation tour isn't what it seems. That he's not with Victoria, and that he'll be at the art charity event. He asked you, Miss Seymour, to meet him behind the banquet hall kitchens at half past eight."

It was all said with such a clinical kind of detachment, a soldier giving a report to a superior. Yet Alice heard the faintest evidence that Miss Jones was warning her to be careful.

"Do you think that he was telling the truth?" Alice asked.

Miss Jones nodded. "I do. From what I can tell he's not living with Victoria, but instead has a room at the Foundation. It's possible he thought aligning himself with her would garner inside information."

Marco swore and shook his head, but Alice couldn't help feeling hopeful.

"I would still advise caution," Miss Jones said. "He's being watched. It's possible Victoria wanted him to get information out to you and that this meeting he's asking for is a trap."

Alice gave her a firm nod. "Understood, thank you Miss Jones."

"Now," Miss Jones said, "back to the matter at hand. This new information. What do you plan to do with it?"

It took Alice a moment to realize Miss Jones wasn't talking about Lionel but the information about the missing supplies at the high-rise and Victoria's reaction.

"Right, so," Marco said, clearing his throat as if it would also help clear his mind, "earlier Alice, it sounded like you're suggesting that someone else is behind the disappearing kids."

Alice took a deep breath and dragged her mind back to the issue of finding Judy. She would have time later to think about Lionel and what he was asking of her.

"Yes, and wanted us to think it's Victoria."

Marco shook his head.

"This is one tangled web."

"And regardless of that fact," Miss Jones said "we still have the matter of a missing child."

"Yes, quite right," Alice said. "We can figure out who is behind the abductions after we've found Judy and taken care of Victoria. Perhaps you could share your former case with me after all this? It might help."

"Sure," he said, giving a grin that reminded Alice of old times.

This is a slippery slope.

"What do you propose we do with this new information?" Miss Jones asked.

Alice snapped back to the present, a small flush rising to her face.

"Yes...right...We need to go to the construction site. If Judy is still there, then we get her out. How many men are there?"

"Uncertain. As of right now, there should only be two night guards. Considering what's been going on though? It could be as many as ten."

"You also haven't considered the fact that Victoria might go there herself," Marco said.

"And lately where she goes, there goes Lionel," Miss Jones added.

Alice mind became crowded with a confusing host of feelings and desires. She wanted Marco to stay. She wanted to talk to Lionel and find out what the hell he was thinking. She wanted to save Judy. She wanted to punch Victoria.

And I can only do something about one of those at the moment.

"Judy is the focus," she said. "I won't let them take that girl anywhere. And besides, even if Victoria is there, I'll be masked, she won't know it's me."

"I'm coming with you," Marco said.

Alice opened her mouth to protest but Marco cut her off.

"Remember the warehouse? It's not a bad thing to have help."

"You're right," she said, a grin tugging at her lips, "it's not."

CHAPTER TWENTY

After a week of freezing rain and snow, Alice was happy to have clear skies as she and Marco made their way to Park Side. They were both dressed head-to-toe in black, their faces covered by balaclavas and their hands with reinforced gloves. She wished she'd thought to bring her batons, but knew even that small detail could be enough to give her away.

Miss Jones drove them close to the border of Park Side. They made it the rest of the way on foot, keeping to the shadows as much as possible. There were a few times that Alice swore she saw someone following them, but when Marco doubled back to check, there was no one there. At last they got to the construction site on the southwest edge of Park Side where Victoria's high-rise was almost finished. Alice took it all in from the condemned building across the street. The upper levels weren't done, but the lower six floors already had most of their amenities, including electricity, and two apartments had lights on.

"They made it fairly easy for us," she said.

"How thoughtful," Marco said. "What's the plan?"

It took Alice a little by surprise to be deferred to so easily, but she took a deep breath and thought quick.

"There will probably be at least some lighting in the hallways, and I'm not sure crashing through a window from the fire escape is the best plan. We want surprise."

"Dark would be ideal."

"Maybe I could help with that," said a voice behind them.

Marco and Alice jumped, ready to attack whoever spoke. When the person came out of the shadows, Alice stared in shock, and then had a flash of anger.

"What the hell are you doing here?" she asked.

Simon grinned. "You think I would let you rescue Judy without me?"

"Yes, I did. And how did you know what we were doing?"

"I'm very sneaky."

"Who is this?" Marco asked.

"I'm Shock Wave," Simon said.

Alice raised her eyebrows. "Shock Wave?"

"Every hero needs a special name, right?"

"You aren't a hero, you are a teenager who's about to get himself killed!"

Simon's jaw clenched and Alice could see determination light up his eyes.

"I can help you, if you'll let me," he said.

Alice opened her mouth to tell him to go back to his room when Marco put a hand on her arm.

"If he can get us in there under cover of dark, that might be useful."

"He's too young and inexperienced! He'll get hurt, and then what?"

"I have a right to be here," Simon said. "Judy is like my sister, and I made a promise, same as you, to keep her safe. I can help, and I want to."

Alice sighed, recognizing the same stubborn streak in Simon that ran in her. He'd somehow discovered what they were doing, he'd followed them without being noticed by either Miss Jones or Marco and now he was a few feet away from rescuing a person he loved. There was nothing Alice could say to make him leave.

So I might as well make sure I can keep an eye on him instead of him running in half cocked.

"Fine," she said. "When we've taken out the guards outside, you—"

"Wait, what's that?" Simon said, pointing at the building.

They turned and saw a van pulling up to the apartments. It was nearly identical to the one Simon had been in. After a minute, a long coffin-like tube was being carried out of the front door of the apartment building.

"No," Simon stood up, electricity sparking on his fingertips, "they're moving her, we have to stop them!"

"Damn it," Alice said, the plan she'd been formulating now gone.

Simon stepped around Alice and Marco, as he if were about to rush right in.

Alice pulled him back, her arm buzzing with energy at the sudden contact.

"You don't just go charging in, that's a good way to get killed."

"But—"

"Patience, kid," Marco said. "There's only...five...no, six of them, we should be able to take them."

"At least we won't be trapped in the building. Alright, Simon—"

"Shock Wave."

Alice sighed. "Shock Wave, when Marco and I have taken out at least four of the guards, you get Judy out of the tube, alright?"

"What? You mean I have to sit back and watch—"

"Yes. If you can't follow orders, you can't be here, got it?"

Alice swore she could almost see his bottom lip stick out, but he nodded.

She and Marco crept out of the shadows as quickly as they could. It was in their favor that the six men seemed completely preoccupied with securing the tube inside the vehicle.

Alice got to the first man on the left side of the van and kicked his knee out from behind. He went down with a shout and she kicked him across the face. She could hear sounds from Marco's attack on the other side of the van, and then the hollow pow-thunk of gunshots. A bullet whizzed past her and she rolled forward, coming up on the balls of her feet. She punched the man in front of her hard in the stomach, seized his gun-hand, and twisted his wrist until she heard a pop. He grunted and punched her with his other hand. She felt the pain across her cheek, but ignored it.

Someone yelped nearby, and the hair on Alice's arm began to stand up from a sudden infusion of electricity in the air. She knew that Simon had come to help.

Blocking another punch by the man whose wrist she'd dislocated, Alice landed a quick blow to his solar plexus, and kicked his knee out. When he went down, she slammed her knee into his face, and the man collapsed.

"No, wait!" Marco shouted around the other side of the vehicle.

Electricity crawled up the side of the van and she heard something slam over and over against it.

She got to the other side just in time to see a man on the ground, his clothes smoking and Simon standing over him, electricity crackling up and down his body.

"What—"

"Behind you!" Marco shouted.

Something slammed into her back, pitching her forward.

"Go, go!" a voice behind her said.

Feet rushed past her, and she could hear Marco and Simon fighting. She rolled to the side as a pipe smashed into the pavement where she had been laying a moment before.

"You are pesky, you know that?" said a barrel chested man.

"So I've been told," Alice said, flipping up onto her feet and delivering a roundhouse kick to the man's face.

The sound of screeching tires echoed behind her, and she could see the van careening away, taking Judy with it.

"No!" Simon screamed, electricity shooting from his hands.

Alice shouted, "Stop, you'll—" The barrel chested man's fist connected with her side and she grunted in pain. He reached back to punch her in the face, but she captured his fist, and with a fluid motion, threw him on the pavement. Two punches to the face and he was out.

The sound of another car reached her ears. She wondered if the bolt of electricity had somehow damaged the van when the sharp report of gun echoed around her. Alice looked up to see Victoria holding a silver revolver, the end of the barrel smoking.

She swore under her breath as Lionel and Baritone stepped out of the car as well.

Marco grabbed Simon, and pulled him away from the apartment building. Alice tried to run after them, but the gun went off again, the bullet just barely missing her. She skidded to a stop and turned to run the other way but Victoria was standing there, the barrel of her gun pointed at her chest.

Their eyes met, and Alice felt as if Victoria could see

past the black balaclava she wore. The villain's eyes narrowed and Alice knew that she was about to pull the trigger. She darted to the side just as Marco slammed into Victoria from behind. Alice saw sparks to her left as Simon kept Baritone occupied.

Lionel met Alice's eyes, a look of torture in them as he ran towards her.

She sprinted away from the apartment and toward the condemned building across the street. Lionel was always fast, despite his size, but Alice hoped he'd give her a break, for old times' sake.

As she rounded the corner at the back of the old building, a large hand yanked on her shoulder. Alice landed hard on her back, the air knocked out of her. Lionel loomed above and she scrambled back. If he was out of control, there was no telling what he might do. Getting to her feet, Alice managed two steps before Lionel's huge arms circled her and she was lifted off the ground.

"No!" she said, kicking her feet. "Let me go!"

"Stop struggling, Alice," Lionel's voice hissed in her ear. "I don't have a lot of time! Damn it, stop!"

Lionel spun her around in his arms, and rippped the balaclava off her head. She arched back and shoved against him at the same time. His arms loosened and she landed on her feet.

Instinct, and two years of anger, took over. She drew back and punched him, twice.

"You son of a bitch!" her voice hitched with a buried sob. "Why didn't you come back to me? Why go to her for help or...whatever it is?"

"It's complicated."

"Why should I believe that answer?"

"Because," his huge hands cupped her face and he bent down.

The kiss was achingly gentle. He whispered her name

against her lips before pressing his mouth more firmly onto hers.

She felt her entire body go warm with the unexpected contact, and couldn't help returning the kiss.

"I've never stopped loving you," Lionel said, his lips inches from hers.

She wanted to ask him why he left, why he'd be so cruel at the Elliot that night. But there wasn't time, any minute someone could come around the corner.

"Come back with me," Alice said. "You don't have to do this, it's too dangerous."

"No, you don't understand what she'll do if I leave."

"Lionel, nothing-"

The sound of running footsteps echoed nearby and the two of them jumped.

"Damn, I have to go."

"No," she said, realizing that she had to tell him about the cure.

"Be careful," he said, sprinting away from her.

Alice thought she should go after him, but her body wouldn't move, and all she could do was watch him flee as footsteps got closer.

To say she was stunned by the turn of things would've been an understatement. When Marco and Simon rounded the corner, her mind finally started working again.

"What happened?" she asked when she saw Marco's bloody arm.

"We got away," Marco said, his balaclava ripped at the chin, which was also covered in blood. "Though this one nearly killed two of the men."

"They deserved it!"

Alice didn't know if it was the shock of seeing Lionel, or being confronted by Victoria or losing Judy, but her control snapped.

She stood toe to toe with Simon, though he was a head taller than her.

"We don't take a life, not ever! We aren't like them, we are better, you understand me?"

He stared at her, shocked by the vehemence in her tone.

"Do you?"

"Yes," he whispered.

"We better get out of here," Marco said, looking back. "I can feel someone coming."

They made it back to the house without much incident, but Alice felt a hurricane of emotions within herself. A deep foreboding sat in her gut from the look Victoria had given her alongside a hopeful desire from what Lionel had done and said.

But I don't love him anymore. And when he kissed me, it was good but…I didn't feel what I thought I would.

"What's wrong?" Marco asked once they'd made into the mud room at the back of the house.

Alice jumped, startled out of her thoughts and felt a flush rise in her cheeks. The last thing she wanted was to tell Marco about that kiss. So she decided to talk about what else was on her mind instead.

"I think…I think you might've been right. I've been too reckless."

"What makes you say that?"

"Victoria, when she looked at me it was like…she saw me," Alice felt her stomach churn and closed her eyes. "What if I've destroyed everything I've done the last two years?"

Marco sighed. "Even if she does know, you haven't destroyed anything."

"But-."

"It might have been better if you'd let Miss Jones go instead, but what's done is done. You can't get stuck on that. Now, you've got to decide how to move forward."

Alice nodded, the feeling that something was going to happen still gnawed at her.

She glanced over at Simon, who had been silent since the fight. Tears lit up his green eyes and his face was tight with emotion.

"C'mon," Alice said to Marco and Simon. "Gerald's waiting for us in the gym."

When they walked through the door, Gerald gave Alice a questioning glance when he saw Simon. The young man stalked to a far wall and slid down to the floor.

"I'll tell you later. Check on Marco, I think he might've gotten grazed by a bullet."

Gerald nodded as Alice walked up to Simon. He hadn't spoken a word on the long run back to the mansion. Now tears made silent tracks down his cheeks.

"I didn't mean…" he said, his voice breaking. "I'm sorry…I just got so mad."

Alice eased herself next to him, and wondered if she'd been too harsh on him.

When she looked at him, something inside her recognized the look on his face, the way he kept flexing his hands into fists. She remembered her first mission, the overwhelming frustration of failure.

And what did I need then?

She put her hand on his arm. "I know…believe me, I've felt what you're feeling."

He shook his head. "I doubt it."

"Someday, I'll tell you about it, but for now, just trust me."

"I was reckless, wasn't I? That's why we failed."

Alice felt her gut twist as truth hit her. "You weren't the only one reckless and at fault. It's not all on you."

"Judy...she is so little, and she didn't trust anyone but me." He began to cry in earnest now. "I failed her! I'm useless!"

She put her arms around him and hugged Simon tight.

"Sometimes...sometimes, we don't win, even though we did our best." The words burned on her tongue, and she knew they weren't just meant for Simon. "But the point is, that we tried, and we gave everything we had in that moment. You can't...we can't, blame ourselves when the fight doesn't go our way. Being a hero doesn't mean you always win. It means you keep trying, even when you lose."

His body shook with sobs, and as Alice held him, she felt something begin to lift, just a little, off her own soul.

CHAPTER TWENTY-ONE

Victoria hadn't said a word on the drive back to the Foundation. Lionel had expected her to rage, or coldly tell him his usefulness was at an end. She did neither of those things.

Which somehow, Lionel found to be even more unnerving.

When he stepped out of the car, rough hands took hold of him and marched him behind Victoria. They didn't go in through their usual entrance, instead taking a small side door that he'd never noticed before.

At first, Lionel was completely lost in the underground maze of passageways. Then he spotted the hallway with the God awful landscape paintings that led to Victoria's private office and wondered if they were just going to rough him up a bit and toss him in his room. But instead of turning down the hall that would take him to his quarters they kept going.

I'm going to pay for those few minutes with Alice. And I don't give a damn.

"Wait out here," Victoria said to Baritone, and then she pointed at Lionel. "You, come with me."

He raised an eyebrow in surprise and followed Victoria through a plain, gray door.

Inside were cold storage chambers against one wall, a sterile table in the center and various trays and drawers full of scientific and medical tools.

He eyed the table, noticing straps that looked several inches thick. A drain sat under it, waiting in thirsty anticipation for his blood.

Victoria unlocked one of the cold storage chambers and pulled out a small box. Without ceremony she set it on the table and took out one of two green vials.

"Do you know what this is?" she asked, her voice sending chills up Lionel's spine.

"No."

"Your cure."

She held it up and Lionel's hand twitched, longing to snatch it out of her grasp.

"I have just two vials. And then it's gone. I never bothered to learn how to make it."

Without warning she smashed the vial to the floor.

"No!" he lunged forward and fell on his knees.

The green liquid seeped toward the drain, glass shards glistening in the bright white light.

"I don't know what you think you were doing tonight," she said, "but you need to remember that I hold your leash. I am your master, and you will not so much as look at her without my permission. Is that clear?"

Lionel stared at the wet floor, limbs hollow.

"Answer me."

"Yes," he whispered. "I understand."

"Good. Now, what did you tell her?"

He clenched his jaw and heard Victoria pick up the last vial of his cure.

"Answer the question. I am in no mood for games."

"I told her that I wasn't really with you," he said, voice harsh. "That I loved her. And that…"

"Yes?"

"Nothing was as it seemed."

"Did she believe you?"

Lionel opened his mouth and stopped.

He was sure from the look on her face just before he ran away that she did believe him. But there was something hesitant in her kiss tonight and it made Lionel wonder if Alice didn't trust him anymore.

I don't have to tell her the truth, I just have to give this bitch an answer and be done with it.

"I think so," he said, not sure if it was the truth or a lie.

He held his breath as Victoria simply stood there, holding the precious vial in her hand. Lionel looked up and swallowed any pride he had left.

"Please, don't. I…I will do as you say but…please."

She stared at him for a long time, eyes hard and cold. Finally, she placed the vial back in its box.

Lionel's shoulders sagged and he sat on the cold floor, sick to his stomach.

"Until the Children's Home fundraiser you will be here at the Foundation, no more excursions," Victoria said. "And at that event, you will be by my side at all times. If you leave…well, you can imagine the consequences I'm sure."

He nodded.

"Now get up, go back to your room and stay there, like a good dog."

In the few seconds it took for him to stand, rage hit Lionel like a blinding hot pulse. He wanted to hit her so much his body shook with the effort of restraining himself. She saw it, because her lips spread in a cold smirk and she stepped closer to him.

"Go ahead," she whispered. "Or have I tamed you too much?"

It snapped his restraint and he pulled back, launching a blow at her perfect face.

She caught his fist and held it, barely straining. With a smooth motion born of years of practice she pushed his arm away and punched him across the face. Lionel felt blood burst in his mouth and blinked back stars in his vision.

"Someone forgot that he's not so special anymore," she said, grabbing a handful of his hair and hitting him twice in the face, then the stomach. "And I hate to admit it, but I'm glad. I needed to get some frustration out."

Lionel coughed out a painful breath and brought his fist up to try and hit her. She dodged out of the way, still holding onto his hair and hit him in the side.

He cried out as pain wrapped itself around his back and he felt another blow land.

"Had enough?" she asked, letting go of his hair.

Lionel stumbled back, legs shaking. Without his fast healing and strength, the blows felt like he'd been hit by a truck. And if it didn't stop soon, Victoria could cause some serious damage.

The door behind him opened and Baritone stepped inside.

"Get him to his room," Victoria said. "And don't forget his next injection."

Baritone dragged him out and down unfamiliar hall-ways. Lionel did his best to ignore the pain wracking his body and tried to memorize where his cure was locked up. When Baritone opened Lionel's bedroom door and threw him in, the vigilante had a pretty good idea of how to get to the cold storage room.

Not that it's going to do much good, I can't get away from anyone in this place...Leave it to Victoria to keep what I want most just out of reach like this.

He laid on his bed, not bothering to ice his wounds and

tried to think everything through without giving in to despair.

When he had agreed to be Victoria's prisoner Lionel had believed that he could help Alice and Marco by being in the thick of things. But in the time he'd been here, Lionel had barely managed to find out anything specific or helpful. The only thing he'd accomplished was to hurt Alice. Again.

And now, Victoria had shown him just how much she had him over a barrel.

"I was so close to it," he whispered, tears falling down his cheeks. "So close…and she…"

He clenched his fist, almost driving it into the mattress.

"I have to have it…if I don't, what can I offer Alice, or anyone? What kind of life could I possible have? And if I do what Victoria wants, how do I help Alice and Marco fight her?"

There was no clear answer except that he couldn't do both. He had to make a choice.

"Alice and Marco. I have to help them finish this. I owe them that much."

Whatever future he'd hoped for, Lionel knew he had to accept that it was no longer possible. He would fight Victoria, and find a way to live with the poison that had changed him so much. If that meant being alone, and never seeing Alice or Marco again, then he'd do it. For them he'd do anything.

CHAPTER TWENTY-TWO

Simon was more emotionally wounded than physically, but Alice agreed that it would better for him to stay the night at the mansion. She wasn't exactly sure that Simon wouldn't go off and try to find Judy without her, and that was something she couldn't allow.

"Are you going to train him?" Marco asked the next morning at breakfast.

Alice sighed. "I don't have the first clue how to help him learn to use his powers."

"I don't think that's what he needs."

"I'm no mother, either."

Marco chuckled around a bite of eggs.

"What? I'm not."

"I've always thought you'd be a good mother," his eyes softened as he looked at her.

In the calm room with winter sunshine falling around them, the smell of coffee and cinnamon rolls floating on the air, Alice found herself unable to look away from this man. The way his eyes shone, the tilt of his lips when he was just on the cusp of a toothy grin, the way his hair looked after he'd tumbled out of bed. It all tricked her senses, and for a moment it was as if the last couple of years fell away.

He's going to leave. Don't forget that.

Alice broke the spell and looked away. She had to stop letting herself think that he might stay after Victoria was defeated.

"You could help give him direction at least. You did well last night," Marco said, his demeanor once again guarded.

Alice chewed her bottom lip and tried not to let Marco's words sink in too far. The problem was, he wasn't saying anything she hadn't been thinking herself.

"I've got to focus on Victoria first," she said, "I can't take him on as well."

Marco nodded.

"You'll think about it after?"

"Yes, fine."

"Can I ask, how are you today?"

"You mean after seeing Lionel?"

"Yes."

She sighed. "I don't know."

Marco looked down at his hands and fidgeted with his napkin.

"Do you think he was telling the truth? That he really isn't working with her?"

The tinge of hope in his voice made Alice's heart hurt. Marco had asked what Lionel had said to her after Simon had gone to sleep last night. She'd told him about all of it, except for Lionel's confession of love.

After all this time, Alice knew that while Lionel would always be one of the people she loved most in the world, she wasn't *in* love with him.

Not anymore. That girl that loved him…she's a part of me for certain. But the woman I am now loves Marco, no matter how much I might not want to.

She shook herself a little to dislodge those thoughts as Marco waited for her response.

"I think he's being honest," she said, her words slow as she chose them carefully. "But I think we have to be careful. We both want to believe it, and that might blind us to what's really going on."

Marco nodded. "I just...he couldn't have changed that much. I don't want to believe he could anyway."

"Me either. But..."

"What?"

"I just don't know how to trust my instincts with this."

"Because you love him."

Something in his voice, a small, barely-there tone made Alice wonder if Marco was asking a deeper question. She looked at him, wanting to somehow tell him the truth of all her tangled feelings. How they could still be this way after all this time was something Alice couldn't understand, but she wanted desperately to try. And if Marco felt something more for her...

"What are you really asking?" she asked.

"If...are your feelings the same, or have they changed?"

Slowly, her heart banging against her ribs and her breath suddenly short, Alice reached for his hand. Her fingers tangled with his and her throat clogged with fear.

"Marco, I—"

The door to the dining room slammed against the wall as Uncle Logan barged through it. Alice and Marco sprang apart, her face flushed.

"What are you—?" she began, but took one look at her Uncle's face and felt her stomach drop.

"Alice," he said. "It's Rose."

Bursting through the hospital doors, Alice sprinted as fast as her cane would allow to the nurses' desk, with Marco right behind her.

"I'm looking for Rose Allen, she would've been brought in last night," Alice said, her voice shaking.

"I'm sorry I don't—"

"Alice!"

She turned and saw Rose standing to the side in the waiting room. Rose's eye was swollen, and her arm was in a sling, but apart from a few cuts on her face, she looked just fine.

Alice threw her arms around Rose and let her tears flow.

"I'm alright," Rose said.

Alice nodded, but didn't let go, even when Marco went to give Rose a hug. Finally, Marco had to escort them away from the nurses' desk so other people could get to it, but Alice kept her arm around Rose's waist.

"What happened?" she asked once they were sitting in the waiting room. "Where's your dad?"

"He's with Derrick in the ICU."

"Oh, Rose, is he alright?"

She shook her head. "I don't know."

"What happened?" Marco asked.

"I...I was supposed to be closing the shop, but Derrick volunteered to do it for me, so I went up to the loft for the night. I heard some breaking glass and saw some men going into the shop, so I...well, I've been working on these gloves that basically help increase the strength of a punch, as well as a chest piece that can take the blows from an enhanced person. Anyway I put them on and went down the stairs.

"When I got to the back door of the shop, there were six men beating on Derrick and he was...God Alice, he was already a bloody mess by the time I got there, and I was down there pretty quick."

"Was it a standard robbery?" Marco asked.

Rose shook her head. "They were asking for me, and Derrick wouldn't tell them. When I showed up they came after me, but between the gloves and the chest piece I was able to put up a pretty good fight. They still got in a few lucky shots though."

Alice's mouth became dry.

"Did you recognize any of them?" she asked.

Rose shook her head. "Not as such, but they were incredibly strong. Unnaturally, I would say."

"Enhanced?" Marco asked.

"Absolutely."

Alice wanted to stand and pace, but her limbs wouldn't work.

"This is my fault," she said.

"You don't know that," Marco said.

"Why would it be?" Rose asked.

Alice told her in broad strokes what had happened last night and Rose's face became hard.

"So, she comes after me to teach you a lesson," Rose said.

"I'm so sorry," Alice said.

"Don't be. This is just fuel to the fire. We've got to finish her, Alice."

The side doors opened and a haggard-looking Gerald came out. Rose stood and met her dad halfway.

"How is he?" she asked.

Gerald shook his head. "It's hard to tell, the mind is a tricky place to heal."

"So, there's brain damage?"

"There's swelling and a lot of internal damage. His left eye is the real problem though. I'm not sure he'll ever recover all his sight in it. I did what I could and I'll keep coming back, but I can't promise anything."

Rose nodded, tears falling from her eyes.

"If I hadn't let him close—"

"Then you'd be dead," Gerald said, his voice breaking. "It's not your fault."

"Dad, I have to tell you something-"

"It's okay," he said. "I know…I saw the gloves."

"Dad—"

"Someday, remind me to tell you about how brave your mother was. Until then, just know that I'm proud of you."

Rose's face crumpled and she fell against her father's shoulder, sobbing. Gerald closed his eyes and held his daughter in a tight embrace.

"Where's your uncle?" Gerald asked Alice, once Rose had stopped crying.

"He's trying to find out anything about the men who attacked Derrick and Rose. But I doubt he'll find anything."

"Rose," Gerald said, "why don't you go to the mansion with Alice, I'll stay here and make sure Derrick gets what he needs."

"I should—" Rose began.

"Get some rest," Gerald finished. "You'll heal faster."

Rose pressed her lips together, and then sighed.

"Fine, but if there's any changes—"

"I'll call, I promise."

Rose hugged her father tight, then followed Alice and Marco out to the car.

"I'm sorry to have to ask this, but—" Alice began.

"Your equipment just needs a little tinkering and it's done," Rose said.

"I know it's the last thing that matters right now, but after this and the fact that the special tour is in a few days—"

"After what they did to Derrick, I want this finished even more," Rose said. "Whatever you need, both of you."

Marco smiled. "Thanks."

Rose nodded. "It's good to see you by the way."

"Yeah, same to you."

"Give me twenty-four hours and I'll have everything done. Then, you can go kick her ass."

Alice squeezed her friend's hand, trying to let go of the thought that she'd almost lost her.

"I'm fine," Rose said. "Angry, but fine."

"I know. I'm just tired of that woman taking things from me."

CHAPTER TWENTY-THREE

The next morning, Alice did her usual training routine, the only difference was that she sparred with both Marco and Miss Jones.

"You seem a little less tense," Marco said, taking a drink from a canteen when they were finished.

"I suppose I am."

She could feel the heat coming off him, smell his sweat, and something familiar underneath it.

Rosemary.

Alice smiled.

"What?" he asked.

"Have you been cooking?"

Marco's olive skin flushed. "Maybe, why?"

She shrugged. "It's nice...I...might have missed it."

"Might?"

Alice slapped his arm.

"Your cook asked for a good marinara recipe, that's all," he said. "And maybe my cinnamon rolls, too."

The thought of having to smell Marco's food after he was gone wasn't something that appealed all that much to

Alice and she wished he'd not even bothered. Or that he'd stay.

Mostly that. Good God! What's happened to me? I don't need him!

Alice tried to ignore the fact that she might not need him, but she sure as hell wanted him.

"So," he said, "you have that charity event tonight?"

"Yep. I'll meet Lionel at eight-thirty like he asked and...I guess we'll see if he's telling the truth."

"I'd like to go with you. To help if things get...messy."

"I'll be fine," she said. "She won't try anything in public."

"Maybe not, but she attacked Rose and Victoria isn't stupid. When Lionel disappeared that night so he could talk to you, she probably figured it out."

"Marco, you can't. If she sees you—"

"I will wait at the meeting place that Lionel chose. It wouldn't hurt to have back up."

Alice frowned, trying to find a reason why this wasn't a good idea.

"Fine," she said, "but you have to be careful. No one can see you."

Shadows flew from his fingertips and wrapped around him in a dense, dark cocoon.

Alice took a step back in shock and stared.

"I'll be well hidden," Marco said, as the shadows spun around him and back into his body.

"Yeah...that's...you couldn't do that before, could you?"

"Not that quick or dense, no."

"Alright, well...you know where the meeting place is?"

Marco nodded.

"Miss Seymour?" Miss Jones said, hanging up the phone on a nearby wall. "Miss Allen is requesting your presence in her work room."

Alice nodded.

"See you at lunch?" Marco asked.

There was the barest hint of longing in his voice. It made Alice's pulse speed up.

"I, um, have an appointment," she said.

"Oh, I…"

"It's a little…um, it's just a lunch with—"

"Lunch with Mr. Parker, to mend fences, as it were, after the symphony," Miss Jones interjected.

Marco's jaw clenched and he took a long drink from the canteen.

"It's just for appearances," Alice said.

"I understand," he smiled, though it was tense. "You have a life here."

"Yes, but trust me, it's not because I actually want to have lunch with him, I just…" she sighed, running her fingers through her long, wavy hair.

"You don't owe me an explanation."

"I know, but I just…I just wanted to."

Marco nodded.

"Miss Allen is waiting," Miss Jones said.

Alice could feel Marco's eyes on her as she walked away, and just barely resisted the urge to look back.

The workroom that Mrs. Frost had originally given Rose was expanded and improved upon with better ventilation, and a separate electric system so she didn't blow the fuses in the entire mansion.

Alice always felt like she was entering a church when she stepped inside the work room. There was something quiet and significant about the place that Alice could never put her finger on.

A small entry room opened into a larger room, where at least a dozen prototypes of various guns and weapons concealed in mundane things, like earrings and telephones, sat on a table. On the next table were three different sets of armored vests. Alice paused by a half-dozen versions of her batons at yet another table, each a different thickness and length.

She saw two strange looking gloves sitting a few feet away and wondered if they were the ones Rose had used to defeat the thugs. Next to them was a strange looking helmet and two different chest pieces.

To Alice's right was a doorway that led to a room with two industrial freezers. Several long tables were laid out with clean clothes dotted by various pieces of things Alice couldn't make heads or tails of. There were two rooms to the left of the main room. One held all the finished gear Alice or anyone else would be using. It was locked with a keypad and Rose had always hinted that the countermeasures if someone broke into that room were not pleasant.

The other room to the left was where the various work tools were kept, including large saws, nail guns, and dozens of other things Alice suspected Rose had created herself.

The genius inventor walked out of this room, her coveralls dirty, and her dark hair swept into a bright green scarf.

"Don't touch anything," Rose said, taking off welders gloves.

"Are any of these mine?" Alice asked, gesturing to the batons.

"No, those haven't had a final test yet." Rose guzzled a canteen of water and motioned to the door on the left. "The finished gear is in there."

It was hard to walk past all the inventions without touching them. Particularly an unfinished version of her suit made of...

"Is that rubber?"

Rose slapped her hand as Alice reached out to touch the suit before walking into the room to the left.

This room was a gorgeously lit space with professional display cases lining two of the walls and a row of seamstress dummies lined up against another.

"How's it going?" Alice asked, nodding at Rose's suit.

"Better than I thought."

"You're not pushing yourself too much are you?"

"My dad healed most of my wounds last night. I think he knew I'd work regardless if I was better." Rose smiled, a glint in her brown eyes. "Would you like to see your new gear?"

Alice bounced on the balls of her feet. "Absolutely!"

Rose led her to a side table and a covered seamstress dummy. Alice felt like skipping, she was so excited.

"These are your new gauntlets." Rose handed them to her. "Lighter, holds six more rounds. The darts are also different, purple clips are for average people, white for enhanced. If you shoot an unenhanced person with one of the enhanced darts it will probably kill them, so be careful."

Alice nodded.

"These..." Rose handed her two, foot-and-half-long, batons, "are your new batons."

Alice held them and noticed right away that they were a little heavier than before.

"There's a button on the end." Rose pointed. "Now, tap them against that dummy over there."

Alice swung it at the dummy and saw electricity zap from the end of the baton.

"Enough to subdue a two hundred pound man, if you happen to not have the darts you need. Just be careful, long term contact might set someone on fire or stop their heart."

"Good tip."

"And, your new suit."

Alice held her breath as Rose uncovered the dummy. Then her face fell a little.

"Looks exactly the same, but it isn't," Rose said. "Instead of a separate chest piece attached to long sleeves, I've developed, with the help of a friend, a new armor type that is thin enough to be sewn between two pieces of leather, creating a reinforced chest piece in your suit. What used to be the vest is now a long-sleeved leather top, still snug around the torso, and just as strong, in theory. And, it's lighter. There's also some protection over the front of your thighs. The boots are the same, plated to protect your shins."

"That friend wouldn't happen to be any of the scientists Victoria had reached out to, would it?"

"She turned Victoria down," Rose said. "And besides, her research was exactly what I needed. I'm a genius, but sometimes, even I need a little help with organic chemistry."

"Can I at least know her name?"

"Stephanie something. Works for Dupont. We're pen pals and she's even working on a few of the problems I've had with my inventions."

Alice ran her fingers over the suit, feeling the difference of the sewn-in plates. "Will it hinder mobility?"

"Shouldn't."

"How many of mine do you have?"

"So far just this one."

"And for Marco?"

"I have an updated version of his suit for him, reinforced like yours. And a new duster. Also, I repaired his grappler gun. I don't know what he was doing with it, but I hope he takes better care of this one."

"You'll have to tell him that before he leaves."

Rose shook her head. "I don't understand you two."

Alice sighed. "It's never felt that simple with Marco."

"It should be."

"Yeah, I know. But right now, it just isn't."

"I'm sorry, I shouldn't have said anything."

Alice waved her hand, hoping to show a nonchalance she didn't feel.

"You want to try it on?" Rose asked, gesturing to the suit.

Alice was grateful for the change of subject and smiled.

"Yes, very much, but I have a lunch appointment."

"Date?"

"More like torture."

The lunch turned out to be much worse than she thought and Alice feigned a headache to cut it short.

As she walked into the foyer of the mansion, she wondered how long she'd have to keep doing this charade of husband-hunting.

Hopefully, not for long.

"You are home early," Miss Jones said.

"It was either that or I poison his fifth martini."

Miss Jones nodded. "Then you chose well."

"Postpone any other lunches or dinners until after the Foundation tour, I need to focus on this."

"Of course. But you do have—"

"Yes, yes, the Children's Home fundraiser tonight." Alice sighed and rubbed her temples. Maybe she really was getting a headache.

"Where is Marco?" Alice asked, trying to keep her voice neutral.

"I believe he said something about testing out the new equipment Miss Allen had made for him."

"He gets all the fun. How long before I have to get ready?"

"Francis will be here in an hour to set your hair, then Jacques will arrive with your dress to help with any final touches."

"I think I'm going to take a bath before Francis arrives."

Miss Jones nodded and disappeared into the library.

The hot water worked the knots out of her shoulders and neck, and by the time the water grew cold, Alice felt ready for the night ahead of her.

When Francis knocked on her door, Alice was starting to look forward to the evening.

At least the getting dressed up part.

Several hours later, Alice walked down the wide marble steps in a simple, knee-length, black cocktail dress that hugged her every curve and flared a little at the hem. Instead of sleeves, it had wide straps that showed off her shoulders and strong arms. The square neckline hung lower than some of her other dresses, though not too scandalous. Long black gloves clung to her forearms and stopped just below her elbows.

Francis had spent two hours winding Alice's thick dark curls up into an elaborate beehive, with a round diamond hair pin at the very center. A simple strand of pearls and matching earrings finished off the effect of a tasteful young heiress off to a fundraiser for orphans.

Alice didn't expect to see Marco waiting for her at the foot of the stairs. He turned as he heard her descending, mouth open to say something that never came out.

Alice took more than a little pleasure in seeing his eyes grow large and his mouth hang open. He swallowed and continued to stare as Alice smiled.

"See something you like?" she asked.

He let out a barking laugh and shook his head.

"I'm sorry. You just...that's one amazing dress."

"Yes, and the woman in it isn't so bad either," Alice said, slipping into her Chimera coat.

Marco's eyes sparkled in a way she hadn't seen in a very long time.

"No, she isn't. I'll see you at eight-thirty. Be careful, please?"

"Trust me, Victoria won't do anything there except posture."

Casting one last glance over her shoulder, Alice walked out the door with a spring in her limping step.

The ballroom of The Grand was stifling with the press of so many bodies. A string quartet played a beautiful concerto that no one listened to, while waiters in crisp white uniforms carried trays of hors d'oeuvres with expert precision.

Alice felt the gaze of dozens of pairs of eyes as soon as she stepped through the doors. This was her first society event since Mrs. Frost's death, and though she was sure everyone still considered her a crippled upstart, not one of them would be forthcoming about it.

Her face transformed into its mask of prim compliance, the curt responses she would normally say were filed away, replaced with mild words and humble nods. With some, a shy smile and feigning ignorance worked wonders. With others it was the pretense of keen interest in whatever they were droning on about.

A few more men paraded their sons, nephews, or grandsons in front of her for inspection. She pretended ignorance in the face of their vaunted business acumen and made sure that they knew how much their advice meant to her.

One got a little too familiar, having already imbibed his fair share of alcohol, and as she moved to the side so his hand fell off her bottom, Alice collided with someone tall and thin.

"I do apologize," she said, staring up into Matthew Marsden's gray eyes.

"Not necessary, Miss Seymour," Matthew said, gaze sliding to the inebriated young man next to her. "Ah, Isaac, I think Suzanne Billings was looking for you."

Isaac burped. "Oh...really? Well, Miss Seymour, I will call you later," he tapped her on the tip of her nose and walked with unsteady feet to find Miss Billings.

"I don't think I've had the pleasure of meeting Miss Billings," Alice said.

"Neither has he." Matthew gave her a conspiratorial grin. "But he won't realize that for quite some time. May I get you a drink or escort you through the crowd to the bar?"

Alice laughed, surprised at her genuine reaction.

"Why not? Maybe you could keep the hungry single men at bay for a few minutes, let me catch my breath."

"With pleasure." He offered his arm and led her through the crowd.

"I don't believe I've ever seen you at any of these events," Alice said.

"No, I've been studying abroad, in Switzerland."

"That's right, forgive my slip of memory. What were you studying?"

"Mostly chemistry and its applications in the medical field, though no one seems to care about that. It's all bombs and weapons these days."

Alice's interest was immediately piqued.

"Have you heard of the Science Foundation that Mrs. Veran is opening next month?"

Matthew nodded. "I just recently took my uncle's place on the board of the foundation. It was a relief to him, he has no interest in anything that doesn't net him a profit."

"But you do?"

"Yes. I may risk sounding like an empty-headed debutante, but I honestly don't have a head for business."

Alice felt the smallest slight from his words, though there was nothing in his tone that said he was thinking of her.

I wish I could shed all this pretense for a few hours and have an honest conversation with Matthew. He seems like a good man.

"What would you like?" Matthew asked once they were at the bar.

"Club soda, please."

Matthew's pale eyebrows rose. "A teetotaler?"

"I don't judge others' indulgences, I just don't participate in them."

Matthew shrugged and ordered the club soda and a dry martini.

As Matthew handed Alice her drink, a familiar voice behind her made the color drain from Alice's face.

"Hello, Miss Seymour."

Butterflies dive-bombed in her gut and Alice had to pause so that she didn't turn too quickly without her cane.

"Matthew Marsden, may I introduce Lionel Lawson," Alice said, hoping her voice didn't sound as shaky as she felt.

The two men shook hands, Matthew smiling politely, while Lionel glared at him with barely concealed hostility.

"You are Jason James' stepson, aren't you?" Matthew asked.

Alice didn't think Lionel could be any more stone faced, but as his gaze hardened, she realized he could.

"Yes."

"I met him once. He has a large research facility in Metro City, they're doing some amazing work with DNA."

Lionel didn't bother acknowledging Matthew and ordered a whiskey sour.

"Are you involved in his business dealings at all?" Matthew asked.

"No."

"Lionel is more of a professional playboy, isn't that right?" Alice said, at once regretting the words.

Both men stared at her. Matthew in surprise and Lionel with anger.

"Well," Matthew said, a smile playing at the corners of his lips, "it was nice to meet you, Mr. Lawson. Miss Seymour, would you—?"

"If you don't mind," Lionel said. "I'd like a moment with Alice."

There was a possessiveness in the way he said her name that brought a flush of anger to Alice's cheeks.

Matthew's gaze was questioning, but she nodded, giving him a smile.

"It was a pleasure speaking with you, Miss Seymour. Perhaps we could do it again?"

"Yes, that would be lovely."

He nodded and disappeared into the crowd.

Alice turned to her drink resting on the bar. She could feel Lionel's gaze on her, but refused to look up.

"Well?" she said, her voice low. "I thought we were meeting in ten minutes out back."

"I managed to get away from her but I'm not sure how long I can be gone before she'll notice."

Alice gave him a sideways glance and noticed healing bruises along his chin.

"What happened?"

"A little warning," he said, fidgeting with the ring on his pinkie finger.

"Why don't you use your powers and get the hell out of there?"

"She neutered me. Some serum she has that takes my

powers away. It's temporary but she's very good about the follow up shots."

"That reminds me-"

A chill raced down Alice's spine as Lionel's hand pressed against the small of her back.

"We need to move this conversation. I'll meet you there in two minutes."

Without waiting for her answer, he sauntered away, smiling at the attractive couples that flocked around him.

Alice sipped her club soda to give Lionel enough time to get out back before her. The last thing she wanted was for someone to see them leaving too close together.

Smiling at the vapid people that made way for her as she walked to the door, Alice took her feelings in hand. She wouldn't give in to his charm. He needed her help and, as much as she wished otherwise, she could use his. That was that.

When she stepped outside, a blast of freezing air hit her, and Alice realized she'd left her coat inside. She saw Lionel waiting for her just beyond the door, his blond hair illuminated by the full moon above them.

Whether because of her nerves or the cold, or both, she started shivering immediately.

"Maybe I should have—"

Lionel pulled her against him and kissed her. All the sensations that she knew she should be feeling were distant. There was nothing except the comfort and warmth of his embrace that chased away the wintry chill from her skin. But there was no fire in her belly, no racing pulse.

Alice put her hands on Lionel's chest and pushed against him, breaking the kiss with a loud smack.

"Don't," she said.

Lionel released her and stepped back, hurt shining in his eyes.

"You don't have to be afraid of me," he said. "Locking my powers away also locked all that rage, it doesn't-"

"That's not it," Alice said, taking a deep, shaking breath. "I...Lionel we..."

How did she tell him that she didn't love him anymore? That it wasn't because of his rage, or that he left, it was because she loved someone else.

"We have more important things to discuss," she finally said.

Lionel opened his mouth to speak when something over her head caught his eye. His face split into a wide, joyous grin and he ran around her, arms open wide to embrace someone.

Alice looked behind her and saw Marco staring at them.

Damn, he saw us.

"Marco," Lionel said, gathering his best friend up in a bear hug. "Oh my God it's good to see you!"

Marco smiled and patted Lionel on the back.

"It's good to see you, too."

Alice ran over to them and they all hid between the large garbage bins and the wall of the hotel.

"What the hell are you doing here?" Lionel asked. "Victoria could catch you."

"I thought it might be a good idea, just in case something happened."

Lionel nodded.

"I'd like to talk but—"

"Later," Alice said, smiling at the two of them. "We'll have time later."

"Victoria, what is she planning?" Marco asked.

"I don't know the specifics," Lionel said. "She's been angry this week. Someone, and I think it's Jason James, has been sabotaging some of her plans."

Alice frowned.

"Why would Jason do that?"

"Apparently he and Victoria were working together until Jason decided to stop taking powers from people and started turning them into weapons. He's the one that kidnapped those kids from your children's home, I'm sure of it."

"Wait, he's doing what?" Marco asked, color draining from his face.

"Do you know where—?" she began to ask.

"No," he said. "Only that Jason has been doing other things as well. It's made Victoria paranoid and she's heightened security a bit more. But I know one thing that might stop her. She keeps a safe in her office at the Foundation, it's full of papers that she's been very worried about losing if Jason broke in. If you can get into that safe, you would probably have what you need to indict her."

"That's...Lionel, that's exactly what we needed!"

"But do it before the tour. Something's going to happen, I don't know what, but something."

Alice nodded "She's clearing the decks, getting rid of the leaders of the city."

Lionel swore under his breath.

"That makes so much sense. Marco did you...Marco?"

Marco was staring at the ground, hand coving his mouth as if he were in shock.

"Marco?" she asked, hugging herself against the cold. "What's wrong?"

"Jason," he said, taking off his jacket and putting it around Alice's shoulders, "I...I think I've seen his handiwork. And it's not pretty."

"We can't do anything about that now," Lionel said. "Trust me, I want to take the bastard out but Victoria is the immediate threat. We get her and we might have something on Jason, too."

Marco nodded.

"We'll get him," Alice said, putting her hand on Marco's

arm. "And we'll get Judy back, too. But Lionel's right, we have to do this first."

"I know…it's…"

"Hard to wait when people are being hurt," Lionel said.

"Do you know what extra security measures have been put in place?" she asked.

"Other than extra guards, who are enhanced in some new and frightening way, no."

"How so?"

"I don't know but they don't talk and when they look at me…it's like they're dead."

Alice shivered.

"I guess we'll handle that when we come across them. Do you know the combination to the safe?"

"It's probably an important date for her, personally, that seems to be her way. Marco might be able to pick the lock, but something tells me she's got a safeguard for that."

Alice sighed. "Alright, we'll have to figure that out then."

"Lionel, about the cure," Marco said. "You have to know that there's a side effect. It will strip your powers."

Lionel stared at him, eyes wide and lips parted. Eventually, he shook his head.

"It doesn't matter."

"What?" Alice said. "Lionel, you—"

"I don't care about my powers—"

"But-"

"I've wasted so much time," Lionel said to Alice, his voice low and fierce. "And I don't care if I don't have my powers anymore. Having the chance to be with you, to be able to live a life without being afraid of myself. That's worth it."

"No," she said, her mouth dry. "No, I can't let you do that."

"Why not?"

She swallowed, knowing that she'd have to break his heart right now in order to save him from a mistake he would regret for the rest of his life.

Alice glanced at Marco, who was frowning at them with concern and little confusion.

"Because I—"

A door close by banged open and the three of them plastered themselves against the wall of the hotel, trying to hide from whoever had just stepped outside.

After a moment, a voice pierced the silence.

"Lionel? Dearest, are you here?"

Victoria's voice held a tinge of menace underneath the concern.

Lionel swore under his breath.

"I'll see you two soon," Lionel whispered before sauntering toward the loathsome woman.

Alice listened to him escort Victoria back inside, heard the door bang shut and knew that she should sneak back in. But even though the cold was seeping into her bones, Alice didn't want to move. She felt sick and desperate.

He can't give this up for me, not when things have changed.

"I should go," Marco said, not looking at her.

Alice nodded. "We should talk when I get back, come up with a plan."

"Be careful. I still don't trust Victoria not to do something."

"And Lionel?"

"I do trust him. You?"

"Yeah, he's...well, he's Lionel."

Marco chuckled.

"Yeah, he is."

Wrapping himself in shadows, Marco ran along the side of the building and out into the night. She stared after him, wondering what he knew about Jason's dealings with powered people that would make the Shadow Master so afraid.

The back door opened again and Alice tensed just before hearing Miss Jones' clear, firm tone.

"Miss Seymour?"

Alice stepped out from the middle of the garbage bins and ignored Miss Jones' raised eyebrow.

"It's time for you and Victoria to speak to the assembled donors."

"Good God, I'd forgotten. Tell Victoria that I'm not feeling well and will be there directly."

Miss Jones nodded.

"The second door would be best, since that hall is where the Ladies' lounge is."

"Thank you."

After taking another minute to compose herself, Alice made her way inside and to the raised dais.

Victoria's smile was cold.

"Where were you, my dear?"

"I'm so sorry, I've been fighting a cold the last few days and it doesn't seem to want to let me go."

Victoria's dove gray eyes were hard. "Some things are like that. Just when you think you've shaken them off, they pop back up."

A chill ran down Alice's spine and a sudden urge to take off the mask she wore was almost too strong to resist. But, eventually, she managed a tight smile and a nod.

They walked to the podium together and Alice siphoned off the fury she felt toward Victoria, saving it for the day when she'd finally visit her in jail.

When Alice came home an hour later, Marco was standing in front of the fireplace in the library, a deep frown creasing his forehead.

"You look even more worried after talking with Lionel than you were before," she said.

"I've been thinking," he turned to look at her. "The risk Victoria took by capturing Lionel and not keeping him under lock and key. Coupled with the fact that she wants him at the special tour, which is so important to her…All of it doesn't add up. She has to know that Lionel will try to stop it."

"I've been thinking about that, too. If she's going to get rid of everyone standing in her way, why have a hero there to stop it?"

"A hero who can lose his temper and-"

Alice gasped and Marco's eyes grew wide.

"Unless she wants him to," Alice said.

"Oh my God. She's just sadistic enough to do it."

Alice sank into a nearby chair.

"He'll never forgive himself for that."

"And neither will the city. They already think we had something to do with Park Side, and if Victoria gets Steel to do her killing for her, the city won't ever trust any of us again. She won't just get rid of any politicians and officials in her way, she'll seal the fate of every powered person in this city."

"And she knows I'm working against her, that's for certain."

"Then there's no reason to wait anymore. We have to do this now."

"Tonight?"

"If she's on to you, why give her the chance to prepare for that? We have the upper hand right now, tomorrow we may not."

Alice felt her body begin to hum with excitement, and just a little bit of fear.

"Alright. I've got a list of dates important to Victoria that might help us guess the combination. We might still need lock-picking gear, do you have yours?"

"Yes, but I think Rose may have more sophisticated ones."

Alice jumped up and walked toward the door. "You get the gear and I'll get the list of dates."

She paused, and remembered her conversation with Rose and Uncle Logan. They had been trying to get her to realize that she wasn't alone in this fight, and that needing others wasn't weakness, but strength.

This is bigger than me or Marco and Lionel. This...this affects us all.

"Alice?" Marco said. "What's wrong?"

"If we fail, we need to make sure that Victoria still doesn't succeed. We need back up. Could you call Uncle Logan, and then ask him, Rose, Gerald and Miss Jones to meet us in the gym?"

"Of course."

CHAPTER TWENTY-FOUR

Rose, Miss Jones, Gerald and Marco stood around the basement gym, making small talk. The tension in the air was thick, as if they already knew what this was about.

Alice felt relief sweep through her when Uncle Logan stepped through the door. Their eyes met and she walked over to him. They hadn't spoken much since the morning of the riot, and Alice wanted to make it right before she left.

"You were right," she said. "About...well, just about everything. I'm sorry I ran. I'm sorry I haven't been honest with you."

Uncle Logan smiled and hugged her. "I don't need to win, Alice. I just want you to be happy."

"I know, but I just wanted to say that I heard you."

"Alright," he stepped back and looked around. "I'm guessing that this is it. You're going after her tonight."

Alice nodded. "It's time."

Uncle Logan hugged her again.

"Be careful."

"Of course."

She stepped back and looked around the room, at the

faces of the people that had been her support, her conscience, her strength through all of it.

Alice took a deep breath. She went over the simple plan, and the equipment they'd need for it. Marco interjected a little here and there, but for the most part it was Alice who laid it all out, and fielded the few questions that came up.

At the end of it Rose was frowning.

"This sounds like a two person job," she said. "Why tell us all this?"

"Because," Alice said.."we may not succeed. If we don't, Victoria still needs to be stopped. And that's where you all come in."

"Us?" Rose asked, her lips turning up into a grin.

"If we don't come back before the tour, I need you all to be there and stop Victoria. I know it's asking a lot-."

"Count me in," Uncle Logan said.

"Me, too," Rose said.

"I think it goes without saying that I will be there," Miss Jones said.

Alice let out a breath she hadn't realized she was holding.

"Thank you," she said, turning her gaze to Gerald, who was silent through all of this. "I know that, though skilled, you're not one for fighting. Can you stay close, offer aid where you can?"

Gerald sighed, relief sweeping his features. "Of course, thank you for understanding."

"And if I may," Miss Jones said, the hint of a smile on her lips. "Well done Miss Seymour."

―――

After a quick strategy session with everyone, Alice followed Rose into her workroom, where her gear was waiting for her.

"Alice," Rose said, her brows drawn in a frown, "be careful, please?"

"Of course, I just asked all of you to help as a precaution. I expect to come back."

Rose nodded. "I know but...I have a bad feeling."

"Hey, I know this is risky, but she's not expecting us. We have the advantage. And even if everything goes haywire, I've got all of you backing me up, right?"

Rose gave her a shaky smile and nodded as Gerald walked into the room.

"Your suit is in there," Rose gestured toward a sleek, black footlocker.

Alice opened it and ran her hands with loving reverence over the leather.

"I feel like all I've done is wait and prepare. Now, it's here...I feel..."

Gerald's hand was heavy on her shoulder. "You're ready. Just come back."

"Thank you for everything, Gerald. You didn't have to do any of it. I wouldn't have blamed you if you'd said no. I couldn't have done this without you."

"I don't know about that. It's certainly felt good to do more than patch you up. I'm...for what it's worth...I'm proud of you. And I think Diana would be, too."

Tears stung Alice's eyes. "That's worth a lot, thank you." She glanced at Rose. "Will you give us a minute?"

Rose threw her arms around Alice, holding her tight. "I'll see you when it's done."

Once Rose had closed the door behind her, Alice turned to Gerald. "If we don't come back—"

"You will."

"But if we don't, my will is in my desk, top drawer. Uncle Logan is my heir, followed by Rose – you're the executor."

"Alice—"

"No arguments. Nothing is guaranteed, even with all of you helping me."

Gerald sighed. "Alright, but I won't need it."

"Uncle Logan might want to charge in early if we're taking a while to get back. Don't let him, stick to the plan."

"I'll try."

Gerald gave her a brief hug before leaving the work room.

Alice took a deep breath.

"Here we go."

The moment Alice slipped on the suit and cowl, she wanted to cry. Without the Serpent, it had felt like she was living with a part of her soul cut out. Looking at herself in the mirror now, she felt whole again.

Rose had made the winding, dark green snake more prominent, per her request. Alice ran her fingers over it, as it twined around her legs, torso, and up onto the cowl, where its head, hanging between her eyes, stared back at her. The boots gave her several inches more height and they felt a little strange at first, but she knew that would soon fade.

She flexed her hands in the new gloves, checked her darts, then checked the batons in their holsters at her waist.

At last, she looked at herself once more in the mirror and grinned.

"This is who I am," she whispered.

"Yes, it is."

The voice was so sharp and perfect that Alice spun around, expecting to see Mrs. Frost, but the room was empty. The voice felt like a blessing, and it filled her soul with strength and pride.

Shoulders back, gait confident, Alice made her way to

the outside garage and the private room where Marco was waiting. She smiled at the sight of her partner in his Shadow Master suit and duster. It had been far too long since they were together like this.

Marco looked up from where Rose was adjusting his new shoulder holster and smiled. His eyes raked over her body and Alice wondered what he saw: the woman or the vigilante?

"It's a good kind of strange to be back in this gear," Marco said, running his hand down the front of his vest.

"You didn't take your suit to Metro City?"

"I did, but after a while it became too damaged to wear."

"If you don't mess this one up too bad," Rose said, stepping back to look at her handiwork, "I might let you take it with you."

Marco gave her a little smile.

"That would be nice, thanks. Are we taking the Lightning?"

Alice's lips spread in a wide grin. She hadn't ridden the Black Lightning in almost two years, but Uncle Logan had kept it in pristine condition. When she tore the cover off, it's black and chrome body gleamed in the low light. She ran a hand over the soft leather seat and up to the handle bars, and then eased onto it. Closing her eyes, she started the engine and it purred to life under her.

She looked over at Marco. "Well, you getting on?"

He settled behind her, hands resting on her hips. An unexpected heat coursed through her as she felt his body press, just a little, into her back. She looked over her shoulder, her face inches from his.

"Hold on tight," she said with a grin, and he grinned back.

The tires screeched as they tore out of the garage, down the gravel drive, and onto the street. Alice opened the throttle, and relished the wind whipping past her body. Marco's hands tightened on her hips as they took a corner at breakneck speed.

She was almost sad when they pulled up to the buildings adjacent to the Science Foundation.

Though the waterfront had become a busy part of Jet City's new nightlife, the Science Foundation was far enough from the loud arcades and bars that two masked people picking the lock of a side door weren't noticed.

At least, Alice hoped that was the case.

The foyer of the visitor center was a huge open space, a concierge desk of blue stone sat on the left, while to the right, were doorways into exhibits talking about the different schools of scientific thought. In the center, a sweeping stair case split the space.

"Victoria's office is down a private corridor," Alice said.

"How do you know that?"

"Memorized the blueprints."

Marco stared at her and shook his head. "I should've expected that."

Footsteps suddenly echoed from above and Alice darted under the staircase. Marco was busy picking the lock as the footsteps drew closer.

A man dressed as a security guard stepped off the bottom step, and Shadow gave Serpent a quick shake of his head to indicate that he wouldn't be done soon enough to avoid detection. Alice took a deep breath and ran toward the man as he rounded the corner from the bottom step. She drew her baton and pressed the button to activate it just as he drew his gun. Before he could fire, a jolt of electricity shot through his body. He jerked and fell to the ground.

"New toy?" Marco whispered as he helped her drag the man under the staircase.

Alice smiled and they both sprinted back to the now unlocked door. They carefully stepped through, the bright lights jarring compared to the dark they'd just left. The hallway they now found themselves in had thick carpeting that muffled their footsteps. There were no doors on either side, and though the hall wasn't narrow, Alice still felt hemmed in. She led Marco to where the hall ended in 'T' and followed the hallway to the left, then to the right.

She was starting to feel like a rat in a maze when, after another left turn, Alice saw beautiful black and white French doors at the end of the hall, signaling Victoria's office. Reaching for the silver handle, Alice opened the door slowly.

The office was huge. A wall of windows sprawled out behind Victoria's desk, giving a magnificent view of the water. The thick carpets were gray, with black couches and chairs, off-setting the white desk and lighting fixtures. Framed works of art, mostly Monet and Rembrant, were the only real source of color in the room. There was only one photograph on the wall: a framed black and white of Victoria's dead children.

"There," Alice said, walking to the photograph.

Feeling along the frame, her finger brushed against a little switch and the picture slid to the side, revealing a plain black wall safe.

And, setting off a blaring alarm.

CHAPTER TWENTY-FIVE

A door that Alice had assumed was a bathroom or closet burst open and out poured four hulking men, who charged straight for them.

Alice drew her baton and hit the button. With a short swing that connected with his chest, she sent an electrical charge into the first man. He shook and fell into the second man behind him while Marco engaged the other two. The men Alice fought weren't down for long, and she somersaulted under the first goon's attempt to grab her. Coming up onto the balls of her feet, she slammed her baton into his face this time. Blood splattered from his broken nose, but he barely reacted.

"Enhanced!" Alice yelled, pushing a white clip into her gauntlet.

She fired at the man with the broken nose, but the dart bounced off his chest. She tried again, aiming for his neck, and missed. Flipping back as the man tried to kick her in the face, she collided into another attacker, who grabbed her from behind. Quickly pivoting, she tossed him over her hip. Still holding onto his arm, she dislocated his shoulder in one smooth move.

Before she could move out of the way, the first goon delivered a brutal punch to her stomach. Alice stumbled back, and tried to breath. She just barely managed to block the next punch to her face, and shot another dart at him. This time, it hit his neck and he went down.

The second goon with the dislocated arm stood up, a blank, cold look in his eyes. He backhanded her, then tried to seize her with his one good arm. Alice swiveled, grabbed his collar and pressed her foot to his knee, throwing him to the ground. He struggled against her just before Alice shot a dart point-blank into his neck.

Jumping up, she saw Marco drive his knee into one attacker's stomach, then land three quick punches to his face before tossing his head into the heavy desk next to them. The man slumped to the floor. Alice realized Marco had been holding back when they had sparred. He fought dirty now.

He ran a hand through his hair, looking around the room at the now defeated attackers. "They're immune to my powers somehow. We should—"

The French doors slammed open, followed by the side door the first goons had come through. Alice and Marco stood back to back as more men surrounded them. They all had the same empty stares as the other four. Alice raised her gauntlet to fire at the nearest man and the group rushed them.

Someone tried to grab her and she twisted his wrist, feeling the pop of the delicate bones, then delivered two swift kicks to his stomach and chest before another man kicked her legs out from under her. He brought a boot down toward her face and she rolled, only to be kicked in the stomach by someone else.

Large hands pulled her head up and drove a fist into her face. She tasted blood and tried to get her legs under her.

That's when thick arms wrapped around her, and lifted her to her feet.

She used her attacker's momentum and pushed off the nearest man to propel them backwards. They landed with a crash on a nearby table and he released her. She scrambled up and saw Marco struggling to get to his feet directly in front of her.

One of the attackers kicked him in the face and she saw red.

The vigilante rushed toward the attacker and managed to send several volts of electricity through his body. It was with no small amount of satisfaction that she saw his shaking body collapse.

Marco and Alice backed toward the French doors, but were blocked by more men coming through. One jab to Marco's face and he was down. Alice turned to help him and was lifted off the ground by two men. One pinned her arms to her sides, the other captured her legs. She arched her body to try and break free, but she was held fast. Two more men picked up Marco and they all headed for the hallway.

Panic built up in Alice's chest. She forced herself to breathe and focus on what was around them. They weren't in the same hallway she and Marco had come down. This one was gray instead of beige, and bright fluorescent lights hummed above them. The crazed guards' clomping steps had a slapping sound, like walking on linoleum. She did her best to count the footsteps before the first turn to the right, then again before another right turn that took them down an incline.

At that point, they came to a gray metal door that opened into a spacious room with large cages that could easily hold a full grown man. Lab equipment sat on neat tables at one end of the room, with three tall filing cabinets against one wall. The men stopped at one of the cages, tossed them both inside, and locked the door.

Alice stared at the men as they left, waiting for one of them to turn around or do something, but they simply marched out of the room, the door lock latching into place behind them.

"Marco?" Alice said, kneeling beside him as he started to move.

His face was already bruising and blood darkened his lips and the skin under his nose.

"I know it's hard to believe," he said, sitting up against the bars, "but I've had worse."

She couldn't help laughing.

His long fingers curled around hers and she scooted next to him.

"What do we do now?" he asked.

"I don't know."

She glanced around the cage, her eyes settling on a set of syringes on a nearby table. Her stomach twisted. What were they going to do to them?

Marco stood up, holding his ribs and wincing.

"These were probably built for her enhanced goons."

"That's my thought, too. So, they're strong."

Marco nodded. "And the room is probably monitored."

Alice looked up and saw a tiny camera in the farthest corner and another behind them.

Marco winced again as he moved to the door of the cage.

"Your ribs?"

He nodded.

"Let me see."

He hesitated, but let her unzip his vest and lift his shirt. There was the tell tale bruising around his left ribs, but his right seemed unaffected. She pressed gently and he gasped in pain.

"Can you breathe?"

He nodded again. "But it hurts."

"I think they're broken, or fractured, at the very least."

"Miss Jones taught you medicine, as well?"

"Basic first aid is what she called it."

Taking a dart out of her purple clip, she carefully drained most of the anesthetic before stabbing Marco in the side.

"That should take the edge off without knocking you out. Hopefully."

She eased his shirt back down and zipped the vest up, noticing how snug it was on him.

"You've gained muscle."

"Rose said I'd gotten fat," he chuckled, then winced. "But I'm grateful for how tight it is now."

"You need more than just this, we have to get out of here."

"I'll slow you down." He slid back to the floor. "You have a better chance without me."

"No," Alice said, examining the bars for any loose ones.

Marco grabbed her hand and pulled her down to him. She practically fell on his lap.

"This isn't a suggestion. You have to get out of here so you can stop her. That's what's important, not me."

"I'm not leaving you."

"When they come for us, I'll pretend that I'm unconscious, when they come in, you run out and close the door."

"No!"

His hands captured her face. "I won't let you sacrifice the city for me."

She opened her mouth to tell him she couldn't lose him, that she loved him and would pay any price to be with him, but she knew it wouldn't make a difference. He was right.

"You'll find me, or I'll find you," Marco grinned.

"And then what?" She hadn't meant to say that, but

now it was out. She ran her hand over his face, thumb tracing the line of his mouth. "I can't lose you."

"You'll never lose me," he said, his hands sliding down to rest on her shoulders. "I'll always be yours, Alice."

"How touching," said a voice from the doorway.

Alice jumped up as all the hate and anger she'd kept contained for so long sprang free. Heat suffused every muscle and joint in her body until she was on fire. Alice let it inflame her gaze, a snarl escaping from the back of her throat.

Victoria gave her a cold smile as her men fanned out behind her. One of them opened the cell and Alice lunged for him, kneeing him in the crotch. She turned to the second man coming through and was knocked to her knees from an explosion of pain shooting through her body.

Her mind was trying very hard to get her body to move, but Alice couldn't make her muscles work, not even as her gauntlets and batons were taken from her. When someone grabbed Marco, she got a hold of the man's ankles only to have that same pain shoot through her body.

"Stop!" Marco said as another jolt was sent through her.

Alice looked up just in time to see the men drag Marco from the room. She groaned in pain, managing to get to her hands and knees.

"Where...did you take him?"

Victoria knelt so she could see eye to eye with Alice through the bars. "To a special place, where magic happens."

"What are you...going to do?"

"You really expect me to tell you?"

Alice fell to her side, half sitting. "What difference does it make now? You have us. And besides, you've been sitting on all this for so long, I think you want to tell me."

A predatory gleam lit up Victoria's eyes and she smiled.

"You're right, I do. However, I want to see how much you've worked out on your own."

"You're going to kill the city's leaders, so you can replace them with men you can control, and make the city afraid of powered people in the process. Then, you'll create your own private enhanced police force, and God knows what else. All in the name of Utopian Science."

Victoria applauded. "Very good. You are intelligent. I wish we could've been partners, we would've made a formidable team."

"If you hadn't become a psychopath, we could've."

"I don't believe I meet the clinical requirements for that diagnosis, but I do see your point."

"What are you going to do with Marco?"

"You know," she said, starting to pace in front of the cage. "I always thought you loved Lionel, and I think you do, in a way. But the one you would be most devastated to lose is Marco, isn't it? How interesting. I wonder how Lionel will feel when he discovers that?"

"He'll tell you to go to hell."

"Unless he's too angry, you know how he can get."

"So, you are going to unleash him at the tour."

"Again, very good. He's the perfect weapon, along with Marco."

Alice felt her stomach sink.

"What do you mean?"

Victoria walked over to a monitor and clicked it on. Alice could see Marco being strapped down onto a hospital bed. Two men in white coats began putting an IV in his arm and after a few minutes, Marco stopped struggling. His glassy-eyed gaze swung to the monitor and away, over and over as if he couldn't quite focus.

One of the men wrote notes on a clip board, while the other wheeled over a bag full of dark solution. They prepared a second IV in Marco's other arm. When the solution began to flow through the tube, Marco's body gave a twitch, then he strained against the restraints, his mouth open in a scream.

"What are you doing?" Alice yelled.

"We've never tried this on anyone powered before." Victoria's voice had a clinical detachment. "And I wouldn't have chosen someone with mental abilities to be the first candidate, but I am very curious to see the results. Usually, I can get about...oh, a week's worth of compliance from my men, before they need a booster treatment. I wonder how long Marco will last."

"You're making him mindless so he'll use his powers on the crowd."

Alice's hands clutched the bars in desperation as she watched, a scream building in the back of her throat.

Marco was twitching on the bed, black tendrils shooting out and coming back into his hands.

"That's interesting," Victoria murmured.

"You could kill him!"

"Yes, I could. And what justice that would be, wouldn't it?"

Alice shook her head.

"I used to feel so much guilt for what happened to your family, as if it were my fault."

"It was!" Victoria's voice broke into a screech. "If it weren't for you they would be alive!"

"No, it wasn't. It was yours. You put them in danger by your choices, and you've been running from that truth all along. Blaming me was convenient, because you didn't want to admit the truth. You killed your family, Victoria. Not me."

Victoria screamed and rushed the bars.

"I had thought to give you the treatment as well, but I think I'll let you be completely aware of everything. I'll put you in the middle of it all, to fight against them. And just before you die, you'll see those you love most become monsters and be put down like monsters."

Victoria flicked another switch, and the other three monitors came alive. All of them showed different angles of Marco strapped onto the bed. She twisted a knob on a nearby control box and the speakers crackled to life.

"Please..." Marco's cries were painfully childlike. "Stop...please don't...no...Ahhhhh!"

Alice's heart constricted, tears stinging her eyes.

"I wouldn't want you to get bored while you wait in here," Victoria said, leaving her alone with the tormented cries pouring from the monitors.

Once the door was shut, Alice let out a scream of rage and panic, tears falling down her face. She pulled at the bars in futility and knew that if Marco didn't survive this, she'd have a front row seat to his torturous death.

When the furious energy of her emotions had been purged, she fell to the cold concrete and sobbed.

"I can't give in to this. It's what she wants," she whispered, a particularly high scream coming through the speakers that made her body shake. "I have to focus...concentrate..."

It took Alice a long time to reach a place where she wasn't overwhelmed by all that had gone wrong. And even then, she couldn't seem to fully relinquish it. Just as she'd find a place of relative focus, a sharp scream from Marco would pierce through, and Alice would have to resist the urge to simply dissolve in tears.

Eventually she was aware of silence, a far more terrifying circumstance than before. She looked up at the screens and Marco was gone.

Clenching her jaw, Alice convinced herself not to think the worst.

"It won't help him or Lionel if I don't stay strong."

She closed her eyes again, staying there until her mind was clear. She began to arrange the resources that she and Victoria had like playing cards in her mind. It didn't take long to see her stack was pitifully small, though she'd learned from Miss Jones that it wasn't the amount of resources that gave you victory, but how you used what you had.

After a while, shuffling the cards, rearranging and discarding some, creating new ones, Alice had no idea what to do.

The door to the room burst open, sending Alice to her feet.

Two men came in and opened the door to the cage, then stepped back.

Alice stared at them, eyes narrowed and body tense.

"I see. Can't have me too fit for the fight."

Running toward the open door of the cell, Alice jumped up, grabbed the bars overhead and launched herself at the first man. Wrapping her legs around his waist, she took him enough by surprise to knock him onto his back. Without hesitating, Alice rammed her elbow into his throat, crushing his windpipe.

His compatriot tossed her onto the floor like a rag doll. She landed on her elbow, pain shooting up her arm. He delivered a swift kick to her abdomen. Alice caught his foot when he tried again and twisted, feeling the bone pop. He barely acknowledged it.

Releasing him and gritting her teeth against the pain in her elbow, Alice somersaulted out of his reach. As the man rushed for her, she used his momentum to toss him over her hip. Pinning him to the floor, she tried to crush his windpipe as well, but the man caught her arm and hit her in the back. She reeled from the stab of pain.

Other hands pulled her up and held her as the man got up off the floor, and the beating started in earnest now

Blows landed in quick succession to her stomach and face until Alice thought she might vomit from the pain.

"That's enough," said Victoria, kneeling down beside her. "We don't want her too damaged. What's the fun in that?"

"You afraid...I'll spoil...your plans?" Alice asked, spitting blood onto the floor.

"I'm counting on you to try."

"I won't...let you down then."

"No, I don't think you will."

Someone kicked her in the face, and all went black.

CHAPTER TWENTY-SIX

The need to vomit was one of the first things that hit Alice after regaining consciousness. Once that was done, her head began to throb and her eyes felt as if someone were trying to push them into her skull. She gently probed her elbow and was thankful that it was just a bad bruise and not a break.

Her stomach was horribly sore, and there were a few bruises around her ribs, but no breaks there either. Her left eye was a little swollen, but she could still see out of it, and the bleeding from her mouth had stopped, though her lip felt two sizes too big.

There wasn't a clock in the room and the lack of windows made it impossible to tell how much time had passed, but Alice knew that she had to be close, maybe within hours, of the tour. And, one way or another, the end of all this was within reach.

She sighed, and leaned against the cool bars. Movement on the monitors caught her eye.

The two men in white coats were escorting someone in a wheelchair to the hospital bed. The sound was still on, and Alice could hear whimpering coming through.

"Now, now," said one of the men. "This won't hurt a bit."

Alice stumbled to her feet, heart hammering in her chest as she saw them lay Marco on the bed. His cries were muffled as he tried to curl into a ball. The men straightened his limbs, once again tying him to the bed.

Marco just laid there and sobbed.

"We've never done all of it in one day before," one of the men said to the other. "How do we know it won't kill him? Or drive him insane?"

"We don't," said the other, hooking up a different IV, "but Mrs. Veran was specific, so we have to try. He's been exceptionally strong so far."

Marco's cries became louder, his voice hoarse as he begged them not to do anymore, telling them he'd obey if they just stopped.

Alice slid down to her knees, great heaving sobs shook her body.

Someone was crying.

That was the first thing Lionel heard when he opened his eyes.

The second was a groan from his own lips as he clutched his head in both hands. It felt as if someone had clobbered him with metal clubs.

When he'd gotten back to the Foundation after seeing Alice and Marco, Victoria had been eerily silent. Lionel knew that she must suspect something and he had braced himself for the fall out.

But nothing happened.

He was escorted to his room, like usual, and started to think that maybe Victoria didn't know anything after all. That's when the vents in the ceiling began to pump gas into the room. Lionel had fled to his bathroom in hopes of escaping it, but it was too late. The last thing he remembered was falling onto the cold bathroom floor and hoping Alice and Marco could stop Victoria.

"What was in that gas?" he mumbled, wishing his head would stop throbbing.

He looked up and realized that he wasn't in his usual cell. Instead of soft carpet, cold concrete was underneath him. Tastefully painted walls were replaced by the gray of more concrete and metal bars. A tight, familiar sensation was wrapped around his body and when he looked down, Lionel saw that he was in a replica of his Steel suit.

"What the hell is Victoria—?"

His words were cut off as the sound of more crying echoed off the gray walls. Lionel looked around to try and see the source of it and his eyes fell on a monitor set on a nearby table. When the screen came into focus, Lionel felt all the air rush out of him in horror.

"Marco!" he cried.

On the monitor, his best friend was writhing in pain as two men shoved IV's into his arms. Marco's hoarse, pleading cries rolled over Lionel like terrible waves. He stared in disbelief.

Was this real? Was it a trick?

Then Marco let out an especially sharp cry and Lionel saw red.

Fury ran through his veins, quick and hot. As he clutched the bars, they bent under his fingers and he let out a gutteral roar that echoed through the stark, bare room he was imprisoned in.

Marco's cries rose, piercing Lionel's ears like knives. With each whimper, Lionel found himself becoming more and more enraged until he could almost bend the bars enough to get out of the cage he was in.

That's when it hit him.

My strength…my anger…

A feral grin took over his features and Lionel gripped the bars tighter, pulling them in an attempt to dislodge them.

"You woke up early," Victoria said, stepping through the door.

She was wearing a perfectly tailored red and black suit and tie, her Phantasm mask dangling in her hands and her blond hair wrapped up in a tight bun.

"You bitch! I'll rip you apart!" he screamed.

"I don't think so."

She released the pin in a metallic grenade and tossed it at him. Sickly sweet smoke began to flow from the cannister.

"No…" he said, horrified as he realized what she was doing.

Victoria grinned at him and slipped her mask on.

"It's show time, and you're the main attraction."

He stared at her and lurched back, desperate to get away from the cannister.

She'd played him beautifully and now everyone he loved would pay the price.

There was no sound in the room except the hiss of the gas being released and Lionel realized that Marco had stopped crying. He tried to look at the monitor through the gas but he could only catch glimpses. Had they killed him? What had happened?

He coughed, the syrupy smell of the gas choking him. Anger flared once more, bright and sharp. He would kill Victoria for this. Imagining her throat in his hand, Lionel reached down to retrieve the cannister. With little effort, Lionel crushed the metal and threw it at Phantasm.

"You'll pay for this," he said, his voice harsh.

"No. I won't."

He took a step toward her, and felt the world tilt. Shaking his head, trying to clear his vision, Lionel couldn't focus any longer. His legs wouldn't obey his command and the concrete room was starting to shift and move. One moment he saw Victoria, the next he saw men in masks, cattle prods in their hands, sparking with electricity. They taunted him, called him cruel names and reached for him. One tried to pull him into a metal box while the other held a wicked looking needle.

"No...Go away!" he screamed.

With desperate fear, Lionel tried to scramble away from them and fell to his knees. Something soft was under him, a sticky warmth covering it. He dared to open his eyes and wished he hadn't.

Alice was laying on the ground, blood covering her body and a desperate gleam in her eyes.

"Help...me..." she said, the sound wet and terrible.

"Oh God...no, no, no..." he sobbed and gathered her up in his arms, burying his face in her tangled hair. "I'm sorry! I...don't go...please don't go!"

A gasping moan reached him through his sobs and he looked up to see that it wasn't just Alice.

Marco lay a few feet away, his body broken at an odd angle.

Gerald.

Logan.

Rose.

They were scattered around him like discarded rag dolls, all of them dead.

Lionel let out a scream, sorrow ripping a hole in his chest. He held Alice tight, unable to let her go as he cried into her hair.

"They killed her," said a woman's voice.

He looked up and saw that he was kneeling in a vast courtyard surrounded by buildings on all sides, like a prison. Unnatural storm clouds swirled above him, and he could hear laughter somewhere in the distance.

"You can still catch them," said the woman's voice.

She sounded so familiar, but the identity of the woman was just out of reach. Not that it mattered anyway. She wasn't the person he was looking for. Whoever had done this, those were the ones he wanted to see. He wanted their screams, their terror as he ripped them apart.

"Where are they?" he asked.

"I'll take you to them, follow me."

CHAPTER TWENTY-SEVEN

Maybe it was the feeling of being utterly beaten. Or maybe it was the knowledge that she was helpless to save Marco or Lionel from their fate at Victoria's hands. Whatever it was, Alice felt a strange calm come over her as the fog of emotion began to lift from her mind.

Knowing that she was likely being watched, Alice didn't move for a long time from her crossed legged position on the floor. Let them think she was done, that all the fight had been taken out of her.

Let Victoria think she'd won.

Eventually, Marco was once again taken out of the room to God only knew where.

Still, Alice sat on the floor, silent and thinking, when a man came into the room with a long hypodermic needle and opened the cage door. Alice sprang at him, ignoring the pain that shot through her body from her injuries. She tackled him and he tried to throw her off, but Alice pinned him too well for that. Grabbing a tray off the table in front of her, Alice smashed it over and over into the man's head until his arms stopped moving.

Her muscles were slow to wake up and she felt tight all

over, especially in her chest. Taking several deep breaths, Alice ran at half-speed down the hall. As she neared the door that led to Victoria's office, she could hear music and applause.

Everything has already started.

Ready to take on whoever might be there, Alice burst into Victoria's office, only to find it empty. She realized that all the enhanced goons were at the tour. She had no idea how many Victoria had at her disposal, but even a handful could do some serious damage. And with Lionel and Marco thrown into the mix it could be a bloodbath.

———

By the time she got to the end of the next hallway, her muscles had loosened, but her head and chest still ached. Skidding to a stop just before the door that led out into the foyer, Alice forced herself to push the pain aside. She could hear someone speaking, and occasional applause.

Then, cutting it all short, dozens of blood-curdling screams.

Alice burst out of the door and heard a loud, wheezing voice come through the speakers.

"Welcome, leaders of Jet City!"

Descending the steps, gas mask gleaming, black and red suit impeccably tailored, was Phantasm.

Alice hung back, not wanting to be noticed just yet. The screaming had died down a little, all eyes on Phantasm as she stood surveying the crowd.

"I'm sorry, Mrs. Veran couldn't make it today, she is indisposed. So, I thought my associates and I could stand in her place."

"What do you want?"

Alice recognized Uncle Logan's voice and felt her stomach drop. She had asked them to be here, but the thought of everyone she loved in harm's way terrified Alice.

"Why, to get rid of you. I thought that was obvious. Shadow Master, if you'd be so kind?"

Marco appeared behind Phantasm, his eyes completely black, a blank expression on his face, as if he were dead inside. He raised his hands and dark, spiraling shadows began building around Jet City's leaders.

Alice stared in shock. It was horrifying and amazing, a writhing mass of nightmares that stretched to the vaulted ceiling. People howled in terror, running and pushing one another out of the way in a chaotic panic as they tried to escape the shadows.

Gritting her teeth against her own fear, Alice ran up to the first goon she saw. She swept his legs out from under him and kicked him in the face. He fell too easily to be enhanced, yet he had the same blank look of the others. Alice felt relief that not every one of them would be difficult to over power.

Darting into the thick of it, she saw Marco now standing at the foot of the stairs.

"Shadow! Stop this!"

He turned toward her slowly, not really seeing her. A spiral of dark power shot from his hands and Alice's mind was plunged into a cold, oily lake of horror. It was so sudden and complete that every shred of self-control was stripped, and she screeched.

She fell to her knees in the midst of the dead reaching for her. The cries of those she loved as they were tormented echoed in her ears and everything was dark. Through all of this, she could see a glimmer of something.

A door.

Her heart beat fast and her chest ached so bad that Alice struggled for breath, a ball of panic starting to build in her throat. She had to calm down, but everywhere she looked were horrors more real than anything she'd ever seen in the light of day. Fears she didn't even know she had were clawing against her fragile courage.

Alice backed away until she was against something solid, but still, hands reached for her. Moaning voices, full of vitriol and fear beat against her brain.

"Calm down, calm down," she said. "They're not real."

She squealed as something brushed against her arm and disappeared.

"Not...real..."

Closing her eyes was one of the hardest things she'd ever done, but if she was going to find that door into Marco's mind, Alice knew she had to calm down. The voices and screams from people all around her, both real and imagined, kept barging through her concentration. But, finally, she could see the door again. She walked toward it, her motions like that of someone in a dream: terribly slow, and then speeding up unnaturally.

At last she was there, but no matter how she tried, her hands kept slipping off the handle.

"You're so weak you disgust me!" shouted a horrid caricature of Marco. "Frightened little girl up a tree! You put on that costume to do what? Keep the nightmares at bay? Beat up your daddy?" She took a swipe at him and he disappeared, though his mocking laughter surrounded her.

It took three more tries before she could get the door open, and when she did Alice gaped at what she saw.

It was Marco's childhood home, the place she'd felt safest in all the world. Except it was a complete wreck.

The wall paper was ripped to shreds, lights blinked on and off, the floors that had gleamed with polish were dull and cracked. Pictures that had hung proudly on the walls, lay in smashed heaps on the floor. A gloom, deeper than midnight without a moon, filled the house. There was a feeling of menace and terrible loneliness in every shadow.

The smell of burned food permeated the place, turning Alice's stomach.

In the distance, Alice could still hear the screams of the people in the Science Foundation, but in the house, there was a louder sound. A mewling, frightened cry, like that of a child.

"Marco?" she called, her voice echoing strangely.

She walked down the hall, stepping over ripped books and broken glass until she was in the kitchen doorway.

The sound of crying was louder here, but it sounded distorted as well, like a warped record.

Alice looked into the kitchen and felt tears burn her eyes. The striped wallpaper hung in tattered ribbons. Glass from the windows littered the floor, along with moldy food and the remnants of the worn table and chairs where she'd eaten cookies and learned bits of Italian. The stove and countertops were covered in a thick layer of dust, while the cupboard doors hung askew or were missing completely. Plates and cups were scattered in broken bits all over.

She walked around the refuse, trying to push aside the grief she felt at the destruction of one of the few refuges she'd ever known.

There was always bread or something baking in here. The smell of roses and herbs underneath it, like a hearth-witches' kitchen.

As if summoned by her memory, the exact smell filled her nostrils, and Alice could swear she saw the stove heat up.

The crying became louder and Alice walked around the kitchen, searching for the sound. At last she found the source: Marco, curled up in a ball inside one of the bottom kitchen cupboards.

A chill filled the room, and what little light there was started to disappear.

Marco cried harder.

She knelt down and tried to touch him but, like in a dream, he was close and still too far away.

Alice didn't know how, but she knew that in order to break the hold of whatever Victoria had done to him, she had to get through to this Marco.

"It's okay," she said, "you can trust me."

Marco wouldn't look at her, and just curled tighter in on himself.

She looked around the wreck of a kitchen and remembered the way Marco used to love helping his mother cook.

"She'd stand there," she said, looking at the cracked, filthy sink. "And wash the dishes while you mixed eggs or—"

Alice stopped as the sink transformed into the white, clean place it had been when Mrs. Mayer was there. A distant echo of someone humming made her smile in spite of herself. And for that moment, Marco's cries lessened.

"You...you and me and Lionel, we'd sit at this table. It was covered with a faded green table cloth...forget-me-nots embroidered around the bottom. And we'd talk and... and...you'd always have a book, and a pitcher of milk."

The shattered table became the warm brown, sturdy one she remembered. With the cloth, book and milk appearing like she'd conjured it. A warm light infiltrated the gloom of the room. The smell of cookies filled the space.

"The curtains were always starched and clean, and even though they were faded, I thought they were so beautiful."

The windows repaired, perfectly starched green and white curtains fluttering in a breeze. "And the breeze was scented with—"

"Rosemary and lavender and roses," Marco said, his voice stiff and hoarse.

She looked at him, now kneeling on the gleaming linoleum floor, though not looking at her.

"And your mother taught you to cook, at the stove."

He nodded. "Marinara…bread…"

The stove and counter tops were suddenly clean, a welcoming heat rolling off the stove as a pot of marinara bubbled, the warm smell of bread mixing with that of the garden. Warm light filled the room now, spreading over the wooden cupboards and into the hallway.

Alice looked up and saw Marco standing at the back door, wearing brown pants and a white shirt. His eyes were closed, tears flowing down his cheeks. She walked up beside him and slipped her hand in his.

"Home," he whispered.

"Home…"

Sunlight filled the yard beyond the door and Alice could see her tree, could glimpse the box where she used to hide her books. Somewhere, three children were laughing.

Marco held her hand tighter. "Home. Safe."

"Yes," she said, reaching up to turn his face to her, "but, it's time to wake up."

"No…" He shook his head. "I want to stay here…with you."

"We can't, not right now. But later…we can come back."

"Promise?"

"Yes."

Marco sighed, brown eyes taking in the kitchen. She took one last look with him, remembering the warmth and safety that filled every corner of the room.

When she looked up at Marco, there was more peace than she'd seen on his face in many years. He smiled at her.

"Alright," he said.

Alice gasped and opened her eyes. She was on her hands and knees in the foyer of the Science Foundation. The dark cloud that curled around her and retreated to Marco, who was lying unconscious on the floor in front of her. She started to crawl toward him when another sound, familiar and yet frightening, rose above the din of terrified screams.

Lionel, in a very good replica of his Steel costume, roared as he charged into the midst of the people. He picked up a nearby man in a pinstripe suit and threw him against the wall. The man's head snapped back in such a way that Alice knew he was dead.

People were shoving each other in their panic to escape. A crowd was around the door, people climbing over each other, while others were banging on windows.

She caught sight of Uncle Logan and, of all people, Oona, fighting hand-to-hand with some of the goons. If Miss Jones was there, she was either where Alice couldn't see her or in disguise. Rose was also nowhere to be found, though Alice was fairly certain she was there somewhere. It was only a matter of time before they encountered one of the enhanced men, or Lionel.

Alice felt exhaustion tearing into her skull, a dull throb behind her eyes, but she was the only one who could reach Lionel before he killed anyone else. If she could reach him, then together they could get her uncle and the others out of here.

C'mon, time to move!

Her body wouldn't respond at first, but after a few more moments, she pushed herself up.

And came face-to-face with Baritone.

"I've been waiting for this," he grinned, the scar under his eye patch deepening.

He threw a punch, and Alice lunged to the side, successfully dodging but also falling to the floor. When she jumped to her feet, Baritone was taking his sweet time sauntering up to her. The fact that he acted as if she weren't a threat made Alice furious. She let loose a yell and punched him in the groin.

When he doubled over in shock, she noticed that he had her batons hanging from his belt.

If I can get those back I can stop Lionel.

"You like these?" he snarled. "Come and get them if you can."

Alice smiled at him, though really it was more of a grimace. Her whole body hurt, and she was suddenly grateful for every torturous training session Miss Jones had put her through.

Baritone advanced on her, punching with his right and left in quick succession. She dodged both punches, ducked down and landed a solid blow to his solar plexus. He gasped, staggering back. Falling forward into a handstand, Alice wrapped her legs around Baritone's neck and twisted her hips. It threw him off balance and he fell hard onto the marble floor.

Her ankles tightened around his neck, and he punched her thigh in desperation for air. The hit made her muscles cramp, and she groaned in pain as she kept the pressure on his throat. Finally, his movements slowed and she let go. Snatching up her batons, she gave him a generous jolt of electricity just to be sure he was out for a while.

Taking two gulping breaths, she stumbled into the panicked crowd.

CHAPTER TWENTY-EIGHT

It was almost impossible to get through the press of terrified bodies. A few of the guests even tried to attack her, fearful of her cowl. She shoved them aside, doing as little damage as possible.

A man stumbled into her path and fell, clutching his face. Alice helped him to his feet and realized it was her uncle. Blood streamed from his nose and his eye was starting to bruise. In front of them, Oona landed a solid side kick to a goon beside her, and then pivoted to deliver a jumping front kick, knocking the man out.

"You really do have a type," Alice said to her uncle.

"Get Lionel," he said, ignoring her comment. "Let us hold some of these back for you."

"Some of them are enhanced, be careful."

He squeezed her arm. "You, too."

Phantasm was still standing on the wide staircase, her wheezing voice directing her minions above the screams of the crowd.

Alice glared up at her, and had a moment's temptation to rush for her when Lionel's growling yell sounded above everything. She cast one last look at Phantasm and could feel Victoria's grin of triumph behind the gas mask.

I have to get Lionel, he's the immediate threat. I'll deal with her after.

Though no one was affected by anything like Fantasy gas, the crowd had been whipped into a panicked frenzy. Anyone that looked different, like Alice did in her cowl, was suspect as evil. Alice had to stun a few of the guests with her baton when they tried to attack her.

As Alice worked her way toward Lionel, she saw Rose, or who she thought was Rose.

Black gloves with gauntlets encased her hands, she wore a tight black body suit under a thick chest piece. The strangest part was the helmet-like cowl she wore. It covered her neck, head and face, though Alice could just see a hint of Rose beneath it all before she took out one of the guards.

She's got this. They all do. Time to do my job now.

Alice ducked as someone threw a baton at her and sprinted toward Lionel, dodging the people who were trying to escape his rage. At last she was near enough to talk to him.

"Stop! You don't want to do this!"

He turned toward her with a snarl, his eyes alive with blood lust.

Alice ducked under his arm when he took a swing at her and rammed a baton into his side. He roared with pain. She thought it would be enough to drop him, but Lionel grabbed the baton from her hands, and tossed it aside. His breath came out in heaves from his spittle-covered mouth as he tried to backhand her.

The sound of glass shattering blocked out everything else as the windows were blown out. People screamed in terror, bunching together even more than they had been.

She looked up and saw Phantasm rush off to a doorway

under the staircase. One of the goons was carrying a still unconscious Marco behind her. Alice jumped up, wanting to run after them but knowing she had to deal with Lionel first.

"This is the police! We are here to help!" said a voice from a megaphone. "Please, make your way carefully to the windows!"

Ignoring the instructions in their panic, people stampeded to the windows, crying and yelling for help. The swell of the crowd pushed against her, preventing her from getting very far and shoving her toward Lionel, who was still in a fury.

He picked up a woman running past him and snapped her neck, throwing her into two more people who fell under the panicked crowds feet.

Alice shoved a young man out of the way as Lionel took a swing at him. The blow glanced off her shoulder, but it was enough to cause pain to shoot down her arm.

As the crowd around them thinned, Alice dodged two more punches. Falling to her knees under a kick from Lionel's massive foot, she somersaulted behind him and rammed her other baton into his back, and then into his neck, until Lionel fell to his knees.

After taking many gasping breaths, sweat dripping off his face, Lionel staggered to his feet and shook his head, as if to dislodge something. His jaw clenched and Alice could see the shock in his eyes when he turned to her.

"You…you're alive?" he said, his fingertips brushing her bruised cheek. "And you're hurt."

"I'm fine."

He stared at her as if he were seeing her for the first time, tears falling down his face.

"Lionel," she said. "We have to move. You can't stay here."

He looked around as if confused.

"Where's Marco? Is he alright?"

"I don't know, Victoria took him through a doorway under the stairs. Do you have any idea where she might have taken him?"

"Probably her lab. C'mon."

***

Lionel took off at a sprint and Alice tried to keep up, but she stumbled when they got to the door. Concern clenched his guts with an iron fist. What he'd seen and felt was still too real, and if Alice was seriously injured, there was no way he wanted her following him into Phantasm's lair.

Lionel ran his eyes down her face and body, taking in her bruises and the blood on her suit.

His jaw tightened.

"What did they do to you?"

"I'll be fine, I'm just a little slower than usual."

Lionel studied her. "You sure?"

Alice nodded. "Let's go."

It was hard to push aside the memory of her dying in his arms, even harder to cast aside the fear that it might still happen. But time was of the essence and if they didn't hurry, Phantasm would escape with Marco.

God only knows what she'll do to him.

Lionel pulled open a door marked "Danger, no admittance!" so hard the hinges groaned. A blaring alarm sounded when they stepped over the threshold and into a narrow corridor with flashing lights. They ran down and around a corner before meeting any of Phantasm's men.

Two goons rushed toward them and Lionel didn't hesitate. Pulling back his fist, he hit the first man so hard that he lifted off the ground. For a split second, Lionel was shocked by the power of his punch, then he grinned, feeling like himself for the first time in a week. Strength coursed through him, every muscle in his body alive as if electrified.

Another man was running toward him, teeth bared and a baton in his hands. The man swung the weapon at Lionel. He blocked with one arm, barely feeling the contact. While the minion stared in surprise, Lionel seized him by the front of his shirt and rammed the man's head into the ceiling. The baton clattered to the floor.

Lionel looked over to see Alice finishing off the last man.

They stood at the ready, waiting for more. But when nothing happened, Lionel took the lead and they ran down the hallway, into a brightly lit L-shaped room that looked like some kind of lab.

"I've walked past this room but..." Lionel looked around for the hallway he was familiar with and saw it through the windows on the other side of the room. "There, that's the hallway I remember."

They made into the hallway just in time to see Phantasm and her men carrying a barely conscious Marco.

"Delay them," Phantasm wheezed, and two men broke off from their little group, running toward the heroes.

My cure is down this hall to the left but she's taking Marco to the right and...Damn it!

Lionel grit his teeth and dodged a blow by one of the goons. He remembered what Alice had told him about the risks in taking his cure and flinched internally.

The punch he delivered to the man's face wasn't that hard from Lionel's perspective but he flew across the hall and slammed into opposite wall.

He'd meant what he'd said about not wanting to live with all that uncontrollable rage, but he hadn't realized until now what a loss not having his powers had been. A sense of being whole again permeated his mind and body. If he lost his strength again, it would be like living without a limb. He'd get used to it sure, but there would always be that phantom pain where a part of him had once been.

He looked down at his hands, dried blood on the knuckles and remembered what he'd done to those innocent people just a few minutes ago.

The goon he'd punched caught his eye. He lay unconscious on the floor, blood flowing from his nose, jaw at an awkward angle.

That wasn't even all the strength I have, maybe not even half. Is it right to sacrifice the lives of others if I lose control just so I can keep these powers?

Lionel knew the answer.

A sense of loss coupled with peace settled on him as Alice knocked out the last man. This was right, even if it was unfair.

"C'mon let's go," she wiped blood from her split lip.

He stared down at his hands and swallowed.

"Lionel? You okay?"

"Yeah," he said, "I'm alright. We have to make a little detour up here. At the end of the hall, we're going left."

She opened her mouth to question him but Lionel took off. He didn't want her to know, Alice would try to talk him out of it, and Lionel couldn't have that.

They bolted down the new hallway. Alice started to limp, though she had a stubborn set to her jaw that Lionel knew very well. She was going to see this through to the end, even if it killed her.

And I'm not going to let it.

"This room," he said, kicking the door down and triggering another alarm.

"Lionel, this doesn't look like—"

He ran forward and yanked open the locked cold storage. With Alice staring in shock, Lionel pulled a huge needle out of the box Victoria had shown him and plunged it into his arm.

"Lionel! What...? No," she rushed toward him before he could press the plunger. "Stop! That—"

"I have to! Please Alice. This…I have to."

Before she could respond he depressed the plunger. The serum was warm, like a perfect bath, at first. But after a few seconds and Lionel swore someone had immersed him in flames. He groaned, his hands bending the metal table with the strength of his grip. His world had become a hell of constant, building pain.

"Oh my God, Lionel!" Alice said, her hands around his face. "Look at me."

He did, her bruised, beautiful face swimming in front of him. Even though he was taking huge, gulping breaths, Lionel still felt like he couldn't breath.

I'm going to die.

The fire in his veins built and the world went black for a second. He screamed so hard that he could feel his vocal cords shredding. Then, when Lionel knew he could bear no more, the fire began to cool. Breath returned to his lungs and he could feel Alice's hands on his face.

"Are you alright?" she whispered.

"I think so," he said, wiping tears from his eyes, discarding his mask in the process. "That…was awful."

"I can only imagine. You rest here, I'll go get Marco."

"What? No, I'm coming with you."

"But, if you get hurt, you won't heal."

He reached down and tore the leg off the metal table he'd bent just a few minutes ago.

"I don't think it's taken effect yet." He forced a grin. "Let's use the little time we have before it does."

She opened her mouth to respond and closed it.

"Just…be careful."

He planted a quick kiss on her forehead and began to walk out of the room.

"Her private lab is down this hall, all the way to the end. It's two rooms and the good news is that this is the only way to get out, so she's definitely in there."

"I'm taking point."

"I'm not made of glass suddenly."

"Not negotiable."

He waved her in front of him.

They were a foot away from the door when out ran two, blank eyed minions.

"How many does she have?" Alice asked, her voice filled with frustration.

One drew a knife, and slashed at Alice's head. She used the baton to block it, and then kicked him in the stomach. He showed little reaction to the blow and drew another blade, jabbing it toward her middle.

Lionel intercepted the knife, feeling the tip pierce his forearm before he snapped the man's wrist.

The second man charged for Lionel, slamming two quick, strong punches to Lionel's midsection. He felt the blows more so than the others he'd received today, but it still wasn't so bad.

He drove his fist into the goon's face, feeling the bones of his nose crunch. The man stepped back, but otherwise didn't react at all.

Time to get a little rough.

Lionel feinted a punch to the man's face and drove his foot down on the kneecap instead. It gave under the might of Lionel's power and the goon fell to the ground.

Not holding back, Lionel kicked him in the head, and the goon was out.

Alice was still fighting the other one, her face bleeding at the cheek and her limp more pronounced.

He was about to step in and help when she rammed her electrified baton into the man's groin and neck at the same time. The goon shook as Alice forced strong electrical charges through his body. Finally, she pulled back and the man fell to the ground, unmoving.

"Well those things are scary," Lionel said.

Alice grinned at him.

"Ready?"

He nodded and pulled the door open, letting Alice go first in spite of his better judgment.

Lionel had only been in this room once at the beginning of his stay at the Foundation. When he'd visited, the room had been lit so bright, it almost hurt his eyes. Now, the lighting was dim, and what little there was glinted off shiny lab equipment, filing cabinets with pad locks and a giant refrigerator. Tables were clean to the point of polished, and everything had a sanitized smell that itched his nose. But there was no sign of Marco.

"Where could she be?" Alice asked.

Lionel looked to the far side of the room and saw a door he didn't recognize.

"That might've been covered up the last time I was here," he said, pointing to it.

As they approached the door, sweat dripped down Lionel's back and chest. A tight feeling began in his stomach and suddenly his muscles cramped. He gasped and doubled over.

That's when he noticed blood on his forearm where the blade had pierced.

That should've healed by now…I must be losing my powers already. Damn it!

"Lionel?"

His gave her a tight smile as the pain ebbed. "It's passing, but I think we should hurry."

"You should stay here."

"Like hell I will!"

"Lionel—"

"He's my best friend, and I'm not sending you in there alone. I'll be okay, really."

She stared at him, took a deep breath and opened the door.

The lights in this room were blazin, the furniture spare and almost monk-like. Not at all what Lionel had come to associate with Victoria's tastes. It was a huge space, with dozens more filing cabinets, a desk on the far side with neat stacks of papers and pens. In the center of the room, tied to a chair and gagged, was Marco.

And beside him—

"Welcome!" said Victoria.

Gone was the gas mask and fedora, but the perfectly tailored suit remained. Everything refined and elegant about her now appeared as cold and hard as the light glinting off the gun she held.

"A gun? Not really your style," Lionel said, doubling over again with a sudden sharp pain in his chest.

Victoria's smile widened. "You found your cure. Have you figured out the surprise yet?"

"Yes," he gasped, standing upright again. "You're a miserable—"

"Now, now," she pressed the gun to Marco's temple, "you wouldn't want me to kill him before he has the chance to see you beg, would you?"

Marco's eyes burned with hate as he looked at Victoria. His fingers kept twitching, little tendrils of power sneaking out and retreating again.

She must've neutered him too.

"What did you do to him?" Alice snarled.

Victoria held up a small syringe.

"It's amazing what science can give us, if only we work hard enough to unlock its mysteries. I wanted a way to suppress mental abilities, and just a few weeks ago my scientists came up with this little beauty. Don't know how long it will last, but at least long enough for our purposes here."

"What do you want, Victoria?" Alice asked, and began to ease herself closer.

"A better world. To protect us from ourselves. And from people like these two, who could wipe us all out if they had the inclination."

"You know who you sound like, don't you?" Lionel said, and started to back up, drawing Victoria away from Marco.

Her face transformed into a mask of fury, as she advanced on Lionel, pointing the gun at him.

"I am nothing like him! I want to protect the weak and innocent! To give the world a peace that will last centuries, and those with a will to create and discover all the resources they could dream of. Hitler killed everything good in his path. I am nothing like him."

"And your children?" Lionel's voice was razor sharp, his words delivered like jabs. "The innocent children of Park Side? The fathers and mothers you've killed? How many of these people would call you a hero? How many would call you a monster? I bet Tony would."

"He was scared..." Her knuckles were white from gripping the gun. "After the accident—"

"That *you* caused. All for what? A failed experiment?"

Out of the corner of his eye, Lionel could see that had Alice made it to to the chair and was trying to get the straps off of Marco's wrists.

"It wasn't a failure. It produced something unexpected, something amazing," Victoria said, tears lighting up her eyes.

"You're insane."

"And you're weak! Influenced by a woman who—"

Before Lionel could distract her, Victoria looked over at Alice and swung the gun around to fire at her.

That nightmare he'd lived barely an hour ago came crashing into his mind: Alice, dead in his arms.

"No!"

Lionel lunged for Victoria, and grabbed her arm. With

his powers, Lionel could've easily over powered her, but all the blows he'd taken today came rushing back to his body, and Lionel was fighting not only against Victoria, but the building pain too.

Alice saw his struggle and ran up to help him. Before he could stop her, the gun went off.

.

The sound of the gun stopped Alice cold. She saw the look of complete shock on Lionel's face, and then the blossoming stain of red on his stomach. He fell to his knees and slumped over.

"No!" she screamed.

Victoria looked at her, surprise giving way to a sneer of triumph.

Molten fury coursed through Alice in an instant. With a roar, she charged at Victoria, who raised the gun at her.

Just before Victoria was able to get a shot off, Alice tackled her to the ground and knocked the gun from Victoria's grasp. With another shout, the vigilante rammed her fist into Victoria's face again and again. Victoria flailed about, raking her nails down the exposed part of Alice's cheek.

She screamed and pummeled Victoria again, blood bursting from the woman's nose. Victoria growled and managed to roll them both to the side, and then pin Alice under her. The villain's long fingers clutched Alice's throat and squeezed. Black spots started to appear in her vision, her throat burned. Victoria's enhanced strength would make short work of this. Alice had to do something.

"You have been a nuisance for long enough," Victoria spat. "I hoped to have you watch them both die, but I'll settle for one."

"Who says...I'm dead?"

Lionel's punch was sloppy and weak, but it was enough to knock Victoria off Alice's chest. He dropped to the floor, as Victoria scrambled toward the gun and Alice dove for it, coughing and gasping for air.

Their hands touched the weapon at the same time, propelling it further out of reach. Victoria punched Alice in the face and crawled after the gun. Pain shot into Alice's already swollen eye, but she overcame it. With a desperate scramble, Alice latched onto Victoria's ankle. She yanked on the villain, but couldn't budge her.

Giving Victoria's foot a vicious twist, Alice heard the ankle pop and her adversary screeched with pain. The vigilante half-crawled, half-ran toward the gun just as Victoria made a frantic lunge for it. An instant later, Alice's fingers curled around the butt and she spun round to face Victoria. Slowly, they both stood. Alice raised the gun, pressing the barrel to Victoria's sweaty forehead.

All the things she'd lost to this woman came crashing into her mind.

Her aunt.

Lionel, and Marco.

She saw the burned and mutilated bodies of Park Side, the broken bodies in the foyer.

The trust she'd placed in her, the symbol of strength Victoria had once been.

"Well?" Victoria hissed.

"Alice," Marco called out, pulling the last of his restraints off, "put the gun down."

Alice's eyes filled with tears. "Everything she's done..."

"But you're better than her, you're different."

Alice pressed the gun harder onto Victoria's head. The anger was so bright, so simple. One bullet, and this vile woman would be gone. No one else need ever be hurt by her.

"I could end it all, right now..."

Her finger tightened on the trigger, but still she hesitated.

"You want to make the world better, but you're not willing to do what's necessary," Victoria said, hate burning in her eyes.

"Kill you?"

"No, let me go. There's a far greater threat coming for you if you don't."

"Alice—" Marco's voice pleaded.

"What does that mean?" Alice asked through clenched teeth.

"There's someone out there who will turn your world into ruin. You made a mistake with Park Side, and look how many died. Don't make another, bigger mistake here."

Her words chilled Alice and her body began to tremble.

"And you will stop them?"

"Yes, I'm the only one who can."

"What about us, you'll just leave us alone?"

"Of course not. But don't heroes sacrifice themselves for the innocent?"

Heroes…I'm a hero…

She remembered what she'd said to Simon, the things that Mrs. Frost had said to her, and the look on every person's face she'd just saved. Alice knew she'd messed up plenty in her search for vengeance, but she also knew that even in her imperfection and anger, she had tried to act like a hero.

And heroes aren't perfect.

"I'll die for this city and those I love," Alice said, lowering the gun. "But not by surrendering to you."

"Weak! Insufferable—"

Alice hit Victoria across the face with the butt of the weapon, taking no small amount of satisfaction from the action. As Victoria crumpled to the floor, Alice tossed the gun aside.

Marco's arms reached out for her, but before she could fall into them, Alice heard Lionel whispering her name.

"Oh, my God."

She stumbled to where he'd fallen. A moment later, Marco knelt on the other side of their best friend.

"Alice..." Lionel smiled weakly.

His face was ashen and there was so much blood coming from his stomach wound that it was starting to pool under him. Alice took his large hand between her small ones, forcing a smile on her lips as tears fell down her cheeks.

"I'll get help," Marco said.

"No!" Lionel latched onto Marco's wrist, tears lighting up his eyes. "I-I'm...scared. Marco, I'm so scared."

Marco looked up at Alice in panic.

"Whatever she gave me..."

"Please?" Lionel asked. "Please, just...help me?"

Marco closed his eyes and Alice held her breath. At first, nothing happened and she was afraid Marco wouldn't be able to take away Lionel's fear. Then tiny tendrils of black seeped from his fingers. They went out and retreated several times before flowing from him and caressing Lionel's body. Alice could see the fear being taken from him, bit by bit, until his face relaxed, an eerie peace coming over him.

Lionel's lips spread in a slow grin and he reached up, fingers grazing Alice's cheek.

"Lemme see you?" Lionel asked.

"This is my fault," Alice said as she slipped her cowl back.

"No," Lionel said. "My choice...you're not the only... stubborn one here."

Alice smiled and Lionel ran his thumb slowly over her lips, as if trying to memorize her face.

"I don't regret my choice," he said. "Except...I wanted

to see what it would be like...being able to kiss you...hold you...every day. It's not fair...We were just...getting started."

"Don't talk like that. You have to hold on, you have to fight."

"She's right," Marco said. "We're together again, the three of us. You can't miss that."

"I'm sorry." His face twisted in pain.

Alice squeezed his hand.

"Breathe, it's going to be alright. Just...keep breathing."

Lionel began to relax, but it was as if that jolt of pain had drained whatever strength was left. His eyes were glassy, his smile slow to return. Alice felt Lionel's fingers wind slowly around hers.

"Do you...remember our...first kiss?"

Alice smiled at the memory of that night so long ago in her childhood bedroom. A scared girl with pigtails and a little boy with scuffed shoes. "Yes."

Lionel gave her hand a little tug and Alice leaned down, placing a light kiss on his lips.

He sighed. "Till next...we meet...sweet."

"No, no, stay with me," she said. "You have to fight. This isn't the end, we've got so much to do. You haven't even seen – Lionel? Lionel!"

He'd closed his eyes, his massive chest still.

Someone came running in through the door, yelling their name but the only thing Alice could hear was the ringing in her head.

Marco sobbed, rocking back and forth on his knees and she grabbed his hands, needing their sold warmth to anchor her.

They were both stretched over Lionel's still body, weeping uncontrollably, when strong hands started to pull her out of the way.

"No! I won't leave him!" She struggled but it was no use.

The next thing she knew, Gerald was there, shoving Marco out of the way.

"He's dead," Marco's voice cracked on the words.

Gerald's face hardened in thought and he closed his eyes.

Marco came to her and they held one another, sobs wracking their bodies.

When Gerald opened his eyes, sweat was pouring down his forehead and he was gasping for air.

"Was he...did you?" Marco asked.

Gerald looked up at them and sighed.

CHAPTER TWENTY-NINE

Weak sunlight filtered in through the gauzy curtains and into Lionel's closed eyes. His entire body felt like one giant bruise, especially his stomach where the bullet had lodged itself.

Patchy memories of being shot and falling unconscious flew through his mind.

No...not unconscious but not dead. Damn close but not... what happened?

His hand moved, searching for something and finding soft cool sheets, a thick blanket and flesh. When he flexed his left hand, Lionel could feel the ring Maria had given him, still wrapped around his pinkie finger.

"Lionel?" said Alice, her voice filled with relief.

Slow and hesitantly, Lionel opened his eyes. Like the rest of his body, they hurt. The sockets felt dry and when the light hit his retinas it felt like knives were being driven straight through them. His eyes snapped shut with a groan.

He felt the bed move and heard the curtains being closed.

"It's darker now," she said.

He opened his eyes once again, his vision fuzzy at first.

Eventually, Alice's face came into focus. When it did, Lionel reached up a shaking hand to touch her cheek, soft light from a nearby lamp casting a warm glow around her worried face. Lionel swore he'd never seen anything more beautiful.

"I…" he winced. His throat was too dry to talk.

"Here," she handed him a glass of water with a straw and helped him sit up.

He gasped in pain as his stomach muscles moved, but thirst drove him past it. After gulping down the entire glass, Lionel put his back onto full, soft pillows and looked at the woman next to him.

Her hair fell in wavy, dark curtains down to her shoulders. Bright blue eyes looked him over, as if in search of further injury.

"Alice," he said, the word like honey on his tongue.

She looked up and met his eyes, a dimpled smile his reward.

"You are a right bastard for scaring us all like that."

"I won't do it again. Cross my heart," he said, doing just that. "I assume, Gerald healed me?"

Alice shifted on the bed so that she was sitting on her legs, a frown wrinkling her forehead.

"It's a bit complicated actually."

"How?"

"Well, the serum did take your powers like we thought it would but for whatever reason, your healing powers have started coming back. Gerald did save your life, if he'd been a second later…but in the last few days, the healing that's going on has been all you."

Lionel stared at her, mind reeling.

"Days…it's been…how long?"

"Almost a week."

His eyes widened.

"I…have so many questions."

"And there's a lot to tell you. But first, do you feel any of your other powers returning?"

"Get me something strong, something you don't mind getting broken," he said.

Alice handed him an ashtray from the bed side table. It was heavy, perhaps an expensive marble of some kind. He grasped it on either side with both hands and tried to break it in half.

It didn't budge an inch.

He tried again.

Nothing.

"I'm sorry Lionel," she whispered, taking the ashtray from his limp hands.

"No it's...At least I'm alive. But why my healing powers?" he asked.

"Gerald doesn't know. Maybe they were the first ones your body manifested so they were the strongest?"

Lionel ran a hand through his hair, words escaping him.

When he'd been shot, Lionel knew that would likely be it for him, and he'd made peace with it as much as he could.

Now, here he was, sitting beside Alice, days after it all and he had his healing abilities but nothing else.

"Are you alright?" she asked, holding his hand.

"I have no idea."

She nodded.

"I could get you something to eat. Marco has been cooking up a storm downstairs. He delayed his flight back because...well, there's been a lot to handle since the attack and he...he wanted to stay."

Lionel looked up a her, hearing so much in what she wasn't saying.

Alice's eyes were down cast, watching her index finger trace the patterns in the blanket, and her bottom lip was caught in her teeth.

"What is it?" Lionel asked.

She hesitated, closing her eyes and Lionel's gut dropped.

"You're still recovering," she said.

"Yeah but I want to know. What's going on?"

"That's a very complicated question."

"Start at what's happened since the attack. Was Victoria arrested?'

"Yes, she's being held in a maximum security psych wing until the DA and her attorney can work out a deal of some kind. The police found all the evidence they needed to charge her with involvement in the Park Side Massacre, and for being Phantasm, which comes with dozens of other charges. We'll see if any of it ends up sticking but...public opinion is pretty much screaming for a conviction so maybe there's hope."

He grinned at her.

"You did it. You got her."

She smiled back and Lionel's heart swelled. God she was beautiful!

"*We* did it, all three of us. Together for one last mission."

Some of the joy melted from her expression and Lionel frowned.

"Wait, why does it have to be the last?"

The door opened and Marco peeked around the corner. When his eyes fell on Lionel, he muttered something under his breath and grinned.

Lionel felt Alice fidget next to him, her eyes lighting up at the sight of Marco.

"You," Marco said, walking over and sitting at the foot of the bed, "are a lucky bastard."

Lionel grinned at him.

"That goes without saying. How are you, after...well, whatever she did to you?"

Marco swallowed.

"It's been hard. I'm having nightmares of the whole thing so...Well, I'm staying at the back of the house so I don't lash out at anyone with my powers in my sleep."

"I'm sorry," Lionel said. "Nothing permanent though?"

"Gerald doesn't think so but who knows?"

"So, why was this mission our last?"

Marco and Alice glanced at each other and Lionel felt like he was about to explode.

"A lot of reasons," Marco said, "but for you it's because the city thinks you're dead."

Lionel stared at the two of them, eyes wide in disbelief.

"Excuse me?"

"We did our best to hide your identity when the police came in," Alice said, the words coming out in a rush, "but someone still managed to see your face and let it slip that Steel was none other than Lionel Lawson. Uncle Logan tried to kill the story, saying it was hearsay but it didn't work."

"Since you were seen socially with Victoria prior to the attack on the Science Foundation, and because you... uh...you-."

"Killed some people, " Lionel finished, the words choking him.

"Yeah. They were going to issue a warrant for your arrest, but Gerald has a connection in the coroners office who faked your death certificate. If not for that, they'd be looking for you right now."

"We're so sorry," Alice said. "I tried to use my lawyer on this one but with the outcry around Victoria, there's no way we could see to get you out of it."

"So you told everyone I was dead?"

"It was Gerald's idea," Marco said. "He asked for a body bag, we got you inside and because he was a doctor no one questioned it when he took your body."

"This is the only safe place we could think of," Alice

said. "No one in their right mind would try to raid the Frost mansion without rock solid proof that you were here and alive, which they won't get."

"And with the funeral arrangements Alice and Logan are making, the illusion is starting to take hold with the police. I only escaped arrest because they found proof that Victoria had drugged Shadow Master."

Lionel fidgeted with the pinkie ring as his mind struggled to process all of this. His whole life was over. Never again would he walk down the street on a summer night. He could never fight beside Alice and Marco, or stick around and just be a part of their every day lives.

He looked over at Alice, her eyes full of grief. Losing her was the worst pain of all. The thought of somehow building a life with her had been a vain hope until the last month when it had seemed that maybe, just maybe, he'd win.

I wish that it had just stayed an impossible thing, beyond my reach instead of almost mine. Then maybe it wouldn't hurt so much.

"I wish there had been another way," Alice said.

"We thought about just having you skip town," Marco said, "but Logan said the chief would likely work with the FBI to coordinate a man hunt. We didn't want you going through that."

"So…" he took a deep breath. "I'm dead then."

Marco and Alice nodded, giving him space to take it in.

"I…I guess I've got to find a place to live, a new identity—"

"I've got someone working on that right now," Alice said.

"You've got…? How? You have a spy network I don't know about?"

She chuckled.

"No, but I have someone who's frighteningly good at this sort of thing. She needs a few days to work it all out, which gives you time to decide where you'd like to go so she can arrange transportation."

Her voice broke a little at the end and Lionel reached for her hand. Then he saw Marco wiping tears from his face and grabbed his hand, too.

None of them said anything for several minutes. They all knew that these were precious times, the last they'd have all together for a very, very long time.

Maybe ever.

"I missed you both so much," he said, tears running down his face.

"We missed you, too," Alice said.

"I'm sorry," Marco said, wiping his eyes. "I tried to find your cure and I-"

"Stop, just stop. No one could've done more. Marco you're my brother, blood or not. And I know you did everything short of dying to get me that cure."

Marco shook his head.

"I just wish things could be different."

"Me, too," Lionel said, "but...we play the hand we're dealt, don't we?"

Alice nodded, wiping tears from her eyes.

"At least Jet City will have the two of you," Lionel continued. "You'll keep the city safe and...maybe some day I can come back."

The tension that suddenly descended on the room was so thick Lionel felt suffocated by it.

Marco and Alice were doing their best not to look at one another.

"You're not staying are you?" he asked Marco.

"I...it's complicated."

Lionel looked between him and Alice. Saw the pain etched in both their faces and wondered why the hell Marco was leaving and why Alice didn't just ask him to stay.

"I should go check on dinner," Marco said, giving Lionel that smile he wore when the pain of wanting was just too much for him.

Alice watched him leave, a deep yearning in her gaze.

That's when something clicked into place for Lionel.

The times she resisted my kisses weren't just about anger. The look on her face when I told her that it was worth losing my powers if it meant being with her...She's not in love with me anymore. She's in love with Marco.

If he hadn't already lost her to being legally dead, Lionel was sure he'd feel like someone had gut punched him.

Or maybe it's because I know how long Marco's loved her and I just want them both to be happy...maybe this is how it should be. If I stay there's no way Marco would do a damn thing. So, if I can't be here to stand by their side, maybe by leaving I can still do something good for them.

It took a few minutes for Lionel to process all this, and he held Alice's hand the whole time. She was once again tracing the pattern of the blanket with her other hand, a wrinkle appearing above her nose as it always did when she was worried or deep in thought. He let himself indulge in a sweet kind of torture as he just look at her and took in the fierce beauty of this woman he'd loved his whole life.

I will always love you, Alice.

"Why haven't you told him?" he asked when he was sure his voice wouldn't break.

Alice's head snapped up, blue eyes wide.

"I don't—"

"I'm pretty sure I haven't got much time until I need to leave, so let's not waste it with lying. You love him. He's always loved you. So why haven't you told him?"

Alice swallowed convulsively and shook her head.

"He left. He only came back to help you, to finish the mission."

"No, he came back for you."

"You don't know what you're talking about."

"I do, actually. He's always stepped back where you and I were concerned, putting us above his own happiness because he thought it's what we needed. But we're not the same people that started all this and," he took a deep, steadying breath, "you don't love me anymore. If you ever did, the way you love him."

"Lionel, I did love you," she said, squeezing his hand, "but it changed, I changed. And…"

"It's okay. I want you to be happy. You would be happy with Marco."

"But he keeps himself so distant. I doubt he'd even believe me if I told him."

"Yeah, he's a stubborn one when it comes to not believing in his own worth. You're just going to have to find a way to convince him."

She laughed, a defensive, sad sound.

"Oh, is that all?"

"Hey," he said, making her look up at him, "you're pretty stubborn and resourceful when you want to be. You'll figure it out."

"Well, I don't have much time. He's leaving after the funeral."

"Which is when?"

"Why, thinking of attending?"

Lionel cringed.

"That would be weird."

"Yeah, no kidding. The funeral is in four days."

"Well, then, you have four days."

Alice looked down at their hands.

"I thought you'd be more upset."

"I'm crying on the inside."

He tried to make it a joke, but Alice's gaze shot up to his and Lionel knew he wasn't fooling her in the least.

"I heard something about dinner?" he asked, desperate to change the subject.

Alice's face relaxed, obviously relieved to not be talking about this anymore.

"Yeah, Marco is making cannoli, lasagna and chicken parmesan."

In response, Lionel's stomach growled loud and long. Alice's eyes widened before she dissolved into a symphony of laughter. Lionel joined her, not able to help it.

"I'll miss his cooking," he finally said.

"Do you have any idea where you might want to go?"

The low lamplight caught the gold of the pinkie ring and Lionel ran a finger over the design.

"Maybe."

CHAPTER THIRTY

Laughter echoed off the walls of the informal dining room from the people around the table. Half empty platters and baking dishes of Marco's mouth-watering food lay on the sideboard. Outside, a winter storm raged, splattering sleet against the windows.

Alice looked over at Rose and Marco on her right, a laugh bubbling out of her throat at their conversation.

"I am going to start charging you a repair fee," Rose said to Marco. "That suit came back and I almost cried it was so wrecked."

"What?" Marco replied with wide grin. "I beg to differ. And even if it was torn a bit—"

"A bit? I had to replace an entire side of the vest."

"I think a little leniency in the pursuit of justice is warranted."

Rose wagged a finger at him and took a sip of wine.

On Alice's left sat Lionel, in conversation with Gerald and Uncle Logan. She smiled at the sound of their voices, savoring the feeling of her family around her.

It was the night before Lionel's funeral, the last time they'd all be in the same room together, and Alice was doing her best to avoid the avalanche of loss that had been dogging her steps for the past three days.

We're burying the past in that empty coffin tomorrow. The good along with the bad.

Alice breathed through the iron grip that grief had on her heart. She had known this was coming, that the reunion between the three of them would be horribly brief. But no amount of preparation was enough to stave off the sorrow that was slowly taking her over.

As she sipped some iced tea, Miss Jones appeared in the door way and motioned for her to come out.

No...I don't want to.

She knew why Miss Jones was back from her trip and each step Alice took out of the room felt impossibly heavy.

When they'd gotten to Alice's private office and shut the door, Miss Jones handed her a large manila envelope.

"I was able to acquire passage for Mr. Lawson to the place he designated, along with all the necessary identification," Miss Jones said. "However, due to the sensitivity of all this and the secrecy, Mr. Lawson will have to leave tomorrow morning."

Alice took a sharp intake of breath and stepped back like she'd been struck.

"I'm sorry," Miss Jones continued, her eyes softening. "I know...I know what he means to you, but this was the only way."

"What time?" she asked.

"Two o'clock in the morning. He must go alone with me or my contacts will not do it."

Alice tried to breath but it came out in a sob. All her attempts to stifle the flood of emotions failed and she buried her face in her hands and wept. Somewhere in the midst of it all, strong arms came around her, and Alice was crying into a chest that smelled of newspaper ink and cigar smoke.

Uncle Logan didn't say a word, just held her until the tears slowed down and Alice could breath again.

When she looked up, Uncle Logan wiped her tears away with his thumbs and kissed her forehead.

"I'm going to turn in," he said at last, his own eyes full of tears. "Give you three time to…."

She nodded and gave him one last hug.

By the time Alice had collected herself and stepped out of the room, the only people left were Marco and Lionel. Their voices filtered out of the library, where Marco was tending the fire and Lionel was pouring the two of them a glass of the good brandy.

"I'll take one of those," she said.

They both froze, staring at her.

"I think one toast," she continued, her voice shaking. "After all it's the last—"

Marco was there in two steps, with Lionel close behind. The three of them held one another, tears falling with silent intensity.

"Okay," Alice finally said, pulling away, "this is our last night and I don't want to spend it crying."

She handed Lionel the envelope and took the glass he offered her.

Lionel stared at it before ripping open the seal. He thumbed through the papers, his face unreadable until he got to the passport and he smirked.

"What name did you get? Marco asked.

"Johnny Danger."

"No you did not!" Alice said, grabbing the passport.

Lionel laughed and shook his head.

"Chance Dayton," Marco read over Alice's shoulder. "That's almost as bad."

"It sounds…" Alice began.

"Handsome? Fearless?" Lionel asked.

"Pretentious."

Lionel shrugged. "I guess I get to make it whatever I want it to be, don't I? Kinda like a 'do-over'."

"So you didn't get enough of those when we played checkers and you're making up for it now?" Alice asked.

"Exactly."

Marco raised his glass between them, the firelight shining through the amber liquid.

"To us," he said, his voice strained, "you two were always the best part of my life, even when I wasn't with you and...no matter how far we go, we'll always be family."

They clinked their glasses together, Alice letting more tears fall down her cheeks. She took a sip and was shocked at how smoothly it went down her throat, trailing liquid fire in it's wake.

"Good?" Lionel asked her.

"Yes, too good."

She took one more sip and handed it to him. The last thing she needed was to get drunk tonight. Lionel tipped the remnants of her brandy into his and went to the record player. After a few seconds, the voice of Aretha Franklin was floating through the air.

They sat on the couch, Alice between them, and just listened to the music for a while. Then Lionel asked Marco about his private investigator practice, and Alice forced herself to be a part of the conversation instead of dwelling on what was coming.

"So," Alice said as the clock chimed eleven, "where are you going?"

Lionel fidgeted with the ring on his pinkie and smiled.

"I met someone when I was in Europe, someone who helped me believe in myself again. She said that if I wanted to, after I was finished here, I could work with her. She gave me this ring to help find her."

"That sounds very much like a spy," Marco said.

"That's pretty much what they are. I'm not real clear on their connections but I know they're doing good work. I think...I think I'd like to do that again."

Alice smiled at him. The heaviness in her chest was suddenly lighter with Lionel's words. She could tell this person meant something to him, maybe something bigger than even he could see right now. And she was glad.

He'll be happy again, he'll have a good life. That's all I could ask.

"Someday, you'll have to tell us all about your exploits," Marco said. "But in the mean time, I have something for your trip. I'll be right back."

Once Marco was out of the room, Alice laid her head on Lionel's chest and let him hold her. The steady beat of his heart under her ear was the sweetest sound she'd ever heard.

"You need to tell him," Lionel said.

Alice closed her eyes.

"Don't wait like I did," he continued. "Take your happiness and hold tight to it, Alice. You've earned it."

"So have you."

"I'll find it, I promise."

She squeezed him tighter and felt his arms do the same. A deep chuckle rumbled under her cheek and she looked up.

Tears shone in Lionel's eyes and he shook his head.

"Do you know how long I've kept myself from really giving you a hug and now I can and...Oh, Alice. I'm so happy and so damn sad all at the same time."

Marco stopped at the door and Alice turned to see a war of emotions on his face. She knew what he was thinking and wanted to scream that it wasn't true. Instead she slowly sat up and made room for him to sit down on her other side.

"Here," Marco said, handing Lionel a bakers box with

twine around it, "I made you all your favorites."

Lionel laughed.

"Hopefully my metabolism is still fast or I'm going to have to change my diet!"

They all laughed at that.

"Well," Lionel said, setting the box on top of his papers, "we still have an hour before I need to pack and I declare a tear free zone until then."

"Then I guess checkers is out," Alice said, laughing.

"I bet I've gotten better since we were kids."

"Prove it."

Six games of checkers, a few of Marco's cookies and some gut busting laughter made the hour go by far too fast.

Alice was looking through the records to see which Lionel would like next when she realized he was no longer in the room. Marco stood in front of the fire, the merriment from earlier gone. In the firelight his eyes looked haunted and grief stricken.

"It's not your fault," she said, coming up beside him and taking his hand.

"I wanted to give him back to you," he said, his voice a broken whisper.

Alice took a deep breath and tightened her grip on Marco's hand. This was her chance.

"What if…what if he's not the one I wanted?"

Marco looked at her, a deep frown hooding his eyes.

"What if," she said, taking another deep breath, "I want—"

The phone rang, shrill and impossibly loud.

Alice jumped and let go of Marco's hand. When she picked up the receiver and heard Miss Jones on the line with someone, Lionel had already made it back into the room.

Her opportunity was gone and it was time for Lionel to go.

CHAPTER THIRTY-ONE

It had been easy to look like she was grieving at Lionel's simple and poorly attended funeral. There was no reception after, which suited Alice just fine. The only people who would truly mourn Lionel were already going to be at her house.

She spent the long afternoon hours in the gym, sweating out the turbulent emotions. It worked for a little while, but restlessness would soon take over.

Marco, who had been everywhere she looked the last few days, was nowhere to be found.

When she asked after him, Miss Jones nodded to the back bedroom where Marco had been sleeping and Alice understood. He wanted to be left alone.

Long after everyone else had gone to bed, Alice lingered in the library, staring into the fire. Loneliness settled around her like a cold fog and she longed for comfort. But from whom or what? Uncle Logan would understand, she supposed, but that didn't feel quite right.

Rose might still be awake for a phone conversation.

That didn't feel right either. So, Alice just stayed in the

chair, her legs cramping with the cold and the position she was in.

When the clock chimed two, Alice sighed. She needed sleep. At the very least, her bed was more comfortable than the chair she was sitting in. But when she climbed the stairs, intending to go to her room, she found herself outside Marco's door, and she knew why. He was the only one who could banish this deep loneliness, the only one she wanted.

"Maybe last night wasn't the only chance I had," she whispered, fear and desire twisting her gut.

No matter how many times she raised her hand to knock, Alice couldn't find the courage to do it. As she turned to go, the door cracked open and her heart gave a lurch.

"Alice?"

She turned around slowly.

"I just...I didn't want to be alone."

Marco looked down at the floor. Bare feet peeked out from loose pajama pants and a white undershirt stretched appealingly over his chest and arms. Hair flopped over his forehead and there was something so vulnerable, and yet strong, about him that it sent jolts of longing through Alice's body.

Marco didn't say anything, just opened the door a little wider and gave her a sad smile.

The small lamp by the bed was the only light, illuminating a rumpled bed and Marco's open suitcase, clothes folded neatly inside.

He's been packing, of course he has. Lionel leaving...it changes nothing for him. What am I doing here?

She turned to look at him and say that she was sorry for disturbing him and goodnight, but then she met those dark sad eyes. They pulled at her and she walked toward him.

"Why don't you ever get your hair cut?" she asked, brushing it back from his forehead.

"Never enough time."

For the first time in a long while, Alice ignored every warning her mind shouted at her. With trembling fingers, she touched his face and shoulder. She could feel the heat from his body. His smell, like baking bread and sweat, filled her nostrils. She wanted to kiss the scar on his nose and run her hands through the chest hair that peeked above the collar of his shirt.

So, she did.

Her fingers dipped under his collar, his skin deliciously warm. With her heart hammering in her chest, Alice dared to look up at him. Marco's lips were parted and his eyes held hers with questions churning in their depths.

Her other hand moved up his chest until it was behind his head. The whole time, Marco didn't touch her, hands clenched at his side.

"Marco," she said, her voice breathy and shocking to her ears. "I—"

Marco's jaw tightened. "You're tired, maybe you should—"

She froze and then pulled away.

"Don't do that! Don't act like the only reason I'm here is because Lionel is gone."

He walked to the other end of the room, shoulders slumped. "You're hurting, I understand."

"Yes, and so are you, but that doesn't mean—"

"Alice please, " his voice was rough and broken, "before we do something you'll regret."

She didn't know if it was the grief giving her courage to finally say everything that had been bottled up inside of her or not, and she didn't care. If she let him go now, he might never come back.

"I know you think that I loved Lionel, and I did, so much. But...I love you, too."

"I know, we're best friends—"

"No. I mean, yes...but, when I say that, I mean..." She closed the distance between them and took his face in her hands. "When I'm with you, I'm home."

He gently removed her hands.

"I know you're broken up about Lionel, but I can't be some temporary comfort—"

"Why can't you just believe me? If Lionel was able to live in Jet City and I had a choice I'd choose you, every time."

He shook his head. "I've spent most of my life seeing the two of you together. Since we were kids, I knew that you were always meant to be with him."

"And I used to think that too, but...I don't know when it changed, just that it did. I'll always love Lionel, but not like I love you."

When Marco still hesitated, she took his hand.

"This will be the last time I ask, and if there was any other way, I wouldn't ask it now, but—"

"Alice—"

"Read me, or look into my soul, or whatever you do. Let me show you and if you still don't believe me or want me, then I'll go." Her voice broke and tears began to build in her eyes. "But please, please just look and see what I feel for you before you push me away."

He opened his mouth and shut it, nodding instead.

Alice closed her eyes and was suddenly jolted back in time, to a tree in a back yard, an awkward boy standing beneath it.

"How's a raven like a writing desk?"

She laughed, and the next thing she knew, they were lying on a worn rug, the smell of baking bread in the air as Marco read aloud to her.

After that the memories were too fast to latch onto, but she lived each of them. Every laugh, every embrace, every time Marco made her feel powerful and beautiful. The quiet afternoons, the battles they fought, the grief of waking in the hospital to find him gone.

Then the connection was broken, and she gasped, her face wet with tears.

Marco stumbled back, toppling his suitcase onto the floor and gulping air.

Alice waited, but the longer he stared at the floor, the more her heart broke.

"I—" she began.

"You love *me*?" He turned tear-filled eyes to her.

She reached for him, but Marco got there first. His hands captured her face and the look of naked love in his eyes took her breath away.

"You love me." His voice was full of awe this time.

No one had ever looked at her like this, like the most precious, most amazing person in the world, and she realized in that moment, the depth of what he'd been holding back all these years.

"All my life," she said.

She had expected a crashing of lips and tearing of clothes. Instead, Marco slowly lowered his head, pausing just above her lips. They shared a breath and her heart beat out a nervous rhythm against her ribs. His fingers trembled as he held her and she closed the last sliver of distance between them. She tasted salt, and didn't know if it was her tears or his.

As their kisses deepened, they exchanged sorrow for hope, loss for love.

A hungry moan escaped Marco's throat, his hands sliding down her back and pulling her against him. Alice relished the feel of his body against hers. Her hands slid down his lean arms, and then the sides of his body. Her fingertips found the ends of his shirt and she slipped her hands beneath. His breath hitched as she slowly ran her hands up the hard planes of his back.

Without a word, he pulled the shirt over his head. She stared at his body and let her hands run slow and deliberate over his chest. Her fingers curled in his chest hair before traveling lower to Marco's stomach. Her eyes and hands trailed over scars that she'd never seen before, alongside the ones she knew very well.

She pressed her lips to the scar where he'd been shot in the shoulder on their first mission together. Then her lips found and tasted a small mark on his bicep.

Marco's breathing became ragged in her ear, and she could feel his body start to hum, like a string pulled taut.

But she didn't rush. She'd waited too long for this. Instead, she kissed and caressed each scar, feeling as if she could somehow heal the years of battle and separation.

She looked up into his eyes and he crushed her lips with his, as he tried to untie her robe.

After a few minutes, Alice began to laugh.

"Damn thing," he breathed, pulling on the silk ties.

"You've got them in a knot. Here."

Before she got too far loosening it, Alice looked up into his eyes and a sudden, playful impulse took over. Taking two steps back, she held his gaze as she untied the sash. His brown eyes were bright as he watched her at last drop the ends of the sash, but as he took a step toward her, she took one back.

Her fingers trembled as she pulled back the sides of the silk robe, letting it fall in a soft pool at her feet. She felt Marco's hungry gaze like a caress.

He stepped toward her, and this time Alice didn't move, aching for his hands on her body.

He started at her round hips, hands slowly gliding up to

the dip of her waist, the sides of her breasts. One hand went around to her back, pressing her close again. The fingertips of his other hand grazed the top of her breasts as he kissed the curve where her neck met her shoulder.

Alice felt a rush of heat fill her body. The more his hands explored, the stronger it became. She couldn't think of anything except the way his lips felt on her bare skin and the growing ache between her thighs.

"Alice," he whispered her name with such longing it almost broke her heart.

Her arms wound around his neck and Alice kissed him, promising with each movement of her lips that she was his, always and forever.

Afterward, they lay entwined on the bed, a blanket hastily thrown over them to keep a chill off their sweaty bodies. She could hear his heartbeat as her head rested on his chest, wiry hair tickling her cheek. Marco's fingers traced absent patterns on her shoulders and back, as he pressed little kisses in her dark hair. Her hand trailed slowly down his side and he jumped a little.

"Ticklish?" she asked.

"Maybe."

She laughed. "All these things I never knew before. I can't wait to learn."

She did it again and he grabbed her hand.

"I know where you're ticklish, you know," he said, kissing her finger tips.

"Not everywhere."

"As you said, there's lots to learn about each other."

She kissed him, relishing the fact that she didn't need to question or suppress those desires anymore.

As he tucked strands of hair back from her face, Marco's eyes became hooded, his forehead wrinkling.

"What's wrong?" she asked.

"I was just thinking…you're going to think this is bad timing, but…about that case I was working before I came here."

"You're right, that is bad timing, but I forgive you."

He smiled. "I've been thinking about it all week and I believe there's a connection, a pretty strong one, between Judy, what Lionel found out and this case, but I'm worried about something."

"And what would that be?"

He swallowed. "There are things about my time in Metro City that I haven't told you. And I worry that you'll—"

"I don't care."

"Alice—"

"I mean it."

She moved so that her whole body was on top of him.

The hair of his thighs was rough against her smooth skin, and she could feel the sweat and stickiness from what they'd just done. With every touch and kiss they'd exchanged, Alice knew that he belonged to her and she belonged to him. Nothing else mattered.

"A lot has happened in the last two years," she said, holding his gaze. "And there will be time to tell each other all about it. But I want tonight," she kissed him, "I want this."

She let her hand travel down, shifting her legs so she straddled him.

"I've waited so long to be with you. Whatever we have to tell each other, whatever troubles and adversaries await us, we can wait until tomorrow to worry about it, can't we?"

Marco kissed her, then flipped her onto her back. "Yes," he whispered. "I think we can."

- The End -

The Vigilantes Universe Continues in
The Heroes of High Tide

AUTHOR'S NOTE

Dear reader,

Thank You for reading Steel's Fate. I hope you've loved the conclusion to the first trilogy of The Vigilantes as much as I did writing it.

If you did, you would be my hero if you left a review on Amazon (even if it's just a few sentences.) Every review makes a difference to an author and helps other readers discover this book.

As for the next part of the Vigilantes story, keep your eyes peeled for Colleen to appear in her very own series, The Heroes of High Tide, in Spring of 2020. Click here to get your copy of book one, Fahrenheit's Ghost.

Lionel will also return in his very own series with Maria and a host of new characters to love in early 2021.

I'm looking forward to continuing the story of the Vigilantes with you!

Sincerely,

Trish Heinrich

Mother Author Hero

ABOUT THE AUTHOR

Trish has been obsessed with stories about female heroes ever since she put on her first pair of Wonder Woman under-roos and spun around. After realizing that fear of failure had been holding her back, Trish became her very own hero and participated in National Novel Writing Month in 2015. Since then, Trish has braved the constant attacks of her nemeses Inner Critic and No Time, in order to achieve the impossible: An artistic life with two small kids!

Trish was one of the co-creators of the super hero comedy web series "The Collectibles". Her first novel "Serpent's Sacrifice" was published in 2017 and is the first book in an Urban Fantasy Superhero series, The Vigilantes.

Trish currently lives in Washington State with her writer/editor/producer husband, and their two geeky daughters.

ACKNOWLEDGMENTS

Thank you to my husband, who soothed my fears and listened with the patience of a saint to all my anxieties. He also read every draft of this book, offering developmental criticism and advice. You make me a better everything!

Hugs and kisses to my children, who have been ever excited about the book and supportive when I needed to work long hours, I love you both so much.

Many thanks to my cover designer and very good friend, Todd Downing. You make me look good!

Thank you to my spectacular editor, Maria D'Marco. Once again she went above and beyond what I asked for and made my book better. You're my hero!

Thanks to the Selling for Authors Facebook group and Bryan Cohen, who continue to be not only professional but also compassionate.

To the friends and family who have been so excited and supportive, you've made me feel like a superstar, thank you!

And last but not least, to all the Advanced Reading Heroes who read my books and take the time to leave reviews. I could not succeed without all of you, thank you all!